THE
CALLING

THE
CALLING

a Novel by

DICK HYSON

University Press of Colorado

Copyright © 1998 by Dick Hyson
International Standard Book Number 0-87081-510-5

Published by the University Press of Colorado
P.O. Box 849
Niwot, Colorado 80544

The University Press of Colorado is a cooperative publishing enterprise
supported, in part, by Adams State College, Colorado State University,
Fort Lewis College, Mesa State College, Metropolitan State College of
Denver, University of Colorado, University of Northern Colorado, University of Southern Colorado, and Western State College of Colorado.

The paper used in this publication meets the minimum requirements of
the American National Standard for Information Sciences—Permanence
of Paper for Printed Library Materials. ANSI Z39.48-1984

Library of Congress Cataloging-in-Publication Data

Hyson, Dick.
    The calling
            p.   cm.
    ISBN 0-87081-510-5 (cloth : alk. paper)
    PSS3558.Y57C3   1998
    813'.54—dc21   98-27488
                                                        CIP

07 06 05 04 03 02 01 00 99 98   10 9 8 7 6 5 4 3 2 1

PREFACE

The High Plains, the Golden Spread, the Panhandle country, whichever description you should use, has always been depicted as a dry, windy, parched
country. This is largely true. But after cowboying and ranching in that country for thirty years, I seem to remember a few, very few in fact, years that it
rained, the grass grew, the wind didn't blow quite as hard, and it was a virtual
cattle paradise. Since this is fiction, to be dealt with at the author's discretion,
it is only natural to portray one of the better years. It was strictly the author's
prerogative.

All physical land descriptions exist somewhere but have been moved
and renamed for the author's convenience. Even the high mesa with the
solitary grave exists. Its location, for reasons of privacy to the landowner,
shall remain known only to those who already know of its existence.

The great state land raids by outsiders happened in the 1960s. Most of
the land eventually reverted back to the state and the original leasers at a
later date, quietly. There was something sinister, if not illegal, going on that
the author was never smart enough to understand. Only now, using the
tried and true veterinarian S.W.A.G. ("scientific wild-ass guess") method, do
I venture to speculate.

It is aggravating to the author that the term "cowboy" is used to describe any wild, crazy, or foolish act or person in the world. The term "cowboy" should in my opinion be looked on as a professional occupation, and
any man who wears the title be seen for what he is: a man who knows the
occupation and has special qualities, i.e., wild, crazy, foolish, . . . Hark! Perhaps I was wrong earlier. I do know that I would be proud if my epitaph
read only: "A Cowboy."

Although this work is not autobiographical, similarities exist between
the author and the storyteller, Frank. This arises from the literary guide-
lines that say that one should write only about what he knows. The author
is not Frank, but he knows him, and was there to watch it happen.

Acknowledgments

Richard Maulsby, Dick Russell, Buzzy Cleveland,
R.C. Chism, John Zurich, Merlin George, Bobby Cooper,
and Max Evans. Cowboys all. Some still living in
the saddle, some gone to the last big gatherin'.

Also, Susan Gleason and Luther Wilson,
who believed.

THE
CALLING

CHAPTER

1

*"I am an ole cowpuncher
and I'm dressed in rags,
But I used to be a tough one boys,
and go on great big jags."*

—from "When the Work's All Done This Fall," author unknown

I watched the sweat drip off the end of my nose. It's not that it was so hot, it's just that I'd been through a bunch of hell the last two trips. I was still looking forward to the next one. I'm a glutton for punishment. I spit on the ground and in the sand there was a mixture of saliva, tobacco juice, and blood. On the last trip I bit my tongue and it felt like I had a chunk of raw liver sitting right in my mouth where my tongue ought to be. I was kind of catching my breath. Damned if I could figure out how he'd done it. Usually I'm not easy to put down. Not that I was such a hellacious bronc rider, too big to be an honest-to-God contestant bronc rider. But I could take advantage of a horse by cheating him and holding on with everything I had, and usually get a trip wallered out. But I was sure having my trials today.

Holding on to that big cotton-braided rein, I looked at this big grulla's left hip and there was a "Cross S" on it. It had been there for a long while. The Boss had gone to the sale yesterday and saw the horse going through the ring, this one in particular that he'd raised. Any horse carrying the Cross S brand, the Boss saw he was going to bring home. The Boss had sold this horse three or four years ago, and evidently the old boy who had him hadn't used him enough and got scared of him. He'd ended up spoiling him.

This ol' horse sure knew what he was doing, and I thought I knew what I was doing. I couldn't figure out where I was going wrong. About then a voice behind me said, "Well."

I turned around and looked at the Boss. He was leaning on the snubbing post in the middle of the round corral. I thought, well yourself, you old fart. If you're waitin' on me, you're wastin' time.

But I threw both cotton reins over his neck and measured my rein. I was going to try and hold his head up this time, the best I could. Very few horses can buck real good with their head up. Holding both reins in my left hand, I reached up and grabbed hold of the headstall with the same hand so I could cheek him around, holding that headstall right close to his eye, so maybe he couldn't see me get on. I did this more out of habit, because this horse wasn't terribly hard to get on. It's after you got on that the shit hit the fan. I reached down and grabbed that oxbow stirrup and just turned it around slightly so I could stick my foot up in it. I eased my foot in, grabbed hold of the horn and quickly swung up on top of him, and got my other stirrup. That big old grulla just stood there quivering. I was waiting and he was waiting. I knew I'd got his attention because both ears were laid back pointing right straight at me.

Now I knew I had to relax. Right then I was tighter than a fiddle string, because I knew what he was going to do. But he just didn't do it. He just stood there. I heard the Boss say, "Untrack him, Frank. Just don't sit there!"

So I turned my toes out, gave him a little nudge with my spurs and the grulla came apart. He went right straight up, came down, and swapped ends. All the bucking he'd done he could've done on the top of a double bed. He was not taking up a lot of space. I was sitting in pretty good shape. Every time he came down it was teeth rattling and bone jarring, but I thought maybe this time I could get him rode. I'm an optimistic son of a bitch.

I looked down and it looked like I was riding a horse that had his head cut off. It's a funny feeling to look down at your saddle right in front of the horn and not see anything but a hank of mane hair. I was pulling with both hands on those reins, but I couldn't pull him up. He was too big and stout. He did his job right there, jumping high, kicking, and coming down and I reached down and grabbed hold of the horn. To stay where I was sitting I'd have to cheat him a little. There was no way in the world that I was going to contest this horse. Every time he came down it was beginning to hurt all over, jarring me up so bad, but I still thought, I've got 'im this time. Directly he took a big lunge forward, taking up some space going straight ahead. He sucked her back, turned back the other way, and then just blew up and lunged forward in a high, twisting leap. I could feel myself weakening, because right then my butt was sitting right against the cantle. One more jump forward and I was completely behind it. I knew I was bucked off.

I turned everything loose and let the inevitable happen. But one more jump and he sent me up pretty high. It was a helluva view! This time I didn't have anything in my hands and my feet were out of the stirrups. I thought, well, I'll just come down in all this sand. Shouldn't be too hard a landing. But he stayed underneath me and made one more high kick. Up I went like a rock from a slingshot. I heard somebody holler, "SHEE-IT!" It could've been me, but I wasn't sure. I must've looked like a feller falling out of a tree, because I was waving my arms and kicking my feet and trying to get control of my body so I wouldn't land on my head and break my neck.

I came down right about the third board on the bottom of the fence, scraped my head from my jaw to my ear. I turned over on one elbow just in time to see the big grulla taking his victory lap around that round corral, with my stirrups swapping sides of him over the top of the saddle. He finally quit on the other side of the corral and just stood and watched.

I heard the Boss say, "Frank, I wish you'd quit swearin'. All the world can hear ya, and there are ladies about."

So it had been me, my own voice. It sounded like something I'd say in a situation like that. As a matter of fact, I always felt that those would probably be my last words here on earth. I was so thoroughly pissed off, I didn't feel like an apology was in order. So I said nothing.

I heard the Boss again. "Well, is the third time a charm?"

'Course, I'm mad. "Hell, no, Boss! I'm just gettin' warmed up. You reckon he's weakenin' any?"

"I don't know, Frank," the Boss said. "I believe he's getting a shade stronger every trip. If you don't quit now, I'm afraid you'll mess up his mind."

I thought, Oh shit! Here he was worrying about messing up that horse's mind, and I had so many cobwebs in mine that I could hardly think straight. He was yet to ask me how I was. But then, that's just the Boss.

I got up and dusted myself off and shook the sand out of my ears. I reached up and felt the right side of my face. Between my tongue, my ear, and the side of my face, it sure smarted a little.

"Well, perhaps you better call Casey Tibbs," I said sarcastically, as I muttered to myself, "fuckin' gruyer," referring to the mouse-colored horse. "Gruyer" was a southwest bastardization of the word "grulla."

"Nah, I'll do one better than that. I'll try to get a hold of Johnny the Twist. I'll leave a message for him at Kitchins. Jerk your kack, Frank. Let's call it a day on this bronc ridin'."

Well, I wasn't too proud of myself. The Boss made me quit. If there's one thing I ain't, it's a quitter.

I could see Tio's face gleaming through the boards on the corral. His face was just as brown as saddle leather. By the big smile, he has sure enjoyed this. I think everybody enjoyed it a lot more than I have. I caught the big grulla, pulled my kack, and headed for the little gate that leads to the saddle house. The Boss went over and opened the big gate and turned the grulla out down the alley.

Tio met me at the gate. "Oh, Frank. She sure ees a good one."

"Tio, it ain't a she, it's a he." I don't know why Tio insists on calling everything on the place a she. Even though I correct him every chance I get, it doesn't seem to make a big impression on him.

I took my saddle in, and put it on the rack. I took off my slicker that I'd rolled up and wrapped in front of the saddle because it doesn't have swells to keep me from going over the front. I use it because I'm partial to slick-forked saddles and use my one saddle for everything: riding, roping, or bronc riding.

Tio walked up while I was taking the slicker off. "Hee, hee, Frank. You should have put eet on the back of the saddle. Maybe eet would keep you from going out the back door."

I didn't see a great lot of humor in that. But it did strike me that it might have made a little sense. Tio was just full of compliments today. "You was sure pullin' the leather, Frank."

"Hell, yes, Tio. I ain't proud. If they'd put that saddle horn on there to pull something with, they'd have put it behind the saddle."

I walked outside and sat on the porch of the bunkhouse, fighting to hold my temper. So far it'd been a standoff. There's a bench that runs the entire length of the porch. I stretched my legs out in front of me and tried to relax. I was plumb tuckered. Losing always has that effect on me. If I'd a'rode him I'd be stepping tall. All I had to contend with was my swollen tongue, scraped head, and aching body.

Tio inspected my head, fiddled with my ear, took off my hat for me. "That needs some juice on eet, Frank. I'll fix you up."

"Uh!" I was beginning to stiffen up. It was kind of a chore to just stand up. I walked off the porch and over to the water tank. Splashed some water on my face. It felt good, especially on the back of my head. I held my nose and ducked my head plumb in.

I went back and dried off on a chicken-feed sack that Tio handed me. He brought out a little bottle of his special remedy, tilted my head over with his hand, and poured it down the side of my face. Godalmighty, I came up off of that bench and did a little stomp dance around there.

"Goddamn, Tio! What in hell is in that stuff?"

I took off my chaps and spurs, and went back in and hung them up. By this time Tio was heading for the house, and the Boss was heading back up the alley from turning the grulla out in a little holding trap.

"Frank, you've got plenty of time before dinner. Run down and get the mail."

I realized how sore I was getting and thought I'd just sit in the shade awhile in front of the bunkhouse.

Where this outfit sits is right down on Long's Creek. The main house sits real close to the creek. It's a big, two-story affair with porches around two sides. Lots of cottonwoods. The bunkhouse is across the road and it's better than most people's houses in this country. We have indoor plumbing. We still had a one-holer out back, but seldom used it, except for Jim, the other hired hand. Every now and then he'd go out there, just for old time's sake. Said it was a good place to think.

Tio's house was just to my left as I looked at the big house. As I looked over this layout, I could see that there was nothing but quality. The fence around the headquarters probably enclosed fifteen or twenty acres. Everything is fixed up nice, mainly because of Tio. You could always see him out puttering, fixing up the flower beds and mowing the lawn, that small space of cultivated grass that lay within the rock wall surrounding the main house, with a push-reel mower. Taking care of everything around here is Tio's job. He's the only one the Boss doesn't tell what to do every morning. He and his wife, Lupe, are both as old as Methuselah. Lupe does most of the cooking and household chores and speaks very little English.

We can get radio out of Amarillo, up out of the creek breaks. Of course, we get the Amarillo paper and the Dorsey *Weekly Wipe*. That's what I call it anyhow. They are really, other than the radio, our only connection to the outside world. The papers are what made the mail such an important thing around here. But most of our information comes by the barbed-wire network. That is, when you go to town or when you meet a neighbor, he'll tell you what's going on around locally. In the telling, truth never gets in the way of a good story.

I went in the bunkhouse, stripped off my shirt, and looked into the bathroom mirror to survey the damage that'd been done. After close inspection, I could see that there was nothing that wouldn't grow back.

The top of my ear had been torn about a quarter of an inch down from the top. And starting at the cheekbone, a deep abrasion ran down to my jaw. The brown stain of Tio's medicine gave it an eerie look. But what the hell, it'd wear off. After it healed up it'd leave a scar. But that didn't bother me. It'd have company, as I have several on my face that I've gotten used to. One over the bridge of my nose has occurred in the same place so many times and become so deep, that I actually worried about it becoming a revolting disfigurement. But as I looked at it now, it wasn't so bad. It took people's mind off my nose, which for my heritage I should have felt lucky wasn't worse. Most Indians are known for their large noses, but for just a half-breed, I feel like I have more than my share. It's been broken four times, never to the point of being flattened, which would have almost been a blessing. But instead it bent, each time more crooked than the time before, 'til the last time, which seemed to more or less straighten it out.

I washed my face again. There was dirt, sand, and dried horse shit in my ears, nose, and eyes. After I'd gotten scrubbed up the best I could, I slicked my hair back. No part, just combed it back to each side and let it fall where it may. After a liberal amount of Wildroot hair tonic was applied and rubbed in, it shined like a raven's wing.

I stood before the mirror surveying myself, six foot two, two hundred and ten pounds. My body was made to stop moving things—human, animal, or otherwise. And that's just the way I'd used it.

I had to smile as I pulled on a clean shirt. My permanent tan had been mistaken for a number of nationalities: Italian, Greek, Mexican, and Jew. Most people seemed disappointed to learn that I was part Indian, sometimes with disdain. You could almost read their minds—a half-breed Indian—like it was the lowest life-form on earth.

I walked out and whistled for Belle. She came arunning. She'd been watching all the bronc riding, too, this morning. Evidently she'd got embarrassed for me and gone off and lay in the shade. But she loved to ride in the pickup we call Ol' Blue, especially up in the cab with me, so we headed for the mailbox.

CHAPTER

2

I was still smarting over the bronc ride, not from the minor scrape on the side of my face, but from deep in my gut. I could feel the blood rise in me and the only known cure was time, hard work, a sudden jolt from fist or hoof, or music. I could feel it now as I squeezed the steering wheel to the point of breaking. I looked at my face in the rearview mirror and my jaw muscles were clenched.

Battling it hard, I turned on the radio. The dial was set on KGNC, a country station down in Amarillo, Texas. I caught the familiar strains of Hank Snow singing "The Golden Rocket." As always, I decided to chime in with him at the top of my lungs. I have this habit of trying to mimic any well-known singer as I sing their songs, trying to do it in their style. The only way I can approach the style of Hank Snow is to pinch the skin up over my Adam's apple, wiggle it rapidly while squeezing my voice through my nasal passages. "You triflin' women can't keep a good man downnnnn."

As I did this, Belle looked at me like I'd caught my foot in a coyote trap. It made me laugh, and I stopped out of concern for her. Already I could feel the tension leaving my body. Music hath charms to soothe the savage breast. I read that once, but I disremember where.

The road to the highway where the mailbox sits is eight miles running due east, straight as a string from the ranch, while the creek angles off to the southeast. The valley is broad, and to me, beautiful.

This part of New Mexico seems to be the bastard child of the whole state. The tourists come through, never stopping unless they have to for gas or food. But this didn't bother me. My business has nothing to do with tourists.

Cattle and horses are what make my world go 'round. This plains country had once been home to the Indian side of my family. My Anglo side traveled the area from Independence, Missouri, southwest to Indian Territory, later called Oklahoma, and settled there. That was a stretch of prairie, harsh and hostile, that had to be gone through in order to find free land suitable for agriculture.

Here a small creek called the Aguacita comes from the north, crosses the road to join Long's Creek, and we have to ford this creek. A couple of years ago during a dry spell we had gone in and poured a cement bottom to the ford. Usually the water runs just a few inches deep. It seldom causes a problem going anywhere, but occasionally after a hard rain or a cloudburst upstream from the ford, we're isolated. As quickly as it rises, it will recede. As we cross the Aguacita we have an uphill climb to get out of its banks and out of the valley to where the land gets tighter, no longer sandy loam like the valley floor, but hardpan dirt that produces mainly buffalo and gramma grass. The only difference, it takes more moisture for its growth. But when you got it, it grew more grass.

"The Wild Side of Life," a song I could sure as hell identify with, was on the radio and I sang along as we approached the highway. As I pulled up to the cattle guard I stopped, just as the Boss had drilled into my head back when I was sixteen. It seemed unneedful, because on approaching the cattle guard you could look down the road either way for at least five miles and see if anything was coming. Nothing was, but old habits are hard to break. I pulled across the highway to the mailbox and opened it.

"Damn," I said to myself. "Ol' Vander Wagon must be runnin' late." I backed up and pulled over to the side of the mailbox, leaving enough room for Mr. Vander Wagon's mail truck. It was unusual for him to be late. Generally you could set your timepiece by him. I sat there with the window open, listening to the radio, scratching Belle's ears. The music stopped and I could hear the Morse code, dot-dash prelude to the local news.

There had been a bank robbery at Tramperos, a small town about forty miles south of us. A broad-daylight robbery, yesterday morning. A lone masked gunman had held up the Sawyer Bank, escaping with an undetermined amount of money. Mr. Sawyer, who ran the bank, had been critically injured from a blow to the head with a pistol butt. Miss Sawyer, the bank's only teller, had been gagged and bound and placed in the vault.

The physical description of the man who had done this despicable deed was sketchy to say the least. His height was approximately five feet six to five feet eight inches tall, weight a hundred and forty to a hundred fifty pounds. Although he had a cap on, his hair was thought to be brown. Outside of that, there wasn't much to go on.

I noticed Belle rise from where she was lying in the seat and peer out the back window. I glanced in the rearview mirror and I could see the mail wagon coming up the road at a high rate of speed. I reckon he had to hustle because his route must be well over a hundred and fifty miles, every day except Sunday. He came in like the "Fireball Mail," timing it just right, slamming on the brakes and ending up right in front of the mailbox. I thought he was going to leave, ignoring me because of his lateness, but was surprised to see him lean across the seat and roll the window down.

"Howdy, Frank. Reckon it's ever gonna rain?"

I gave him the standard reply. "Well, if it don't, Mr. Vander Wagon, it's gonna be a hell of a dry spell."

"Yep."

"Say," I said, "I just heard about the bank robbery down at Tramperos. Did you hear about it?"

"Sure did, Frank. Terrible, terrible thing. Mr. Sawyer'll be lucky if he pulls through. It's been robbed before, back about ten years ago, if I recollect right. You gotta admit, it's just ripe for the pickin's sittin' out there all by itself filled with money."

I thought about what he'd said, and replied, "I reckon."

"Say Frank, when I come by the crossroads back yonder, there's an ol' boy down there sittin' under the trees. Just asittin' there. Don't have any idee what he was doin' or wantin'. But I thought I'd better tell ya."

"Thanks. I'll run down and check on him. I appreciate it."

Vander Wagon leaned over closer and peered out the window at me. "My Lord, Frank! What happened to your face?"

I reached up and touched the scrape. "Ah, nothin' serious, I fell down in the bathtub."

Vander Wagon straightened up in his seat, and as he shoved the pickup in gear said, "What in hell was in that bathtub, Frank, bobwire?" And with that he was gone, scattering gravel all over Ol' Blue.

I topped the rise and after crossing the steel-girder bridge over the creek, I could see the trees down at the corner still several miles off. Somebody had planted those trees as a haven for weary travelers. In the eight years that I'd been around they'd not gotten any bigger. They were elms that had grown to about a height of twenty feet and then just stopped. They leaned permanently toward the northeast because of the prevailing southwest wind that always seemed to blow, and would remain that way.

As I approached the trees I could see somebody sitting in the shade. He was lucky. These were the only shade trees for miles. Not that it was so terribly hot, it was just a good place to stop and spend a spell. I made a U-turn and pulled up under the trees myself, and looked him over.

"Howdy," I said.

"Hi," he smiled, real friendly.

"Where ya headed?"

"I don't know."

"How'd ya get here?" I asked.

"I caught a ride with a man in a pickup. He turned and went down this road," pointing to the highway that ran west, "and I wasn't sure whether I wanted to go that way or not. So I had him let me out here."

This fellow was a puzzlement to me. He was young, probably twenty-four, twenty-five years old, dark hair, rather dark complected. But at the same time, pale skinned, like the sun hadn't hit him in a coon's age. But what was really noticeable were his clothes. He had on a heavy thatched, cheap, farmer-type straw hat, a tan long-sleeved work shirt, and a pair of blue jeans. Not Levis that we all wore, but blue jeans, loose fitting with a pair of Acme curb-kicker boots on his feet. He looked like he just purchased everything from J.C. Penney's. He was sitting on two suitcases. *Those* did not look cheap. As a matter of fact, they appeared to be leather, or a damn good imitation of it.

I opened the door to get out. As soon as I did, ol' Belle hit the ground and headed straight at him. She had that habit. I knew she wouldn't bite the man. But he showed no fear as he smiled and held out his hand as Belle approached. She stopped, smelled his hand, and then damned if she didn't lick it as she turned her attention to his suitcases, sniffing around.

I walked over and squatted down on my haunches.

"Where ya from?" I said, knowing damn well he wasn't from anywhere near here.

Again he smiled pleasantly. "Back East."

I started to ask him to be more specific. It could mean anything from one mile to several thousand. But I figured it wasn't any of my business. It was the code of the country not to pry. I had an idea this fellow wasn't acquainted with that code, but I'd honor it anyhow.

"Is there anything in particular I can do for ya?"

"Well," the stranger said, "I'm looking for a job."

Now we were getting somewhere, I thought. "What kind?"

"A job on a ranch. A cowboy."

"You have any experience?"

"No. But I catch on fast. Where do you work?" he said.

"The Piedra Ranch," I replied.

"Where is it?"

"Well, part of it is right on the other side of that fence behind ya."

The fellow turned around and looked. "Are they needing any help? And would they be interested in hiring me?"

I knew the Boss had been thinking of hiring an extra hand for some projects he had in mind this summer. But whether they'd hire him, I seriously doubted. I pulled out a chew, a plug of Brown's Mule, bit off a hunk, and offered it.

"No, thank you."

There was something about this fellow. He wasn't a gunsel. A gunsel is a fellow that tries to make you believe he's something he isn't. This fellow made no bones about the fact that he didn't know much and that he was willing to learn. And he was friendly. He had soft features, maybe too soft for a hardworking job. But I'm talking more about his eyes. If what I saw in his eyes I'd job in a horse, I would call it "soft eyed."

"Do ya know what you're gettin' in for?" I asked. Without giving him time to reply, I said, "We work from daylight 'til dark. It's hard, physical work. And the Boss is very demanding. He's particular about how things are done. He's got his way, and his way's the only way. But if you're willin', I guess I can drive ya up, let ya talk to 'im. The rest is up to you."

The fellow stood up, and so did I.

"Thank you," he said. "I'd appreciate it. By the way," as he stuck out his hand, "my name is Roth, R.C. Roth."

I took his hand. "Mine's Frank Dalton."

While he was shaking my hand, he smiled real big. "Frank Dalton. Wasn't he . . . ?"

"Yeah. He was an outlaw in the 1800s. We ain't no kin. Everybody asks me that. It's just a curse I've gotta live with."

"Well," he said, "it's a good, solid name."

"Thanks. Grab your suitcases. Throw 'em in the back, and I'll take ya to meet the man."

I thought about the hand that I'd just shook. It was small and soft, like that of a girl's. He didn't look like he had what it took to make it in this country. But who was I to judge. At least I'd give him a chance. If nothing else, he might be able to wrangle a free meal out of it. He looked like he could use it.

As we turned off the highway we went under the tall overhead pipe that held the sign "Piedra Ranch" with the +S on each side of the large letters carved into a heavy slab of wood.

"Pie . . ." he struggled, trying to pronounce the ranch name.

"Piedra," I said. "Means rock or stone in Spanish. Matter of fact, the owner's name is Boss Stone."

"Is that the reason for the name?" he asked.

"No, it's because of a rock landmark on the ranch. A coincidence, I guess."

"What's the Plus S, your logo?"

I damned near laughed. "No. It's a Cross S, our brand."

"Oh," he said. "This is really unusual country."

I allowed it was. Where we'd been coming through is just as flat as it could be. "I think you'll like the place. It's about the prettiest place in these parts. Everything is done up to snuff. That's the way the Boss wants it. And if I can give you any advice on gettin' the job, it's just to say 'Yes, sir' a lot and tell him you're full of try."

CHAPTER

3

We were going over the last cattle guard and you could see a whole bunch of cottonwoods up there on the steep bank. R.C. seemed to be just as relaxed as he could be.

We pulled up in the circle drive and I parked Ol' Blue. "Get out," and I started walking toward the kitchen door. "Why don't ya sit on that stump over there? Just move the dishpan, the soap, and the towel off. I'll go talk to him and see if he's hirin'."

I walked in and the Boss was sitting at the dinner table, along with Miz T. and Jim. They were about half through eating, and the Boss said, "Frank, you're late."

"Sorry, Boss. The mail was runnin' late, so I waited."

"Well, I appreciate it," he said.

"Uh, Boss, I met a feller on the road down there that's lookin' for a job."

"Oh?"

"Yeah. He doesn't look like much, but he seems to be a pretty good feller. Says he's a quick learner."

The Boss laid down his napkin and got up. "Well, let's have a look at him." He walked over to the window and looked out and there's R.C. sitting on the stump where we always wash up at.

"Good Lord, Frank. That feller looks like a gutted snowbird."

"I know, Boss. He was sittin' out there at the crossroads and I hated to just leave him there. He said he wanted a job."

"Trot him in here and we'll feed him. I'll talk to him and send him on his way, or hire him, one."

"Okay, Boss."

I went outside. "Well, the Boss will talk to you. Are ya hungry?"

R.C. smiled at me. "Yes, I haven't eaten since yesterday."

"Well, wash up here."

I walked over to the spigot and filled up the washpan and brought it back and set it on the stump, and commenced to wash myself. I rolled up my sleeves, soaped down real good, and dried off. R.C. just stood there looking at me. I threw the water out and said, "You do the same."

We walked through the screen door into the entryway and stepped into the kitchen. The Boss got up and walked over to R.C. and said, "Howdy."

R.C. said, "Hello, sir."

"I hear you're lookin' for work?"

"I sure am."

"Well, we'll talk about it. Are you hungry?"

"Yes, sir, I certainly am."

We went over to the table, and the Boss said, "This is my wife, Teresa Stone."

Miz T. smiled at him and got right up and went to get another plate. The Boss said, "This here's Jim."

Jim stood up and leaned across the table and shook hands.

"Sit down, and put on the feed bag, son," said the Boss.

I went over to where I generally sit, started lighten' in. Miz T. started to bring some things that she'd kept warm. Almost everybody was through eating except me and R.C., and I was picking it up and putting it down, as good as my butchered tongue would allow. I was wanting to get out of here and let R.C. and the Boss have their talk. I sure didn't want to hang around and listen to it. It might be brutal.

R.C. took a napkin, shook it out, and laid it across his lap, picked up his fork, and went to eating like he was plumb civilized.

"Certainly is a nice place you've got here, Mr. Stone."

"Well, thank you. We've been working on it for a good spell. I kind of like it here myself."

Miz T. said, "Frank, will you slow down. The pasture isn't on fire. I swear to goodness, you're always eating too fast."

I could tell by looking at her she was rather pleased with R.C.'s table manners. Not many hired hands come down the pike that have the table manners of this gentleman.

Miz T. is such a pleasant lady, always has a smile. She can't be over five foot three, pretty well rounded on the edges, snow white hair. I reckon she was a beauty in her day. And she's still mighty pleasing to look at. Now, the Boss, he's just as white-headed as he could be, too. His hair's just as thick as the day he was eighteen years old. He's a tall, proud-standing man and always wears khaki pants. I don't believe I've ever seen him without his pants stuck down a pair of short-topped boots. Sure enough a cowboy. I'd heard a lot of tales about the man, and even though he was hard, and awfully demanding, anybody I've ever talked to has always considered him fair.

I was about done eating and I looked up at Miz T. and said, "May I be excused, ma'am?"

"Of course, Frank."

"It sure was good, ma'am," as I took my plate to the sink.

I headed out the door. Jim had been sitting there taking in all of this, kind of eyeballing R.C. When I left, he decided it was time to go, too. So we both headed for the bunkhouse.

Along the way he said, "Tell you what, Frank, you sure brought a ripe one."

"Ah, hell, Jim, I know it. But I felt sorry for the guy. He was sittin' out there and I asked him where he wanted to go and he didn't know. I don't think he knew where he was. So I decided to bring him on up here."

"Well, it don't look like he can stand a great lot of hard work, but maybe he's good at tinkerin'. Maybe he's mechanical. We can always use somebody around here. Hell, what if I should happen to get sick or die? Nothin' would ever get fixed."

I shook my head, and Jim and I went on in the bunkhouse. There were eight single cots, and only two that were occupied. I had one by a window, and on down three cots, Jim had his bed. Every bed had a little chest of drawers. There were pegs across the room that you could hang whatever on, your rope or spurs or chaps. A small table with four chairs was at the end.

Jim was pulling off his work shoes. He had on some lace-up brogans that he wore when he was afoot or horseback. After he pulled off his boots, sprawled out on the bed, and let out a big sigh, I knew if I didn't talk to him real quick, it was going to be too late. That man could go to sleep quicker than any man I ever saw.

"I heard on the radio that the bank was robbed."

Jim rolled back over. "Ah, shit. That's all the Boss needs. With it bein' dry and the cattle prices slippin' he sure ain't gonna be happy about that. He's been doin' business with them since the first fire was lit in this country. And, accordin' to him, it's one of the few home-owned banks left in the country. Depression closed most of 'em up. Hell, the Depression for that matter damn near closed everythin' up."

I'd heard the Depression tales forever and was born in the middle of it, but it never affected me a great lot. My family left Oklahoma when I was just a button and went over on the western side of New Mexico on the big reservation and that's where I grew up. If there was any hard times outside of just your normal, tough-to-get-along times, I never knew anything about them.

"Jim, you reckon I oughta tell the Boss about the robbery?" For once he wasn't sound asleep. He was kind of staring at the ceiling, thinking.

"Nah, I'll tell 'im. It's gonna be terrible upsettin' to 'im.

"Jim, you've got the job, 'cause I don't relish tellin' him."

While I was lying there thinking, I wondered about old Jim. He was a pretty good cowboy. His strong point, though, was building things. That old feller, and I didn't reckon that he was all that old, maybe fifty or somewhere thereabouts, could do it all. Anyhow, most of the buildings and the houses, this bunkhouse for that matter, were built by Jim.

In looking at Jim now as he was snoring away with his hands folded across his chest, I couldn't help but notice those hands. They were just as gnarled and brown and as hard as a rock. They'd held many a hammer and pushed a lot of trowels, handled a lot of well-ropes and bridle reins.

I asked Jim one time, "Jim, you ever been married?"

He just chuckled. "No, Frank, I've been vaccinated for it."

About that time the bunkhouse door opened up, and in came R.C. with a big smile.

"Well, how'd ya do?" I said.

"You're looking at the new hired hand."

"I guess congratulations are in order. You'll never get rich workin' here, but the grub is sure good. Gotta good roof over your head. You ain't gonna get a great lot of sleep. But if that makes you happy, I'm proud for you."

R.C. said, "Where should I put my things?"

"There's six empty bunks. Just pick one out that suits ya that's got a little ventilation."

Damned if he didn't say, "How about this one right here next to you?"

"Well, it's a free country."

"Do you have any objections?"

"No. Not unless you go to fartin' real regular. One thing I can't stand 'til I go to sleep is fouled air."

He grinned and said, "I'll remember."

He threw those two suitcases on the mattress, and said, "Shouldn't we go to work?"

"No, not quite yet. After dinner we get awhile to let our dinner settle and catch a little shut-eye. What did the Boss tell ya he wanted ya to do for the rest of the day?"

"He told me to tell you to show me the ropes and how everything lays, whatever that means."

I was kind of glad to hear it. I could stand a little rest and relaxation. I told R.C. to unpack whatever belongings he had and take a dresser right there on the left of his bunk. I was going to grab a little shut-eye. When he got done, he could holler at me and we'd take the grand tour.

I lay there on my side and kept watching this R.C. feller. He sure seemed eager. Through half-closed eyes he was kind of hard to study. But I always do my best studying lying down. I could see in his face he was full of questions, and raring to go. And just as I suspected, he started in with the questions.

"Did you grow up around here?"

"No, I come from over in the western part of the state."

"Well, were you born and raised in New Mexico?"

"No, originally I come from Oklahoma. When I was born I had a little feather stickin' out of my hair, and it stayed. I'm part Indian and I don't really pass that on to everybody that comes down the pike. Bein' an Indian isn't one of the more respected nationalities in the country. A lot of people still figure an Indian is a 'red nigger,' or I've even heard them referred to as a 'prairie nigger.' And if they get to talkin' that way long enough, they're sure goin' to get my fightin' side up. It's better just left alone."

"What kind of Indian?" R.C. said.

"Plains Indian," I told him.

R.C. seemed to accept it.

Well, Jim started stirring, coughing and wheezing, and sat up on the side of the bed. He stretched real big, reached up on the dresser and grabbed a sack of Beechnut chewing tobacco, and loaded up his mouth. I favor plug tobacco myself, or a little snoose.

He got up and headed for the door and said, "You boys gonna sit on them beds all afternoon? Me, I gotta go back to work."

I decided I'd better get at it, too, so I pulled on my boots and stuck my pant legs down the top. I glanced over at R.C. and he isn't missing anything. I just knew this feller was going to be full of questions and I just hoped that I could answer some of them in a decent way.

Belle had been lying out in the shade. She got up and stretched and we started down toward the barn. "How big is this ranch?" R.C. asked.

"I don't know. What difference does it make?"

"Just curious," R.C. said.

"A word to the wise," I said. "Never ask the Boss that. He'll say 'None of your damn business' and more. I've seen it happen before."

"Why?" R.C. asked.

"It's personal, like askin' how much money he's got."

"Oh." R.C. seemed to understand.

We walked on over toward the new barn. It'd been there maybe ten, fifteen years. That's where we kept all the cake. And I told R.C. about that.

"Cake?" he said.

"Yeah, cake. Winter feed."

"What's that?"

"It's forty-one percent protein and it comes in little seven-eighths-inch pellets that's broke off into three-inch lengths."

There was some cake on the floor. He picked some up, rolled it around, and damned if he didn't take a bite out of it.

"Boy, this is hard. How does a cow manage this?"

"They manage pretty well. They waller it around in their mouth. It's sure pretty good eatin'. Look at Belle over there." She had one up in her paws like a cat holds fish and was chewing and gnawing on a piece of cottonseed cake.

We both grinned at what she was doing. Just looked like she had a little old bone that she was proud of.

"Is that all you feed in the wintertime?" he said.

"Nah. We keep enough hay on hand where we can feed thirty days if we get covered up. A lot of snow comes through here horizontally because of the wind, but very little of it stays on the ground except in drifts. I've heard it said that during an honest-to-God 'blue norther' blizzard the snow could pack a barn through a single nail hole."

R.C. looked at me in disbelief.

I showed him around in the barn where we had an old DC welder partitioned off. I asked R.C. if he knew anything about welding.

"No," he said. "But I think I could luhn."

"You think you could what?"

He repeated the last word, "Luhn."

"Oh, you mean learn?" I questioned.

"Yes," he said, slightly embarrassed.

I had noticed from the time I picked him up that his manner of speech was different from mine. He seemed to pronounce r with an h, unlike myself who leaned hard on the r and rolled it. He had not done that with my name, Frank. I wondered why. Perhaps because of the way I pronounced it had led him to do the same. He either had a hell of an accent that I had never heard, or a speech impediment.

We walked over to the old barn. I don't know how old that barn was. It had been there many a year. Its sides were made out of rock and had a gambrel roof. Inside was just everything that had made the ranch go on for the last fifty years. We walked around to the west side of it, and that side was the saddle house.

It had a porch with a roof that came out over the door. It had hitch rails in the front. I opened up the door of the saddle house and walked in, and R.C.'s eyes got big. He just stood there and looked around. Right then I figured this feller appreciated the same things I did. It never ceased to fascinate me.

"I could spend a lot of time in here," R.C. said. "I hardly know what any of this stuff is."

"Can't learn it all in a day. All of it has a use. You'll find that out probably sooner than later, provided you last."

He looked up at with me with another one of those smiles and winked. "I'll last."

We went out the door and shut it. We were walking by the round corral, and he noticed the shape of it, too.

"What's this for?" he said.

"If anybody's ever after you, you run in there, and they'll never get you cornered," and I grinned at him real big like I'd made a joke. By the way he took it, I allowed that I had.

"Do you work horses in it?"

"Yeah. You get their complete attention in that thing. You can get one to goin' around in that thing and change directions. And you don't get boggled up in a corner," I said.

"What's out there in the middle?"

"This ya gotta see." I opened up the gate to the corral and we walked inside. We walked right up to the snubbing post, and you could tell by looking at it that it was old and it'd been used. There were deep rope burns all over it, the top anyhow, and it was weathered and bleached.

And, of course, R.C. said, "Well, what do you use this for?"

"If you're workin' horses, you can run a horse in here from any of the corrals outside or any of these little traps. There's a lane comin' in." I pointed over to the big gate. "If you have to rope him, you can. Then take a turn around that snubbin' post, and talk to him. Maybe you can get him to come a little closer and you can get him shortened up. You can get where you can touch him, handle him, and get him saddled, and eventually get him rode. Sometimes ya gotta choke 'em down to get a halter on 'em. We don't break horses around here until they're four years old."

"Why is that?"

"Well, 'cause the Boss does things the old way. When they come four years old, we put 'em in here and just waller it out."

"Do you ride broncs?"

"I've ridden a few. Matter of fact, that's what I was doin' this mornin'. That's the reason I'm missin' a little hide," as I touched the side of my face.

R.C. was still standing there looking at that snubbing post. He put his hands on it, kind of rubbed it like he was touching history. I didn't know how he knew, but he sure enough was.

"I wonder what kind of wood this is?"

And I had to be right truthful with him. "I don't know. The Boss said he brought that with him when he first came here, and that his daddy had it when he first came to this country. They brought it from back in east Texas. But, I'll tell you what. It's sure enough hard. You can take a piece of metal and whack it, and it'll draw sparks. It ain't petrified, but it's about as hard as iron. If there's one thing on this ranch that the Boss looks at with great fondness, it's that snubbin' post. As a matter of fact, it comes close to bein' sacred.

"Well, come on, I'll show you where the chore bucket is, and show you ol' Rat, the milk cow. I have a feelin' you're gonna get pretty intimate with her." I winked at him. "Maybe more than jerking a tit, though I doubt it'll become real social. She can't dance."

CHAPTER

4

"What, what?" Somebody was shaking my shoulder. I opened my eyes and the moonlight was shining through the windows. It had to be the middle of the night. Whoever was shaking my shoulder was doing a good job of it, because he hadn't stopped yet.

"Frank, Frank."

"What?"

"Listen."

Coming out of a sleep, I realized it was our new man, R.C.

"Listen, Frank," he said.

I lay there and listened. All I could hear was Jim snoring.

"What's that?"

"Hell, that's Jim asnorin'."

But I sat up and listened real close. You could hear coyotes howling. "R.C., those are just song dogs."

"What?"

"Coyotes."

"Really? It sounds like there's a million of them."

"No. A few of them can sound like a bunch."

"They're all over."

I listened. You could hear them to the south, and then a bunch up north that answered back. From all points they chimed in, letting another clan know they were still alive and kicking.

"I didn't realize there were so many coyote-ties in the country."

"There's lots of coyotes in the country, and R.C., they're coyotes, not coyote-ties. Nobody but old Tio calls them coyote-ties. That's kind of a Spanish pronunciation. We just call 'em coyote, period. Now go back to bed and get some sleep. We're gonna have to get up pretty quick."

"I'm sorry," R.C. said. "It just sounded like so many of them, I thought you ought to hear them."

"I hear 'em every night."

I rolled over and faced his bed. He was still sitting on the side of his bunk, just fascinated by the sound of those coyotes. As I drifted back to sleep, I opened my eyes and it seemed like he was still sitting there.

That morning I had my turn. Jim was up, grumbling about it. Had the light turned on, and I was pulling on my britches. R.C. had finally gotten over his coyote scare and was sleeping like the dead. I walked over and shook him. His eyes popped open like he didn't know where he was. Sat right straight up in bed and said, "What now?"

"Time to get up," I said.

He looked around. 'Course the moon had gone down. "It's the middle of the night."

"Nah. You may think so, but it's time for breakfast."

"At this hour?" he said.

"Yep, the standin' rule around here is never let the sun catch you eatin' breakfast. So get up or you'll be late."

We started out the door and down at the house you could see a light burning in the kitchen. Jim started first, and I fell in behind him, and R.C. was last.

"You follow us. It's darker than the inside of a bruised crow out here. If you don't know where you're goin', you're liable to trip over somethin' and fall down."

Lupe was around pouring coffee for everyone before we sat down. Had the table piled high with good food. The Boss was already at the end of the table, and I could see by the look on his face that he knew what had gone on down at Tramperos. He did look a mite worried.

About that time young Tres walked in. School must have been out for some reason and he'd come to the ranch. He lived in town during school. He was just a young button, about twelve or thirteen. The Boss introduced R.C. to him and to Lupe. He was proud of that grandson. Lupe had already smiled at R.C. and decided she'd take him under her wing. Couldn't really see what everybody saw in this new feller, but everybody, including my dog, thought he was sure all right.

After breakfast, while we were sitting there drinking our coffee, the Boss said, "I'm going to take Tres and go down to Tramperos and try to find out what happened. Don't mind telling you I'm worried. I've been doing business with the Sawyers for many years. Sure don't believe they deserve all the unfortunate things that have been happening to them. So, I'll be gone part of the day. Tres told me last night, Frank, that the windmill in the Martinez is down. Looks like the crows have been working on it, too. You take R.C. up there and see what you can do."

"Okay, Boss. We'll get right at it." Could tell the Boss was in a hurry to get going. The sun was just beginning to come up, and it was time for him to be somewhere else.

R.C. and I went on up to the big barn, started loading up the power wagon. It was a World War II army pickup that was four-wheel drive. We had everything you needed to fix a windmill. Got in and warmed her up, backed out of the barn, and headed west.

One good thing about having R.C. along, I was not going to have to open any gates. I was driving and he was sitting on the cushions, so he could open the gates. It was plumb light now. The sun had just cleared the eastern horizon. And R.C. started in with the questions.

"Who's this Tres?"

"That's the Boss's grandson."

"Where are his mother and father?"

"I don't know. I never knew his daddy. Evidently he went to the war. Talkin' to Jim I understand that the Boss was always real hard on him and they never got along. Always seemed to be a little bad blood between them. He got every dirty job on the ranch. I guess it was the Boss's way of makin' him into a top hand and a good man, accordin' to Jim. But his son just couldn't take it. He got to drinkin' real bad. 'Course the Boss was forever on his back about that. One day he just got up and left.

"All I know is that Tres was just a baby when a woman came by here claimin' to be Mrs. J. W. Stone, Jr. She couldn't keep Tres and wanted to leave him with them, since they were his grandfolks. They quizzed her quite a bit on where their son was and what had happened. I guess her answers were good enough that they accepted that he was their grandson. I think J. W., Jr., 'Sonny' they call him, left her and the boy. That was back East somewhere. She was goin' to California.

"Whatever mistakes they made with their son, they sure weren't goin' to make with Tres, because of all the dirty jobs, all the ranch-hand jobs, and the windmillin' and all this, he only does his work a-horseback. The boy is practically a-horseback ten hours a day. The Boss showed him how to use a rope. As a matter of fact, he's the only thing outside of Miz T. that the Boss has shown compassion for and a great deal of love."

"What does he do when he's horseback?" R.C. asked.

"Aw, he just prowls. Sees things that are wrong and comes back and tells the Boss so we can go fix 'em like this mornin'." We stopped at the gate going into the Padre pasture. R.C. got out to open it. I could see he was pondering what I'd just told him. As I was sitting there watching him open that gate, I got plumb tickled. All our gates were so tight you could play a tune on them. But R.C. hadn't mastered opening a wire gate. He pushed on the gate stick and tried to get the bale up. His feet came practically off the ground, and he backed off and pushed again. I thought we would never get any work done unless I helped him.

"Can you get it?"

"I'm trying," he said.

"Let me show you how to do this." I grabbed the gate stick and got my elbow and forearm straight with the top wire and shoved all my body weight against it. I just bumped it with my left hand and lifted the bale up and open it came.

R.C. looked at me with amazement. "How'd you do that?"

"Nothin' to it. It's all in the way you hold your mouth."

I went back and drove the power wagon through and sat there and watched him in my rearview mirror. He grabbed hold of the bale with his right hand and got the gate stick with his left hand and lined everything out. I'll be damned if he didn't do it just like I had opened it. One quick little push and he shoved the bale down and the gate was closed. By God, maybe he was right. He learned faster than I thought he would.

He climbed back in the pickup and we headed on up the creek.

"What's this pasture called?"

"We just got into the Padre pasture. There's an old mission up here. It's been abandoned I reckon for a hundred years. Used to be an old settlement here. Peralta is what they called it."

You could see the big mesa we call the Piedra. Sandstone rising out of the valley floor. Must have risen two or three hundred feet and flat as a flapjack on top. Just solid rock.

I pointed it out to him. I said, "There's the Piedra. That's what the ranch is named for."

I glanced over at R.C. and he was taking it all in. As we went by the mission, he looked it all over and said, "I sure would like to know the history of that place."

"You bet. If it could talk, it would be quite a tale to tell."

We had to cross Long's Creek right there to the south of the mission. There's always been a ford there. I guess that's why the mission was built where it was, mainly because it was a handy place to cross the creek. It was on the trail between Tramperos and Dorsey long before there was a town by either name or graded roads anywhere in the country. You could see wagon tracks and a dim trail coming down through the breaks and crossing the creek going to the mission. All around the mission were crumbled adobes. Everything was long since rotted. There was a well there. It was the only hand-dug well on the place.

"Why would they dig a well? The creek is right here, not a hundred yards from the church. Why didn't they get their water from there?" asked R.C.

"I suppose they did, but that well water would be a lot cleaner than the water that's in the creek, wouldn't it?"

He shook his head, like he believed that was true fact. I stopped just before going into the creek and pulled her down into four-wheel drive. The creek wasn't running much, but on that creek it could sure get awful "quicky." It was mainly a wet-weather creek, but always had a trickle, and the holes, which were numerous, remained full. Sometimes when it rained up to the head of it, God, the water would come down in torrents.

Long's Creek wasn't that big. Maybe thirty yards across, but it was the lifeblood of this ranch. Saved a lot on windmills. It ran through almost every pasture the way the Boss had it set up. If the wells did break down or it became unusually still like in August—that's about the only time the wind didn't blow—the stock would have water.

"It sure is pretty country," R.C. said.

"Yeah, this part of it is," I said. "These are the breaks." Kind of a windy road going through here and there's lots of juniper. Matter of fact, those were the only natural trees on the place outside of the cottonwoods along the river. But when you got up on top on the prairie you could find places where the homesteaders planted trees, elms mostly, with a few fruit trees. I think that was probably the first thing a homesteader did when he came into this country, planted some trees.

We topped out of the breaks on the prairie and stopped at another gate going into the Martinez pasture. This time R.C. got out and whomped the gate and open it came. Had no trouble at all. Driving out on top of the prairie, all of a sudden, R.C. hollered, "Stop, stop, stop!"

God, I slammed on the brakes like I was fixing to run over something. "What's the matter?"

"Look! There's a bird with a broken wing."

I looked out there, and sure enough there was a curlew, and it was awobbling off with its wing dragging the ground. R.C. was already out of the car door taking after it.

"What are ya gonna do?" I hollered at him.

"I've got to help her."

"Come back here."

I drove out there to get him and he was after the bird and the bird just kept amoving.

"R.C., come on back."

Finally he walked back. "She'll never make it if we don't help her."

"She ain't hurt."

"What do you mean?"

"She's laid some eggs around here. You see them doin' it all the time. They start draggin' a wing and actin' like they're crippled and they'll lead you off from that nest. If you follow 'em, I suppose they'll lead you plumb to the Gulf of Mexico. Then they'll quit you and fly back to the nest.

"They lay those eggs in the buffalo and gramma grass out there and they kind of hang around until the eggs are hatched and their young'uns can get up and run around."

They're an awkward-looking bird. They did have long legs. I don't know where they came from. But they came back every year to the prairie to lay their eggs and raise their young. It seemed like it was always the first part of May, so when the curlews came you knew it was sure enough spring.

We drove on down to the Martinez well, while R.C. still pondered the flight of the curlew. We pulled on up to the windmill, and sure enough, I could see that Tres was right. Right up under the wheel under the stub tower was a big wad of wire. The crows flew off as we drove up, and I knew they were building a nest. They did it every year, especially on this well, and I didn't know why.

We piled out and I said, "First things first." I pulled back the seat, grabbed a pair of coveralls, and told R.C. to do the same. Always kept a couple of pairs of coveralls in the back. "Put on those John Deere chaps, and let's go to work."

I threw him a pair of wire cutters and got myself some. The wind wasn't blowing much. There was just a slight breeze. I told him if we both went up and did it, we'd sure get through a great lot faster. I went over and pulled the brake down on the mill. It pulled the tail over and shut it off, and I started up the ladder with him afollowing me.

The tower was an old wooden one with four-by-four legs, a wooden ladder, and a platform built just below the angle-iron stub tower. We got up on the platform. There was just room enough for both of us to sit on opposite sides of the tower and go to cutting.

"My God, this thing is huge," said R.C.

"Oh, they've just begun." The nest was made all out of wire. With wire cutters, "dikes" we called them, you could reach up and start snipping. They wove that wire around the angle-iron legs and tightened the nest down where it was a real pain to get off. We spent the better part of an hour just cutting, pulling, and throwing down the bits and pieces. Finally we got to where we could peel it off. We crawled down off the tower and examined it.

We were both squatting there on our heels looking at it. "This is a wire collector's dream," I said. "Look at all the different types of wire in there." And there were little short pieces of barbed wire of all kinds, baling wire, bedsprings, fence. Just any kind of wire that you'd want. I picked up a piece of flat wire, and said, "Look at this. This is the old XIT fence." It was about twelve inches long and kind of a ribbon shape. It was galvanized and had points that were popped on top of it. "Wherever they got this, they must have got it fifteen miles east of here. That's the only place I know where that old XIT wire is still standin'.'"

"Where did all this old wire come from?" R.C. asked.

"I guess these crows go salvage around those old homesteads and pick up all this junk. Sometimes it'll fall between the sucker rod and the pipe, and get down in the checks and under the balls. It'll quit pumpin' and the first thing you know, we're out of water. If somebody isn't around checkin' it, well, somethin's goin' to go thirsty."

It took most of the morning to get the well fixed and to see water flowing from the lead pipe. Since it was dinnertime we pulled out our lunches, got on the shady side of the power wagon, and commenced to see what Lupe had fixed for our lunch.

While we were sitting there eating, looking out over the prairie, R.C. started in with those questions. Cows were starting to come in to water. A few of the calves were coming in with them. But quite a few calves were left out there. Always a cow stayed with them, babysitting.

"All these cows seem to be the same color," R.C. said.

"Yeah, this here is Hereford country, strictly Hereford country. You'd have to burn the prairie and sift the ashes to find somebody runnin' somethin' other than Hereford cows."

"How come?"

"Ah, I don't know. Just tradition mainly. You'll find some steer outfits runnin' Mexican cattle, Corrientes we call 'em, with a lot of color to 'em. But these Hereford cattle are an English breed brought over here in the late eighteen hundreds, some say by Colonel Goodnight. They adapted to the prairie and plains real well.

"The story goes that the Boss's daddy started out with eleven head of real good Hereford heifers. Bred 'em up and bred this cow herd all from them eleven head."

"Do you raise your own bulls, too?" R.C. said.

"Nah. The Boss mainly buys outside bulls. Try to keep the cattle from gettin' inbred that way. All them cows, you'd have to look real hard to find a cow that weighs over nine hundred. You don't find big cows out in this country. They say a cow is doin' her job if she'll wean a calf half her weight."

"So," R.C. said, "the calves'll weigh around four fifty?"

"Oh, the steer calves'll weigh about that and the heifers anywhere from twenty-five to thirty pounds lighter. 'Course, dependin' on the year. If it's dry like it is and stays dry, we could come up with weanin' an awful light calf crop. In the fall we'll get all of 'em up, wean 'em, and turn 'em out in the weaner pastures. We'll dry winter 'em and keep 'em all 'til next summer. Then sell 'em as yearlin's."

"That's fascinating," R.C. said.

CHAPTER

5

Had this good sorrel horse that I had started pretty well. I figured he'd seen enough of the inside of that round corral, so I thought I'd take him out and show him some sights. Had a pretty good handle on him by this time. I'd been working on him off and on for a couple of weeks, with three other young horses. As we headed out west, toward the Padre pasture, saw R.C. peeling posts. Stopped by and visited with him a minute.

"Have you found out what your duties are yet, R.C.?"

He just smiled. He knew what I was talking about. The second day here he asked what his duties were, and Jim had told him, "If there's somethin' special the Boss wants you to do, he'll tell you at breakfast. If we've got a big project goin', and he don't say nothin', you go out and stay on that project 'til he pulls you off or you get finished, either one. If you don't have nothin' else to do you go up to the post yard."

"Well," I asked R.C., "how do you like it so far?" That was kind of an unfair question, with me sitting a-horseback and him standing on the ground peeling posts.

He grinned that easy grin. "I didn't come here to peel posts. I want to learn more about this country and about cowboying. When do you think the Boss will let me get on a horse?"

"Spring brandin' is comin' up here pretty quick. You're goin' to need to get a-horseback. Can you ride a horse?"

"Certainly. I've ridden before."

I had my doubts about that, but if he picked up horseback riding as quick as he had everything else, there wasn't a doubt in my mind that he'd be making a hand before too long.

"Next time I get a-horseback, I'll take you with me."

"I'd sure appreciate that, Frank. This peeling posts is getting tiresome."

"Well, hang in there, pard. I'll see you later." And I headed on out.

Feels good to be a-horseback. I've always enjoyed this part of my work, probably more than any other kind of work I've done. That's one thing I don't care about working here on the Piedra, it's a ranch-hand job. When our neighbors to the west here, the C Slash C, the Cannon outfit, hired a man on for a cowboy job, that's where he stayed. They had a windmill crew. They had a fencing crew. All a cowboy had to do was get a-horseback every day, prowl his cattle. They were big in the yearling business. They ran a bunch of Mexican Corriente steers. If I could have my choice of what I do, that'd be it! Strictly horseback work.

I was standing up in my stirrups, and we were heading out at a long trot, going by the old mission church. When I went across the old wagon road at the ford, I noticed tracks, pickup tracks to be exact. I wondered who in the world could be coming down in here. The Boss was real particular who passed through the ranch. The gates weren't locked, but you just didn't do that in this country.

So I thought I'd take a look. The mission had been fenced out, just a little five-wire fence going all the way around it, to keep the cattle out mainly. I hobbled Sorrely and went in to take a look. Whoever drove in there had driven right up to the gate and got out. There were two sets of boot tracks. Fairly easy to see there in the sand, especially on the road.

It wasn't unusual for some of the Mexican folks to come and visit the mission, because there was a graveyard connected with it. Some of their people were buried here. There were tracks around the little cemetery, which was on the north side of the church. It was fenced off by a little handmade, wrought-iron fence. It wasn't high. Rather ornate, with little points like spearheads on the top of each post. Like all graveyards, you could see where somebody had put some plastic flowers around the graves. I didn't imagine the cemetery had over forty graves.

The cornerstone on the old mission read "1852." It was a little over a hundred years old. I opened the door. It still worked. Walked in. It wasn't inhabited by anything except maybe rattlesnakes and a bunch of pigeons. All the windows had long since gone. Don't imagine they ever had any glass in them, just wooden shutters that had all fallen in disrepair.

I hadn't been in a great lot of Catholic churches, but this one was very similar. It was long and narrow, made out of adobe and plastered with some kind of a whitewash on the inside. I could see a number of shelves and recesses in the wall up toward the front of the church where religious articles had been placed and long since removed. I walked on up to where the altar should have been. There were a fair number of tracks around there. Off to the left was a door leading into a small room that might have served as a bedroom or an office. I didn't know what.

I didn't realize it until I looked back, but Belle had come in with me. And what I saw startled me a little bit. The hair on her back stood straight up and she had her nose to the ground. I didn't know if some wild animal had been in there, or she was upset by the scent of whoever had been in there.

I backed out of there toward the front door, stopped in the middle, and took one more last look around. Looking up you could see that the crossbeams were made out of, I suspected, a pine pole, peeled long and straight. The rafters had been hand-hewed, and the roof was still on and in pretty good shape. All in all, if it hadn't been repaired since the late 1800s, the place wasn't in all that bad a shape.

It felt good to get back outside and into the sunshine. I don't know why I'd been uneasy in there. It was supposed to have been a house of God, but it seemed like God had left it years ago and forgot to come back.

Whoever had been here had walked around a great deal. They left tracks everywhere. They even went over to the old crumbled adobes. Could have been that they were just looking for arrowheads. I knew they were plentiful up and down the river. Had to be kind of lucky to run into any up on the prairie. But down here in the breaks you could find them. I know, because the Boss had a coffee table in the living room with a glass top. Underneath that there must have been two hundred perfect arrowheads of all shapes and sizes.

Everyone knew, especially me, that the Comanches and Kiowas had roamed this country for years and years. There was even a tale that Comanches had raided this little village and pillaged it, and that's why it had no longer continued to thrive.

Walked on over around the adobe houses and they were in a sorry state of repair, all crumbled down. As I walked in and out of them, you could notice some of the timbers that had held the roof up had been charred. Looked like there had been a big fire. As close as everything was together, I guess if it started on one house, then it would have spread to the other houses. There were maybe fifteen or twenty separate structures, and all of them in shambles. Belle and I just wandered around through them. There were tracks going in every one. Whoever had been here had spent a good deal of time looking, but I couldn't see where they'd disturbed anything.

I walked back to my horse and took the hobbles off, got on, and fixed to leave. Couldn't help but wonder who had been here. Could have been those Mueller boys. The Muellers lived up north of here, on a little bitty place. Just scraped out a living. Those boys had always been a little suspect, but they'd never been caught at anything. I knew a few neighbors around had been missing a few cattle, and everybody wondered if it might be them.

I hit a trot and pushed it out of my mind. Crossed the river and on up through the Martinez. Got on the south side of the breaks and headed west, just putting some miles on this young horse who was getting an education. His ears were no longer laid back. Occasionally one would be back and the other one would be forward. That meant his mind was split in the middle. He was watching me and paying attention to what was up front. As soon as I got those ears forward, I knew that I would have accomplished something. He didn't need to be watching me. He needed to be watching the country and watching cattle. If you watched a horse, he could tell you a great lot.

We were pretty high up on the west end, and I stopped to take a look around, survey the country. I was right close to the west fence that borders on the Cannon Ranch. I could see somebody way over on the north side of the breaks, a couple of miles off, a-horseback heading south. I wondered if it might be my friend, Poke. I hoped it was. I hadn't seen him since I'd gone over and helped the Cannons when they were branding. I just hoped it wasn't Top Darcey, the foreman. I'd had enough of him to last a good long while.

Whoever the rider was, was coming slow. He kind of acted like he was riding fence, which I didn't see any need of. The fence that separated us from the Cannons was the best fence the Cannons had surrounding their place.

So I thought I'd amble on down, kind of stay out of sight and watch him. I sure hoped it was Poke, because I could stand some good-natured conversation and good laughs. Every time we were around one another we always hoorahed one another pretty good. Poke was quite a philosopher. Anything that came out of my mouth I'd heard from somebody.

Poke, now, he had original thoughts. Sometimes they got pretty deep. He came from down in Sanderson, Texas, off a ranch. The funny part about it was, it was a sheep ranch. He'd gone up to Texas Tech to further his education. He spent most of his time chasing girls and drinking whiskey and beer. When his daddy got his grades, he told him to go to summer school and to jack up that car, take the wheels off it, and ship them home. Which he did. His grades didn't improve any, and he had a wonderful social life. But he was afoot, and didn't appreciate it. So, he just packed his belongings and caught a ride out west and had gone to work for the Cannons.

I rode on down and stopped at a cave—off on the edge of the creek, probably about thirty foot above the creek. I sat by a lone cedar and waited for him to come out. Began to wonder if he hadn't circled around behind me. But directly old Sorrelly pointed both ears and looked straight ahead, and sure enough, out of there he came.

It was Poke. He was looking around like he knew somebody was watching him, but couldn't figure where. He threw his reins to his horse's head and let him have a drink. All of a sudden that old bay horse he was riding jerked his head up and looked right square at me. I could see a big grin spread across Poke's face and he reached up and kindly tipped his hat at me. He went on up the creek a little bit, crossed, and met me there at the fence.

"What are you doin' hidin' behind that cedar tree, pullin' your pud?"

"Nah. I'm just watchin' you. You lookin' over here on the outfit tryin' to find a heifer that maybe you could rope and hump on a little bit?"

"Maybe so," Poke said.

We both laughed. "You in a big hurry, or you got time to visit a little?" I asked.

"I'm just prowlin' around. What happened to your face? Sackin' wildcats and run a sack short?"

"Yep." We both got off, hobbled our horses, and sat down across the fence, and commenced to lie to one another.

"Frank, you been anywhere worth talkin' about lately?"

"Nah. I haven't been to town in several weeks. I sure need to go. I'm so horny I honk."

Poke smiled. "Well, I'll give you a name. When you get to Dorsey, you can look her up and she'll dehorn you."

"I don't want no note, I want a personal introduction. I've never noticed the ladies flockin' around you. As a matter of fact, I've noticed that when you and I walk down the street all the young things we're meetin' cross over and walk on the other side."

"That's because they can see you're a gut eater, pure savage. And no self-respectin' lady's got any use for them."

"I don't believe that's so, Poke. I think they smell sheep-dip." We both laughed at that.

"Heard about that jailbreak back in Oklahoma?"

I allowed I hadn't.

"Three sure-enough desperadoes headed west on 66, holdin' up fillin' stations and grocery stores, and anything else that might have a little money, 'til they hit an Amarillo roadblock. Two were killed, but one got away. Ain't never been caught since. Old Sheriff Gaither's a former Texas

Ranger. If anybody can get him, he will. Them Rangers don't never give up."

"Did they give any kind of description on these boys?" I asked.

"The radio said all three of them were young fellers. They broke out of El Reno. I guess they was double mean. They put up a fight. The one that got away was supposed to be in his early twenties, dark-headed, about five foot ten and a hundred and fifty pounds. Leastwise that's what the radio said."

"What have you heard about the bank job?"

"Jack Cannon come back from down there tellin' that the spinster Sawyer said that all she could remember was that the feller had a pistol, a cap, and a scarf tied around his face, just like the Old West." He grinned real big. "She said the pistol wasn't a revolver. Said it had a big hole in the end of it. So, evidently it was a .45 automatic."

'Course, Poke was big on guns, and knew all this stuff.

I stuck a stem of gramma grass in my mouth, and was picking my teeth.

"Frank, between you and me, I think this outfit I'm workin' for is in trouble. These boys are pretty heavy in debt. They've never got the bank paid off."

"Well, hell! I didn't think you were ever supposed to pay the bank off. That's the way you build up credit."

Poke looked at me with one eye squinted and said, "I betcha Boss Stone don't owe nothin' at the bank."

I allowed that might be true. "Everybody always said the cow business was a great lot safer than the yearlin' business. If you hold on to an old cow's tail, she may drag you through the mud a few times, but she'll always pull you up on dry ground.

"You know, Poke, it's funny. You ought to have the job I have and I ought to have the job you have. Of course, they always say the grass is greener on the other side of the fence."

Poke laughed. "Hell, I am on the other side. And just look, it ain't no greener over here than it is over there."

"I know. But you're interested in genetics and in building up breeds. Me, I'm interested in horseback work and workin' steers, and not having to get off my horse.

"Poke, do you think the Cannons will be able to hold out 'til fall and get their cattle sold? This bunch they've got now may get them all healed up and cover all the debt."

Poke shook his head and looked at the ground. "I don't know. I hear the place is up for sale now. They've got a couple of hot-shot lawyers up in Santa Fe interested in the place. But you know lawyers. Anytime they get involved in anything, they get to nitpickin', wantin' boundary surveys and the like. And all that costs money, and the Cannons don't have it to spend. I think what they'd like to do is sell it to these lawyers and lease it back 'til fall, 'til they get their cattle gone.

"What kind of music you hearin' on the radio lately that you like?" Poke asked.

"Oh, myself, I'm gettin' partial to Hank Thompson. Have you heard 'The Wild Side of Life' yet? You know I believe if that Hank Thompson was singin', there isn't a son of a bitch in the world that could whip me!"

He nodded. "Well, I'm kind of partial to Frankie Lane. Boy, he does a job on 'Jezebel.' But I still think 'Muletrain' is my favorite."

You could tell that Poke's and my preference of music ran a little different way. I preferred the hard country music and he had a preference to top-ten hit parade music, "popular music" we called it.

Poke said, "Hell, I'm gettin' lonesome. Is the 'Bullet' runnin'?"

He was referring to my 1949 Ford that looked like it had a bullet headed straight forward in the middle of the grill. "Oh, yeah. Runs like a top."

"You got the weekend off?" he asked.

"Yep."

"Me, too. I can get loose Friday night and I don't have to be back 'til Monday mornin'."

"Ride on over and spend the night Friday," I said, "and we'll go to town Saturday mornin'? By the way, got us a new hand."

"Sure 'nuff," Poke said. "Where'd you find him?"

"Found him down on the highway, a couple of weeks past. Pale as a ghost and hardly knows straight up from straight down about the cow business. But he's workin' at it and seems to be fittin' in."

Poke seemed real interested. "Where'd he say he come from?"

"I didn't really ask."

"Feller mighta been in jail. You sure don't get any suntans in jail."

"Whoa! That's one thing I hadn't thought of."

"Well, I better start makin' tracks. Top will wonder where I'm at," Poke said. "He's circlin' around on the other side. I'm supposed to meet him back west of here."

I'd known Top since first coming to this country and asked about him.

"He's the same arrogant bastard he always was. But you got to admit, he is good. He knows what he's doin.' I go to school on him quite a bit. If I can just live through all the barbs he throws at me when he's talkin', I'm sure I'll come out ahead. But if I don't git, he'll be talkin' to me like a stepchild. I'll see you Friday night, Frank."

"All right, Poke. Now, don't get none on you."

He looked back over his shoulder as he was climbing aboard his horse. "And don't you get lost."

"No chance. Belle will always lead me home."

CHAPTER

6

On Thursday night we were out looking toward the west and a big bank of black clouds that had gathered up. It looked like it might rain. We looked at the big house and quite often we saw the Boss out on the front porch looking toward the west. If we didn't get a rain out of this batch of clouds, we sure were going to miss a good chance. To the west about a hundred miles the Sangre de Cristo Mountains rose up to ten to twelve thousand feet elevation. It had been common theory for everybody in this country that Pacific fronts brought in a lot of moisture, picked up some steam, hit the west side of those mountains, bounced, and didn't come down until they were over east of us in Texas. But occasionally it came down short. When it did we were grateful.

Sometime during the night a big clap of thunder raised me about a foot off the bed and scared me to death. I could hear soft rain coming down, and I tell you it was music to my ears. I didn't know how long it'd been raining, but already it was beginning to smell so sweet. You could smell the outdoors mixed in with all the body odors, saddle sweat, screw-worm medicine, blood-stopper powder, and all the other odors that would come out of the bunkhouse. Above all of them, you could smell that sweet freshness of the rain. I closed my eyes and went back to sleep. I woke up in another hour or two and heard it raining some more.

Again another hellacious clap of thunder, and I could hear Belle at the door whining. I think the only thing Belle was really scared of was thunder and lightning. She didn't understand it, and she wanted to be near the only thing she had faith in, which was me. I got up and let her in. She generally sleeps on the porch. But tonight it wouldn't do. She had to come in and sleep right by my bed.

It seemed to me like it rained all night long. Not hard, mind you. But soft rain. And those were the kind that did us some good. When it rained hard, and came a real thunder-buster, this country could shed rain just like a slicker. Bring the creek up, and most of it would wash away. A soft rain like we were having this morning would go in the ground and turn the country completely around.

I was sound asleep when all the lights came on and I heard the Boss hollering. "Get up, boys! Get up! It's a great day in the mornin'."

Very seldom did you see the Boss smile real big. I'd never seen him just out and out guffaw and laugh. But this morning he had a grin on his face as big as all outdoors. He even pulled up a chair around the table and sat and talked to us while we were getting dressed.

Jim asked the Boss if he'd checked the rain gauge. "You, bet. I've been checkin' it since midnight. The last time I looked, we had an inch, ten. And it all fell just right. That's the important part."

R.C. chimed in. "Sir, it sure will be nice to see all this country green."

With that the Boss looked up at him and said, "Son, this country ain't supposed to be green. It could rain a foot and it would never turn green."

"Why is that, with all this rain?" R.C. asked.

"Well, you see, that's why they call this country the Golden Spread. It's supposed to have the brown, golden look to it, 'cause we save our grass. Green grass mixed in with the old grass makes the best feed in the world. This is a wonderful, wonderful country. A fellow has just got to respect the country, know what it can do, live with it and not fight it."

The Boss seemed to be enjoying himself immensely. I guess he considered himself on a roll. So, he continued to expound on the virtues of this country.

"I'm tellin' you, the best country in the world is where the buffalo ran, on the east side of the Continental Divide, out here on the prairie. Anywhere you find old buffalo country, even though they're gone now, that's ranching country. We're only supposed to get about twelve inches of rain a year. But I've been here a long time and I don't know where they got the average. Don't seem like we ever get that twelve inches."

He smiled and I could tell by his eyes what he was fixing to say was going to have some irony to it.

"You know most of the firstcomers into this country, the settlers, claimed it was the best 'next year' country in the world. And I suppose that's true. They came from the Midwest where they had lots of rain. They homesteaded this country on hundred-and-sixty-acre plots. And all it was was the government wantin' to populate the territory. You take a hundred and sixty acres and put it back in the Midwest and you just might have somethin'. But you take a hundred and sixty acres out here on the prairie, and you do well to run two billy goats. What the government did was bet these poor boys a hundred and sixty acres against their lives that they couldn't make a livin'. And let me tell you boys, the government won most of their bets.

"There were two kinds of settlers that come out here then. Those that had a little money and wanted to make it, and those that didn't have any money and had to make it. I don't mean no offense, Jim, your daddy was the hardest-workin' man I ever saw. Spent his whole life walkin' behind a moldboard plow and a span of mules, tryin' to eke a livin' out of this country doin' day work on the side. And doin' anything he could to bring in a little money, sellin' cream. He did it all, didn't he, Jim?"

Jim just hung his head. "I guess so, Boss."

"Anyhow, when the thirties came along and the wind began to blow and the dust rolled in from Colorado and all those plowed-up fields, some of 'em got so depressed they couldn't stand it anymore and they just left with washin' hangin' on the line and a pot on the stove. They just left those claims and headed out. Walked down to the train station, begged and borrowed enough to head back where they came from, with a broken heart.

"Well, boys, Lupe's waitin' breakfast on you. I had breakfast over an hour ago. I'm goin' to saddle up old Spud and take a look around. Even though there's just been about an inch of rain, it seems like there's been a foot of lightnin'. Gotta check around and see what damage lightnin's done, not that it'll do any good. If it's hit any cattle at all, I'll gladly sacrifice a few head for a good rain like this. You boys stay dry today. We're goin' to brand toward the end of next week. So get all our brandin' paraphernalia organized, sharpen needles, knives, oil up some saddles. And say, Frank," with a wink, "don't forget those harnesses. Weather's been cold and I don't want 'em crackin'."

I understood what he meant, and I nodded to him. And with that, out the door he went.

We looked around on the rack for a slicker that'd fit R.C. Got him one that was a shade big, but it sure would shed the rain. He had long since taken up wearing an old felt hat that somebody had left around there that was a size or two too big and sat right down on his ears. But it had a little character to it. R.C. was taking shape. I noticed in the past two weeks he was getting some color to his cheeks, and getting a few calluses on his hands. He was wearing an old pair of worn-out gloves that somebody cast away. Jim had advised him not to wear gloves, just do it barehanded. If you get in the habit of wearing gloves you'd have to buy a new pair. New gloves cost money, where hide grew back. But R.C. appreciated the gloves and old hat. We all stomped down to breakfast and God, did it smell good outside. After breakfast we gave Tio a hand with some of his chores. Tio never wore any overshoes. He just wore the old brogans and faded Levis, faded gray work shirt buttoned at the very top button at the collar. Everything on the old man fit loose, just like a pup tent. He didn't wear a slicker, he wore an old oilcloth poncho or serape, or whatever they call them.

R.C. received his final lesson on milking old Rat, the milk cow. He'd been working on it off and on for a couple weeks under Tio's supervision. At one point Tio had told us that he thought he was trying to pump the milk back up in the cow rather than pull the milk out. He was getting along real well with it now.

Later in the saddle house, we commenced to saddle soap, and wash off all the sweat and grime that had accumulated over half a year of riding. We generally worked these saddles over once in the spring and once in the late fall after delivery time, usually on a day like this when it's best to stay inside.

There were two saddles that no one ever rode. They were high-backed, high-cantled Fraiser saddles. One of them was an old center-fire saddle. Never knew who it had belonged to. Had a suspicion it might have belonged to the Boss's dad. And another double-rigged saddle, the one known as "Sonny's saddle." None of the two had been ridden that I knew of. So they didn't need a lot of cleaning, but we oiled them faithfully twice a year. Sonny's chaps and spurs still hung where he'd hung them up years ago.

I asked Jim, "Do you think Sonny's ever comin' back?"

"No. No, I don't believe he will, Frank. He's been gone too long and he was sure terrible to drink. I imagine by now he's been long dead and buried somewhere. The Boss has never received word from him and I guess all of Sonny's things will hang right where they are, at least until the Boss is gone."

About that time Tres walked in and we had to change the subject. I hated that, because I liked to find out more about the Boss's son, John W. Stone, Jr. Always seemed a mystery to me why a man would have a ranch like this coming to him someday, and he'd blow it all and walk off from it. Whiskey to me had always been a pleasurable thing, but I guess it's got its demons. But maybe that wasn't the whole story. Maybe it was the way the Boss had taken it upon himself to make Sonny tough and to ride him so hard.

Since we'd knocked off a little early, Jim pulled off his boots, and was lying down taking a nap. I pulled out my old Harmony guitar that I'd had since about 1945, and was playing a little bit for R.C. and Tres. I knew all the old cowboy standards, like "Git Along Little Dogie," "When the Work's All Done This Fall," "The Strawberry Roan," and "Zebra Dun." I knew quite a few songs that were on the latest cowboy hit parade. I'd listened to them on the radio so much that I'd memorized the words. Those fellers never seemed to tire of hearing them.

We heard somebody out on the porch of the bunkhouse, hollering, "Would you fellers let a poor humble stranger in out of the rain?" and I knew by the voice it was Poke Mahone.

"Come in and get dry. What are you doin' over here so early?" I asked.

"Hell! We're goin' to town, ain't we? You said you had this weekend off."

"I do, but I didn't expect you so early."

"Well, things were runnin' a little slow 'cause of this good rain, and I thought I'd get over here while there was still a little light to see by. As much lightnin' as there was last night, I'd sure hate to get caught out in it tonight. A big bolt might come down and strike my horse as dead as a hammer."

"What in the hell would happen to you? You're sittin' on top of him," I said.

"No chance, Frank." And with a big grin, "I'm insulated."

"Let me go out and help you put your horse up."

"Nah, I've already turned him in."

"Why don't you wash up. We're fixin' to go down for supper."

"Nah, no need to wash up. I'll use a fork," Poke laughed. "You reckon that the Boss'll feed an old worn-out drifter like me, or do you reckon I'll have to chop wood for my supper?"

"Oh, Poke," Tres said, "you know Papa has said more than once having you stop in is a pleasure. You'll be as welcome as a spring rain."

"I hope so. You know, I don't know as to how I'm not totally responsible for this rain that we're all agettin'. I've concentrated all my thoughts on just what lay under the Cannons' fence. I was really surprised when I came out and got on the Piedra and found out it was rainin' here, too. I promised the good Lord if it'd rain on us, I'd carry water to you folks in a bucket."

I laughed at him. "All this rain proves, Poke, is that it rains on the just and the unjust alike."

Jim reared up wondering what all the noise was about. "Well, Poke Mahone from over west. How are ya, my lad?"

Poke walked over and shook his hand. "Hell, I'm doin' all right, if you let me be the judge."

Jim smiled. "You mean I've got a say in the matter? I thought you elected yourself judge."

They both laughed. 'Course, just like Tres said, the Boss and Miz T. were sure glad to see Poke. The Boss shook his hand and Miz T. give him a hug. Both of them called him Louis. I knew that was his given name, but hardly anybody ever called him that. I hadn't seen the Boss in such fine humor in a long time. It's amazing what a good rain will do for the soul of a cowman.

We hadn't got back to the bunkhouse any more than to just let the door slam and Poke started in talking about getting to town.

"Damn, Poke," I said. "If we go to town now, since it's been rainin' all day, we'll get stuck sure as hell."

"I've got a surefire remedy for not gettin' stuck."

"Well, I'd like to know what it is."

"It's simple. Don't stop!"

"Well, shit! Poke, that makes a lot of sense. But sometimes you slip off the road and can't get no traction."

"Hell. Wind it up. The faster you go, the less likely you are to stop."

Jim didn't think it was too good an idea, either. "The way I see it, we've got eight miles of muddy road. Then we gotta cross the Aguacita, and it's liable to be runnin' high. Since me and Frank are the biggest fellers here, I have a feelin' we're gonna end up pushin' the car the biggest part of the way."

"Besides that," I said, "when we get there, the last picture show will be started. They've shut the town down by then."

"Hell," Poke said, "we ain't goin' to town to see a picture show. The Water Hole'll still be open, and the bar at Kitchins. I just cain't hardly wait to see Sally."

"See Sally? Listen, I want you to keep your eyes off her while we're up there. I'm goin' to try to get all her attention."

"Over my dead body," Poke said. "She likes me better than she does you."

"Oh, you think so?" I said. "Well, to be right truthful with you, she ain't showed either one of us the time of day. But I keep hopin' one of these days I'm gonna get lucky. I figure she's got a hell of a lot better chance of noticin' me because of my great size and stature, than she will a little horny cow pimp like you, Poke."

"Shit! I shall overwhelm her with my charmin' personality, my wit, and my commandin' use of the vocabulary."

We all laughed. "What do you think the chances are of Tres comin' up here and sittin' in with us awhile?"

"Slim and none," I told him. "I don't think the Boss is gonna let Tres come up here while you're here. He's pretty particular about the words that might drift into that young boy's ears, especially with you bein' here."

"Well, I tell ya what," he said. "I'm goin' to the saddle house to get my clothes. Be back in a minute."

Directly Poke came in. He had all his belongings wrapped up in a small canvas tarp that he tied on back of his saddle. He brought his saddle-bags in, too.

"Looky what I got, boys." And he pulled out a pint of Jim Beam whiskey.

Now this made me nervous. I knew the Boss's feeling about drinking on the ranch. He just would not have it. It didn't seem to bother Poke or Jim either one. So I figured, what the hell? What's good for the goose has got to be good for the gander.

Poke broke the lid on that fresh bottle and passed it around and we all took a little nip. I opened the lid to the stove and stuck it down inside the stove, out of sight.

"I reckon," Poke said, "I can wait one more day to get to town, providin' old Bullet even runs."

Everybody kind of stretched out on their beds. R.C. was just taking everything in, when I realized that nobody had ever really introduced R.C. and Poke.

"You know, I'm plumb forgettin' my manners here," I said. "Poke, this here is R.C. Roth, our new man."

"Oh, there wasn't no introduction necessary. R.C., I've heard about you."

R.C. smiled. "I'm pleased to make your acquaintance, Poke."

"How're you gettin' along here, R.C.?"

"Oh, fine, fine. I sure do like it here. I'm trying to learn all I can."

"Well," Poke said, "this is a good place to do it, and excludin' me, you couldn't have better teachers around you. Are you goin' to town with us tomorrow?" Poke said.

"Yes, if it's all right with you fellows. I'd like to get some new clothes. The clothes I'm wearing make me stick out. I'd feel a lot more comfort-able if I just blended in."

"I'll tell you what," Poke said, "Frank, here, and myself, will outfit you tomorrow. What are ya aimin' to buy?"

"Well, I thought I'd get some of those western shirts like you wear, and some Levis."

"That's a good idea. Those pants you're awearin' are a might high-water, and although it's rained all night and all day, I don't think the water is gonna get high enough to threaten your pants." All this ribbing R.C. took with good nature.

"I'd like to get me a good felt hat, too, and a belt like you wear with those fancy buckles."

"Well," Poke said, "you can get a buckle like mine almost anywhere. Now, if you want to wear a fancy buckle like Frank's, you're gonna have to win an event at a rodeo, because they just give those to you when you're a champion."

R.C. looked my trophy buckle over. "I didn't realize that."

"Yeah, I won this bulldoggin' in '51."

R.C. still hadn't completed his wardrobe in his mind. "I'd also like to get a pair of boots. Authentic cowboy boots, and maybe a saddle. I'm hoping to get to ride here pretty soon. Frank's promised he'll take me horseback the next time he goes."

Damn, I hated to hear him say that. Just the other day the Boss had been talking to me and told me that maybe R.C. better spend branding time on the ground, since he didn't know the lay of the country and didn't know how well he could ride a horse.

"Well, R.C.," Poke said, "I'll tell you what we're gonna do. We're gonna fix you up. Old Frank and I are connoisseurs of western attire, and you can betcher bottom dollar that when we get through with you, you're gonna look as genuine as the best cowpoke a comin' down the pike. But a thought just occurred to me. All of this is going to take a considerable amount of money. Have you got that much money?" Poke asked.

"Yes, I believe I do."

"R.C., I hope so, 'cause you just drawed your first paycheck tonight. If you don't have a lot more money than I thought you had when you signed on with this outfit, that paycheck won't even start to go around what you're thinkin' about buyin'," I said.

"Well, I think I can handle it. Oh, I want one of those scarves you guys wear around your neck, too."

Poke reached up and fingered his wildrag. "These scarves is what we call wildrags."

"Well, they make great decoration. You guys certainly do look authentic with those wildrags around your neck."

Poke sat up on the bed. "Decoration, hell! These things are essential to our profession. Why, there's any number of things that this wildrag is good for. I tell ya what, Frank, I'll name one use for a wildrag and you give another and we'll just see how far we can go. First off, if you're ridin' drag behind a bunch of cattle and it's drier than a popcorn fart, and the dust is foggin' up behind those cattle, you can pull it up around your nose so you don't have to breathe all that dust."

I thought for a minute. "Well, if you're out and break your arm you can make a sling out of it."

"You can also hobble your horse with it," added Poke. "Just loop it around one leg, twist it three or four times, and then tie a square knot on the other leg."

"If it's real windy, you could put it over the top of your hat and tie it under your chin like a stampede string and hold your hat on."

"If it's cold you could put it under your hat and over your ears to keep your ears from freezin' off."

"If you get bit by a rattlesnake they make a wonderful tourniquet."

"And if you forget your belt, they'll help hold your pants up," Poke said.

By this time R.C. was grinning and seemed to be enjoying the play on the wildrags. I said, "One thing they're especially good for, if you're ridin' an outlaw, you can blindfold him with it while you're gettin' on."

"Another good thing you can do with it," Poke said, "is if you've got to take a shit and there ain't nothin' around to wipe your ass on, they're pretty handy that way. Damn sure beats a dry cow chip."

"Yeah, and they also are fine things to clean your nasal passages out on."

"You can even use the thing to hog-tie a calf, use it as a piggin' string. They're made out of one hundred percent silk. And they're strong. They'll keep your neck warm in the winter. I ain't never had a cold since I've been wearin' one in the winter. I put it on in October and double it, and don't undouble it 'til May. Throughout the summer I just wear it tied single around my neck in a square knot," Poke said.

"Another thing you can do, R.C., if worse comes to worst, you can put a slipknot in it and tie it to a tree and hang yourself," I said. And this was the cue that Poke had been waiting for.

He looked over at R.C. and said, in kind of a sly voice, "If you're short of dollars, you can always pull it over your nose and rob a bank."

R.C. looked at him kind of funny and innocent-like. "I didn't know there were that many uses for that scarf, or wildrag, I mean."

"You bet!" says Poke. "It's part of the equipment of a cowboy. We'll fix you up tomorrow. With what you've got in mind, while you're cashing that paycheck maybe you'd better rob the bank first, if you haven't already robbed one."

R.C. just grinned and shook his head. "No, I've never done that. Never even crossed my mind."

Jim popped up and said, "Reach down in that stove and pass that puddin' around, will ya, Frank? That stuff's gonna spoil if you leave it down there."

Poke looked over at Jim. "I hear, Jim, that you've got Kitty Wells on your mind when you go to sleep at night."

Jim grinned kinda sheepishly and said, "Well, I tell ya what. I wouldn't kick her out of my bed for eatin' crackers."

Poke lay back, with his hands behind his head. "As far as these country lady singers go, Patsy Montana would be awful hard to beat. Sure do like her singin' 'Cowboy's Sweetheart'!"

"Me," I told them, "I'll just take old Sally up at the Water Hole."

"Damn you, Frank. We're talkin' about girl singers and she ain't no singer. Now, if you can't stay in harness with everybody else, why don't you just not say nothin'?"

"I just thought I'd get dibs on her for tomorrow. That'll make it a double dib, to kinda keep you out of the way, Poke."

We walked on out to the end of the porch. Poke whispered to me, "Where do you suppose R.C.'s gonna get all the money to do all this buyin' that he's talkin' about?"

"Honest, Poke, I don't know."

Poke thought a little bit. "Don't that make you kinda suspicious?"

"Well, yeah, it makes me wonder a little bit. But I've been around the guy a couple of weeks now, and he sure seems to be all right. He tries hard and he works hard. And he's learnin' fast. He seems to be an alright feller. I'll admit the little conversation we had up on the fence put me to thinkin'. But now that he's got some color in his face, I just can't hardly imagine R.C. bein' in jail and bein' in trouble with the law in any way."

Poke looked over and winked. "Always expect the unexpected."

"It's what a feller does and the way a feller acts that counts with me." We headed back in.

"Boys," said Jim, "let's hit it so we can get a start in the mornin'. It may take us all day just to get to town with that muddy road." With that, we all turned in.

CHAPTER

7

Next morning at breakfast we declared our intentions. Tres asked to go with us, but the Boss wouldn't let him. I think we were all kind of relieved at that, 'cause our plans didn't include a young boy like Tres. We didn't want him to get into any bad habits at such a young age.

We asked Tio if he needed anything in town. He said he would appreciate it if we'd bring him back some twelve-gauge birdshot. Old Tio had an old double-barreled shotgun that was his prized possession. I'd looked at it and couldn't tell who'd made it. It was so old that I didn't know if it would take these new shotgun loads, but he seemed convinced that it would. Why he needed the shells, I didn't know, because I'd never seen him fire that shotgun. I'd seen him clean it a million times. But, if he wanted shotgun shells, shotgun shells he'd have.

I just started to drive down to the gas tank and Poke said he'd drive down with me.

"Ya know what, Frank? I think there's somethin' bogus about this R.C. feller."

"Oh, godalmighty, Poke. What in the world would make you say a thing like that?"

I started filling her up. He came out the other side and met me. "I went around the back of the bunkhouse and stood at the side of the window there. R.C. walked over to the bunk and looked around toward the front door. Then he pulled that suitcase out from under the bed and opened it up. He had pajamas in it."

"What's so unusual about that?"

"That ain't all," Poke said. "He pulled out a sock and reached in there and took out a wad of money that would choke a horse. Bills, they was. I couldn't tell what denomination. But he peeled off four or five and stuck 'em in his pocket. Before he put those pajamas over the top of it, he pulled out another sock and just felt it. Frank, I'll swear there was a gun in that sock!"

"What made you think so?"

"If you stuck a dehorn saw in a sock, you could tell what it was. Same with this. It was flat and didn't look like it had any cylinder in it. Like one of those automatics I was tellin' ya about."

"You haven't even been drinkin' this mornin', have you?"

"I'm tellin' you what I saw, Frank."

"He could have saved it. Maybe he has some rich kinfolk."

By this time the tank was full, and Poke had given plumb up on me. Went around and got in the passenger side. I started Ol' Bullet up and stopped in front of the bunkhouse. Poke and I both had to get out 'cause it was only a two-door, and let Jim and R.C. get in the back. I looked out the window after everybody was in and Belle was sitting there wagging her tail, if you want to call it wagging her tail. Her whole butt was shaking, looking at me with those anticipating eyes. She wanted to go, too.

"Belle, you can't go this time, now. Hold down the fort."

She was still sitting there when we drove off.

"Now, remember what I told you, Frank. If you don't stop, you won't get stuck," Poke said.

Jim piped up. "This road has got a good caliche base on it. We ain't gonna sink in it, but it's slicker than snot."

With that I let the hammer down on Bullet and we made a run for the main road. We did a bunch of fishtailing. Two or three times we got off in the barrow ditch. Every time I did, all I could hear was Poke hollering, "Don't stop! Don't stop!"

Finally we came to the cut where the maintainer had pulled up out of the barrow ditch, and I got back up on top again. I tried to keep a head of steam up the best I could. But, boy, it sure was slick.

"Don't stop! Get back up on top again," Poke was screaming.

We made it plumb down to the crossing of the Aguacita. From there we stopped, decided we'd better have a look-see. See how deep the water was running across the ford. Without getting out, Jim allowed that maybe it was running two and a half, three feet deep, but it wasn't very wide. Maybe ten yards across. You just got down in real quick, and it came out real quick. It could get pretty deep right in the middle. Poke didn't think it was that deep. Thought our best chance was just to get a running start and blaze right on through it. Well, we didn't take a vote on it, but I decided if we were going to get to town, there wasn't any other way to do it. So, I pulled her down in low gear and popped the clutch and headed for the water. When we hit it, it went all over everywhere. But we did come out the other side, asputtering. We lost our speed and momentum and lost our engine. The motor had plumb quit on me.

I didn't know what to do, but we all got out and Jim and R.C. popped the hood on it and got underneath it. Went to drying off those things that were so wet. Everything was soppin' underneath there. Poke and I sat on the back fender and chewed and spit and looked back over where we'd come. We could see the tracks back for a mile or so and it looked like somebody plumb drunk had been coming down the road. If anybody saw it besides us they'd swear we were three sheets in the wind.

Pretty soon I heard Jim say, "Now, give her a spin, Frank."

I got in and turned her over two or three times. He'd say wait a minute and tinker a little bit more. Finally it kicked over. Now, if we could just get over the creek bank here, we'd be on our way. But we couldn't get any traction. So, as Jim said, it was me and him apushing. R.C. got out and was doing the best he could, but he was the lesser of the two work-horses. And, of course, Poke, he drove. With lots of falling down and cussing we did get some traction and got it on up the road. Poke finally did get her to going, and he didn't stop until he topped clear out of the draw. We had to walk about two hundred yards on that slick caliche to get up to him. All three of us were as muddy as we could be. I told Poke to move over, it was my car, I'd drive it.

Finally we got down to the main highway. I stopped and looked both ways.

"Why in the hell do you do that?" Poke said. "There ain't nobody that ever comes along this road. You can look down here at the crossing for miles. If nobody's comin', just keep right on goin' and pull out."

"The day I do that, the Boss told me, a big cattle truck would come by and mash me flat. So, I make it a habit to always stop."

With that we turned north and headed to Dorsey. There was a lot of gravel on this road, with a pretty good base on it. We could sickle along at a pretty good pace. R.C. started in with the questions, as expected. Wanted to know what kind of place Dorsey was. We all put in our two bits. Up ahead you could see the twin mounds, and I told him that those twin mounds were a landmark for the Santa Fe Trail.

"Honest?"

"Sure. I can take you up there and show you the trail. You can still see the wagon-wheel road all those wagons made that came for years and years over the Santa Fe Trail. They'd just go from one landmark to the other. That particular landmark was easy to see because all the country around it plumb back into Kansas was as flat as it could be. All you had to do was just keep in line with those.

"As for the town of Dorsey, it was just a little old bitty place, maybe twenty-five hundred people. All those people in town, merchants, everybody depended on the cattle market and the cattle people. When the market was bad, their business was bad. When it was good, their business picked up. It was an honest-to-God cow town."

R.C. wanted to know how long it had been there. None of us knew for sure. All Jim could think of was that the railroad had gone through there long before there was a town. They called it the Colorado Southern Railroad. Tramperos had the Southern Pacific/Rock Island Railroad going for it. Neither town had been there until the railroad had come through. And Dorsey had been the main land office for the homesteaders when they were claiming up on all this land.

It had everything in it that a cowboy'd need, except whorehouses. They'd been outlawed by the good citizens of Dorsey many, many years ago. But all in all, it hadn't changed a great deal since the early 1900s. If anything, it had probably lost a little in population. As far as supplies, and the needs of the cow people, it had everything you needed.

We crossed the bridge at Corrizo Creek, came out the north side of it, and headed up out of the creek draw. Got up on top and we could see Dorsey up ahead of us about twelve miles. The clouds were clearing and the sun was out and it looked like it was going to be a beautiful day.

Poke pulled up his pant leg and pulled out what was left of the pint that we had started last night.

"Here boys, you'd better finish this one up. I'm gonna hold off myself. I've got a cravin' for scotch."

"Where'd you pull that bottle from, Poke?" R.C. asked.

"Out of my boot. That's what pint and half-pint bottles are for, R.C. Did you ever notice the backside of 'em? They's kinda concave, while the outside is kinda round? That's made where you can slide it down between your leg and your boot. Pull your pant leg over it, and the preacher won't know if you got anything in there if you meet him on the street. Pretty handy, huh?"

We passed the bottle around and Jim took a big share of it. And I sure took my share. R.C. took a little snort. As we pulled on into Dorsey, we crossed the railroad tracks and got over on the main highway and headed north into town.

"Well, what's the plan?" I asked.

"Why don't we go to Kitchins," Poke said.

The old Kitchins Hotel was built in the late 1800s, around 1880 I'd say. It was built out of rock blocks. Pretty ornate. Three stories high, by far the largest building in town. And I guessed it had what you'd call a false front on the very, very top. Still made out of stone. Even had a flag flying at the top, kind of like a courthouse. Instead of an awning coming out across the sidewalk and in front of the street, it had a little porch built out of the second floor surrounded by wrought-iron railing. It had fallen on hard times. It wasn't near the grand place that it once had been. The downstairs was divided in half. The left side of it was the bar and the cafe, and on the right-hand side was the hotel lobby with its check-in desk and some soft cushioned chairs facing the street. On upstairs were all the hotel rooms.

We went through the bar door. "Is this a saloon, Frank?"

"Ah, I reckon you could call it that."

R.C. looked at the big door. "I thought all saloons had double swinging doors."

"Well, you'll find those connectin' the bar and the hotel lobby. But those swingin' doors don't keep out the cold wind and all the dust that blows."

Pete was behind the bar. Called us all by name, except R.C. We all walked up and shook hands. "You boys haven't been to town in quite a spell. Beginnin' to miss you."

"We missed you, too, Pete. A feller can get mighty lonesome out there. Also, awful thirsty and we aim to fix that right now."

"Well, belly on up and name your poison."

Poke, he ordered him some scotch with water. Jim and R.C. and I just had a mug of draft beer. Pete looked us over real good. "How in the hell did you boys get to town? Did you crawl on your hands and knees? There's mud all over you."

"Nah. We got stuck gettin' out to the main road," I said.

"I guess I don't have to ask who was drivin' the car," Pete said, as he looked at Poke.

Poke was grinning. "You bet, Pete. Somebody had to be the pilot. And I figured I was the best qualified."

I reached in my pocket and pulled out a dime and slapped it on the bar. R.C. and Jim did the same. Poke, since he was drinking that scotch whiskey, had to shell out a half a buck. While they were visiting about the rain with Pete, I noticed R.C. looking around taking it all in.

"Quite a place, ain't it, R.C.?"

"Sure is, Frank. I don't believe I ever saw a bar that didn't have stools around it."

"This is a stand-up bar. Even's got a brass footrail," and I pointed underneath the bar. "This old bar has got a lot of history to it. I'm talkin' about the bar itself, not the building. I understand they brought this bar down from a minin' camp up in Trinidad. It was made in Europe, shipped over here in pieces, and found its way down here to Dorsey."

We looked the bar over and it was quite ornate. Made out of something that looked like rosewood, with pillars on each end and a mirror in the middle. A lot of gingerbread wood carving, real ornately done, over the back bar.

On the other side of the room were booths. There were three tables out in the middle of the floor and they were toward the back end of the bar. On all the walls were pictures of cowboys working cattle, riding broncs, roping steers, all of them old pictures taken back in the 1800s.

The ceiling was one of those tin ceilings with squares in it. I told R.C. to walk with me down toward the end of the bar. When we got down there I pointed up and showed him two bullet holes up there. "When was that done?" he asked.

"Oh, I don't know. Back when the West was wild, I guess." You see those tin ceilings in a lot of old buildings. Even they were ornate. But this ceiling had long since turned to a kind of grimy yellow color. The whole place was kind of getting run-down. But it was still the meeting place for anybody that came to town.

We all ordered another beer. Poke, he was still nursing his scotch. Sometimes he'd even stick out his little finger, when he grabbed a glass. I kidded him about it. I asked him if he was waiting for someone to hand him a donut.

"You boys gonna be spendin' the night?" Pete said.

"I thought we would, Pete," I said. "Can you put us up?"

"Sure. What'll you need?"

"Oh, a room with two double beds will do us, I reckon."

"I can do that. When you finish your drinks, come around into the office and I'll check you in."

We finished our drinks and headed on into the lobby. Went through those swinging doors I was talking about. Pete came around and fished out a set of keys to room 210. "One of you boys will have to sign in. It's the law."

I stepped up and signed the register. "Pete, I'd better pay you now. I might not have any money when I leave town."

"How does ten bucks sound?" Pete asked.

"Fair enough."

Since we were all going to have to take a bath, Poke said he'd go down and bring our warbags up. Jim and I kept our stuff in World War II duffle bags we called "warbags." Of course, R.C. had his suitcase. We thought that was mighty big of Poke, since he was the only one that was clean.

Jim told me and R.C. to go first, and he'd go last. It'd been so long since he'd had a bath, he might sit in that hot water and soak a little.

We walked down the hall. There was one door marked "Men's Water Closet" and one marked "Men's Bathroom." I went in and started running water in the tub and peeling off all my muddy clothes. Didn't take long for me to take a bath. I was in a hurry to get out and get on the town.

"Well," Jim says, "I need to cash my paycheck."

"Me, too," I said, "or we're not gonna have enough money to eat on. Then I think we'd better go eat dinner, 'cause it's liable to be a long time before we get up to the table."

While he was finishing up eating, Poke said, "Well, we gotta outfit R.C. here. R.C., are you sure you can stand the damage we're gonna do this afternoon?"

"Yes. It's real important to me that I get outfitted right. I think I got enough money to handle it."

"Let's start at the top and work down."

"That sounds like a good idea to me," Poke said. "Where to? Steinbach's Mercantile?"

"That's the place," I said.

We got up to pay our checks. Underneath the glass where the old brass cash register sat was a cigar case. Pete kept two rolls of toilet paper in saucers under there that he'd add a little water to, to act as a humidor for his cigars. I never had gotten used to cigars, but every time Poke got to town, he wanted him a cigar. So, he bought himself three or four Roitans, stuck them in his shirt pocket, and left with one thing in mind, to outfit R.C. like a sure-enough cowboy.

As we walked in, Mrs. Steinbach howdyed us and told us how glad she was to see us. I had a feeling that she was going to be a lot gladder and a shade richer by the time we left. We started by looking at hats.

"You gonna buy two hats?" I asked.

"Well, I need one to work in and one to dress up in. You guys have two hats, don't you?"

Poke and I allowed that we did.

R.C. said, "I never have understood why you guys wear your hats so far up on the sides."

"R.C., that's easy," I said. "All cowboys do that so more of them can sit in a pickup seat together."

R.C. began to look at shirts, and then he told the lady he needed some Levis. She asked what size he wore. He said he didn't know. So she got out the tape measure and went to measuring him. He looked a little goosey while she was measuring the inseam. She went to rummaging through all the Levis she had stacked up on the table, and finally pulled out a pair.

"R.C., you gotta buy Levis two sizes too big. Ain't that right, Mrs. Steinbach?" Poke said.

She wisely nodded her head.

"You gotta wash 'em. They'll shrink up and fit you like a glove."

He looked at us both with sad eyes and said, "Well, I wanted to wear them today."

Poke thought a minute and said, "I think we can get that done. Go ahead and buy 'em."

Then R.C. tried one of his hats on and looked at himself in the mirror, one of those three-way mirrors. Believe you me, he caught every angle. I think he kind of liked what he saw. I know from my viewpoint, it was a hell of an improvement.

He went over and asked our opinion about wildrags. I told him, "Well, you gotta get a black one, R.C. It's the code of the West."

He did take a black one, but wanted another. And damned if he didn't pick a red one. Poke spoke up. "You know when we were talkin' about all the things you could do with a wildrag, R.C.?"

He nodded his head.

"There's one thing we forgot to mention. With that there red one, you could flag a freight train!" We all laughed at that, including the Steinbachs.

R.C. came over and sat down with us. "Boys, I need some boots. Some for now, and I want a custom-made pair." We finally picked out a pair of Tony Lama boots. And we told him it would probably take awhile to get boots made. When he decided he wanted something, he wanted it right now! Odd part about it, he acted like he was used to getting things right now.

When we walked out of Steinbach's Mercantile, R.C.'s pocket was a great lot lighter.

We went on up the street to Tony Bono's. He was the boot maker in town. Finally R.C. decided on what he wanted with some coaching from Poke and me. He got high heels with a deep scallop on top. We assured him that he'd look real good with his pant legs stuck down his boots with those deep scallops. He wanted his initials on the front and the back of each boot. He got them made in black calf leather, with yellow inlaid initials and just the prettiest green and red stitching going up the sides you ever saw. He thought all that stitching was just for decoration. Since he'd got tall-top boots, sixteen inches high, I had to laugh and tell him that if it wasn't for the stitching going up the side of the boots, that nice soft leather would just fall down around his ankles just like an old pair of socks.

The boots were going to cost him a hundred dollars, and he had to put twenty-five dollars down. Down at Steinbach's he'd paid for everything out of his right pocket. This time he'd gone to his left pocket and I had an idea he had money scattered in each of his pockets, so when he pulled it out it wouldn't look like it was such a big roll.

We headed to Jake Martin's Saddle Shop. We looked over a couple of old Fraiser saddles. I think that's what R.C. really had in mind, those old-timey, high-cantled, slick-forked saddles. Finally we did find an old Prosser-Martin saddle, and it was a fairly recent vintage. It was a good-looking saddle, with flowers stamped all over. But he had a whale of a price on it, too.

"I need a pair of spurs, don't I?" R.C. asked.

"Yes sir, a pair of chin lifters," I said, "is just what you need. Ain't nobody rides slick-heeled in this country."

I told R.C. I preferred Crocket spurs. Poke, now he was partial to Kelly spurs, but I think all three of us eyed that pair of Blanchard spurs at the same time. Poke picked up one and I picked up the other. Those Blanchard spurs were real popular. They were made out of old, cold-rolled steel. They would rust, and that was the rage of the age right now.

"I'd buy these spurs myself," Poke said, "if I had the money."

"Me, too," I said.

That was good enough for R.C. He snatched them up right now.

Now we had to get a belt and buckle. Jake showed us everything he had, even the trophy buckles. R.C. wouldn't have any of it. He said before he wore a trophy buckle, he'd have to win it. And he looked over at me and winked. That boy was catching on fast.

What finally caught R.C.'s eye was a pure sterling silver ranger-style buckle. This was the buckle that R.C. wanted. He told Jake that he wanted just a plain leather belt right now to go on it. Nothing fancy. So Jake went in the back and went to cutting him a belt out of some latigo leather.

Spending that much money in one day had almost made me sick. I figured I'd helped him as much as I could. So, I gathered up some of the packages, walked out the door, and stood on the street while R.C. was settling up. When he came out he was packing that saddle on his hip, had his new belt on, and even though he was wearing those old pants, Poke had made him stuff his pant legs down those new Tony Lama boots. Poke was carrying a hatbox and a couple of sacks. We headed back to the hotel to put all of it up. When we got to the car I asked R.C. if he wanted to throw the saddle in the back.

"No." He thought he'd take it up to the room and adjust the stirrup leathers. It was going to take considerable unthreading of all the lacing to get them where he wanted them, and he wanted to put those oxbows on real quick. I told him I didn't see why, we weren't going to do any horsebacking today. But that boy was as happy as if he had good sense. So, we let him take it on up to the room.

I couldn't help but feel happy for R.C. He threw his saddle on the floor, scattered all his stuff out on the bed. Then it hit him.

"Oh, my God! What are we going to do about my pants? Poke, you said you knew how to fix it."

Poke lit up a cigar and thought a little while. "I do, I do. But it might be a little painful."

"Painful?"

"I'm afraid so," said Poke. "There's just one way to do this that I know of." Then it struck me what he was talking about. And I thought, oh my God, that boy is going to be miserable tonight if he takes Poke's advice.

"You're gonna have to take those Levis down and soak 'em in the bathtub. Then put 'em on. And don't take 'em off 'til they're dry. Get outside and walk around and let the sun hit 'em. Get the fresh air on 'em. Might be a little uncomfortable, and chafey a bit. But when they're dry, they'll fit you like a dream."

R.C. shook his head like he understood, grabbed a pair of those Levis, and took off down toward the bathtub. Poke hollered at him, "Make that water in the bathtub as hot as it can get. It'll help shrink up those Levis all the more. We'll meet you down at the bar."

CHAPTER

8

As Poke and I walked out of the lobby and into the bar, we stopped and looked around a little while. Things were picking up. Looked like Pete was going to do a land-office business this evening. There was a big crowd of fellers down toward the end of the bar and I knew that one or two things were happening. Either two fellers on the floor were wrestling or Egg Robbins was holding court and telling one of his stories. Since I couldn't see, could only hear, it had to be Egg.

He was a little bitty red-headed feller, and high-tempered as hell. They called him Egg, but his real name was Edgar. I guessed it had something to do with his last name, Robbins. He took all this in good stride. He had his own place up on the dry Cimarron. He was a real good hand, and was usually one of the fellers that the Boss asked to come down and help brand.

We walked over to the crowd just in time to hear Egg's story. He had a big grin and a wild look in his eye. And he was going through all the animation of the story he was telling. And then just died laughing and so did everybody else.

Poke and I stepped up to the bar, got a drink, and surveyed the crowd. We knew practically everybody that was in there. Looked over in the back corner booth and could see that Nick Compton was having a drink with three of his buddies. I hated to see old Nick. He and I'd had a go-round a couple of years ago, and I'd whomped up on him pretty good. He was the cheap-shot artist of the country.

About that time the front door opened and Ira Turner walked in. He was another one of the fellers that owned his own place and would come help the Boss brand. He had a son named Clay that was fast becoming a real good hand.

He saw us right away and waved. Before he did, he walked up to Pete and said, "Pete, I sure like the flag that's flyin' up there on the porch above the street."

Pete looked at him kind of dumbfounded and said, "I don't know what you mean, Iry."

"Somebody's flyin' their britches off that steel gratin'."

Poke and I looked at one another. I said, "Oh, my God, Pete. I'll take care of it. I have a feelin' I know what happened."

Shook hands with Iry as I went by him. I ran up to the second floor to our room. R.C. was sitting on his saddle testing out his stirrups. He'd taken off those roping stirrups and put on his oxbows, and was trying to get them set at the right angle. He had on his boots and his shorts, his hat and new shirt.

"My God, R.C.," I said, "did you hang them pants out over the street?"

He looked up and grinned and said, "Yes. The only way I could get them dry in a hurry. They sure soaked up a lot of water. I go out to try them on about every fifteen minutes, but they're still way too big."

I looked over to the bed and he'd been trying on his hats, and he had one of his hats sitting on the bed. That absolutely horrified me. I walked over and picked up the hat. "Let me tell you somethin'. Don't ever lay your hat on a bed!"

R.C. looked at me kind of with wonder.

"If there's anything that's bad luck to a cowboy, it's that. Now I don't particularly care what might happen to you, and what bad luck it might bring you, but the problem is, I might be with you when it happens. That bad luck might get both of us. So keep your hat off the bed! Understand?"

I'd never talked that way to R.C. It kind of took him back a little. He nodded his head okay. I told him to go get his pants. I didn't think that Pete Kitchins appreciated him flying them off the porch above main street.

"Let them dry a little and put 'em on. Either that or wear your old pants."

R.C. shook his head. "Everybody makes fun of those high-water pants I wear. I'm not going to put them on."

"Then stuff your pant legs down inside your boots and nobody will know any difference." That brightened R.C. up, and he said he would.

So with that taken care of I went back downstairs. Pete and Iry were in a big conversation. Iry's name was spelled Ira, but so often country folks turned anybody's name that ends with an a, they put a y on the end of it.

I walked back to my drink and Iry looked up in my face where I had slid into the corrals. There was still a dark mark up there alongside my face and ear.

He grinned at me. "I heard about your bronc ride."

That was one subject that was a little touchy to me. I didn't really want to talk about it a great lot. I figured Iry would hoorah me a little bit about it.

"A feller that never's been bucked off ain't never got on many."

Iry wisely nodded his head.

"You know the Boss stopped by and asked me to come to a brandin' next week," he said. "Sure lookin' forward to it. I wish I had his place and he had one better."

"Then I'd be workin' for you. I don't know as how I could handle that, Iry. I hear you're a hell of a taskmaster and awful hard to please."

Ira winked at me. "I couldn't be any worse than the Boss, and you know it."

We all laughed and allowed how that was true.

Poke pulled out one of his cigars and stuck it in his mouth, offered one to Ira. Ira looked at it longingly, and then shook his head. "No thanks, Poke. I'd like to, but don't believe I will. I come to town today to borrow some money, and if I smoke that damn cigar, first thing you know, I'll be wantin' to lend some." Old Ira had a way with words.

You could hear Egg starting up with another story down at the end of the bar. Ira looked down. "Egg is tellin' stories. Guess I'll mosey over and catch a few. I love to hear that feller tell jokes. I haven't had that much to laugh about lately. I'll catch you boys in a little while."

Poke noticed that a booth had opened up. "Frank, come on over. I've got to do some figurin'." Poke pulled out a paper napkin and went to figuring, asking me if I remembered how much R.C.'s hats had cost, putting down the boots and trying to remember what this and the other had cost. Had all those figures added up, held it up to me.

"That man spent three hundred and twenty-five dollars, at least, today. I saw him take out four maybe five bills. Frank, they had to be hundred-dollar bills!"

Now I figured that was probably true. "Don't forget his paycheck. He cashed his paycheck."

"Hell, that couldn't amounted to much. I don't know what kind of wages he's makin', but that couldn't amount to a hundred-dollar bill. Closer to fifty. What do you think?"

I figured that was probably right, fifty dollars a month and room and board. He might be getting a little more, but I doubted it. A feller sure couldn't get rich on cowboy wages.

Poke asked me, "Did you see him pull out a hundred-dollar bill when he was payin' for anything?"

"No, but it seemed like he had money in several different pockets."

Poke thought awhile. "He had to change those hundred-dollar bills to smaller bills."

"He did go to the bank. He could've changed some there."

"Yeah, or he had to have purchases come close to a hundred dollars before he'd give a hundred-dollar bill, so they could make change for him. Let's go ask Pete."

So we both walked over to Pete. He was busier pouring drinks than a one-legged man in an ass-kicking contest. Had his sleeves rolled up, his apron tied on.

"You know that feller we introduced you to this mornin' when we came in? Did he happen to change a large-denomination bill with you?" I asked.

"Yeah," Pete said.

I said, "Well, when?"

"You fellers had gone up to your room. He came back down and wanted to know if I could change a hundred-dollar bill. I told him I could, seein's it was Saturday, and I knew I was goin' to have pretty good business."

On Poke's insistence we checked every store where R.C. had made a purchase. Sure enough, a hundred-dollar bill had been used to make the purchase, which didn't prove a damn thing except for the fact that this feller had a hell of a bunch of money.

We walked back down the street and I remembered the shotgun shells that Tio had asked me to buy for him.

I went to the hardware store and got a box of number seven-and-a-halfs. That's birdshot that would make a pretty wide pattern. No better than Tio could shoot or see, I figured they'd probably do him more good than any other kind of shot I could buy. Besides, that's what Tio said he wanted.

I threw the shotgun shells in the front of Ol' Bullet as I went by, and caught up with Poke back in the bar. We sat down at a booth and decided to have a talk about R.C.

"Now, let's look at this logically," Poke said. "We know at least three one-hundred-dollar bills that he's passed in this town."

We sat and looked at one another for a few seconds. I said, "What does that prove? Not a shittin' thing!"

"Well, from my point of view, he's either rich or he robbed a bank."

I thought about that. "If he's rich, why in the hell is he workin' for wages? And if he robbed a bank, again, why in the hell is he workin' for wages? I know if I robbed a bank, I'd be as far from here as I could possibly get. And I damned sure wouldn't come to town, for fear somebody would recognize me."

Poke stuck up his finger. "Yeah, but this is the first time he's been to town since he's gone to work out there on the Piedra. Can you think of a better place to lay low than back there in the breaks of the Piedra? They did have about a half-assed description of the feller that robbed the bank. And R.C. fits that description, as far as size, height, and weight."

We both thought a little while. I said, "Well, in this country aren't you innocent until proven guilty?"

"Oh, that's straight out of Government 101. You did learn somethin' in college, Frank. I always had my doubts."

"There's not much we can do about it now. Hell, let's get drunk and be somebody."

Poke thought that was a good idea. We ordered another round of drinks. Looked up and who should be walking through the door but Top himself, Poke's boss. I looked him over real good. You couldn't help but admire the man. He was tall and lean and twisted just like a rope. He had a belt buckle on that said "Champion Calf Roper," a pair of those Bluecher boots that was hard to miss—had a big yellow butterfly on the front and back. He didn't have his spurs on, and it's a wonder. He seldom took them off.

Top seemed like he knew everybody in the bar by their first name. Stopped and shook hands and visited a little while with each and every one down the bar. He finally noticed us sitting over in the booth.

He walked over and shook hands with me. "Frank."

"Top," and we let it go at that.

He pulled out the makings and started rolling himself a smoke. I don't know what there was about Top. He'd always been a shade aggravating to me. And I think the feeling was mutual. There was a little uneasiness between us, a little animosity. It all stemmed from when I was a kid and he was the top hand on the Piedra. I'd never gotten over it. Top always made you feel a little bit inferior. He sure enough was a cowboy's cowboy. The problem was that he knew it. And he had just enough age on Poke and me to kind of lord it over us. I don't know how old Top was. Thirty-five I imagined. But he'd been damn near everywhere and seen damn near everything. Nothing ever seemed to surprise him.

He cocked up his leg and took a kitchen match and struck it on the side of his Levis, lit his smoke, and looked down at us.

"Looks like a hell of a hickey on the side of your face, Frank. What happened?"

I looked Top right square in the eye. "I got bucked off, Top. But, I'll tell you what, that Gruyer horse that bucked me off didn't git no cherry."

Top never changed expression, but changed the subject. "You guys gonna make a night of it?"

Poke said, "Yeah, we planned to, Top. Wanta sit down? We'll buy you a drink."

"Nah. Couple of fellers I gotta talk to on business. You boys goin' out to the Water Hole and go dancin' tonight?"

"Yeah, Top," I said. "Thought we would."

He blew a big smoke ring and looked down at us. "Would you boys like me to piss on your leg so you'll smell like cowboys?" With that and a grin, he just turned around and walked off.

Poke and I looked at one another. "Goddamn!" I said. "I don't know why that man irritates me so. I do respect him, but Top's got to be the most irritatin' man I've ever been around!"

Poke raised an eyebrow and looked me right square in the eyes. "Hell, Frank, you oughta work for the son of a bitch!"

We had some time to kill, so we took our time and discussed what we had been talking about in our speculations about R.C. We still didn't come up with anything solid enough to be just purely what I said, speculation.

After we ate we went up to the room and checked on R.C. He was still fiddling with his saddle and getting everything just right. He'd made it back from Jake's and he was sure proud of a pair of light tan shotgun chaps. He'd had Jake cut out his initials. Instead of putting his full initials like "R.C.R.," he just had "R.C." put on them. They were fringed clear from his butt down to his heel. He was a little skeptical about those fringes. Thought it looked maybe a little feminine.

So Poke told him, "Nah, most shotgun chaps are fringed somewhere or 'nother and them fringes come in handy."

You never knew when you might cut one of them off to use for a little wang leather to tie something up or add on to a piece of leather that broke.

We asked R.C. whether he wanted to go down to the Water Hole with us. He still was complaining that his britches weren't dry yet. He'd spent most of his afternoon standing out on the porch on top of the entryway to the bar letting the breeze blow through them. But they were beginning to pull down on him, so he told us to go on. He'd catch up with us later. Since this was his first trip into Dorsey, he didn't know where to go. But it wasn't hard to give directions in a one-stoplight town. We just told him to go down to the corner and head north.

CHAPTER

9

We were all going to the Water Hole. That was the name of the honky-tonk out on the edge of town. It was just far enough out where all the rowdiness and carrying on didn't bother the people that wanted to act human on Saturday night. It sat off by itself. And unlike Kitchins, it wasn't a landmark. It looked better at night with all the neon on. In the daylight it was just a dingy old cinder-block building with some of those glass, semitransparent blocks surrounding the door.

There were a number of cars, pickups, some with trailers, some with horse racks on back of the pickup. Some of the horse trailers had a horse or two in them.

A goodly crowd was gathering on a Saturday night. We figured it would. After a good rain over the entire country, there'd be something to celebrate.

What you'd call the Water Hole was just an old, puredee honky-tonk. You opened the door, walked in, and it was just like the song says, "dim lights, thick smoke, and honky-tonk music." Since it was about eight o'clock at night and the band wouldn't crank up 'til nine, we were a mite early. But they had the jukebox going full blast. The bar at the Water Hole wasn't anything spectacular. It had stools around it where you could sit down. It also had booths all around the sides, and a few tables sitting off from the booths toward the dance floor. Right smack in the middle of the whole outfit was sure enough a pretty good-sized dance floor. A feller would have a terrible time roller-skating on it, but for dancing it was just about the right size.

The main attraction had always been the bartendress, Sally. In the afternoon when things were slow she tended bar and waited tables. When things picked up, like on a Friday or Saturday night or something special going on, she'd call the owner and he'd come in and bartend. I don't know quite what there was about Sally, but there'd been many a night I'd spent in the bunkhouse thinking about her, about bedding her down and wallering around on her a little bit. She wasn't what you'd call beautiful. As a matter of fact, she had a scar over her left eye. And for some strange reason, that scar didn't detract from her looks. In some maybe tragic sort of way, it even made her more intriguing.

Ever since I'd known Sally, she'd been involved in some trying love affair. I know for a fact that she'd been married at least three times. She was a very friendly lady, I guess is about the best way to put it. If you happened to hit on her just right, why, she'd go to bed with you. She'd never gone to bed with me, but who knew, tonight might be the night. She always wore gabardine pants and short-sleeved women's western-style shirts, and some sort of curio-store moccasins with some beadwork on the top of them. Had short, brown, curled hair, and always a smile, and soft, kind eyes. You could tell her your troubles, and she'd listen and sympathize. If there weren't too many people in the bar she'd match you quarters for the jukebox.

Poke and I sat down at a booth. When we first walked in we noticed that Top had been there awhile and he already was starting to lay it on pretty thick with Sally. I'd always kind of thought that maybe Top and Sally had something going at one time. Knowing her, it was just probably an off-and-on thing. You could tell that he was sure trying to get her attention tonight. And from where we sat, it looked like he was getting the job done.

She saw us sit down, and came over and called us by name. Put her hands on both of our shoulders and gave us a little shake, and with a smile on her face scolded us because we hadn't been in for so long.

Poke and I began to sour up immediately. Both of us had designs on getting her alone one of these nights, and it looked like Top already got to the head of the line.

Poke said, "It looks like Sally is in fine fettle tonight."

"When have you ever seen her when she wasn't?"

"Ah, hell, Frank. I'm just pissed because Top's here. And besides, I ain't wantin' to marry the lady. But who knows, maybe we'll get lucky tonight."

We looked around, and there was a crowd beginning to gather. There was a number of girls that came in from out in the country that were old enough to be legal in the bar. If you wanted to polish your belt buckle and get close to the ladies, this was about the only place in town to do it.

Sally brought our drinks back to us, and as we were paying for them, Bob Wills's band cranked up on the jukebox, with Tommy Duncan singing "Faded Love."

With all my charm and suave personality, I said, "Sally, how about dancing this one with me?"

"Frank, I'm sorry. I'm just too busy right now. I'd love to, but I've just got to keep workin'. Maybe we'll find time to do some later."

At least she gave me a glimmer of hope, but I was fairly let down. I thought, hell, I'm not gonna waste "Faded Love." So I went over to a booth where some girls were sitting. I knew them vaguely, but it didn't make any difference. If they didn't want to dance, they wouldn't have come into this outfit.

I picked out the prettiest one I could find, and asked her for a whirl. And she obliged me. Turning, I almost ran over Poke 'cause he was standing right behind me. He gathered him up one too, and we hit the dance floor. It sure is nice to hold a young, sweet thing that smells nice, and get up close to her and swing her around that dance floor. Some folks call it a mating ritual. I don't know how it ever started, dancing, that is. I couldn't dance a great lick, but I sure loved to hold them girls while they tried.

I don't know who was pumping the jukebox, but whoever it was, I sure admired their taste. Those good songs came awhistling out of that lit-up machine like you never heard. Webb Pierce, "There Stands the Glass," even old Hank Snow and "Tangled Mind." But when "Any Time" with Eddy Arnold came around, I had to leave a drink and get up and make another run at those girls. Picked me another one this time. Not that any of them were getting lonely. They were getting their share of attention from about all the single boys in the bar. But while we were out on the dance floor this time, I noticed the inevitable Nick Compton had shown up with three of his buddies.

I knew he was going to show up here tonight. He was a dancing fool. He was known all over the country for being light on his feet and getting the job done with the girls.

But I hated to see the little bastard show up. Not so much because he was going to muss my hair, but I hated to see him take advantage of some poor feller that didn't know exactly what he was getting into. He walked by our table, swaggering in that cocky way of his, slightly bowlegged. Stopped by and said, "How ya, boys? Say, Frank, where's that gunsel partner of yours I seen you with earlier today?"

Just for pure orneriness, I looked him right square in the eye and said, "Ah, he'll be along directly. Nick, ya know, he saw you today and he asked me how come you was so bowlegged, and I told him it was because you wore wet didies when you was little."

You could see a look come over Nick's face like you'd just poured a bucket of water on him, but he wasn't dumb enough to take issue. We'd already had our issue, and he knew better. He just grumped and walked on off, and settled down with his boys in a booth. It wasn't long 'til he was up, taking the girls one at a time out on the dance floor. Some of the fellers out there looked like they were stomping snakes. Others looked like they were having sort of a jaked-legged fit. The majority of everybody out there danced pretty well. But you can cut your capers, stack your duds, and you'll find no flies on Nick Compton. There'd be times when everybody'd just move back and give him room on the faster tunes, and watch him do his stuff. He was good, and he knew it.

We'd gone through several drinks, and had several fellers sit down and bullshit with us. The band had set up, tuned up, and was playing, and I was beginning to wonder what happened to R.C., that maybe he just wasn't going to show up at all. But sure enough, after a little while, in he walked. And he was something to look at, I'll tell you what! His pants were still wet, and hadn't quite shrunk down to size yet, but they were tolerable. You could tell as he walked over to our table with a big smile on his face, that everything he had on was just as new as a spring calf, from his boots plumb to his hat. He'd a' looked like Cousin Minnie Pearl if the price tag had been left on. We had him stop before he sat down, and turn a dido for us so we could look at him from all angles.

"That's a great improvement over what you've been awearin', R.C.," Poke said. "You ought to be proud of them duds."

R.C. grinned real big. "I am. I feel like I belong."

I told him, "Well you need to get a few miles on those boots, get those Levis faded a little bit, and get some character put into that hat, and you will, shore 'nuff, fit in. But right now you could go stand in the winda at Steinbach's Mercantile, and if you didn't blink, and didn't move, you'd look like one of them dress-up dummies that they're displaying clothes on."

R.C. grinned and sat down. "You're hard to please, Frank."

"Ah, I'm just hoorahin' you, R.C. You shore do look nice."

Sally came over to get his order. He ordered a beer. I paid for the beer, thought I'd give him the first one on me.

"You think some of these girls in here would dance with me?" He'd been watching the dance floor pretty close. I guess he figured he could do the shit-kicking stomp as well as anybody.

"It's a free country," I said. "Get up and get after 'em. If you catch a wild one, holler for me, and I'll mug her down while you get ahold of her."

I'm not sure he quite understood what I meant, but he got up and went over to the table where the ladies were sitting, got him one, and got out on the dance floor.

Everything went pretty smooth for about an hour, when I noticed Nick and R.C. talking out on the dance floor. I didn't figure they'd have much in common to be talking about. I'd just gotten over being chewed out about buying R.C. several drinks.

"Damn it, Frank, quit buying him drinks. I wanna see him get in his pockets and jerk out that money. I wanna see if there's an end to it, see if he has any more of those hundred-dollar bills. I want him drunk so he'll talk more."

"Poke, there ain't no chance he's gonna pull a hundred-dollar bill in here. I imagine they could change it, but there ain't many men that come in here and flop a hundred-dollar bill down and expect to buy a round of drinks."

"Give him a chance to try!"

When R.C. sat down, I asked him what Nick had to say.

"Nothing to be bothered about. He was recommending that I quit dancing with his girl. I told him I'd danced with all four of them, which one was his. He gave me a big smile and said, 'All of 'em.' "

R.C. had confined his dancing to just those four ladies. There were a lot of other girls in the bar, but he found one that he'd gotten comfortable with and was making a habit of going over and dancing with her. So I didn't figure it'd be long before Nick had something to say about her, and he'd surely make the one that R.C. was dancing with his favorite for the night.

And sure enough, after a while Nick swaggered over to the table and stopped just short of R.C. Standing up, looking down on R.C., who was sitting, he said, "Sonny, you ain't payin' attention to what I've been tellin' you, so I'm gonna have to tell you again. Leave my sweetie alone and quit dancin' with her."

Right then that Indian temper of mine began to kind of get away from me. "Nick, we ain't lookin' for trouble here at this table. But if trouble is the only damn thing that'll do, you shore 'nuff come to the right place."

Nick looked over at me. "I don't have any truck with you, Frank. This here is just between me and this pal of yours."

"That don't make any difference. We came in here together. He's a peaceable sort, and new in the country. And he ain't lookin' for no trouble."

R.C. said, "I can speak for myself, Frank." Oddly enough R.C. didn't seem scared or worried. He just looked up at Nick and said, "I don't know who you are, or care, but as long as the young lady is willing, I'm going to keep doing what I've been doing all night long."

Nick was taken aback a little bit by this. I suppose Nick thought that he'd get this new feller in the country, this slight young feller, to crawdad a little bit and go to running backwards. Real cocky-like, he looked down at R.C. "Well, suppose you and me step outside and we'll just settle this thing right now."

With that, Poke popped up and said, "What about your three buddies over there? If you think you're goin' outside and have a three-on-one ass kickin', mister, you're wrong."

"Nah, nah, Poke. I'm tellin' ya, it's just between me and this feller here." To R.C., "If you've got enough guts, you'll get up and foller me outside. I'm headin' out there right now. If ya don't show up in five minutes, I'll figure ya got jello for a backbone, and come back in and just spank you like a stepchild." With that he turned on his heel and marched outside.

I noticed that his three buddies had been paying attention. For that matter, everybody had kind of quieted down, 'cause it had gotten a little bit loud, at least Nick had. So everybody in the outfit thought, "Well, here we go!"

Sally was still waiting tables and had called in the bartender. But nobody seemed to care what happened, as long as it didn't happen inside. "Take your trouble outside" was the motto around the Water Hole. And a lot of it went on outside, quite frequently.

I looked at R.C. "You don't have to do this. I think I'll step outside with Poke and skin ol' Nick up."

What happened next sure surprised me and I'm sure it surprised Poke, too. R.C. was calm, still smiling, and had a glint in his eye. He said, "You don't have to do that, Frank. I can take care of myself."

"You don't know this Nick Compton," I said. "I do. He only picks on people he thinks he can whip. He'll kick, he'll bite, he'll jab his thumb in your eye, he'll grab you by the ear, try to rip it off. If he can get you to lookin' the other way, he'll blindside you. He's what you call an alley fighter, and kind of an opportunist. Don't tell me you think you can handle that."

"I believe I can."

This was plumb amazing to me. Here sat a feller in brand-new duds that didn't look like he could beat shit with an eggbeater, and he was going to step outside his first night in town and take on the town trouble-maker. I leaned over and looked at R.C. "Can you fight a lick, R.C.?"

With quite a bit of confidence, he looked right back at me. "I have been schooled in the art of self-defense a little. I think I can handle myself so you won't be ashamed of me."

"You're bound and determined to go through with this, then?" Poke asked.

"You bet!"

I pushed back my chair. "Well, let's go! Let's don't keep the gentleman waitin'."

When I got up, it seemed like every man and a few women made a rush for the door. Poke and I had already started for the door, and all of a sudden we realized somebody was missing. Our scrapper and the man who knew the art of pugilism was still sitting in his chair.

I walked back to R.C. "Aren't you comin', or did you change your mind?"

"No, I'm coming. But I'm having trouble."

"What trouble are you havin'?"

He looked at me kind of sheepishly. "I've got an erection."

I didn't believe my ears. I leaned over a little more and said, "A what?"

"I've got an erection."

I looked at him in disbelief. "You mean you've got a hard-on?"

He smiled. "Yeah. I can't get up. And if I did I'd be at a disadvantage."

"My God, R.C.! You're goin' out there to fight him, not fuck him!"

"Yeah, I know. But this sometimes happens when I get real excited."

"Well," I said, "what are you gonna do?"

"I don't know. I guess I need something to calm me down."

I don't know why I did it, but the only thing I could think of was, hell, his pants are wet already. So I just reached over, got my drink, and poured it right on R.C.'s crotch, ice and all.

With that he stood up real quick. "Godalmighty! Why'd you do that?"

"Well, what kind of shape are you in now?"

He reached down and pulled at the crotch of his pants and smiled real big. "That did it. Everything's under control now."

And I thought, Oh, God, what next? "Well, are ya comin'?"

"I'm right behind you."

When we hit the door and got outside, there was a sizable crowd gathered around. I hadn't noticed, but old Egg Robbins had come. Even though Egg was short and small of stature, when he spoke he did command respect. When he saw us come through the door, he began to give directions to everybody to back up and give us room, and laid down ground rules. There wasn't much need for that. Anything'd be fair. What he didn't want was anybody else jumping in on somebody. You'd be surprised how quick a full-scale, knock-down, drag-out can happen when two guys start fighting. All of a sudden it's contagious.

Egg allowed that everybody there was a spectator and nothing else. So everybody backed up. Nick was up rolling up his sleeves, flexing his muscles, swinging his arms around, kind of halfway warming up.

R.C. turned around to me. "Are you watching him?"

"You bet I'm watchin' him," I said. "I'll not take my eyes off of him."

So while R.C. had his back to him, and there was a good space between them, he said, "Here, Frank, hold my hat and my shirt. This is my brand-new shirt, and I'd sure hate to get it torn or messed up."

Well, there I stood, holding his hat while R.C. was taking off his shirt. He had on one of those sleeveless undershirts that we all wore, and he left it on. He handed me his shirt.

Nick popped off and said, "What's the matter, boy? 'Fraid of gettin' your shirt all bloody?"

R.C. just turned around and looked at him and smiled. "It isn't my blood I'm worried about."

And that flat threw old Nick into a rage. He started dancing toward R.C. and R.C. went out to meet him. I noticed he was balanced well on his feet, had his knees bent. For some reason or other I had a feeling that this wasn't going to be one of those wild haymaker, swinging bar fights. There was going to be a little bit more to this one. And Lord, I was sure enough right.

R.C. began to move around to his left in a boxing crouch, with his left extended and his right arm cocked, chin kind of tucked down underneath his shoulder. When they got close enough, Nick let loose with a great big haymaker you could see coming from a mile away. R.C. just stepped underneath it and pounded a short right to Nick's belly that damned near doubled him over.

Nick backed up and straightened up with a surprised look in his face, mumbled some swear words, and took in after R.C. again. This time R.C. just kept his left out there. He had the prettiest jab you ever saw. Got all his weight behind it, stuck it out there, and every time it went out, it landed somewhere around the vicinity of Nick's nose.

Nick began to flail away with both hands, which R.C. wasn't having any trouble getting out of the way of. Ducking, bobbing, dodging. He'd whack a little bit on Nick's belly, and come up with a left hook to his ear, back off and jab again, and come around with a right cross.

And then it dawned on me. I don't believe R.C. had ever been in a bar fight or an alley fight. But he had some considerable experience boxing. He was putting on a display of boxing that you just couldn't believe. I don't believe Nick ever touched a hair on his head.

Finally, out of frustration, Nick backed off, and I could see it coming. He let go with a kick, aimed right at R.C.'s balls. R.C. slipped it off to the right, just like he would a jab or a cross, and caught the heel on the way up and just kept pushing. The first thing to hit the ground was the back of Nick's head. By this time, Nick's nose was bleeding. His lips were puffy, and I had an idea his front teeth were getting loose. He began to swell over one eye and I could see he was going to have one hell of a shiner in the morning. And he just wasn't making any headway at all. You could see the steam fast going out of Nick Compton.

When Nick finally got to his feet, he brushed himself off a little bit and had the audacity, and I mean au-dass-ity, to say, "Well, have ya had enough?"

R.C., with a smile, said, "Not nearly. I'm just getting warmed up. I don't even believe I broke a sweat."

You could see by the look on Nick's face that he'd been whupped. But I guess he decided to make one more lunge at it. If he could get R.C. on the ground and take him down, he might have one card left in the deck that he could play. With that, he made a wild running lunge, head down, trying to tackle R.C. and take him down. R.C. was way too quick. He sidestepped and as Nick went by, gave him a healthy shove. Nick ran head on into the side of a pickup door, made about a three-inch dent in the door, slumped to the ground, leaned up against the pickup truck, and turned around with a dazed look in his eyes. And I have to admit, it was a funny sight. Blood dripped off of him, damn near everywhere. It was all over.

Egg made the announcement. "Well, we've all seen the fun. Let's get back inside and carry on. The night's still young."

With that everybody began to file back into the Water Hole. I was one of the last to go back in. R.C. was putting on his shirt and tucking in his shirttail. He had several people slap him on the back and tell him he'd done a hell of a job. One feller stopped and told him he sure admired his fisticuffs. R.C. thanked them all. Pretty humble for a feller that had just knocked the living whop out of Nick Compton. I was pretty proud of my boy.

R.C. put his hat on and we went back inside. Nick and his three buddies never did come back in. We got a fresh round of drinks. Even Sally smiled at R.C. with a different light. Kind of like she'd found a new puppy. I had a feeling she collected stray dogs and cats and anything that needed a little lovin'.

R.C. began to wonder what Nick might do, and everybody at the table agreed that once Nick was whupped, that would be the end of it. He wouldn't go home and get a gun or a knife. He was capable of anything. But with this many people around, you could bet it was over for the night. He might screw up his courage again, and try some other day. But that day was down the road.

Even Top came over, introduced himself to R.C., and shook hands with him. He pulled up a chair, and was about half-sociable for the first time in a long time.

"Where'd you learn to fight like that?"

"Well, I did some boxing when I was younger."

Top seemed to accept that all right. "We don't often get to see an exhibition of boxing like that. It was downright entertainin' to watch." With a wink, Top gave him a pat on the shoulder and got up and went back to the bar.

R.C. was a might uncomfortable. He was wetter than when he started out, and he'd started out wet. His knuckles were skinned up some and one knuckle in particular began to swell up on him a little bit. But Poke and I had big dreams of getting a bunkmate for the night. We'd thought we'd make another run at some of the ladies and see if we couldn't find one of them to take us home with her.

After another half hour of Poke and me dancing with different ladies, and hinting about what we might like to do, we didn't get any takers. R.C. was so miserable, we decided, well, hell, we'd just head back to the room. All three of us went out and climbed in Ol' Bullet. We stopped and got us a bottle, just in case we ran onto a snake.

We went up to the room, got us some ice, and began to ice down R.C.'s knuckles. Pete had long since closed up the cafe, and was fixing to close down the bar.

After we got R.C. all doctored up, he'd had just enough to drink to make him sleepy. Poke and I had enough to make us wound up like an eight-day clock. While R.C. pulled up the covers, you couldn't have counted to ten any quicker and counted him out, he was sound asleep. Poke and I propped up on the bed, passed the bottle back and forth occasionally, and started in like always, lying to one another.

Poke said, "Wasn't that some kind of an exhibition that ol' R.C. put on tonight?"

"It damn sure was. I didn't think he had it in him."

"Hell, he's good. And he didn't come by that by accident. Somebody went to great pains to teach him to fight like that. Where do you suppose that was?"

"I don't know." There was nowhere around here that I could think of that a feller could get that kind of training.

"Don't they have boxing teams in prison?"

I thought about it awhile. "Yeah, I've heard of that."

"Well, that just makes our case even stronger."

Somehow I just couldn't figure it. I know there was a lot of funny things going on, but prison and R.C., it just didn't add up. He was a mystery. With all the goings-on, outlaw business down in Amarillo and the bank job at Tramperos, deep down inside when I figured R.C. in that, I just came up with one answer, and that was, No way.

"Poke, how did you come by the nickname of Poke? Who was it that give it to you, your Daddy? Was you his little cowpoke?"

With that Poke started giggling, and the more he giggled the more I smiled and pretty soon he was just having a fit laughing. I guess laughter is contagious, so I laughed with him, but I didn't know what in the hell was so funny.

Finally I got him settled down. "What's so funny?"

"It's a secret. Not many people know."

That really got my curiosity up. "We're friends, aren't we?"

He giggled some more. "Yeah. But I don't know as to how we're that close of friends."

"Come on, Poke. If there's something I need to know, I want to find out about it."

"Pass me the bottle and let me get another little nip here. It's kind of a long story. I think you'll enjoy it.

"You know my family's Irish, just as Irish as Paddy's pig. And we still have some distant kinfolk that live in Ireland." You could see him pause a little bit, and he turned and looked at me. "Frank, what I'm gonna tell you, you gotta promise you'll never tell another soul, 'cause I don't want this gettin' around."

He got real serious. "You gotta promise, cross your heart and hope to die?"

"You bet," I said.

"Well, my older brother, Collin, was in World War II and did some fighting in Germany at the tail end of the war, and got shot. He got a Purple Heart, you know."

"Nah, but get on with your story."

"They sent him back to England to the hospital. After he'd recuperated enough to where he could get around, he got a pass and went to Ireland to see if he could trace down some of our relatives. During these travels he picked up an Irish phrase that was used in part of the region where he spent a lot of time. And the phrase was 'pogue mahone,' but it sounded like 'poke mahone.' Guess what 'pogue mahone' means in the Irish language."

"Poke, I don't have any idea."

With this he just broke out in gales of laughter, giggling and snorting. "Frank, it means 'kiss my ass.' "

I laughed until I was sick. "You've got to be kiddin' me."

"No. Honest. I don't know exactly what the spelling is, but that's what it means. And when my brother came home, that's the handle he hung on his little brother. He said it seemed to fit. Frank, outside of my brother and you, nobody knows. 'Course everybody in our part of the country has got a nickname. If a feller's gotta have a nickname, I'll take Poke and let everybody think it's short for cowpoke, rather than Dip, and let everybody think it's short for sheep-dip."

With that we began to laugh and giggle, and the more I thought about Poke Mahone and kiss my ass, the funnier it got.

First thing we knew, we could hear R.C. up and stomping around and, God, he got up just like he would at the ranch, at the crack of dawn. Both Poke and I raised hell with him and told him to at least get out of the room and go get coffee. On Sunday morning, let us try to sleep it off. We both felt like hell. My mouth felt like a whole band of red-dog Apaches had marched through it barefooted.

We caught a little sleep off and on, 'til the middle part of the morning, and then got up and went down and drank as much coffee as we could hold. The restaurant and bar were closed up at Kitchins, so we had to go down the street to the Riteway.

Made you feel kind of funny sitting in the only cafe in town that was open, and seeing people come in with their Sunday-go-to-meetin' clothes on, and you had on your Saturday-night clothes. Everybody else seemed to be on their way to church and afterwards a big Sunday dinner and family gathering. Kind of made you feel lonesome, kind of made you feel left out.

'Long toward evening we thought we should head back toward the ranch. We still hadn't run onto Jim, but I figured he'd find his way back some way or another. So, we didn't worry about him. Besides, we had to get home so Poke could get saddled up and ride on back to the Cannon outfit while there was still plenty of daylight.

Poke and I were somewhat hung-over and R.C.'s knuckles weren't in the best of shape. But all in all we'd had a fairly successful night on the town. For a cowboy, a night on the town will give you the strength to carry on for another week or two. A little bit of excitement never hurt anybody.

Somewhere during the night I heard Jim stumble in. I don't know why, but it didn't surprise me. Jim was always there when it was time to go to work.

CHAPTER

10

The next morning when we went to breakfast, you could tell the Boss had heard what happened in town. Now the Boss, he loves a winner. As a matter of fact, if there was anything he did hate, it was a loser. He'd never want the particulars, or come right out and ask R.C. what happened. He took a little extra time with R.C., smiling and examining his hands and kind of grinning. Had an idea that the Boss had been some kind of a rounder in his day, too. Funny part of it is, I'd never seen him in Kitchins bar or cafe, he and Miz T. together, or he alone. And I had sure never seen him out at the Water Hole. He just didn't frequent those places. He seemed to have put all that behind him.

I'd heard stories, but never put much stock in them, about how the Boss was when he was a young man. But by the gleam in his eye and some of the tales that he told, I knew that in his day he'd gone on some big jags, and knew what it meant to walk on the wild side of life. He frowned upon drinking, in public at least. But I had an idea he knew where us boys were coming from.

Later that morning, I was trying to teach R.C. the fine art of horse-shoeing. We gathered up a couple of head of horses that needed their shoes reset. R.C. watched me pull the shoes, take a foot and shape it, shape new shoes, and nail them on. And I was talking to him and in-structing him as we went.

We got to the point where he was pulling shoes and using the nip-pers trying to get the foot fairly flat, when we heard somebody drive in. I was looking for a good excuse to quit and get a drink anyway. So I peered over the fence and there was an old, beat-up pickup, faded in color, and it had seen its better days. A young, slight feller got out of it and was walk-ing up toward the house. I wondered who it was.

The Boss evidently had been expecting him because he met him, shook hands, and they went on inside. Curiosity was getting the best of me, so I called Tio over. He was working in the flower gardens there in front of the house. Asked him if he knew who that feller was.

"Why chure, Frank. Thees guy ees Johnny. You know, the one who rides the bucking horses, the Boss calls Johnny the Twist."

Well, finally we were going to get to see a show. I'd sure been looking forward to it. I'd heard of this feller for a long time. But we went on about our business and got the horses shod.

We could hear the Boss coming. We were in the saddle house when they walked up on the porch, so we went out to meet him. No last name, just introduced him to me and R.C. as Johnny.

Johnny was friendly enough. Shook hands. Real strong hands, but real small hands. He was very small in stature. He was a shade too big to be a jockey, but not by much. He stood around five-five, five-six and weighed about a hundred thirty pounds, I'd guess. The clothes he had on seemed like they'd seen better days. Had on a pair of gray, I supposed they'd been black at one time, real high-topped, high-heeled boots, with a deep, deep scallop. And on the back of those boots were a pair of Jerry Ambler–style Crocket spurs that looked like they'd been put on the day he bought the boots and never taken off since. An old work shirt, a belt with just a plain ranger-style buckle, no trophy buckle, a black wildrag, and a black hat that was shaped like one you'd seldom ever see in this country. Had a wide four-inch brim, with the top crown of the hat open except for a dent facing forward coming down the hat, and a fairly tall crown. But that one dented crease in his hat made that old black hat look like it had a forehead sloping toward the back. The odd thing was the way the sides were shaped. The left side had very little curl and roll to it, while the right side had a very distinctive upper roll and curl, even the edge of it in toward the crown of the hat. It was dished low in front and low in back, and just covered with dust.

The Boss held most of the conversation, with me chiming in and R.C. occasionally with a question or a statement of fact. Johnny answered most questions politely, but wasn't much for words. He had a way about him, and he was very confident in what he did. I guess rightfully so, because I heard what he did, he did awfully well.

The Boss told me to get a-horseback and run out to the horse pasture and bring in that old Gruyer. We'd just turned him loose and he'd been out in the horse trap getting fat. I gathered up one of the horses we'd just got through shoeing, and hit a lope. Didn't take long to get around the grulla and a couple of others and run them into the round pen. The Boss had the gate set. We cut out those that I'd brought in that we didn't need, just leaving the grulla.

Johnny said, "I'll go get my truck and drive it up here fairly close, so I don't have to pack my kack a long ways. Then I'll go to work, Boss, if it's all right with you."

"This is your deal, Johnny. He's in the pen, you have at him."

While Johnny was gone, we all squatted down and rested our backs on the fence, trying to get in the shade a little. The Boss said, "Frank, I want you to watch careful. And you, too, R.C. I think you boys are liable to learn somethin'. John's awful good with a tough horse, but this time, he just might have met his match."

I had a feeling that since this old grulla carried the Cross S on his hip, maybe the Boss was pulling just a little for the horse, instead of Johnny. Oh, I know he wanted the horse broke, and wanted to get to riding him again. It was a waste of horseflesh to let that good a horse just ruin. But I guess it was the pride in the bloodline that made him pull a little bit for the old grulla.

Johnny had thrown his kack up on the fence, along with a halter and a long braided-cotton rein. I looked his rig over real careful. I had supposed that instead of a slick fork that he would be riding what we call a "bear-trap," a bear-trap being a saddle that had swells that swept back and was deeply undercut, and a high cantle that gave you support from behind, and where you could shorten up your stirrups, jam your knee and thigh up underneath the swells.

But surprisingly, that's not what he was riding. It wasn't a slick-fork, but it looked a great lot kin to this committee rig that the RCA had accepted as a standard bronc-riding saddle. It did have considerable undercut under the swells, but not anything like I'd supposed. The cantle wasn't near as high as I had thought it might be. It was an old saddle and had seen lots of use, but it'd been well taken care of.

Johnny was pulling on his leggings, and you could tell by looking at them that they weren't leggings that were used in rough brush to protect your legs from cholla cactus and brush. They were made out of a real lightweight suede leather. They weren't the showy type of chaps that bronc riders use, the big batwings. They were ordinary leggings. But you could see dark patches right above the knee, and I imagined that was where he used a little rosin, and rubbed it into his chaps, and also applied it to the underside of the swells of his saddle.

The Boss got up and walked over to him, gave him the story about the horse. Johnny walked up and caught the horse with no problem, talking to him low. He didn't move quick or sudden. Slow and easy, he slipped the halter over his neck, up over his nose, and buckled it on. He led him over to his saddle, threw the blankets on, and threw his saddle on, ever so quiet, ever so slow. Everything deliberate. Cinched him down. And he didn't pull him in two like a lot of fellers would. If you pull a horse real tight, he'll have a tendency not to buck quite so hard.

Johnny pulled him up just about a notch over snug. And since it was a double-rig outfit, he snugged up his back cinch just enough to keep the hay from falling out. He led him out toward the old snubbing post, made a circle around it. Then reached up very slowly, put his hand on the back of his hat, his left hand on the brim of his hat, and pulled it down as low as he could.

He reached up and grabbed the side of the halter, and about that time the Boss said, "Be careful, Johnny. That ol' horse's mama comes from buckin' stock."

Johnny didn't even turn his head, but answered the Boss just as he stepped aboard. "Don't fret, Boss. I come from bronc riders' stock on my daddy's side."

The words had no more than cleared his mouth when he was sitting right in the middle of him. Just like with me, Gruyer never moved a jump, never quivered, just stood there with his ears laying back.

Johnny had a quirt that was looped around his right wrist. He sat there quietly for a few seconds, and I thought to myself, man, this feller has the guts of a bank robber. It's so easy for a horse to rare up and come back over on you, with him standing still. I thought he'd untrack him as quickly as he could. But he just sat there. He gave Gruyer a nudge with the spurs. He still didn't untrack, but humped up considerably. Another nudge. He still didn't move. Johnny raised his right wrist and with that braided rawhide quirt, laid it right down where the colt would suck, right under his right leg. And ol' Gruyer exploded.

Johnny was everything that they said he was. Ol' Gruyer pulled the tricks that he pulled on me, but Johnny stayed up there just like a giant tick on a hound's ear. And believe you me, Gruyer was doing his best. He was doing a lot of bucking and not taking up a lot of space. Johnny seemed to let him have his head. He gave him all the rein he wanted. And he wasn't contesting the horse. He wasn't going to the shoulders with the spurs and back to the cantle. But every time the horse's front legs hit the ground, Johnny's feet were in front of him, and that quirt came down on the ass end of Gruyer.

I guess that it was getting so painful for Gruyer that he began to take up more room. There's a song called "Zebra Dun" that in it somewhere the words go: "You can see the mountains under Dunny ever jump, but the stranger, he was growed there, just like a camel's hump." Well, there weren't any mountains around this place, but from my vantage point, squatting down there alongside the fence, I could see the top of the fence under Gruyer's belly. So I can tell you, he was flat chinning the moon!

He swapped ends, rolled his ol' belly up to the sky, and Johnny never lost position. He never changed expression. Then he did something that was hard to believe. He was under such control and balance, he was able to slip the quirt off his wrist onto the saddle horn. For a moment I thought he was holding onto the horn, trying to help himself, but found out it was only to hang up the quirt. Having done that, he reached up and grabbed the brim of his old black hat and went to fanning the horse across the head, old-fashioned style, sacking him out while he was riding him. It was impressive. I'd never seen it done before. Now I had my explanation of why his hat had been shaped the way it was.

At last you could see the Gruyer weakening. He slowed down to running and bucking, finally crow hopping, and finally just some running around the arena.

The Boss was leaning on the snubbing post, turning his head to watch him as he made his circles, and R.C. and I hadn't had to budge from the edge of the round corral. When he finally began to talk to him, he let up on the fanning, let up on the spurs, and just began talking to him in a steady calm type of voice. After putting his hat back on and pulling it down low, he plow-reined around a time or two. And every now and then Gruyer would get a wild idea that he'd take advantage of him, and he'd blow up again. But every time he would, here would come those spurs, the rowels catching him in the shoulders.

I guess ol' Gruyer finally put two and two together; if I quit this nonsense, he'll quit ajigging on me. So finally they hit a standoff. I won't buck, if you'll let up. And Johnny seemed to know right when to let up. Directly he didn't even have to plow-rein him. The horse was neck-reining around in pretty good shape, still going fast. Johnny even stopped him.

The ol' Gruyer still had his ears laid back. Johnny started him off again, loped him around the corral a time or two, pulled up and stopped him, and started off again. You could tell the ears were beginning to come forward. He began to turn him into the fence. Finally he rode over to the snubbing post, and just as quickly as he got on, stepped off.

"What do ya think, Boss?"

"Well, Johnny, I believe you've got him conquered." He looked over at me. "Frank, grab your kack and take him outside."

Johnny had pulled his saddle when I got there with mine. I didn't even tie the slicker on the front of the swells this time. I just threw my saddle on him, cinched him up, put a plain grazing bit in his mouth, got on him, and circled the corral a time or two, while Johnny, R.C., and the Boss stood out in the middle and watched. I told R.C. to open the gate. I headed for the horse trap.

It seemed like ol' Gruyer had had all he wanted. His manners had improved considerably. I rode him around the big old horse trap and let him cool off 'cause he was lathered from his ears to his tail. And I headed back in. I'd ridden him for about an hour, and I figured that was enough for one day. I didn't believe I'd have any more trouble with him from here on out. And I wanted to get back. Maybe Johnny was going to stay for dinner. I'd like to learn a little more about this feller that rode wild horses for a livin'. He sure had gained my admiration, and I'd like to hear him blow his breath a little bit.

But when I got in I saw that the old pickup was gone. I asked about him, and the Boss just shook his head. "Johnny's not one to impose. I asked him in to dinner. I even had Tess go out and ask him to please stay, but he seemed embarrassed and seemed like he needed to be on his way. He's a loner, that boy, and prefers it that way. I paid him what he asked, and gave him more, and still felt like I got a bargain. I believe the only thing that ol' Johnny is comfortable with is horses, and riding the wild ones. People tend to make him nervous. And he isn't big on conversation. If a bad one don't get him, or he don't get hurt bad, the boy's found his niche for life. 'Course a bronc rider's life ain't long. Not that he's gonna get killed. But he'll soon find, as he grows older, that that life is over, and he'll have to find another. For Johnny, that'll be hard. As a matter of fact, he may not be able to handle it at all."

We didn't have any trouble staying busy the next few days because the big branding was coming up, starting Thursday morning. It kept R.C. and Jim and me humping to make sure that everything was ready, all our equipment and our holding pens. R.C. had connived Tres into giving him some lessons on how to rope. During the spare time we had in the evenings you could see Tres out there helping R.C. learn to swing a loop, coil a rope, throw a flat loop.

You see, the Boss was a master with a rope. I'd heard people talk about him. He grew up with one in his hands, and there's no telling how many calves he'd dragged to the branding fire by the heels. He was a better man on heeling cattle than he was on heads or horns. He was still in great demand by some of the local hotshots. Everybody wanted him to heel for them at the local rodeos. He seldom entered anymore, just occasionally to let everybody know he still hadn't lost his touch. Everything the Boss knew, he'd take great pains with and pass it on to Tres. And Tres took to it just like a duck to water.

For a young feller, Tres was about the best hand with a rope that I'd ever seen. I just hoped that someday that rope wouldn't get him into trouble. I knew that I'd gotten into some considerable wrecks with a rope, and I found Tres was just like myself. He always had a rope in his hands when we were working cattle. I would tell him, "Now don't go ropin' anything." It just seemed like he could not keep that rope off something.

He was showing R.C. how to get it done. It was kind of comical at first. R.C.'d hold that loop and Tres would show him where to grab it where the honda would be balanced with the loop. He'd swing it over his head like he was waving a flag on a stick. So Tres worked with him until he got his wrist coming down on the down swing. And you could see R.C. was learning his lessons well. He was beginning to curl that loop around him and keep it open, and he began to rope a bale of hay. R.C. seemed obsessed with learning to swing that rope and learning to handle it right.

He was also on my case about getting a-horseback. So I asked the Boss if it would be all right if I took R.C. out.

"Yeah, Frank, go ahead. But watch out for the boy. He may not know nothin', and I want you to be responsible for him."

Damn, I hated to be responsible for somebody. It was all I could do to be responsible for myself. I'd been used to working around cowboys where everybody was just responsible for themselves. To take on the responsibility of another human being really wasn't down my alley. But who knew. He said he could ride. He might be better than what I thought, and I'd be in for a pleasant surprise.

The Boss did tell me not to put any ideas into R.C.'s head about getting a-horseback and helping us when we started branding. He said he needed him worse on the ground, and he didn't want him getting in the way. So we'd break him in easy on this horseback deal 'til he could finally make a hand.

It tickled R.C. plumb to death, when after breakfast one morning I asked him to go with me horseback to check the yearling pasture. His eyes lit up like it was Christmas. "You mean it?"

"Shore. Let's break in that saddle of yours, and those chaps."

Nearly all the horses were fairly gentle, though it took a cowboy to ride them. They weren't kid ponies. We didn't even have one of those on the place. But I gave him about as dependable and gentle a horse as we had, for a Hard Twist bloodline, that is.

R.C. seemed to know where everything went. Got his breast collar on and back cinch snugged up. Had given him a bridle that he'd have control of, but that he could hardly hurt a horse's mouth if he was heavy-handed. I thought this the best way to start out and we'd just see how much this feller knew.

He got his chaps and those good-looking Blanchard spurs on. "Well, step on and let's go," I said.

He reached up, grabbed the saddle horn with his left hand and the back of the cantle with his right hand, and climbed aboard. And right there I began to coach him.

"Don't grab ahold of that saddle with both hands so far apart. Either grab the saddle horn with your right hand, and the neck with your left hand, and swing on, or grab the saddle horn with both hands. The main thing is those reins. Keep control of those reins, 'cause that's your steering wheel and your brake."

He was listening to me and paying attention. I also noticed the reins and the way he was holding them. They were coming out the top end of his hand by his thumb. I told him to turn his hand over to where his thumb was pointed down toward the front of the reins, and slip the split reins between his thumb and finger.

"Why?"

"Because you're going to control the horse that way. It's all right to turn your hand around if you're going to jerk his damned head off. If you hold them the way I tell you, then a horse will neck-rein better."

We started out at a trot. I watched him and he was doing considerable bouncing up and down, and it looked like he was doing it on purpose. I couldn't quite figure out what he was doing. I widened out from him a little to get a better view of him and every step that horse took, he'd sit down in his saddle and then stand up in his stirrups. Me, I was just standing up in my stirrups since we were going at a high trot.

Finally I pulled down to a walk and said, "Are you doin' that on purpose, or is that horse throwing you up into those stirrups like that?"

He looked at me with a frown. "I don't understand what you mean."

"I noticed you're standing up in your stirrups and then you're sittin' down."

"Oh, I'm posting."

Then a frown and a quizzical look came on my face and I asked him just what in the hell posting was.

"That's when you have a horse at a trot. The only riding I've ever done is in an English saddle. I've never ridden one of these western saddles before."

So with a little bit of disgust I said, "I don't know what postin' is, but it looks like if you're gonna do that all day you're gonna be worn to a frazzle. Sit down in the saddle. Keep your feet in front of you, your heels low, your toes out, and get with him."

He tried that. But as the horse was going up in the trot, he was coming down, and as he was going up the horse was going down. They were out of rhythm. So we had to pull up again, and I had to explain it in better terms. I didn't quite know how.

"Stand up in your stirrups and hold onto the horn at a high trot, and sit down and get with him at a fox-trot, a traveling trot. I'll show you what I mean. Watch me."

He did as he was told. Standing up in the stirrups at a high trot came easily. He had trouble at a traveling trot until he finally relaxed, put more weight in his stirrups, and got with him. Since this is the way we traveled practically all the time, in order to make a hand he'd have to be comfortable at this fox-trot. Finally I could see he was getting the hang of it.

"Kick him into a lope," I said.

R.C. looked at me blankly. "A what?"

"A lope. Watch." I touched the spurs to my horse, he broke from the trot into a slow lope. R.C. had considerable problem with this. He couldn't get in time with him. I wondered what to tell him, then realized the perfect explanation.

"Let your hips move back and forth just like you're humpin' some ol' girl. You understand me? Your pelvis comes forward. You keep your feet in front of you and your butt and pelvis keep movin' forward right with the horse. I hate to bring fornicatin' into the picture here, but that's the best way that I can explain it. Get the picture?"

R.C. glanced at me sideways and grinned. "You gotta stay in rhythm if you're gonna get the job done."

We started out at a trot again and I watched him. And by God, he was getting the hang of it. We hit a high trot and we stood up in our stirrups. Then we hit a lope. In the beginning, he looked like a bear cub playing with his peter, terrible clumsy. But now that was gone. He'd caught on.

It was a standing rule around this place that you never walked a horse unless you were examining something, or trying to figure out something. But if you were going to or coming from someplace, you hit a trot. It didn't wear your horse out, and when you got where you were going, you had plenty of horse left to do whatever needed to be done. You also didn't go whooping and spurring and riding at breakneck speed. When you worked for the Cross S and the Boss, you rode his horses his way.

We were beginning to see a few deer, as it was still early in the morning, and they hadn't brushed up yet. Quite often you'd see mule deer down in the breaks among the juniper and down along the river. But you seldom saw them when you topped out and got up on the prairie. Up there you were apt to see lots of antelope. That morning we had the good luck of running into a herd of twenty, twenty-five head.

I kept pretty close watch on R.C. as we traveled through the country and he was taking to the horse in good shape. He was kind of a natural, you might say. This R.C. never ceased to amaze me, how quick he caught on to things. I remember the words he first told me when we met down under the elms on the corner. He'd said, "I catch on fast." And he hadn't lied to me. He paid attention, and was always watching. You only had to tell him once, and he didn't take offense when you corrected him or told him how you'd do it. And there he was, sitting on one of the good Cross S horses, just as big as you please, with a good-looking pair of chaps on, spurs that fit the country, and his hat made him look like he belonged. I'll tell you what, this gentleman had come a long way since I'd first laid eyes on him.

CHAPTER

11

It didn't take long for branding day to roll around. At four o'clock in the morning it was pitch black, and people started stirring. Egg Robbins and his son Wade had come in the night before. Wade, he was staying at the bunkhouse with us common folk. 'Course Poke and Top had ridden in from over on the Cannon outfit the night before. There was going to be quite a crew. Iry Turner and his son Clay, and Horace Crockett was going to bring his boy Ike. Another good man, Bob Chisum, who everybody called Jingle Bob, would be in with the Jaramillos.

The Jaramillos had a place over south and west of us. The old man, Diego, was quite the gentleman in the Spanish-Mexican tradition. English, being his second language, was spoken very correctly and very deliberately. The word "ain't" was not in his vocabulary. He not only was the owner of the Jaramillo ranch, but also the patriarch of the entire clan, which resided in a small village at the ranch headquarters. Although much older than the Boss or Miz T., he was her half-brother; same father, different mothers. He and the Boss were extremely close. Whenever Diego or his two sons were over, Joaquin and Miguel, they had a kind of familiarity to them like kinfolk do. All the Jaramillos (Diego, Miguel, Joaquin) stayed at the big house with the Boss and Miz T.

It was something to see, to feed seventeen people with the appetites of bitch wolves, all at one sitting. The big table in the dining room was pulled out and the slats put in, and they had a big table out on the porch. Everybody howdyed everybody else, and shook hands all the way around.

The Boss, even though he was getting a little old, could be, if you twisted his arm hard enough, persuaded to put on a heelin' exhibition, which was looked forward to by all of us.

There was always a feeling of excitement that early in the morning. Even though it was late May, it was still cool enough to be a shade crisp.

We all were anticipating the gather and the branding, and all the unexpected events that happened. We'd probably laugh about them if they were serious or not. That was just the way things worked in this country. It took something almost fatal to keep the laughing down, and to keep a serious pall over a bunch of cowboys during branding.

We all saddled up and gathered at the gate Jim was holding open for us. We were going plumb to the back side, riding right through the Padre pasture. Long's Creek passes through the bottom, and up on the bank of the creek where the Martinez and the Holderly have a common fence between them, were two pens.

It was a pretty good ride to the back side of the ranch. Took about an hour. As we split up the Boss was going to take part of us, and he gave Top the honor of gathering the Martinez pasture.

The Boss picked his crew to work the Holderly and started off to the northwest. 'Course Top was left with the rest of us and I was in his crew. So we went through the Martinez gate, then stopped and had our own little private confab. Top asked who was riding green horses. 'Course I was, and Poke needed some miles on his horse. So our job was to take the outside circle. Those riding older horses could take the inside circle.

I rode west until I could get to the fence. This was the part of the cowboy life that I loved the best. The sun just coming up and everything fresh and clean, just like the day the world was born. The birds asinging, the cows bawling, horse sweat, the creak of leather, everything about it suited me. And I really believe, deep in my heart, that this was my calling, the reason God put me here.

Wasn't long before I could see Poke coming down the south side of the pasture heading toward me. We met up there on top and had a chew. Poke was tickled also. That early morning riding does something for a feller. They say that the best thing for the inside of a man is the outside of a horse. And I believe it.

We headed back, taking a shorter circle to pick up what might have been left behind by the guys on the inside circle, just kind of a double-check. We both started back in the same direction in which we'd come, only riding a little tighter to the inside this time. The sun was up good and high and you could see the dust trails heading down into the breaks, cattle bunched up by the dozens, heading down for the creek to where it got flat and we could gather and pen them.

Up there on high I could see Jim and R.C. and old Diego, who by all rights could be called "Don," a term of esteem in the Spanish language. He was a fine old gentleman, a wise man and an honest man. He and the Boss had a lot in common, only I had a notion that Don Diego Jaramillo was not quite the taskmaster that the Boss was. Had a feeling he was of a gentle nature and had a much more relaxed attitude about operating a ranch than the Boss did.

It appeared that we'd done a good job of gathering. Everything came together down at the bottom. Top was on the point and kept them strung out. Didn't push too hard and let them file into the pens. We worked them easy, they knew where they were going, they'd been there before. We didn't separate the calves off their mothers and put them through undue stress when we worked them. Left them right on their mothers, heeled them and drug them to the fire and let them go back. It was wonderful how peaceable everything could stay when you worked quick and smooth.

Although we still did everything the old way, there'd been some improvements. We no longer used wood for our branding fire, or cow chips. Our brand burner was a ten-inch pipe welded shut on both ends with a hole cut in it to where we could stick a pipe coming from a rubber hose off a butane bottle. The whole thing was portable.

The Boss preferred to make the X for the Cross S brand out of bar irons to prevent blotching. Of course the S was just bent into a regular S brand. I imagine the bar and the S were about four inches in height, with long handles and a ring at the end of the handle.

It was always a privilege to rope at one of these brandings. As a general rule you didn't rope your own cattle. You delegated that to your good friends. The kids seldom got to rope, with the exception of Tres. The Boss loved to show him off. Maybe toward the last day and the last pen of cattle, some of the sons would get to rope. But the chance of me getting to drag any calves while we were working there on the Piedra was less than slim. I'd get my chances when I went to help and repay these other fellers. I didn't mind. My time would come.

I asked the Boss if I could start flanking with R.C. Kind of felt responsible for him. We had our leggings on and our gloves. Always kept our gloves on because there would be some grabbing of the tail, and every now and then that tail would be full of cockleburs.

While we were waiting for our irons to get hot, I told R.C., "Watch Poke and me, then you'll get the idea of what to do."

"Come over and help me flank a few," I hollered at Poke.

Poke came over, pulled on his gloves that he'd had tucked in on the wang string between his chaps. Top and Jingle Bob, already tied on hard and fast to the saddle horn, had their loops, and were sitting there visiting.

Boss walked by and looked at the irons and said, "They're hot, boys. Go to 'em."

So real slow, one of them went to the left, one to the right. They eased into the cattle. A couple of cranks with the rope, a good hard loop thrown, set up in a trap on the hind legs. They turned and Top was coming to the fire, and Bob was right behind him.

Poke and I took the first one. Bob had come to our side. He came at a high trot right between us, both hind feet caught. Poke grabbed the rope, I grabbed the tail. We popped him down, I lit on his neck, holding the front leg up. Poke plopped down on the ground, stretched the bottom leg forward and held the top leg back, took off the rope. Jingle Bob was shaking out another loop, going back to the herd.

It was a bull calf. So Egg stepped in and cut off the end of the bag and pulled out the nuts, squeezed them out, you might say. Gathered them between his fingers, gently stripped them back a little ways, and took his knife and kind of rubbed the tissue, 'til it came apart. Tio came with a "nut bucket," and Egg dropped both sets of nuts in the bucket, and took the little furry part that he'd cut off the scrotum and handed it to Diego. He was going to keep track of how many steer calves we had, and Tio was taking charge of the nuts. That meant we were going to have a big calf fry one of these days.

Poke and I didn't have to do it long 'til R.C. thought he'd caught on to it. He watched the boys go out into the herd and throw their loops. Occasionally one of them would miss, but not too often. This was really the easiest time to be roping, because practically all the calves needed roped. There were always those snaky calves that would slip in behind their mamas and curl in behind to try to stay out of the way. And the tail end was always the toughest to get.

Between the dehorning, the cutting of the bull calves, the branding, the vaccinating, and the ear marking, it didn't take us over forty-five seconds a calf, sixty at the longest. Everybody had a job to do, everybody knew their jobs, and the jobs were interchangeable. Anybody was capable of doing anything, although some were better at some things than others.

The smell of burnt cattle hair was just like Chanel No. 5 to me. But it was considerable hard work flanking because you had to keep holding and keep a strain. You dare not let anything go. There's too many sharp knives and too many hot irons, too many people could get hurt. This is the one fear that I had that R.C. might make a slip-up. But he was doing fine. He'd caught on to the flanking method.

He and Tres were working real good in double harness there 'til by some accident, and I'd warned R.C. and told him not to let anything go, his hand slipped off the top leg while Egg was a cutting a bull calf. The calf jerked his leg up and jerked it back down so quick that Egg couldn't get out of the way and that sharp knife put a pretty good gash in his thumb. Egg fell back, landed on his back, and got up and looked at his thumb. The Boss, who had been doing the branding, stopped. And believe you me, R.C. was fighting for his life to get ahold of that leg, which was churning back and forth like a pump handle.

When he finally got ahold of it and reared back, he looked at Egg and said, "I'm sorry. It won't happen again."

The Boss looked at him. I believe this was the only time I ever heard him really get on R.C. And it didn't take him many words to do it. "If it happens again, you're gone!"

But Egg, he was a pretty good sport about it. He shook his thumb, sucked it a little. Even though there was calf blood all over it, it was clean blood. He walked over to where we kept the cutting knives, stuck his thumb down in the Lysol, pulled it back out, and glanced at it. "Ah, hell, it's all right, Boss. It's a long way from my heart."

'Course, the Boss had to make a fuss. "We've got a first-aid kit in the truck there, Egg. Do you wanna put a bandage on it?"

"Nah. It'll quit bleedin' directly. There's so much blood, it won't matter no how."

He had to finish the job he'd started, so he figured he'd better get at that calf so he could get him up and back to his mama. While he was finishing, he looked over and winked at R.C. "Don't think a thing about it, son. I've had worse than this on my lips and never did quit whistlin'," and gave him a big smile. You could see that R.C. was accepted by the entire crew.

At midday everything had been worked. We kept the cattle up and let them graze since there was plenty of grass in those pens. We pulled back and visited. Those of us that had been doing the strenuous work took off our chaps to cool off, walked over to the fence, squatted down, and leaned our backs against the fence to rest. R.C., doing the same, had thrown his chaps over his shoulder. He was squatted down by Top as we all made small talk of the morning's work.

When it happened, it happened so fast everyone was caught by surprise. For no apparent reason, Top quickly reached over, slapped R.C. up beside the back of the head, and sent him sprawling into the pens, face down. Nobody understood until the dreaded word was uttered, "Snake!" It seemed as R.C. leaned against the fence he had aggravated a rattler on the other side that had coiled and struck through the fence. Top, being the only one seeing what had happened, did what he had to do. Quick as greased lightning, Top leapt up to grab the snake, which now was laying on top of R.C.'s back. With a quick motion he grabbed the snake by the tail, swung him around his head, then reversed the swing like cracking a bull whip, and practically separated the head of the snake from its body. Then with a fling, slung it out of the pen to where it had come from.

R.C. still didn't know what was going on. We quickly crowded around him and found the chaps thrown across his back had saved him from serious injury. We found two holes, small but deadly, in the chaps. R.C. seemed in a daze. He couldn't believe what had happened. After he realized, he repeatedly thanked Top.

"You better watch where you squat next time," Top said.

Only Egg brought comic relief to the situation when he said, "It's a shame you had those chaps over your shoulder, son. Now I'll always wonder where we'd a'put the tourniquet." There was deadly silence for a moment before everybody saw the humor, even R.C.

After we mothered up everything, the cattle seemed to settle down. We just eased out of their way and let them drift on back to the pasture they came from, and headed in for dinner.

It was early afternoon when we finally got in. We put our horses up; the work had been done for the day. We had started early and worked hard. Now the time was to catch up on a little gossip, a little storytellin'. I imagine with some of the older fellers the discussions got pretty serious. Things like cattle markets and imports. But us younger fellers and the kids, we tried to find ourselves a way to have a good time.

Believe me, washing up was the big project. That washpan got used over and over again, 'til all the grime and blood and dirt and sweat was scraped off. Then we went in to eat dinner, and those branding dinners were banquets in themselves.

Miz T. and Lupe had outdone themselves. Francesca, the Jaramillo brothers' sister, Don Diego's daughter, had come over to help. I hadn't noticed Francesca at breakfast. She had spent most of her time in the kitchen.

Since moderation wasn't one of my strong points, as usual I overdid eating until I made myself miserable. I wasn't alone. So after dinner some went to the bunkhouse for a nap. Some of us didn't even make it to the bunkhouse. We just laid down under the shade of the cottonwood trees, out on the lawn. Some of the older fellers got the cushy chairs in the living room, but everybody sprawled for a mid-afternoon nap or a rest.

I sprawled out on the lawn and R.C. came and sat down beside me. I had all the intentions of snoozing, but R.C. wouldn't let me. He was too involved in finding out who the beautiful lady—his words which I would agree with—was that was serving us. I acted like I didn't know who he was talking about, and had him describe her.

"Ah, you know, Frank. That beautiful girl with the long black hair pulled back in a ponytail and clasped with a silver comb. She's really slender, with a white peasant-type blouse that had all the frilly lace on the bodice."

I grunted and groaned, rolled over a little bit. "What's a bodice, R.C.?" You could tell he was getting frustrated with me.

"Ah, Frank. Dammit." I believe that was the first time I heard him swear. "The girl who was serving us. You know who I'm talking about."

"Oh, yes, I think I do remember that girl. Let me see."

"Come on, Frank!"

"R.C., that's Miguel and Joaquin's sister. Her name's Francesca. Everybody who knows her well calls her Kika. However, if you meet her, I'd suggest that you call her Francesca, or Miss Jaramillo, for that matter."

"Why? Have you got designs on the lady? She's the most strikingly beautiful lady I've ever seen. I'd like to get to know her better."

"Didn't you meet her this mornin' or hasn't somebody introduced you to her?"

"No. Will you?"

"Shore, but not now. Right now I'm so full I can't move."

With that he laid down and propped himself up on one elbow. "Well, what can you tell me about her, Frank?"

"Ah, I don't know. What do you wanta know?"

And I should have expected it. "Everything."

"All I know is that she's the youngest in the family, and she just has the two older brothers, and you've met them. Her mother passed away a long time ago. But she's been educated. She was sent back to Indiana to prep school and to college at St. Mary's. I think it's the women's counterpart to Notre Dame. I don't know if she ever finished school back there or not. But she's come back home. Born and raised on the ranch over there on Ute Creek, and has taken over the role as the head woman of the household for the Jaramillos. She's a good woman, R.C. The Jaramillos are good people. As a matter of fact, the best family I can think of. They're very proud of their Mexican heritage."

R.C. sat up. "Why do you call them Mexican? Don't they take offense to be called Mexican?"

"I don't think so. That's what they call themselves. I've heard Diego refer to himself as Mexican. I've heard him say that his people have been here over two hundred years. I think their ranch was part of a Mexican land grant, and they still observe many of the Mexican customs that their people brought to this country when there wasn't nothin' but buffalo and Indians runnin' all over the prairies and the canyons. So, no, I don't think they take offense to being called Mexican. Maybe it's in how you say it that matters."

Things were quiet for a while. I knew R.C. was thinking. I had my hat pulled down over my eyes, and was just about to drop off to sleep when R.C. said, "Well, I'd always thought that if you called somebody a Mexican, and he wasn't from Mexico, that it was considered derogatory."

I lifted up my hat a little bit and looked at him with one eye. "You mean like callin' somebody from back East a 'damn Yankee'?"

"Yes, kind of."

"I guess you could call them Mexican American. I don't knows to how it makes any difference. The Mexican tradition is very rich. As a matter of fact, the people that came into this country, the Anglos, a lot of them were poor and lower-class farmin' and ranchin' people that were looking for new land and a new lease on life. Where some of these families like the Jaramillos were high-classed people when they came. Like this ranch we're on now, it was the Martinez Ranch at one time. And they were conquerors and explorers, and set out to bring a new culture and a new religion to this land."

That satisfied R.C. "Well, I want you to introduce me."

"R.C., the first chance I get, count on it!"

"I don't want it to be the first chance you get. I want it to be today."

"Ooh, boy, you're gettin' awful serious, awful sudden, aren't you?"

"Frank, I know a good thing when I see it."

"Well, it ain't gonna be easy. She's not the kind of girl you can just go up to and say, 'Hi, sweetie, you wanna go to the picture show?' For the Jaramillos, there's a certain protocol. You will have to be properly introduced and show respect. That's just the way they do things. Do you think it's worth it?"

There wasn't any hesitation when R.C. told me, "You bet! Whatever needs to be done, I'll do it."

About that time Miguel and Joaquin came up and kicked me lightly on the sole of my boot. "Frank, you sleepin'?"

I raised my hat up so I could see. "Well, I was thinkin' about it, but my friend here keeps jawin' at me. Gettin' where a man can't take a decent nap in the afternoon."

"We're headin' over to the Piedra. We want to get up on top of it and check out a grave. Do you want to go with us?"

Now this kind of took me back. "A grave? What grave?"

"Dad told us that one of our relatives was buried up on top of that Piedra. He's been up there. He asked us if we'd go check it out. Do you want to go?"

"Why sure. I've been workin' around here for a good while and I've never heard of any grave up there. I've never even tried to crawl up on top of the rock. How are we gonna get up there?"

"Dad told us that on the south side there's a trail that you can get up," Miguel said, "but it's a pretty hard climb."

"Does the Boss know about this?"

"Oh yeah, he and Dad are inside talkin' about it now. Very few people even know about it, evidently."

With that we got Ol' Blue and all of us piled in the pickup. We kept it kind of quiet. We didn't want the young boys going with us. So, it was just Miguel, who I more often than not called Mike, and Joaquin, who for short we just called Quin, pronounced "keen," and R.C. and I.

It was late afternoon when we got over to the old mission, and it wasn't half a mile to the Piedra. We could drive up almost to the base of it, because there wasn't any gradual upslope to it. It was just on the sandy bottom of the drainage of the creek, and from there rose right straight up, red sandstone. But the rock had crumbled off on the south side, and there was a trail. Nothing that I could tell in the way of tracks had ever gone up there. Certainly no deer or antelope, cattle or horse tracks.

So we started up. The leather-sole boots didn't make the climbing the easiest in the world. As we rose up along this rock slide, we curled around the mesa. We came to a place where a large slab of sandstone, probably four feet thick, had broken off and fell across the trail. It really wasn't a trail. It was just a ledge of broken rock that we had to pick our way through. But we had to pass under this slab of rock for maybe thirty, forty feet to keep going.

We stood there and examined where this rock had fallen. Decided it had fallen long ago, and looked like it was anchored pretty well and wasn't going anywhere.

R.C. didn't seem to have any fear of anything, so he started first, and Mike and Joaquin fell in behind him, and I brought up the rear. We had to duck down to get through, but soon broke out on the other side. There weren't any switchbacks. We just followed this clear to the top. As we got closer to the top, the going got harder. We had to use our hands and knees to crawl around and scramble from rock to rock, and finally got up on top. We stood there on the edge and looked over where we came. It was quite a sight to see. Sure had to be three hundred feet right straight down. And on top, just pretty flat. Slabs of sandstone, a few soapweeds, and a few shrubs that had taken ahold in some low places where some blow sand and dirt had accumulated.

I imagine that the whole surface of the top didn't cover over five acres at the most. And low and behold, there stood the grave. It had the same wrought-iron fence around it that was around the little graveyard down at the old mission. We walked over to it. It had a gate, and it creaked as we opened it. The fence didn't cover much more than just the grave site. It had square wrought-iron uprights with little points pounded into spear points on each. They were spaced about six inches apart, with some very artistic scrollwork made of iron in between the top crosspieces and the bottom crosspieces.

The amazing thing was, there was a marble headstone ornately carved with the name "Estabio Tomas Martinez, 1874." None of us had said a word since we'd walked up to the lonely grave. But upon entering the gate, both Miguel and Joaquin dropped to one knee, made the sign of the cross, brought the hand that made the cross to their lips, and just knelt there silently.

R.C. and I just stood dumbfounded behind them, and stared at the headstone. Finally the boys got to their feet and we backed out, closed the gate, and stood there leaning on the fence looking everything over. It appeared like this gravesite had been picked where dirt had blown in. And I had no idea how deep the dirt was before you came to solid rock.

"I wonder how they got all this up here?" Miguel said.

"Well, getting all this up here sure would have been a chore," I said. "But how do you reckon they got *him* up here?"

So we began to scout around and walked the edges to see if there was some way a body, a coffin, panels to a fence, a large marble headstone, could be either carried or hauled up. Surely all of this wasn't dropped from the heavens.

Joaquin said, "Dad's got some explaining to do."

"I'd appreciate it if you'd let me in on how they got all this done, if you can find out," I said. "Eighteen seventy-four wasn't all that long ago if you stop and think about it, boys. Surely the story has been passed on as to how all this came about. I don't believe there's been anything up here in a long time, except hawks and eagles." I was almost afraid to say what else was on my mind.

The view was magnificent. You could look practically right down upon the old mission church, and the little village that had once been.

You could see up to the tops of the breaks in the Martinez, and the Holderly pasture that we had worked today. You could even see clear to the north to the Mueller place, follow Long's Creek and all the cottonwoods down to the headquarters where the house was. And see clear on east where the valley opened up, into what I figured was Texas.

I knew I'd have to come back up here. I'd probably bring Poke with me. But not for anything in the world would I disturb that grave. I figured the outlying areas could stand a little more inspection. I took a good look at the headstone again. Outside of the name and date, there was a Spanish inscription on the bottom of the stone. And with no more Spanish than I knew, didn't mean anything to me. I figured it was probably the Spanish version of "rest in peace" or something similar that you'd find on Anglo graves. I didn't want to ask Joaquin or Miguel. They were quite solemn, as if they were having some religious experience. Which I could understand. This was some relative of theirs and I knew they'd find out all they possibly could about how all this had come to be.

After we passed underneath the big slab, and got down to the bottom, we all stood and looked straight up. "I can't believe I've worked on this place all these years, and didn't know about that. You'd have thought with my inquisitive mind I would have tried to climb up there, just to see how far I could see. There sure are some questions I'd like answers to."

"Amigo, you aren't the only one," Miguel said.

We noticed that there was quite a bit of activity going on up at the corrals. The Boss was showing off the Gruyer that had dumped me so many times, and that he'd had Johnny out to top off. He was explaining to everybody what a terrible injustice it had been to let this horse go to waste for such a long time.

Horace, called Hoss by most, said, "J.W., as big and stout as that horse is, you're always gonna have to watch him, especially bein' a grulla. He's liable to get it in his head anytime to turn sour on you."

"You're right, Horace. Ain't nobody ever knows what goes through one of these dumb brutes' mind. Anybody ever put complete trust in a horse is a plumb fool. But with the sackin' out that Johnny give him, and now Frank's ridin' him pretty regular, I don't figure it'll be long 'til even Tres can use him. Sure be a great horse to rope big cattle on. Well, I suppose it's time for us older fellers to retire to the house. Come down for supper about six, boys. Frank, bring your guitar and entertain us a little, and maybe we can get Joaquin to play us a tune or two."

We were all up at the bunkhouse when we heard the dinner bell ring. I grabbed my guitar to oblige the Boss and we all filed down for what I knew would be a social outing and an informal supper.

You could tell Tio was manning the dinner bell, because it was hitting on all three sides with great vigor. It wouldn't last long, because the metal bar that it took to ring it was so heavy Tio couldn't stand up under the strain. We didn't use the dinner bell much. It was only used on special occasions. So when that bell rang, and it wasn't anywhere near time to eat, everybody in hearing distance came arunning, knowing something was wrong.

The Boss had told me that his dad had brought the old bell with him when he'd left the last wagon he'd been running and started out on his own. I call it a bell, but it really wasn't. It was a triangular-shaped piece of round steel that had been tempered and bent to make a triangle, but not closed on one end. The clanger was made out of the same material, and attached to a chain at one end. The idea was to stick the clanger in the opening of the triangle and start circulating, whacking the triangle on all three sides as fast as you could. And with the temper of the metal, it let out a loud ring that could be heard all over the headquarters.

R.C. pulled up beside me on our way down to the big house. "Don't forget the introduction, Frank. I have to meet this girl."

"Relax, R.C., I won't forget. You've been remindin' me all afternoon."

I leaned the guitar up beside the wall on the porch. I wasn't going to perform 'til somebody requested it. Then I'd act a little bashful and see what kind of a response I could get. Not that I wanted them to beg. I was more than happy to entertain them. But it just made a feller feel a little more in demand and that his audience would appreciate him.

Everybody filed into the living room where the Boss, Egg, Hoss, Diego, Jingle Bob, and Iry had already taken seats and been discussing cattle affairs. It was a treat to get into that part of the house. The hired hands were seldom invited in.

R.C. grabbed me by the arm before we started in, and we held back until almost everybody was into the living room, and he told me, "Now, Frank, now!"

Francesca Jaramillo was still preparing food along with Lupe and Miz T. in the kitchen. So I called Francesca over, and she came with a smile on her face.

"Kika, we were so busy goin' about our business today, that I don't believe that anybody has introduced you to R.C. Roth."

I looked at R.C. "R.C., may I present Francesca Jaramillo."

Francesca stuck out her hand, which R.C. eagerly took. "It is an honor."

As they began to make small talk, I stood there and looked at Francesca, and I, too, admired her beauty. I stood almost a foot taller than she. She was slender with the most beautiful, rather olive complexion that she and I seemed to share. Her complexion was clear, the features so soft, with large brown eyes and even white teeth. She was almost regal in bearing.

I was the third cog and needed to be somewhere else. I went into the living room just in time to hear the Boss start one of his stories.

The story he was telling now always amazed me. The Boss had everybody's complete attention, for he always seemed, outside of Diego, to be in a class of his own. Of course, Egg, Iry, Hoss, and Jingle Bob were men of substance, had their own places, branded their own brand. But they still did not occupy the stature in the country the Boss did.

The Boss was warming to his story. "Boys, when I was about thirteen I was workin' with my dad when he was runnin' the wagon for the Capitol Syndicate, known as the XIT, down by what is now Hartley, Texas. It was my job to get up with the cook at about three in the morning and get out and jingle the horses." Everybody there knew that "jingle the horses" meant to gather them and bring them in for the day's work.

The Boss continued. "The sun was just coming up when I felt somebody nudge me with their foot. It was Papa, and I realized that I'd overslept. Papa stood over me as I lay in my bed, you see we were camped out and sleepin' on the ground, Papa said, 'Son, I see that you like that bed awful well. So, I'll tell you what. See that you stay in it for the rest of the day. I believe that we can manage without you. I'm tellin' you, don't get out of that bed 'til it's time for you to go to work again.' "

He looked around at everybody. "And I knew what that meant. Boys, let me tell you, it was a miserable day. It was in early summer and my, that bed did get hot. There were no shade trees around. We were just camped out on the bald prairie. I lay under those covers under that tarp all mornin', all afternoon, and all night. And I guarantee you that I didn't have any trouble gettin' up at three the next mornin' to jingle those horses."

He laughed and everybody laughed with him. And that's what always amazed me about this story, that the Boss told it with such admiration for his dad. I figured that anybody that would do a stunt like that had to have a mean streak running through him.

The room we were in showed evidence of that admiration. Above a fireplace that would hold practically a whole cedar post for firewood it was so big, on a brass gun rack, was an old octagon-barreled, .38–.40 Winchester lever action that had been his papa's saddle gun. He had let me take it down and inspect it. I didn't know a great lot about guns, but I did know this model '92 Winchester. I had asked him if he had ammunition for it, and he had looked at me rather indignant, and said, "Shore. But it'll never be fired. The last man to pull the trigger was my papa, and that's the way it'll always remain."

I once had the opportunity to go upstairs to the Boss's office. I had noticed an old Colt, single-action Frontier model revolver that was quite worn, a .38–.40 caliber. Also hanging on the walls were batwing chaps, and a twisted rawhide riata at least sixty feet long. It was not braided and was the only twisted rawhide riata that I had ever seen. Even a beat-up, old sweat-stained felt hat was on a peg. All these things had once belonged to his papa, and were now memorabilia that he looked on with great fondness.

The only thing in the room that applied to the Boss himself was a silver and gold belt buckle mounted in a picture frame under glass on the wall. It was a trophy buckle in a rectangular shape, with square sharp corners, that pronounced: "J.W. Stone, Champion Calf Roper, 1922 Las Vegas Roughriders Rodeo." All these things, except the buckle, I thought were monuments to a hard man. I wondered if the Boss hadn't been just as hard with his own son. The son that had left, never to return.

As I was mulling over these thoughts, the Boss said, "Frank, I hope you brought your guitar." I allowed as I did. "Well, get it and give us a tune."

I noticed as I went back through the kitchen to get my instrument that R.C. and Francesca were still talking and seemingly enjoying one another a great deal. All this over a cup of coffee, while the other two women worked.

As I was tuning up, the ladies and R.C. came in from the kitchen. Some of the boys got up from the many cushy leather, overstuffed chairs and let the women sit. All the couches and chairs in the room and in his den were made from fine leather. He had told me once that since leather was what held his cattle together, was what he sat on when he worked, it was also what he preferred to sit on when he rested.

I was sitting underneath two original C. M. Russell paintings that hung on the wall. Everybody was scattered out all over the room, some sitting on the floor leaning against the wall. Egg, he squatted cowboy-style on his haunches.

I decided to stick with traditional cowboy tunes, so I laid a little bit of "Blue Prairie," "Riders in the Sky," "Tumbling Tumble Weeds," and this sort of music on them. I stayed away from the popular music that was making the country charts about drinking and broken love affairs. Those kinds of songs were for another time and place.

I had everybody's complete attention, and they seemed to enjoy it immensely. After I'd run through my repertoire of songs, I asked Joaquin to take over, knowing he was the musician of the Jaramillo family. He was reluctant to do so, but finally agreed. We played the same guitar but we played it a great lot different. His rhythms were totally different from mine. Of course, they had the Latin flavor.

At one point he turned and said, "Kika, come sing with me."

She got up and walked over to Joaquin. Those two sang in harmony. They gazed into one another's eyes, and I had a feeling as a musician, they did this to stay in connection with one another as their singing went. I don't know how much practicing they had done at home, but it was amazing to me how one could take the melody, the other take the harmony. Singing these beautiful Spanish love songs, they watched one another's lips so closely that they could feel when to start and when to stop and when to pause, as if they were one.

I looked over at R.C. and the look on his face was that of bliss. I don't think he had ever heard Mexican music sung with such feeling. I had a very strong suspicion that the boy was in love. But because of Kika's responsibility, and I suppose because of her nationality, her religion, and the strong traditions of her family, this boy was going to have a rough row to hoe if he expected to make any headway. But then, he had been surprising me all along.

After a while we drifted on back to the bunkhouse, everybody tired. We had one more day of branding. As I crawled under the covers, R.C. said, "Frank, I just met a wonderful woman tonight. It's amazing. I talked to her and seemed like I'd known her for years. She's quite a lady."

"Yeah, R.C., she is. But I'll tell you what. You'd better get her out of your mind and hit the sack, because it's not goin' to take long to spend the night on the Piedra tonight."

The lights were out but I knew R.C. was going to have trouble sleeping, and four o'clock the next morning the same thing started all over again.

CHAPTER

12

R.C. and I were to do the payback work to all the fellers that had come down and helped us out during our branding. So at noon we started pitching in everything we needed to take with us in the back of Ol' Blue.

We got to the highway and headed north. We went to Dorsey and turned over east toward the Oklahoma state line, then going right straight up until we hit the Dry Cimarron, and back west a ways until we got to Egg's place. All the country that was going by our window sure looked good.

When I realized that we were about ten miles north of the twin mounds, it was just getting sundown. If I stomped on Ol' Blue we might make it in time to see something I'm sure R.C.'d be interested in. So I cranked Ol' Blue up and R.C. quit his deep thinking and looked over at me.

"What's the hurry all of a sudden?"

"I've got somethin' I want to show you up here."

You had to watch real close, because if you weren't watching, you sailed right on by it and never knew. But sure enough, I could see it. I pulled Ol' Blue over to the shoulder of the road. We both got out and walked in front of Ol' Blue. As I loaded up with a chew, "Do you notice anything in particular?"

We were just standing out there on the prairie. "Well, I can't see anything but the twin mounds, a few windmills, and these barbed-wire fences along the highway. There isn't even a house in sight, nor a tree."

"No. Look to the west and the southwest and see if you can't catch an outline on the ground."

R.C. looked out as I told him. "Yeah, I can see where there's kind of a gully cutting through here."

"R.C., that ain't no gully."

He looked at me kind of quizzical, and said, "What is it?"

"You're standin' right flat dab in the middle of the Santa Fe Trail."

"No kidding?"

He glanced back to the east, and you could see it until it faded out of sight. He looked back to the west where the sun shone on it better. You could see the path the wagons the pioneers had used, those big old prairie schooners, Conestogas, had taken so many years ago. It was about fifty yards wide, about two, three feet deep. There wasn't just one wagon rut, or one road. It was a wide trail, and more or less just a depression that just went on and on west. It was all haired over. The grass had come back.

You could tell R.C. was impressed. As he looked to the west, I thought to myself, you know, that's the way I looked the first time I saw it. I didn't look back toward the east with much concern. I looked west. I'd worked cattle over on Ira Turner's outfit, which was almost due north of the twin mounds, and crossed it a-horseback many times. Once you get to working on it, you really don't pay that much attention to it. But you're riding on so much history. Whenever I did realize it, when I looked down the trail, I always looked west, never back east. Maybe it's because I'd always had a yearning to go on west, never to go back to where civilization came from. Keep aheading away from it.

I was jogged out of my own thoughts by R.C. when he said, "Wow! How come this place isn't marked, Frank?"

"I don't know. It's just a dirt road that's used by people like us. It isn't a tourist trail. Even on the highway goin' through Dorsey, the trail crosses it way over toward the mountains. But, as far as I know, there's no marker for it. We could get a-horseback right here, R.C., and ride this trail and follow it plumb to Wagon Mound. I suppose we could follow it plumb on to Santa Fe."

"I'd like to do that someday, Frank. Would you go with me?"

"Hell yes, R.C., I'll go with you, if you'll open all the gates."

Egg didn't have near as big a place as the Boss, and he hadn't had nearly as easy a time of it. He'd had to scrape, hustle, and work-slap together everything he could scrape and borrow to put his place together. But he lived life with such gusto and such a sense of humor that the workings tomorrow would be a great lot more relaxed. It was a long way to go, but he and the Boss were good friends, and distance between friends didn't mean a great lot.

I could see something was troubling R.C. and finally he brought it up. "Do you think he's forgotten that I turned that calf loose on him, and getting cut?"

"Well, I doubt if he's forgotten it. I think he's probably going to have the scar for the rest of his life. But," and I had to laugh, "Egg ain't one to carry grudges. Seemed to me you had earned his respect by the time our brandin' was over. It wouldn't surprise me a bit, however, if he let you drag some calves."

And with that R.C. damned near went into shock. "Oh, my God. What'll I do?"

"Hell, I'll tell you what I'd do if somebody asked me to drag calves. I'd get my rope down, and tighten my cinch and take in after it."

"But, Frank, I've never done it before."

"There ain't no time to get started like the present. You'll enjoy it. One more thing you might remember if you get a rope in your hand. Swing a big loop."

"Why?"

"The bigger the loop, the more apt somethin'll fit in it. You might take some hoorahin', but you won't miss as many. As a matter of fact, if I have a philosophy of life, that's it. Swing a big loop."

As the branding crew began to file in for breakfast the next morning, Egg went to introducing R.C. to everybody because this was a whole new set of people.

When we got all the cattle gathered, the first thing right out of the box, Egg come over to R.C. and said, "Pull your cinch and grab your rope, R.C. You can get this thing started," turned around and walked back to the irons that were getting hot.

I could tell R.C. was about to melt and run down into the tops of his boots. So I walked over to him and I told him, "You've seen it done, you can ride the horse. Just get out there and take your licks. No better place to learn than right here. Somebody will be aropin' with you. If you miss a few, build you another loop and keep athrowin'."

R.C. gave me a weak smile, walked over, and got his horse. Egg had matched him up with another heeler that I'd been around before that was sure pretty tough. So we wouldn't be short of cattle if R.C. had a little trouble gathering some heels.

I heard old Egg holler, "The irons are hot. Go git 'em."

With that R.C. tugged down his hat and went to the cattle. He looked pretty natural out there. He moved into them slow. I saw him throw his first loop, saw him pull up on that slack and come up empty. He went to build his loop and he was in such a hurry he dropped the whole thing, all the coils, and had to coil all the rope back up again, build another big loop. As he was doing that he glanced back over his shoulder at us. And, really, nobody but me was paying attention. His roping partner had already brought a couple in by the time R.C. had connected on his first calf. And he came bringing it in at a high trot.

As he went by me he gave me a big grin and said, "I'm catching on!"

As I watched him throughout his turn, it was amazing. That feller could catch on to things quicker than anybody I ever saw. He made a hand that day. He was accepted by everybody. Hell, who couldn't like a feller who went around with a big smile on his face all the time and listened to everybody's wild stories.

Only once did he make a mistake, and I happened to be watching. He threw his heel loop, caught only one heel, turned his horse to the left, and started to the fire. But not fast enough. He didn't take up his slack. The calf headed back to the herd, and when he hit the end of the rope, circled back to R.C.'s left bringing the rope underneath the tail of R.C.'s horse. When that happened, all hell broke loose. The rope tied to the saddle horn, coming across R.C.'s leg, had him pinned to the saddle. And, believe me, his horse was chinning the moon, coming straight at the fire. I was already on my way, as was everybody else that saw what was happening.

I grabbed the horse by the headstall and mane, just as several others did. A couple were knocked away. Others ran to the rope, taking the pressure off of it while somebody else reached up, jerked the pigtail on the rope, and got it off the horn. Soon as the pressure on the rope was relieved from the horse, he began to settle down, though he was blowing his rollers and wallering his eyes around in his head like a booger had just bit his butt. He'd scattered things a good ways, knocked the fire over. But really, nobody was worse for the wreck. And in a way, it broke the monotony. Only R.C. seemed to regret the happening.

Egg laughed it off, saying, "It happens in the best of families. Go back and git another. The irons are still hot."

As we were heading back to Dorsey, R.C. was all smiles. "You know, I really enjoyed that one." Then a cloud came over his face. "Except for that one dumb stunt I pulled."

"You mean the wreck?"

"Yeah," he answered, averting his eyes to the floor.

"Hell, don't feel bad. It's happened to me. It's happened to almost everybody. And it'll probably happen again. As far as draggin' calves, I believe that's about the second of my most favorite things to do that I can think of."

"The second? What's the first? Riding broncs?"

I winked at him. "Nah, riding broncs is third. I'll let you guess what the first one would be."

Then he caught on and laughed. "Frank, you're the shits."

"Thank you, R.C. That's what I always aim to be. Keep workin' at it, and in time, you'll be the shits, too."

We'd left Egg's place right after dinner. Had another forty miles back to Dorsey, and then had to go out west to Bob Chism's place. The Chism place was about twenty miles west of Dorsey and ten miles north, on the headwaters of Ute Creek. If you followed Ute Creek south, about thirty miles, I reckoned, it'd take you right through the Jaramillo place.

As we went through Dorsey, you could see a storm brewing up out west, and we weren't five miles out of town before it started raining like a two-cunted cow pissing on a flat rock. It rained so hard Ol' Blue's windshield wipers could hardly keep up with the water. R.C. kept a watch out the side, telling me where the side of the road was. All I could do was just keep at a slow pace. He kept coaching me on how to stay on the road. It didn't last but about fifteen minutes. And when it stopped, we were going on completely dry pavement.

I looked around at him. "One of them shotgun rains."

He grinned at me, figuring it was another one of those practical jokes or sayings. "Explain that."

"A shotgun rain in this country is what they call a rain that you can lean a double-barreled shotgun up against a fence and it will fill one barrel up where it's runnin' over and leave the other one as dry as a popcorn fart. All in all, it'll average out over the year, to where most every place in the country gets their share of rain. I don't think the good Lord's gonna take it out on anybody that ain't been livin' right, although sometimes I wonder about it."

R.C. shook his head. "No, Frank. It's just the laws of nature. I don't think they're to be trifled with."

By that time we were almost to Jingle Bob's. He was another good one. His daddy had come from Texas, after working for the XIT. Found some country he liked and homesteaded on it, and began to add to it.

Jingle Bob was a damned good cowboy, a good hand, and an enjoyable man to be around. It's been said, out of his hearing distance, that the only curse on him was that he never had any sons, only daughters. He had five daughters, and all of them in their teens. I hadn't seen the oldest girl in a good while. Roberta, I think was her name. Even though Jingle Bob didn't have any sons to help him work the place, he turned all his girls into good hands. And with the help of neighbors, they got by.

Up in the distance, probably about five miles away, you could see the Chism headquarters. It was a pretty little place nestled down in a small valley that Ute Creek ran through. You could see some low hills way to the north that were the beginning of the Chico Mountains. They weren't really mountains, just fair-sized hills.

Jingle Bob had a good spot, even though Ute Creek had a tendency to dry up here at the headwaters and go underground at times. But it still had holes in it where cattle would always have fresh water. There were some breaks and a few cedar trees that would provide protection for his cows in the wintertime. As Ute Creek went on south and went by the Jaramillos', it gathered in size by what few tributaries ran into it, and what springs might feed it. All in all it was really a wet-weather, seasonal-type creek until it got on down toward the Canadian.

"Frank," R.C. asked, "why do they call Bob 'Jingle Bob'?"

"R.C., didn't you notice the spurs he was wearin' when he was down helpin' us brand last week?"

"No, I guess I didn't. Sometimes there's just too much for a man to take in, in a short period of time."

"Well, the next time you get a chance, take a look at his spurs. He wears jinglebobs on 'em."

"What's that?"

"Little balls shaped like bells with metal that go through the rowel hole on a spur. When you walk, it'll jingle. They used to be quite the thing back in the old days. Bob still wears 'em."

"It'd be hard to sneak up on somebody with those jingling spurs."

"The size of Jingle Bob and the reputation he's known for, he don't have to sneak up on anybody. I've always heard that he'd drive five miles out of his way just to get ahead of trouble, so he could meet it head on. But, he's one of the most gentle-natured men that you'd ever want to meet. In contrast to old Egg, who's always promotin' something, Bob's quiet, smiles a lot, and seems to enjoy life to the fullest. I guess that's the attitude you'd have to have to be surrounded by five daughters and a wife. All that many women, and running a petticoat outfit would kind of temper you a little."

We were getting close to the house and it was late afternoon. Yes sir, Jingle Bob had a nice place. It wasn't as fancy as the Piedra, but it was built to last and definitely showed a woman's touch. The yard had lots of grass and flowers and lots of trees. A few cottonwoods down along the creek, but they'd also gone to the trouble of planting fruit trees.

Up ahead I could see Bob walking toward the house from his outbuildings and corrals across the road. He waved and waited for us. He met us with a big smile.

"Glad to see you boys get in. Did you come through a rain?"

"Sure did, Bob. Looks like it missed you here."

"Yeah. That one did, but we've been gettin' our share. Sure don't have anything to complain about."

I had my back to the corrals and barns. I heard a voice behind me holler, "Daddy, do you want the horses left up, or do you want to turn them out?"

Bob looked up. "Come on down, Roberta. Look who's come in."

I remembered Bob's oldest daughter, Roberta. I was right about the name. But I hadn't seen her in three or four years. She was just a tall skinny kid. But when I turned around and saw her coming down from the barns, my mouth stood open. There, walking toward me, was an honest-to-God cowboy's dream. And the closer she got the better she looked. She had on clothes any cowboy would wear. Tight Levis with the pant legs tucked down the top of high-heeled boots, spurs, with a loose gray work shirt that even though it was loose didn't conceal what appeared to me to be a magnificent pair of mammary glands. Gold hair, blond I'd guess you'd call it, with the sun shining on it, hung down in ringlets. And perched on top of her head was an old, soiled felt hat.

She walked up and Bob said, "Frank, I don't know whether you know my oldest daughter. Roberta, this is Frank Dalton and R.C. Roth, from down on the Piedra."

She just smiled, the most beautiful smile you ever saw. White even teeth, sprinkle of freckles across her nose, and hazel eyes that were large and even glinted with a touch of humor.

She stuck out her hand. "Yes, I know Frank. I don't think he remembers me, though," as I took her hand. With that, she turned to R.C. and shook hands with him, then stood back, put her hands on her hips, rested most of her weight on one leg, and waited for me to respond.

I had a hard time getting my mouth closed. I can't ever remember being quite so speechless. "Sure. I know Roberta. I can't remember when I saw you last. Where have you been?"

With a smile, she said, "I've been away at college. Just finished up my second year at Fort Collins, at Colorado A & M."

"Boys," Jingle Bob said, "come on down and get something cold to drink. R.C., I want you to meet my wife."

"You guys go ahead. R.C., go with Bob. I'll check our saddles and see if anything got wet and put 'em in the saddle house, if it's all right with you, Bob."

"Sure. Go ahead. Give him a hand, Roberta."

That was just exactly what I'd hoped he'd say. As they started on down toward the house, I turned back to Roberta and I had a feeling I was about to make a fool out of myself.

"My. You've sure grown, Roberta."

"Frank, I think that's what you'd tell your niece or nephew when you haven't seen them in a year and they're under eight years old."

I kicked the dirt with my boot. "Nah, I don't reckon that came out right. You've changed. I know you've been away at school, but you've been home in the summer, haven't you?"

"Mostly I stay out here and help Dad. I've never been much of a socializer. I've seen you around. I don't think you saw me, though. I don't think you were looking real hard."

"That's my mistake."

As we talked, I noticed I could almost look eyeball to eyeball with her. I had to look down very little to look right square in her eyes. I've always been partial to tall, lanky girls. And this one filled the bill.

My directness in speech had always been considered a curse by myself. All of a sudden I blurted out those very things I was thinking. "How tall are you?"

She must have read my mind, because she had a ready answer. "Five foot twelve, in these high-heeled boots. Would you like to know my weight and my measurements?"

I had to duck my head. "Roberta, excuse me for being so forward and personal."

"That's all right, Frank. I've been trying to attract your attention for many years now."

I looked up. "You have?"

She sighed. "Yes, but you didn't even know I was alive."

Somehow I had a feeling I was losing control of this situation and I really didn't give a damn. All I could tell her was, "Well, I'll tell you what, you've got my attention now."

"So I see. Are we going to stand out here in the middle of the road all day, or do you want to go put your saddle up?"

"No, you're right. We'd better get out of here and get on with what we're doin'. Will you give me a hand?"

"I thought you'd never ask."

I drove Ol' Blue on up to the saddle house. Pulled the tarp off our saddles and bedrolls, and everything had made it through the storm in good shape.

After we finished putting everything up, we sat on a bench outside the saddle house and I said, "Tell me about yourself. I have a feeling there's a lot I need to know."

"Well, like what?"

"What are you majoring in at A & M?"

"Not agriculture. I get enough of that here at home. I'm working on a degree in education. Seemed like the thing to do. The world always needs schoolteachers. And, who knows, I may grow up to be an old-maid schoolteacher, and I have to have a way of supporting myself." She smiled and looked at me out of the corner of her eye.

And I had no doubt who was in control. "Fat chance," was my only reply to that.

"This is the first branding that I've been back for in two years, 'cause Dad always brands early. This year he waited until I got home. But I was always around, Frank. It's just that you never noticed. And I'm kind of a loner, you know?"

"Yeah, I'm kind of that way myself."

"No attachments, Frank?"

I shook my head. "No. None. How about you?"

She smiled and shook her head. She took her hat off and was undoing a red handkerchief bandanna she'd tied around her neck. You could see where she'd been sweating along the temples and that's where the hair hung down in ringlets. It was a little longer than shoulder length. She appeared to mess it up, but the more she ran her fingers through it fluffing it out, the prettier it got. She had the most beautiful hair. I noticed light skin with a copper tan. She'd spent a lot of time outdoors in the sun, you could tell on her hands and on her face. Small waist. Very sexy flair to her hips. She was the most beautiful thing I'd ever seen. And looked like we were starting a mutual admiration society. I didn't know if my life would ever be the same after this day.

"Come on down to the house. They'll be wondering what we're doing." And smiled.

So with our hands in our pockets we strolled down to the house. They didn't have a bunkhouse, so R.C. and I were going to stay upstairs in a guest room. It wasn't until I'd almost gotten to the house that I realized I needed to wash up. And I thought, good God, of all the times I had to look like I look now. We were in work clothes and dusty and dirty as could be. I realized how grubby I was. But Roberta didn't seem to take notice. If I had showed up all spit-shined, I'd probably look like a feed salesman. So maybe it was better this way.

Roberta and I stayed talking that evening, well into the night, even though we knew we were going to have to get up early and start branding the next day. She was so easy to talk to, and I didn't normally find girls easy to talk to. I could bullshit them and had a better than average line for picking them up. But just to make conversation, interesting conversation, and find out about one another, was something that was as foreign to me as wearing lace-up shoes. But with her, it was so easy.

The next day as we were branding, she pitched right in with her four sisters. She was doing the branding on one side of the fire, handling the irons, being the oldest. And Bob was doing the branding on the other side. I was doing some dehorning. The four younger sisters even flanked some of the littler calves and ran the vaccinating needles. We were done by noon.

I kind of hated to leave, but somehow I had a feeling we would be seeing a lot of each other. So just before we pulled out to head back home, I said, "Roberta, would you consider going out with me?"

"I thought you'd never ask."

"How about a movie the Saturday after next?"

"What time?"

"Six."

"Do you know where our house is in town?"

"Yep. I don't have any idea what the movie will be."

She looked back and smiled. "Who cares?"

Bob shook our hands and said how much he appreciated it. I think he had a feeling that something was going on by his handshake and his smile. I had a feeling he was on my side in this affair, and I wasn't getting much resistance from the lady. I'll tell you what, things were looking up! It would be a new experience for me. Outside of Belle, I've really never cared about anybody, or anything, in a long time.

R.C. drove and I pulled my hat down over my eyes and slunk down in the seat, daydreaming, only the dream I was having had long blond hair and lanky legs. All of a sudden I heard gravel hitting up underneath the underside of the pickup, and I came up out of that seat bracing myself for a hell of a wreck.

When my eyes got focused in, we were just headed down the highway, "Goddamn, R.C., the road's as straight as a ruler. What are you doin', goin' to sleep?"

R.C. smiled at me. "No, I just wanted to see if you were sound asleep or just daydreaming."

I looked out the window and watched the fence posts go by. "She makes a hell of a first impression, I'll say that for her."

"Looks like you're having a struggle with this, Frank, and I can't understand why."

"I'll tell you why. I like things just the way they are right now. Like to keep things simple. Roberta is quite a woman, and that's the problem. She's too good, just too good."

"What do you mean by that?"

"It's hard to explain. But many a good cowboy's career has been ruined by a good woman."

"Ah, that's nonsense, Frank. I'll bet it's just the other way around."

"I don't think so. It complicates things too much. I like the way I live. Right now, if I get ready to leave, all I've got to do is piss on the fire, grab my saddle and roll, throw 'em in Ol' Bullet, crank her up, and leave."

"Do you always want it to be that way?"

I had to think about it for a while. Always is a long time. "Nah. Not always. Someday, sometime, when I'm ready."

"When do you think you'll be ready, Frank?"

"Hell, I don't know. It's just that I'm not ready for things to get too complicated right now."

"You could do worse. She appeared to me like a good one, a keeper."

Hell, this guy was even beginning to talk like us. "Yeah, that's the problem. She is a good one. She's the right kind. She's no boogie mama or a honky-tonk angel. She is the kind. When you run into those kind, it can get complicated. That's what's causing me the problem. I've got a date with her for a week from Saturday. We'll just take it from there and see how it goes."

I flipped on the radio. It was nice to know that Eisenhower was still the president, not that I gave a damn. And some smart-ass senator from somewhere was accusing someone of being a communist, and they were getting all upset about it. That didn't make much sense to me. I couldn't figure out why they just didn't tell him to go to hell. They got into the regional news, and something made me sit up and really take note. I hadn't been paying that much attention, but the announcer was talking about capturing a man in California that had slipped through a roadblock a couple of months ago on Highway 66 in Amarillo. This fellow was supposed to have been one of several who escaped from an Oklahoma prison. But this fellow had been caught in a holdup, and Sheriff Gaither of Potter County, Texas, was having him extradited back to Amarillo.

I listened real intent, trying to make sense out of all of it. We were just about into town, so I told R.C. to stop at the drugstore. I wanted to go in and see if I could find a paper. Sure enough, there on the front page of the *Amarillo Daily News* was a picture of this fellow they'd arrested in California. I read the whole article as we headed on back to the ranch. When I was through, I laid it down and thought about it a little while.

"Why were you so interested in this paper?"

"See this headline here?"

"Yes."

"All of this took place a short time before I met you down by the trees on the highway."

R.C. shrugged his shoulders. "So what?"

"So, I'd just heard the news about the Tramperos bank robbery. And I just wondered if this guy might be you."

R.C. had a big laugh over that. "What in the world made you think that I was a desperado?"

"Well, you weren't from this country. The way you were dressed, like you just purchased it. You hadn't had any sun on your skin, like you hadn't been outside in the weather. Besides, the physical description fit you pretty good."

"When did that happen, Frank?"

I caught the date on it. "Well, just damn near two months ago. It was in the last part of April."

"You've known me now for two months, Frank. Do you think I'm some sort of bad guy?"

I said, rather sheepishly, "No, no I don't, R.C. But at the same time, the bank down at Tramperos was robbed. They're tryin' to tie this fellow into the bank job. So far they haven't had any luck. Have you ever robbed a bank?"

He smiled and shook his head. "Not guilty."

"Well, a feller has to do something to pass the time. You know, you're still kind of a mystery. I really don't know where you're from. Don't know anything about you, except we've been together almost night and day now for two months. You've become a friend, and you're the fastest-learnin' feller I was ever around. You're makin' a good hand. You do an awful lot of watchin' and very little talkin'."

It had been rather a joke up to this time with R.C. As I started talking serious to him, I could see him starting to clam up again.

"I appreciate what you said, Frank. I consider you a friend, too. But there are some things that are better left alone."

I could respect that. There were some things that I didn't care to talk about. And every man has got his private side. So I told him, "Fair enough. When you're ready to talk, I'll listen. But to tell you the truth, I'm relieved to find that they've finally arrested the man they were lookin' for. Let's just let it go at that."

"Good enough."

Still, in the back of my mind I wondered about the bank, and the pistol R.C. was carrying, and I knew he had a good roll of money. Those questions still needed to be answered. But in my heart I just couldn't see R.C. pulling a stunt like that.

As we turned off the highway and headed home, I loaded up with a chew, stretched real big, and rearranged myself. "Well, one more big jag, and cattle workin' will be over for the spring."

We pulled across the cattle guard and into the headquarters. Belle came out to meet us. "Slow down, R.C., goddamn it. Don't run over my dog!"

She ran along the passenger side, jumping as high as she could about every other bound, trying to see in the pickup, 'til we got in front of the bunkhouse. Jim was sitting out on the bench in front, resting after a day's work. Lupe waved and Tio, he came over to greet us and find out how everything went.

"Hell, Jim, we've been up before dawn, acrackin' it and makin' a hand, and done more work in the past four days than you've done probably all month."

With a big grin, Jim said, "I hope you waddies got one more big circle left in you, and you ain't wore your ropes out."

"Nah," I said, "we're still rarin'. What's the plan?"

"You and R.C. supposed to head over to the Jaramillos' the day after to-morrow to help them work their calves, and then it'll all be over. Nothin' but white meat for the rest of the summer."

"I reckon I can stand that."

R.C. chimed in a might too quick with a "Me, too."

I saw that something was bothering Jim, because he turned serious. "Say, Miz T. told me that when you guys got in, come on down to the house. She wanted to have a talk with you."

This kind of straightened me up. "Is the Boss here?"

Jim looked down at the ground. "Nah. He hasn't come in. Wasn't he up there with you?"

"Yeah, he made a showin' at both Robbins' and Chism's. Never roped. As matter of fact, never got a-horseback. Stayed awhile. Didn't see much of him."

Jim said, "You better go down and have a talk with her."

"You reckon I got time to put our stuff up?"

"I'd go now, if I was you," Jim said.

When we were out of earshot of Tio and Jim, I said, "Godalmighty. I hope we don't get hit in the ass with a paycheck."

"What do you mean?"

"I mean fired. I don't know what the hell we've done. Probably ain't you, it's probably me."

But thinking about it, Miz T. wouldn't fire anybody. If anybody was going to do any firing, it'd be the Boss, and I couldn't think of anything

I'd done terrible wrong. Very seldom did I do anything just right to suit him, but I was always somewhere in the neighborhood, halfway being right. I couldn't think what on earth Miz T. would want to talk to us about.

We walked into the kitchen. I rattled around in the cupboard and found a coffee cup and poured myself a big cup of coffee and that brought Miz T.

She came with a saucer and cup. "Hi, boys, glad to have you back. Did you happen to see Roberta?"

"Yes, ma'am, I did."

"Isn't she a lovely girl?"

"Yes, ma'am, she is," and glanced out of the side of my eye to R.C. who was standing there smiling at me.

You could see she was quite preoccupied with something, and I'd just as soon we'd get on with it and not prolong it.

"R.C., would you like a cup of coffee?"

He saw the teakettle on the stove and noticed Miz T.'s cup. "Are you having tea, ma'am?"

"Why, yes, I am. Would you care for some?"

"Yes, ma'am, that would be quite nice."

As I sat down at the table I thought, Jesus Christ, a cowboy! Just when I think he's making a hand, he walks in and partakes in a cup of tea, for godsakes, with the Boss's wife! Tea!

Miz T. fiddled with her cup a little bit. "I suppose you boys are wondering why I wanted to talk to you?"

We both nodded our heads. "Yes'm."

"I really don't know where to start, and it might not be anything at all. But I thought I'd ask. J.W. did show up at the brandings for Egg and for Bob, didn't he?"

We both nodded yes.

"Did you notice anything unusual about him?"

"Like what, ma'am?" I asked.

"It's probably nothing. But for the past couple of weeks there's been times when J.W. just doesn't act like himself."

"Perhaps," R.C. said, "he's just got a lot on his mind, Miz T., and he's preoccupied."

"Maybe you're right. He was upset over the Sawyer bank closing down at Tramperos. But the rains have been good, the cattle prices seem to be holding steady, and Tres is here all the time. And you know how the Boss dotes on Tres. He's the light of his life."

"Yes, ma'am, I know. But I couldn't see anything peculiar in the way he acted the times I saw him in the past week."

That seemed to relieve her mind a little bit. "Well, it's probably just me. And you're right. He's probably preoccupied."

With a smile she asked, "Are you looking forward to going over to the Jaramillos'?"

"Oh, yes ma'am, we can hardly wait."

"Well, I think J.W. plans for you boys to ride over and hook up with Top and Poke day after tomorrow."

"That'll be fine," I said. "That's what we usually do."

"J.W. and I and Tres will go around by the road. It's been a long time since I've been to a branding at Diego's. We have a lot to catch up on, and I'm sure we'll have fun."

When we got back to the bunkhouse, Jim said he had gone through the same thing with Miz T., and that he hadn't noticed anything out of the ordinary with the Boss. But then, none of us were as close to him or knew him like Miz T.

"Frank, didn't you see some unusual happenin's over at the old church awhile back?" he asked.

"Yeah. I could see where some people had been prowlin' around there. Never could figure out who it was."

"Well, it's happenin' again."

"Oh? Like what?"

"Oh, tire tracks around the church and the old village."

"Did they come across the ford?"

"Yep."

"Well, it'd almost have to be a pickup then."

"The water's not runnin' real deep across there right now."

Somebody that knew what they were doing and had been there before could make it across in a car all right. "Could you tell what they were after or what they were doin'?"

"Nah. There were tracks inside that little cemetery, around the old building, in the church."

"It probably doesn't mean nothin'. I'm sure the Boss wouldn't like it, but it's probably just some neighbor lookin' around." Yet I knew that any neighbor of ours wouldn't come in there and go to poking his nose around, without at least telling us.

CHAPTER

13

Evidently the Boss had come in sometime last evening. The next morning at breakfast he was his usual self. He told R.C. to get our gear together and he'd haul it over to the Jaramillos' for us. He told us to head out over to the Cannon headquarters where Top would be expecting us. We'd spend the night there and go on over to the Jaramillos' where we'd start bringing the cattle in.

The Boss wanted me to ride the Gruyer. He asked me how I'd been getting along with him since Johnny had rung him out. I told him sure pretty good. He said that Tres was anxious to ride him. The Gruyer was a good-looking stout booger. I could see where it might pump up Tres's ego a little bit to be riding what was once considered an outlaw.

Jim was going to stay and keep things agoing at the home place. R.C. and I got up our horses, and I reset the shoes on the Gruyer, and made R.C. do the same on his little dun horse.

Right after dinner we were ready to ride. Tied our slickers on back and made sure we had everything and headed out for the Cannon outfit. We stopped at the old church, and looked around, and sure enough, you could still see where someone had been nosing around.

From our headquarters over to the Cannon outfit was just about fifteen miles. And fifteen miles to a good set of ponies like we had wasn't hardly any jaunt at all. As we climbed up out of the Martinez and went through the gate over into the Cannon pasture, the country changed considerable. It was like our yearling pastures, mostly tight land. Good strong buffalo and gramma grass, a few soapweeds, very few trees and very few breaks in the terrain. So we hit a fox-trot and rolled into the Cannon place in late afternoon.

The Cannon place was nothing fancy. It was just built for a purpose. Corrals good and stout and high. Typical yearling place. There was a main house, but it wasn't much since both Jeff and Jack Cannon never spent much time out here. They stayed down in Amarillo most of the time. And their wives wouldn't be caught dead out here. Even though that's what put bread on their table.

So Top stayed in the main house, along with Poke. They had a cook they called Ol' Tom and a couple of wetbacks working fences. They stayed in a small bunkhouse. Pretty simple really.

We were getting up close to the fence that surrounded the headquarters, R.C. and I riding neck and neck. Thirty yards from the gate, I put the spurs to the Gruyer, jumped him and loped him up to the gate, swung off, opened the gate, and let R.C. through.

"What'd you do that for?" R.C. asked. "I'd open it."

As I was putting the gate back, "That's a bit of range etiquette that you need to remember. If you're ever ridin' with a bunch and you come up to a gate, you'll see some of the younger fellers waitin' to get a reasonable distance from the gate to jump out and open the gate. Like they're eager to please and showin' respect for the older fellers. They appreciate it. I've even seen a horse race or two in order to open the gate, while the older fellers will hold back."

"It's an honor to open a gate for everybody?"

"Yeah. It's a way of payin' your dues."

"I'll remember that."

We rode on up to the house. Didn't seem to be anybody around, but we stood out in front and hollered into the house. Finally the door opened and out stepped an old, grizzled cowboy, his boots run over on both sides, bowlegged as sin, with about a week's growth of gray beard, an old greasy hat on top of his head. He had an apron tied on around his waist. It was just as greasy as his hat.

"What's all the ruckus goin' on?" he asked.

"Hello, Tom. Long time no see," I answered.

He squinted through weak eyes. "Frank Dalton! Top told me you were comin' tonight and to fix some biscuits for supper."

"Sounds good. Where is everybody?"

With that he looked off to the west where the sun was slowly sinking. "They're still out. They ought to be along anytime now. You boys put your horses up, come on in, the coffeepot's on. You know where to find the oats, don't you, Frank?"

"Yeah. Thanks, Tom, we'll do it."

I turned and we rode on over to the barn. When R.C. dismounted, you could see him waver just a shade. I realized this was the longest trip, probably, that R.C. had ever had a-horseback. I thought a little good-natured ribbing might be adequate.

"Feelin' a little weak-kneed, are you there, R.C.?"

He began to bend his knees, raise his legs. "Oh, just a little, Frank. That was pretty far coming across there."

"Well, you get used to it. You've seen old cowboys walkin' like boots hurt their feet. I don't believe that's so. I think they just miss the horse that's supposed to be underneath 'em. Their old bones'll kind of lock in place to the contour of a horse's back. They ain't real comfortable walkin' any distance."

R.C. was still doing his calisthenics. "I believe it!"

"How's your butt?"

He reached back with both hands and grabbed both cheeks of his ass. "Not too bad. Like you told me, I'm riding with a lot of weight in my stirrups. I think my legs just need conditioning. Kind of dreading tomorrow already."

"It's just like gettin' drunk and usin' the hair of the dog the next mornin'. The best thing for those legs will be to crawl back on and take another long sashay tomorrow."

We put our horses in a water lot, scattered out a gallon of grain apiece for them, was pitching some hay over the fence, when R.C. said, "Here comes somebody horseback now."

We looked up to the northwest and still a few miles off we could see a rider coming in at a trot. Couldn't tell who it was, but I was hoping it was Poke. I wanted to do a little visiting.

I went over and squatted down beside the barn on my haunches cowboy-style. R.C. squatted down after taking a good look around and underneath the barn, for snakes I suppose.

He said, "This feels good on my legs."

"Yeah. It'll even feel better when you get up."

"Frank, this Cannon place. Is it mostly like all the country we've ridden through this afternoon?"

"Yeah. Pretty well watered, with fairly shallow windmills. But there's no trees to amount to, except where Long's Creek cuts through the northeast corner. Kinda pretty up here. Pretty good tight land, yearlin' country from here on south. Might get a little tough in the wintertime tryin' to winter somethin'. If a blue norther comes through and the cattle get to driftin', there isn't anything they could get behind for any protection. Mainly they let it sit fallow all winter. Then they stock it up with yearlin's from the spring 'til October."

"How big do you think this outfit is?"

"Well, you know, being's it's impolite to ask, I don't rightly know. But I was over here when we were workin' their yearlin's, and I do know they're runnin' around twelve hundred yearlin's. I heard Top say that they were givin' 'em fifteen acres. So, put the figures together, and what do you have?"

"Eighteen thousand acres. Whew. That's a pretty good-sized outfit."

"Yeah. But the money in runnin' yearlin's is volume. You gotta run a bunch of 'em. Some years you might only make ten dollars a head. Hell, you might lose a hundred dollars a head. The yearlin' business is a very risky business."

I'd been so busy talking that I didn't notice that Poke had come into the yard gate and was heading to the barn at a high trot. He stood up in his stirrups. "Well, well, look at what the dogs drug up."

"Howdy, Poke." I looked at his horse. He was fairly lathered up. "Looks like you've been makin' lots of tracks."

He swung off and walked over to us. "That's my job."

"How's everything goin'?" I asked.

"Hell, all right, I guess. Things are goin' so perfect around here, I don't know why they need me. How you doin', R.C.?"

"Good, Poke. A little stiff and a little sore."

"What from?"

"That ride over here this afternoon."

Poke winked at him. "Hell, if you're hurtin', never admit it. How did everything go up north for you boys?"

We told him all about the branding up at Egg's and had to tell him about R.C. adragging calves and his wreck. We all got a laugh out of that. I had to do a little animation and carrying on to imitate Egg and his reaction to it.

To get even with me, R.C. had to bring up Roberta Chism and my infatuation with her.

Poke, still holding the bridle reins and squatting down, said, "Oh, my. There's gonna be hearts crushed all the way from the Arizona line to Amarillo. How serious is this, Frank? Please tell me it ain't so, please."

"Oh, shit. It ain't nothin'. We just got along real good."

"Are you gonna see her again?"

"Yep. I got a date with her a week from Saturday."

"Well, there's one consolation. That leaves old Sally all to myself."

"Why don't you put your horse up," I said, "and shut up?"

"I do believe I will. My stomach is layin' on my backbone. All I've had is a windmill soda and a little bit of jerky. A couple of Ol' Tom's biscuits will drop on you quicker than a frozen horse turd." And with that he went to jerking his saddle and putting it up, while we waited on him.

I thought it was as good a time as any to bring it up. "Say, have you heard the news?"

"What news?"

"They caught that feller that got away from that roadblock a couple of months ago down in Amarillo."

Poke had his back to me when I said that. He was pulling his saddle off, and he hesitated a few seconds. "They did, did they? Tell me more."

"R.C. and I heard about it on the radio. Stopped and got a paper in town. And sure 'nuff, there's even a picture of him handcuffed. They're gonna bring him back to Amarillo and try him. I imagine he'll end up back in Oklahoma behind bars, where he started. Probably with an extended visit."

Poke still hadn't turned around. "You're sure, then?"

"I'm sure."

About that time R.C. popped up. "Hate to disappoint you, Poke, but it wasn't me."

Poke turned around and looked at me, and then looked at R.C. "I reckon not. You're sittin' here, out in the middle of nowhere, and that feller is behind bars in Amarillo, I guess. And besides, who in the hell ever said it was you?"

R.C. shrugged his shoulders. "Well, I kind of figured that maybe you and Frank thought . . ."

I interrupted him. "I told him what we thought, Poke. Hell, it was natural. I run into R.C. the day after it happened."

Poke jerked his saddle up on his hip and started in the barn door. "Huh. I never thought it was."

I looked over at R.C. and grinned.

We followed Poke into the barn while he was putting up his gear. He had given me a frown and shook his head like he had doubts about our conversation and R.C.'s apparent clearance of wrongdoing.

R.C.'s eyes fell almost immediately on an old saddle. "Wow, where'd this thing come from?"

Poke looked over. "Oh, that's Ol' Tom's, the cook's."

R.C. was looking at that saddle very closely. "I don't believe I've ever seen a saddle exactly like this."

It was one of those old-timey kacks. Great big square skirts, slicked fork that sat up high, and a great big high cantle.

"Ol' Tom's cowboyed from Montana south," Poke said. "And there's no tellin' where he picked that up. Lookin' at it, probably up in the north country."

We went over to the saddle and began to look for the saddlemaker's stamp, which we found right below the gullet. It was almost faded away. But turning it into the light, we could see "Cogshall, Billings, Montana."

"Yep. It's a Montana kack, all right."

It was an old one, and showed considerable wear. R.C. stood by the saddle, his hand resting on the fuzzy saddle horn. Curiously, he said, "I wonder how they made this?"

"Made what?" Poke said.

"This leather, hair-side-out horn cover."

Both Poke and I laughed. It was Poke that said, "Underneath it's probably a nickel or a brass saddle horn. Ol' Tom at some brandin' somewhere took the end of a cod sack and put it over his horn. It shrunk up and dried, and that's what you're lookin' at."

R.C. removed his hand quickly. "Cod sack?"

"Yeah," I said. "You know how they cut off the end of the bag when you castrate a calf?"

R.C. nodded.

"He just took that end and put it over the horn."

"Oh," R.C. said, with wonderment.

I walked outside with Poke. He curried his horse down and let him cool off a little better.

And in a low voice, "You're sure, are you, Frank?"

"Yeah. I told you I read the paper."

"That still don't explain the bank business."

"No. But after bein' around R.C. these past two months, I can't believe that he's in on somethin' like that."

"How do you explain all the money and that Colt .45?"

"I can't."

"Maybe he didn't, maybe he did. But, I tell you I can feel it. He's hidin' somethin', and I aim to find out what it is."

We inspected a few more of Ol' Tom's trappings. There was a pair of angora chaps with the wooly outside that was quite a sight to see. I'd heard about them, but I'd never seen a living cowboy wear them. There were a couple of silver-mounted spade bits that Tom had collected along the way. All this stuff showed signs of buckaroo country, northern cowboy. Texas, New Mexico, High Plains cowboys, as far as I knew, had never gone in for equipment of this sort.

"I'd sure like to visit with Tom for a while," R.C. said. "I'll bet he's got a few stories he could tell."

"Oh, can he. The man could talk for days and never repeat himself."

About that time we heard somebody coming a-horseback, walked up to the door, and Top was sitting there, rolling himself a cigarette. "Hello, Frank. How you and your pard?"

Both R.C. and I howdyed him. It was funny how Top could be so damned cocky and obstinate at times, and so friendly and easy to get along with at others. While he and Poke were discussing what had gone on during the day, I watched Top and thought about how our relationship had changed.

When I first started coming to the Piedra and working for the Boss, Top had been there, and I'd learned a lot. Probably more from him than anybody I knew of. Why, I could break a horse to ride, nothing to it. Just brute strength and awkwardness and get him broke, bridled, saddled, and then just step on him and leave. I could guarantee you, when I got through with him he'd be broke to ride and be broke to rope off of. But he wouldn't have much of a stop to him or much of a handle to him. And that's where Top came in. He made a science out of it.

He also showed me where to be and where not to be when we were working cattle. He'd kind of taken me under his wing. The first few summers, Top had been my coach and mentor. Then it got to the point where Top wasn't working full time for the Boss. Maybe he'd work a month in the spring and a month in the fall, during branding and shipping, like he was restless. But over the years it seemed like Top had taken exception to me, like I was some sort of rival to him. I didn't feel that way at all. Perhaps he was as close to the Boss as any man. Maybe he got to feeling that I thought the same way about the Boss, as somebody to look up to, sort of an idol, and that's where the rub came in.

Top seemed to be in good humor today. When he was unsaddling, he said, "Frank, what time did you and the professor get in this afternoon?"

"Oh, about an hour ago."

"When you said 'professor,' " R.C. said, "were you referring to me?"

Top looked at him with a big smile. "Yeah. No offense."

"None taken. Kind of curious as to how you came up with professor."

And Top, with that air he had about him, took a deep drag off his smoke, blew a ring, and said, "Well, you know when anybody new comes into the country, everybody takes notice of him. And everybody I've talked to that's been around you has noticed how much attention you pay to every detail that's goin' on, and all the questions you ask. I've never seen anybody quite so curious. So, I've been studyin' on it a little bit. And the only thing that I could come up with is that you're fixin' to write a book about this here country. Nobody could have the curiosity and want as many answers as you do, without havin' a motive such as that behind him." And with that he cocked an eye and looked right square at R.C., like he expected an answer.

R.C. looked dumbfounded but stared right back at Top and never batted an eye. "You got me. How'd you guess?"

Poke and I looked at one another. That was something that we'd never thought of.

Top looked rather proud of himself. "Let's go to the house, boys, and see what Ol' Tom's got on the fire."

Top had put his arm around R.C.'s shoulder. "Now, in this here book, surely you're aimin' to make me the hero, ain't you? Leastways, I ought to be the one that gits the girl."

He looked back over his shoulder at Poke and me, and winked. Poke and I hung back, Poke acting like he had a few more chores to do before he went to the house.

After they were out of earshot, Poke said, "Do you believe that shit?"

"I don't know. Makes sense. You just said he was up to somethin'."

"Well, I never figured that!"

"Me neither."

"Old Top had to get that crack in about gittin' the girl. He's referring to Sally, sure as shit!"

"Oh, don't get so cranked up, Poke. He seems like he's in pretty good spirits today. Let's don't take issue with him. We gotta work with him the next few days."

When we got to the kitchen, Top and R.C. were having a cup of coffee, and Ol' Tom was puttering around his stove, cooking up a storm. Poke and I poured ourselves a big cup of coffee and sat down to join them.

I took a sip and it was sure stout enough to float a horseshoe. Even though Ol' Tom had a bunch of modern conveniences, like a gas stove and electricity, he had out his old Dutch oven and cast-iron skillets, and range coffeepot, and that was what he was cooking on. Just because he was indoors, you could tell he wasn't the type that was going to change.

Ol' Tom kept aworking at the stove, with that cigarette in his mouth. The ashes he dropped off, I figured they got into everything that he was cooking. But what the hell, a few ashes never hurt nobody. At least they'd been cooked.

Directly he turned around with a big toothless grin, and that old greasy hat sitting on top of his head. "Since we got company, I fixed you boys a special treat for tonight."

"What's that, Tom?" I asked.

He winked at me and said, "Spotty dog. How about that?"

Hell, I knew what was coming. R.C. said, "What's that?"

"I swear, son, don't you know nothin'?"

"That's Ol' Tom's specialty," Top said. "It's cooked rice with raisins in it. Believe me, it's sure larapin."

Then we had to clarify the term "larapin." 'Course this was right down Top's alley, 'cause he figured if the boy was going to write a book, he had a lot of explaining to do, and maybe get a little credit.

Directly Ol' Tom in his bowlegged, broken-up gait walked to the door and squalled out to the bunkhouse. "Andale, hombres! Comida!" at the top of his lungs. Came back in and slapped everything down on the table. Those two wetbacks were there by the time it was all set down.

There wasn't much said between anybody except hello when they walked in. Top was a pretty good hand with what we call "ranch Mexican." He could make himself understood and carry on a half-decent conversation. In between bites and swallerings, you found out how it had gone during the day. Seemed like the head honcho for the wetbacks did all the talking. Top seemed pleased with the progress.

After eating, Tom said, "Boys, let's pull our chairs out on the porch. I gotta git off my feet. Goddamn, they're killin' me!"

We sat on the porch and chewed and smoked, looked at the sky. This country is a great place to look at the sky. The air is so clear that you can almost reach up and touch the stars. And the only sounds you can hear are the coyotes. Not long after the sun went down, the coyotes would start howling back and forth from all directions, making connection with their kin I reckon.

Ol' Tom looked at R.C. "Son, I noticed you gittin' around kinda ouchy, like an old man, myself for instance. Either you been a-horseback way too much or not enough."

"It shows, does it?"

"I reckon. You'll get used to it. And directly you'll feel more comfortable a-horseback than you will sittin' and walkin'."

"Well, I wasn't born a cowboy. I just decided to be one." And this started the old man off.

"Hell, none of us was born to be a cowboy, that is, in the beginnin'. There's some fellers growin' up on ranches now that their daddies are tryin' to turn 'em into cowboys. They may be worth a damn, and they might not. Time will tell. But most of us just got the callin', just like a preacher. It gits on your mind and sinks in, and that's all ya think about. It becomes all ya want to do. If ya got enough guts, ya leave and go do your callin'. And ya better be careful or ya'll wind up like me."

"How'd you get the calling, Tom?" R.C. asked. "Were you born here on the ranch?"

"Hell no, I was born on a big ol' dryland farm in east Kansas, just south of Topeka. I was one of eleven kids, and we was havin' a rough time. Me and my pap didn't git along very well. Nobody got along with ol' Pap too well, includin' my ma. However, they musta got along well enough eleven times. After a big scrape with Pap, I decided I'd light a shuck and head out. So, I just packed what few things I had and told my ma I was leavin'. She shed a tear, but didn't try to stop me. And I just walked off on down the road.

"As I's agoin' down that road, I passed my pap. He was behind a span of mules, walkin' in plowed ground, comin' toward me. When we met, he never looked my way, he never waved, never said yea, nay, go to hell, or nothin'. I just kept on walkin'."

"How'd you get out west?"

"Well, I worked some and I stole some, just enough to git by, you understand. Hopped a freight, just kept aheadin' west. Got off in Elkhart, Kansas. Got a few odd jobs around town, and ran into some cowboys that was workin' for the Matador. They was runnin' some steers in the Panhandle, and they asked me if I wanted a job. I told 'em sure."

"You started cowboying right then?"

Tom chuckled. "Hell, no! My job was gatherin' prairie coal."

You could see a puzzled look on R.C.'s face. Top leaned over and said, "Them's cow chips, dried cow chips for fire."

"That's right. My job was to gather cow chips. There wasn't no firewood. I worked for the cook and I paid close attention to 'im. That's where I picked up all my cookin' skills, by watchin' that damned ol' Matador cook. Pretty soon he put me to lookin' after the cavvy, the horse herd. I'd git 'em in early in the mornin' and put 'em in a stake corral. The wagon boss would stand out in the middle and rope each cowboy's mount, threw a good hoolihan he did.

"Finally I hooked onto a cowboy job. At that time the Matadors was still runnin' steers up in Montana. All the big cattle drives were already over. They were shippin' 'em by rail, so they loaded us on a train and sent us up there to take care of a bunch of steers.

"I'll tell you boys, when I got to Montana, I thought I'd found heaven on earth. Never had I seen so much good, green grass. I'm tellin' ya it was an absolute cattle paradise. Steers got fat and we shipped in the fall, and then I found out what Montana was really like. Boys, it's hell in the winter. I don't reckon I ever got warm. I'll tell ya boys, that winter was longer than a whore's dream. And cold. It was colder than the end of a polar bear's prick. But then spring comes and for some reason, it makes you forget all about winter.

"It's a lot like a drunk, boys. You had a hell of a time while you're drunk, and you're standin' up in your stirrups, and you're whoopin' and hollerin' and you're sure feelin' good. And then comes the hangover. You swear ya'll never get drunk again. As soon as that hangover's gone, the first good chance ya get, somebody hands ya a bottle and ya get rip-roarin', knee-walkin', snot-flyin', wild-eyed agin. Just the thing ya swore you'd never do. And that's the way Montana was.

"However, the winters was three times longer than the summer and after about five years, I packed her in and drawed my pay and headed back south. I liked that Wyoming country. Had me a good camp job on an outfit just east of Chugwater, and was doin' fine. Then ran into a little trouble."

Well, by that time he had us all hooked. I said, "What happened, Tom?"

"Well, I went to town sober and got drunk. When I sobered up, I was married."

Top looked at Tom. "No shit, Tom. I didn't know you was ever married."

"Yep. I sure was. Goddamn, when I was drunk, she was the prettiest thing ya ever laid eyes on. Sweet, my heavens. But after I sobered up there was never a meaner, ornery old bitch that ever lived. I took her out to the camp where we was livin', and she did nothin' but bitch and moan all the time we was out there. Hell. I even had a kid, a boy."

Top looked at him. "Where did you find this girl?"

"In a saloon."

"If you found her in a saloon, she might have had wicked ways."

"Oh, she did, she did!"

"Well, how do you know that kid was yours?"

Tom stretched back in his chair a little bit. "Well, he was born just about nine months after we was married. And I'll tell you boys, for that first nine months, what time I wasn't on it, I had my hand on it. So, I know he was mine!"

"What happened to your wife and baby boy?" R.C. asked.

Tom looked kind of far off and turned his head. "Well, it's kind of a sad story. But, dammit, she had it comin'. I told her I was gonna be off two days ahelpin' over at another camp. A storm came up and we couldn't do our business, so I come back home. And damned if I didn't catch her in bed with one of the other hands."

"What did you do?" R.C. said.

"Well, I shot the son of a bitch."

"No kidding? Did you kill him?" R.C. asked.

"Damn right I killed him. Deader 'n hell."

"Whew, what happened, Tom?" I said.

"What do ya think happened? I got on a horse and rode to town and told what I'd done. I figured a man was within his rights to protect his own property, not that I owned the lady, but she was supposed to be mine. I guess I'm stretchin' the truth a little by callin' her a lady."

I had to ask him what happened next.

"What generally happens when ya shoot somebody. They throwed me in jail, and they had a trial and they didn't see it my way. So I spent five years over at Rawlins in the state penitentiary. I was paroled and when I got out I didn't spend much time in Wyoming. I headed on back south."

"What happened to your wife and the baby?" R.C. asked.

"I don't know. I never heard of her agin. Never think of her no more. Sometimes I wonder what happened to my boy. But at the time it didn't bother me much. I was wild and reckless and still had the callin'. I drifted back into Texas and worked for the Matadors agin.

"So, I rode the rough string for the Matadors 'til too many horses and too many bad wrecks had me crippled up so bad that I couldn't do it no more. Then I just started cowboyin' for 'em, ridin' cattle, ridin' fence, and when the longs hours in the saddle started gittin' to me, like all cowboys that keep the callin', I went to cookin'.

"But even this country would get too cold for me in the winter. Hell, I was never out of a job. I drifted on south. Matter of fact, that's where I met up with Top, down in Wilcox, Arizona. He talked me into comin' back here and helpin' him out. Hell, I just come.

"I've had a hell of a good time. I ain't made much of a livin', but I've lived on what I've made."

"I sure wish I had some of your experience," R.C. said. "I wish there was a way to get it."

Ol' Tom looked at him. "If wishes was fishes, we'd have a big fry. And if horse turds was biscuits, we'd eat 'til we die." With that, he laughed. "If you boys is gonna git up and be over to Diego's at daylight, ya better settle down in them sougans. I'll have breakfast in the morning."

You could hear his old bones creak as he got up out of his chair and shuffled inside.

Top looked over at R.C. and winked. "He'll give you somethin' to put in your book."

"Top, I let you in on that secret because you guessed it. But I'd appreciate it if you don't tell anybody. None of you boys. Kind of keep it to yourselves, because I'd hate to get it around. People might be afraid to talk to me and tell me about things if they thought it was going to end up in print."

Right quick ol' Top said, "You can count on me. I'll not say a word." And we all agreed.

"Well, I'm gonna turn in," Poke said.

"Me, too," Top said. "Mornin's comin' early."

He told R.C. and me where we could bunk down. We waited just a little, until everybody was out of earshot. I leaned over to R.C. "Goddamn, R.C.! Why couldn't you tell me? Looks like as much as we've been together and close as we've grown, that you could tell me what you was doin'."

"Frank, I'm not writing a book. I've never written anything but a term paper or a book report, and they weren't worth much. I just told Top that to get him off my back. I didn't rob any bank, and I'm not writing any book, and you already know I didn't escape from any prison."

"If there was anything I needed to know, you'd tell me, wouldn't you?"

R.C. looked at me as sincere as a feller can look. "Frank, you'd be the first to know."

"Good enough for me, pard. Let's hit it."

CHAPTER

14

It didn't seem like I'd hardly laid down and closed my eyes, 'til I could hear some banging around in the kitchen. I pulled on my britches and boots and R.C. reared up out of bed. "What are you doing?"

"Must be time to get up. I can hear Tom in the kitchen."

Without a word he crawled out of his bed and started doing the same. When we walked in, Ol' Tom had that cigarette that he'd rolled stuck in the side of his mouth. "Mornin' boys. Help yourselves to the coffee."

"I've gotta go out and throw those horses some grain," I said. "I'll be back."

"Nah, go ahead and sit down and enjoy your coffee. I've already done grained your horses. And they had plenty of hay. Everythin's in good shape and we'll have somethin' in your belly here directly."

Top came in sticking his shirttail in his britches. "Did you tend to everything, Tom?"

"I did."

"Tom, you must have been up quite awhile," R.C. said.

Ol' Tom grinned real big. "Oh, I got plenty of sleep. I had to git up."

"What for, Tom?" I said. "Did you have to take a leak?"

"Nah. But I lay down for a little while and, God, these ol' bones git to achin' so damn bad, I just cain't stay in that bed any longer."

I was the only one that was paying close attention to Ol' Tom. He had him a big cast-iron griddle he'd put on top of the stove that covered two burners, and had been spending considerable time adjusting the flames on both burners. Directly I saw him lean over that griddle and spit. And when the spit hit the griddle, it just went to bubbling and sizzling, and I saw Ol' Tom watch it, down close like his eyes were fading on him. Directly he stood up and said. "Ah, she's just right."

With that he went to pouring pancake batter out and making flap-jacks. I tell you what, it kind of turned your stomach to know what he'd done. But after you got past that first jolt, he made the best flapjacks I'd ever eaten. Light and fluffy, with eggs and bacon to go with it, and plenty of strong coffee.

Top reached out into the middle of the table after we were done and grabbed the toothpick can, and passed it around. "Here, you want a quitten stick?"

R.C. picked one out and looked at it, raised his eyebrows, and passed them over to me. We talked a little while and kind of let our breakfast settle on us.

Finally Ol' Tom said, "Boys, if you're gonna git on to that fence, you better fork your horses."

"Tom, I'll see you in a couple of days," Top said. "Hold the fort down."

"You bet."

We hit a long trot and had a few miles to go. Whoever had coined the phrase "it's always darkest before the dawn" damn sure knew what he was talking about. The night was so black we couldn't even see each other. But we followed Top's lead, riding four abreast. It was his country and he knew where the gate was. Leastways, I figured he ought to, or they wouldn't be calling him Top.

Sure enough, he slowed to a walk. "Careful, boys, the fence is right up here in front of us. Don't run into any wire." Directly he pulled to a stop. "I do believe the gate is right here."

R.C. stepped off his horse without being asked, went forward and grabbed the fence, and started feeling around for the gate.

"Walk to your right. You ought to feel the gatepost."

Pretty soon R.C. said, "Here it is." You could hear him opening the gate. "Come on through." So, we single-filed it through.

As R.C. was putting the gate back up, I was looking back over my shoulder and there was just a thin line of silver back in the east, separating the ground from the sky. "It looks like the sun is gonna come up today, after all." I'd begun to doubt it.

"Well, we're a mite early," Poke said. "But I'd rather be early than late."

Off to our right we heard a voice. In Spanish, "Quien es?"

So we all called out: "Top Darcey, Louis Mahone, R.C. Roth." When it got to me, I said, "Frank Dalton, por qué?"

It was lightening up now, and we could see a shape moving toward us. And here came Miguel leading his horse, with a big grin on his face.

"Well, I've been waitin' for you. Glad you could come over. This here ain't gonna be a great big deal. Just these last two pastures to work, and we'll be set for the summer. But we wanted you to come for this last circle, because we're plannin' a big fandango tomorrow night. I sure wouldn't want you to miss it."

With that, a look of concern came over his face. "We should have a hell of a time, providin' we can get Dad out of the doldrums."

"What's the matter with Diego?" Top asked.

Miguel shrugged his shoulders. "Oh, some trouble has popped up. Some legal troubles. I don't think there's anything to worry about, but anything that comes up like that that Dad doesn't understand, it tends to upset him. He's gone to Santa Fe to check into it. We've been workin' cattle, so I haven't really got the latest. But, like I said, I'll fill you in on it later."

"Miguel, he hasn't been talkin' to the Boss, has he?" I asked.

"I'm sure he has. Those two do a lot of talkin' together. They've even had a meeting up in Dorsey with a lawyer, and I think the Boss went with him."

"Well, Miz T. seems to think that the Boss is actin' kind of strange and preoccupied. Maybe the same thing with your dad is gnawin' on the Boss, too." I said.

"Maybe so. They're pretty close."

It was getting light enough to see now, though the sun hadn't come up. I was anxious for R.C. to see this country, because it would be totally different from anything he'd seen so far. None of us had realized that coming through the gate we'd passed within several hundred yards of a bunch of the Cannon brothers' yearlings that had been bedded down. And as daylight came they started getting up and stretching and grazing.

Miguel noticed them and told Top, "I've been watchin' your Corrientes, Top. They're doing sure pretty good."

"Yeah. They're beginning to fill out every day. They're shapin' up all right."

"You know, when those first came in, I sure felt sorry for 'em," Miguel said.

"Sorry for 'em! Why in the hell would you feel sorry for 'em?"

Miguel looked back at Top. "Because they had three strikes against them when they got here."

"What do you mean?"

"Well, they're poor, they're Catholic, and they're Mexican." With that, Miguel laughed at his own joke.

Miguel had a very easy way of giving orders. He told Top, "If you want to, Top, head back south down the fence line 'til you can see Juan, then start movin' west. We'll string out toward the north and drop off in sight of one another and we'll start down into the breaks. Push everything to the bottom."

We hit a trot heading north. The sun was just beginning to break the horizon to our right. As I looked over to the west, you could see what most of us called the Caprock. It was a large escarpment standing six to eight hundred feet high. It wasn't made by the Ute Creek drainage. It was an honest-to-God caprock that rose on the west side of Ute Creek to another plateau of prairie that stretched on to the Canadian River breaks. It was prairie on up to the foothills of the Sangre de Cristos.

We were, perhaps, half a mile from where the breaks on the east side started down into the Ute valley, and it was very rough country. Steep canyons, years of erosion, and lots of grass and quite a few piñons and cedar trees. From where we rode you could look over the entire valley heading south toward the headquarters. And you could see a break in the escarpment to the north of a canyon where Ute Creek dropped into the valley.

With a motion of Miguel's hand, any one of us could drop off and head west. Miguel had a pretty good idea when he'd see the first rider on the north. As long as we stayed in sight of one another, we wouldn't let any cattle slip in behind us.

Poke dropped off, then myself. R.C. went on with Miguel. With the sunlight shining across on the caprock, and not a cloud in the sky, it made for a beautiful morning. Fresh and clean. And with the sunlight hitting the grass, you could actually see the green. You could hear the call of the meadowlarks, and occasionally a jackrabbit, startled, would cross our path.

As I started down into the breaks, I saw a coyote that looked like he was heading back to his den after a night on the prowl. It wasn't long before I began to run into a few head of cattle, and I pushed them off. They went easy. The hard part is you had to go over and look into another canyon, and look good. We tried to stay within sight of one another. I could see Poke. He watched me. If he saw me ride to the top of a rise and look down into a canyon, then he wouldn't bother, because I'd taken care of it. I did the same with R.C.

On our way down we picked up more cattle. We had to pick our way. You couldn't ride just anywhere. Some of it got so steep that I got off a time or two and threw some rocks down to get some cattle started. Once they started and lined out, I was pretty sure they'd continue on. I might have to go off the other side to find an easier way down. I could see cattle streaming down to the west through the canyon single file, when a covey of blue quail got up right in front of the Gruyer. He liked to've turned wrong side out! He didn't lose me, but I didn't realize a horse could turn that quick. He also never bucked a jump, but for a few seconds there I had a runaway on my hands. I had to turn my hands around and rare back and get my feet in front of me. I gave him a couple of good, hard jerks to get his attention 'cause he was "shittin' and gittin'." A puredee runaway! I finally got him slowed down and turned around. I realized all the holes weren't out of him yet.

We scared the hell out of those quail. Blue quail will usually run on the ground. This covey got up like a bunch of bobwhites, so I knew they were surprised, but not near's surprised as old Gruyer! Scared the hell out of me too, but I wasn't going to run off about it. The Gruyer just stood there trembling. I untracked him and started back to where we came from.

When we got to the mesquite bush that they'd all come out of, he went to sidling off to the right. And I thought now was a good time to teach him a little lesson.

Took about five minutes to get him up close to the brush and make him stand with his nose facing it, all the time him wanting to run backwards, snorting and blowing his rollers. Finally I got where I could track him around the brush, then I could feel the tension go out of him. I decided he'd learned his lesson. Or at least, I hoped he had.

Then I saw R.C. down on the bottom trying to break up a bullfight! This is something I hadn't thought to tell him about. All I could think of was I'd better get over there and tell him to back off quick. So I undered and overed the Gruyer, with the end of the reins, and we came right down straight off that canyon rim. Rocks, brush, and all. I was hollering at him, but he was busy hollering himself, and waving his hands, and he had his rope down whopping his chaps, getting way too close to the bulls. And he couldn't hear me.

I was heading for him at a dead run, when what I was afraid was going to happen, happened. Finally one bull had had enough and decided to leave the country, and when he did, R.C. and his dun horse were right in the way. The bull connected with the dun horse, just behind the saddle and below the hip, and spun the horse down and flattened him out, and R.C. along with him. He was leaving the country!

'Course, the worst was yet to come! The bull that had just won now had the advantage, and he was right after his vanquished foe. He, too, ran right over R.C. and his horse. I kept going as fast as I could go. It was a relief to see the dun horse get up and move away slowly. R.C.'s foot wasn't hung in a stirrup, and that was a relief. But R.C. hadn't moved!

I put on the brakes, and the Gruyer squatted down and made a big eleven in the ground as I stepped off and ran to R.C. I stood there in a crouch and looked at him, trying to think what to do and assess the damage.

He was bleeding over his left cheek. His lip was bleeding some, and the worst thing, his nose was laying over, under his left eye. Obviously broke all to hell. His eyes were open, but glazed and unfocused. He was bareheaded. His hat lay off ten feet from his head, and was fairly smashed. He was lying on his right side, with his left arm stiff and bent at the elbow, with fingers extended and quivering slightly.

I was afraid to touch him. He might have a severe head injury, might even have broken his back. About that time I realized I wasn't alone. Miguel had pulled up at a dead run.

I started talking to R.C. "R.C., are you all right?"

I couldn't think of anything else to do but the old cowboy remedy for anything, and that's fan him with my hat. You could see the tension go out of R.C.'s left hand and it quit quivering. His eyes began to focus, and I could see him blink.

I knelt down beside him. "R.C., can you hear me?"

He didn't answer right away. But different parts of his body began to move a little bit. I kept hollering in his ear, "Can you hear me?"

Finally a weak "Yeah. Quit hollering," came from his lips.

"Where are you hurtin'?" I asked him.

With a grunt, "All over."

"Does it feel like anything's broke?"

"Unh uh."

Then he went to feeling around and trying to get up. Both Miguel and I pushed him back down. "No. Don't get up, don't get up. Just lay there."

By that time he'd rolled over, flat on his back, and looked up at the sky, blinked his eyes a few times. "What happened?"

"Oh, you just had one hell of a wreck!" I said.

"It must have been."

I held my fingers in front of his eyes. "How many fingers do you see?"

He gave me the right count. I asked him his name.

He frowned a bit. "Raymond . . ." Then slowly, "R.C . . ." and said, "Roth."

"What's my name?"

And without any hesitation he said, "Frank Dalton."

"Do you know where you are?"

"Yeah. Frank, I'm all right. Quit asking me these stupid questions!"

"Well, I thought you might of had a head injury. You're bleedin'."

I pulled out my handkerchief and dabbed at his nose. "Is there anything else hurtin' you bad? Does it feel like anything's broken, other than your nose?"

With that he began to test his arms and wrists, moved his shoulders and his ankles, bent both knees. "No. Everything's all right. I just hurt all over. Help me up."

So Miguel and I each grabbed him under the arm and helped him up. He was a little unsteady on his feet.

"Looks like you're all right, pardner," Miguel said. "You're lucky. Let me catch your horse and see what happened."

R.C. looked at me with clear eyes now. "I don't know what happened."

"A valuable lesson. Whenever you start gatherin' cattle and the bulls are turned out in them, it gets them stirred up and their blood hot. They each have their little harem and their peckin' order. And when they start gettin' choused, they decide to challenge one another. Stay out of their way 'til it's over, then throw 'em in with the bunch."

"Now you tell me!"

"How in the hell was I to know that this might come up?"

Miguel came leading the dun horse up. He was a little gimpy on the rear end, but he'd weathered it a sight better than R.C.

R.C. went over and took the reins from Miguel, stroked Dunny a little bit, and reached back and ran his hands softly along a scrape that'd knocked the hair off Dunny's thigh. He led him around in a circle, talking to him a little bit. I went over and got his hat, brought it back to him, and handed it to him.

He looked at it. "Oh, shit! It ruined my hat!"

Right then I knew he was going to make it. When a cowboy is more concerned about his horse and his equipment than he is about himself, he has a running start.

"I'm goin' back after those bulls," Miguel said. "They're heading payah."

We looked up the draw, and sure enough, they were heading away from the herd, the winner abellering and trying to catch up, and the loser just trying to get away.

R.C. wanted to get on and help him. But I figured it was a good idea if he led old Dunny on down the hill a little bit and got the blood flowing back into his brain and his legs.

It wasn't long until we could hear what sounded like a shot coming from up the canyon.

"I didn't know Miguel had a gun!" R.C. said.

"I don't think he does."

A look of horror crept over R.C.'s face. "My God, I hope he doesn't think he has to shoot that bull that ran over me. It wasn't his fault. It was mine!"

"You got that right. I don't think he's gonna shoot anything."

Directly we saw him coming down the draw and he had both bulls at a dead run. He had his rope down, only he wasn't using the loop end. He'd taken the other end and had tied a leather popper to the tail of his rope. He had about thirty foot dragging behind, and in one graceful long stroke, he'd roll that rope forward like a bullwhip and bring his arm back just as it reached the end. It would crack like a .30-.30.

I watched him with admiration and said to myself, "God, I wish I could do that!"

The big circle had already closed in around all the cattle and had them headed down the valley. R.C. and I were just poking along, mainly to avoid any further injury to old Dunny. When we got to the creek, I told him to get off and wash up a little bit.

He took his handkerchief, wet it good, and dabbed around on his lip and on his eye where a considerable goose egg rose up. He felt for his nose, and had to hunt some before he could find it.

"Don't worry about your nose. It'll still work." I told him to soak his hat a little bit, and shape it up, if he wanted to.

"Won't it ruin it?"

"Hell no. It'll do it good. Stayin' in the water will shape it up. Steam's best, but in a pinch, water'll do. You gotta have your hat lookin' right for your lady friend down the creek."

R.C. hadn't thought of that. "Oh, God. I wonder what she'll think of me coming in looking like this?"

"Well, you'll probably get more sympathy than you deserve. And it just might get you out of a hell of a lot of work."

As R.C. fiddled with his wet hat, dipping it in front and in back, and seeing that both sides were level, he said, "Speaking of work, wasn't that a sight this morning with all the cattle coming down off both sides of this valley? Did you ever see the likes of cowboys?"

"Yeah. And we're probably the only outsiders invited to this shindig."

"Oh, really? Who are the others? Where'd they come from?"

"Family, mostly," I said.

"There sure were a lot of cattle."

"Tell you what, that wasn't even a piece of it. They've been brandin' all month, off and on, right here on the home place. You don't have any idea how big this outfit is, do you?"

"I guess not."

"Well, I don't rightly know either, but I bet you there's upward of five thousand mother cows. This is one of the better, larger outfits in the country. You can find some ranches that are a great lot bigger here in New Mexico, but very few that'll run more cattle. This was part of a Mexican land grant. I don't know much about it, but if you're interested in history at all you ought to get Diego set down and have him tell you the story from the beginnin'. I wouldn't mind hearin' it myself. I've just got bits and pieces of it over the years.

"Today will clean up all their spring work, and tomorrow will be mostly fun and games. They really didn't need our help. They could have done this all by themselves. It's an honor to be included in on the Jaramillo festivities.

"Not only," I said, "are the Jaramillos known for their good cattle. For years and years their horses have been praised far and wide. Diego has buyers that come from as far away as Montana and Mexico to buy horses from him. I'll bet Diego runs a hundred brood mares and stands four to five stallions a year. And he doesn't stand these stallions to any outside mares. Except, of course, to the Boss. I don't know which he takes more pride in, his cattle or his horses, but my guess would be his horses."

By the time we'd gotten to the pens, they were all set up and ready to go. People everywhere. Lots of young boys to run irons, flank calves. Diego and the Boss, Joaquin and Poke and Top, all of 'em came over, expressing great concern about R.C.'s welfare. He assured them he was all right. But Diego wouldn't take no for an answer, or the Boss. Told me to take him on down to the main house and get some ice on the knot on his head. It was about to close up his left eye.

Diego told me, "Let old man Pedro down at the corrals take a look at Dunny. He's as good as any vet," he declared. "He understands the horse, he'll take good care of him."

R.C. put up a feeble argument, but lost. It was just a short ride on down to the headquarters, and it was impressive. It never ceased to amaze me that something that had been there for so long could be kept in such good repair.

The lane up to the house was lined with trees that must have been over a hundred years old. Great cottonwoods that you had to extend your arms around three times to get around to where you started.

We found old Pedro, unsaddled our horses, and he immediately began to feel and touch the dun horse to find out just exactly what ailed him. R.C. and I walked up to the house.

It was a true Spanish adobe home, but of huge proportions, with sandstone steps leading up to the door, wrought-iron latticework, and wrought-iron yard fence and gate.

Francesca met us coming up the steps, and ran toward us with skirt flying. "Oh, R.C.! Joaquin rode down to the house and told us what had happened. Are you all right?"

"I think so."

She put her arm around his waist, he put his hand on her shoulder as if he needed help. Hell, he was walking along on his own pretty good, I thought, but he seemed to be weakening now. I suggested they pull off his boots so his spurs wouldn't tear up the fine leather couch. Kika dismissed it as if it didn't matter.

I turned around and backed up to R.C. and had him stick his foot between my legs, and told him to push on my butt with his other foot. And by grabbing the heel and toe, worked his boots off. After we got both of them off, Kika laid him back on the couch. She had things organized by now.

"It's just a suggestion," I said, "but you'd better put some ice on that nose, and not on his eye."

Kika gave another command and here came Maria, a short, stout woman. She hustled. They put ice in bread wrappers and laid it across the bridge of his nose and up on his eye.

"Frank," Kika said, "had we better take him to town? What are we going to do about his nose?"

"I can fix his nose."

Kika looked at me with doubt.

"I've been around a lot of broken noses. I can fix it, if he can stand it. What do you say, R.C., do you want to leave it like it is, or do you want to try and straighten it out?"

"How bad is it?" he asked.

"Oh, most of your nose is layin' over on your left cheek. If we let it go, it'll grow that way. It'll probably stay that way forever, unless you do the same thing again and let them bulls come from the opposite direction. To tell you the truth, it gives your face quite a bit of character just like it is."

Kika frowned at me. "Frank. Don't tease him."

"The only thing," I said, "is if he's had a concussion."

Kika looked at his eyes to see if his eyes were dilated. "No, I don't think so. They look normal to me. He has the prettiest gray eyes."

"How do you feel, R.C.?" I asked.

"Pretty good. I've got a headache."

"Do you want me to straighten out your nose the best I can?"

"I guess so."

"Well, you're gonna have a hell of a lot more headache, soon as I'm done. Kika, grab ahold of his wrists and hold 'em to where he won't reach up. I'm gonna kneel down at R.C.'s head and clamp his head with my knees. Then I'm gonna push that nose over where it's supposed to be. Don't give with the pressure. Fight the pressure, R.C."

He mumbled, "Okay."

I reached down and placed one thumb underneath his nose aside his cheek and the other one across his nose from the opposite thumb and looked up at Kika. Our noses were about four inches apart. "Are you ready?"

She nodded.

"Here goes." And I pushed with all my might toward the center of his face. You could hear gristle popping and bone grinding against bone. You could hear a muffled groan from R.C. and Kika was holding on with all her might. By this time the blood was squirting. I gave it another shove, straightened up, and eyeballed it to see how straight it'd gotten. It'd straightened up considerably, but it still had a bend between the tip and the bridge of his nose.

I eyeballed it one more time. "I think that's the best that I can do."

We rolled R.C. over and stuck his head over the washpan. Every now and then, big, thick globs of dark blood would come out. I didn't realize until then that we'd had quite an audience. All the ladies from the kitchen had come in, and all of them were standing with their hands to their mouths holding their breaths.

Poke just stood there, wide-eyed.

"What are you doin' here?" I said.

"I thought you might need some help, and I was just gettin' in the way up there. But, it looks like you've taken care of it."

Kika was holding a damp cloth to R.C.'s head, and he was on his all fours, letting it bleed. The blood concerned her.

"Frank, I'm afraid he's going to bleed to death."

"No, I've never heard of nobody bleedin' to death over a nose. Just let it bleed awhile. It'll clean it out."

She looked back at one of the girls and nodded her head. And directly she was back with cotton balls and swab sticks. With ice behind his neck and ice over the bridge of his nose, the bleeding slowed a great deal. I had him lay back down and I packed some cotton into some gauze and rolled it up and stuck it up his nose.

I got up. "I think I've done all the damage I can do."

"Help yourself to some brandy," Kika said. "Or get a cup of coffee. I'll take care of him now."

We walked out onto the patio. There were tables, chairs, and shade. Poke and I spiked our coffee with a good shot of brandy.

Leaning back and enjoying his spiked coffee, Poke said, "Frank, where did you learn to do that?"

"Well, I've had it done to me a number of times, and I've seen it done to other people. So I just followed their lead." Looking around I said, "Isn't this the damnedest place you ever saw?"

"You bet it is!"

"How old do you reckon this place is?" I asked.

"There's no tellin'. A hundred years, maybe older."

"Did you ever notice the rock wall in the front yard, right off the road? It's still got tie rings for horses and carriages. I bet they built this house about the same time they planted those big cottonwood trees down the lane."

"Probably so," Poke said. "It looks just like a hacienda that you'd find in Santa Fe."

"Yeah. The walls have got to be three feet thick, all made out of adobe."

The shape of the thing was kind of built like a fort. The front of the house was two stories, all adobe, with the vigas sticking out on the outside. It had wings that ran back from it that made it into a U shape, and a coyote fence with large, peeled cedar posts, big enough to be corner posts, eight feet high and set side by side going across the back side.

On the inside was a grass placita or courtyard, with a hand-pumped well in the middle. I'd never seen them use the well, but I knew it wasn't decoration. If I went over and started pumping on the handle, I was sure I could draw water.

We looked around us. There was a porch, a sandstone sidewalk that enclosed the entire inner circle of the placita. Each room had a pueblo-type fireplace. It was the kind where you laid the wood in standing up, rather than laid it down on a grate.

From what I'd seen of the house, it was decorated in the utmost of Mexican taste. Imported Mexican tile throughout for floors. Numerous large Navajo rugs were placed strategically on the floors, along with a rough Chimayo or Truchas weave rug. For window tapestry they had the lighter, finer Chimayo weave. Some of the finer weavings hung as wall decoration, along with what I was sure were valuable paintings and old artifacts brought down through the family for years, that held some great significance to their forefathers.

146

Diego's den was a veritable museum. The only drawback I saw to the whole outfit was at the very back of the U-shaped compound. In order to get out of the rooms and get into the main house, you had to step outside and walk along under the porch until you got to a door that led to the main house. And then you had to go from room to room to get to the front of the house, because there were no hallways.

Down at the corrals they had an adobe structure built on the same principle as the house, with a porch and with stalls all around three sides. And the middle, instead of being a placita, was more of a corral, which they kept spotless.

CHAPTER

15

You could call the Jaramillo headquarters a village. There were about fifteen houses scattered up and down the east bank of Ute Creek, all of them almost within hollering distance. Unlike most large ranches, they didn't use line camps where somebody would go out and spend the winter looking after his little portion of the ranch. The Mexican people like to cluster together, probably stemming back to the days of Indian raids where they would band together for protection. All in all, it looked like a good working situation. And was probably the most self-sufficient ranch I'd ever been on.

Poke and I went to the kitchen with the coffee cups. We headed back into the room where R.C. was, and were surprised to find the entire Jaramillo clan, along with the Boss and Miz T., standing very solemnly, almost like at a funeral.

All seemed to be listening to a very small, old Spanish lady who was seated on a chair beside R.C. The old lady was dressed entirely in black, even with a black shawl across her shoulders. And she was talking directly to Francesca, who stood with folded arms looking down at her. She wasn't receiving a scolding. But the woman definitely was speaking her mind, and doing it in Spanish. And I couldn't even catch a word.

For some reason the old lady reminded me of someone, with the brown, deeply wrinkled lines in her face, and a fairly long, sharp nose, and brown sparkling eyes. She was making a point, and there was no doubt that she thought she was right.

I edged over to Joaquin and whispered, "What's goin' on?"

Like two boys whispering in church, Joaquin cupped his hand over his mouth and whispered back to me, "She's saying that she should have been called first for her opinion. She has medicines she could have given him. For years she's been taking care of our aches and pains and was the midwife of everybody that was born on the place for the last fifty years. I think she feels slighted and needs to get it out of her system."

"What would she have given him?" I whispered back.

"She is an herbalist. She knows the plants and the remedies to make one well. She already mixed up a cup of brew, a tea-like solution, and made R.C. drink it. I don't know whether it'll do any good."

About that time the old lady rose, and with her head bent and her hands clasped in front of her, left the room.

Francesca shrugged and looked at her dad. "I didn't think of her at the time, Dad. Frank and I just did the best we could."

Diego nodded. "Don't give it another thought. It looks like things have turned out well enough. He is a lucky man."

The Boss spoke up. "From where I stand, Frank, he looks pretty good, providin' there's nothin' else wrong with him besides his nose."

"It was a pretty bad wreck, Boss. I saw it. He could have some cracked ribs, or he could be bruised up inside a little bit. I guess time'll tell."

R.C. appeared to doze off from time to time, but was awake now. So I walked over to the foot of the couch.

"How you feelin', pard?"

With a weak smile he said, "Not bad, considering, Frank. Oh, I know. Don't tell me. You've had worse than this on your lips, and never did quit whistlin'!"

That made me smile. "You're catchin' on."

The whole bunch had turned to talking among themselves. I heard Joaquin and Miguel tell their dad they'd go on down, handle the branding, and finish up.

"Good," Diego said. "J.W. and I need to talk. We still have business."

"I'd better go back down with you, too," I said. "I haven't popped a cap this mornin' or helped a lick. I feel like I'm lettin' you down."

Diego waved his hand in the air. "It's better that you take care of your friend, Frank."

Before everybody left, Miz T. walked over and patted R.C. very lightly on the head. "I don't know where to touch you. I'm so sorry, R.C." And gave him a weak smile.

"Thank you, ma'am." And returned the smile.

We asked R.C. if he was hungry, and he shook his head no. "I don't know what was in that potion that the old lady gave me, but I'm sure feeling a lot better."

"Well, stay there and relax," Francesca said. "Frank and I will get something to eat. Then we'll get you some clean clothes."

After we got in the kitchen we could talk openly. All the help had gone down to feed the crew. "Kika, what do you suppose was in that potion that the old lady gave R.C.?"

She shrugged her shoulders. "Who knows? She gathers all sorts of things from right here on the ranch. Different herbs and plants that I don't know the name of. She also sends over in the Rio Grande Valley for some other things. She's a big help to us."

I decided that I'd see if I could find out a little bit of what was going on between the Boss and Diego. "Has something happened recently that has upset the Boss? Miz T. seems to think there's something wrong with him."

"No, Frank. It's Dad. He and J.W. are so close, they're both trying to figure out a reason for what is happening."

"If you don't mind my asking, just what is happening?"

"I don't know myself. It gets complicated. Dad got a letter from the state land commissioner that upset him a great deal."

"Well, what was it?"

"I read the letter. He wanted to know what I thought. Evidently someone has become interested in our state lease up on top." She pointed upward, west above the caprock. "As we understand it, it could be put up for sale. Which, of course, we don't want to happen. We have leased that land from the state ever since New Mexico became a state in 1912.

"But worse than that, someone has been poking around," she said, "and claims the taxes were not paid on this ranch for a period of time. Since this ranch has been handed down from generation to generation, and Frank, this is what is killing Dad, they say they can find no proof of Dad's birth, no birth certificate in Santa Fe. Since this was once a Mexican land grant and was passed from my grandfather to my father, if he cannot prove who he is, he has no claim on this ranch, our home."

I screwed up my face. "Can they do that?"

"That's what we don't know. Dad and J.W. have been to see a lawyer, and they even went to Santa Fe. Since then they have been talking among themselves. I think they think some kind of a conspiracy is going on, and they don't know who started it. It's upset both of them. I have a feeling that maybe tonight or tomorrow, whenever Dad decides to let it come out, we'll get the whole story. Outside of reading the letter, and an inquiry to Dad to please produce a certificate of birth, I don't really know what's going on."

"Hell!" I said, "they can't do that, Kika. This is the 1950s not the 1850s. They just don't take something away from you that's yours!"

"Well, Dad's lawyer doesn't think so either, that it's just something to cause Dad trouble. But at his age, he doesn't need it. I don't want to tell you the whole story. I'd rather you hear it from his lips than mine. I think you're right. They can't take this place away from us. We've been here too long. I don't know what I'd do if they did. We have our own cemetery where my mother, grandmother, and my grandfather, and those before them, were buried. We have our own church. We have our own life that we made out here on these plains. I've heard the story before, and perhaps Dad will tell it to you."

"What's that? Diego's life story?"

"No. Well, yes, that too. But the story from the beginning. Our heritage, Frank."

"If you're gonna talk business with Boss and Diego, maybe they'll include Top. But, Kika, I'm just a hired hand. They won't want me or R.C. or Poke in on the family discussion. Or any business discussion for that matter."

She looked at me. "Oh, yes they will. They both think a lot of you, Frank. I know Top's older and they value his opinion. But I think they want you, Poke, and R.C. to get in on this."

"Why us?"

"Well, you're young, you hear things, and Lord knows, you're quick to act on things. And you might just have more insight than the older ones. Besides that, you all have become a part of us."

With that I had to duck my head. I really didn't know what she meant. "Thank you. I'll take that as a compliment."

"It is a compliment. When I speak of our heritage, I speak of the past, but I speak of the future, too. And you'll be a part of that. I think you'll stay in this country, Frank."

I shook my head. "I don't know about that, Kika. I don't think much past tomorrow."

"I know you don't, but you're the type of man that was made for this country."

I motioned my head up toward R.C. "What about him?"

"I've only known him a short while, but I've become very fond of him."

"That's very evident."

She smiled and shook her head. "I know. And I know nothing about him."

"I know. I'm the same way. I have no idea where he came from. I don't know where he's going. And I don't know what he's got on his mind. I just do know one thing."

"What's that?"

"I think he's a good man."

She nodded her head. "Yes. Yes, he is that. And that's a certainty!"

Later we all congregated in the living room. It had been a long day. The talk was quiet. I paid my respects to Miguel's and Joaquin's wives, for I hadn't seen them in a good while. Everyone was tired, and there seemed to be an air of tension in the room.

At supper, again Kika had taken over along with a lady she called Tia, and what they prepared was simple but quite adequate. The conversation ranged from the accident that R.C. had to the festivities to take place tomorrow.

There was no question that Kika was the lady of the house. I watched her closely. She even asked her father to say grace before we ate. She handled everything with an uncanny grace and ease. And it showed that she had been doing this for years, even though she was just a young woman.

When the meal was over, Diego arose and asked all the men to join him in his office for brandy and to smoke. As we all rose to go with him, Kika brought R.C. another cup of that tea potion.

We all piled into Diego's office. Besides a large desk with a comfortable chair behind it, there were several old leather divans and stuffed leather horsehair sofa chairs to sit in. Lining the walls were books, so actually it could be called a library, not just an office. I had had no idea that Diego was such an avid reader. But knowing him for the gentleman that he was, and for the isolation in which they lived, I could understand how someone would become quite attached to reading.

He opened up his liquor cabinet and produced a fine bottle of brandy and glasses, and bade everybody to help themselves. He opened a box of cigars that lay on the corner of his desk and invited anybody that had the notion to partake.

We all gathered around, and no one said much. They all just enjoyed their smoke and their brandy. I looked at Diego and could see the worry in his face. He was a handsome man, with the gray hair and the white mustache. You didn't see many mustaches in this country. But I think he would have looked out of place without it. It was a part of him.

He sat down in his chair, folded his hands in front of him, and studied his glass. He had on an old gray work shirt that was buttoned clear up to the top button at his neck, as if he was going to wear a necktie but had forgot to put it on. I'd noticed before that he did this. It was the style in which he dressed. I got to feeling a little uncomfortable because I thought somebody needed to say something, but it sure wasn't going to be me.

Finally Diego cleared his throat. "I'm not the type to air my problems in public or to wear my heart on my sleeve. But recently I have been confronted with a problem. I would like to discuss it with you, my friends. If you will bear with me, I will try to explain my predicament.

"J.W. and I have discussed this problem at length. I know some of you in here are young, much younger than I. Maybe you have an insight or know something that I don't. I consider you all my friends, and that is why I would like to share this, with your permission."

He acted so humble and was so sincere, everybody aside of the Boss mumbled some sort of appreciation.

Finally Top said, "What's the problem, Diego?"

Diego wrung his hands. "I don't know where to begin."

Top blew smoke from his cigar. "I think the best place to start is always at the beginning."

Diego studied a minute. "All right. About two weeks ago I received a letter from the commissioner of public lands. It was an inquiry. It pains me to speak of this, for we Jaramillos have always been a proud people. Perhaps too proud. The letter stated that the taxes on this ranch were not paid from the year 1848 until 1880, a period of thirty-two years. And it also stated that there was an inquiry, from a party that he did not identify, as to the legality of my birthright."

We were all listening intently. "I don't understand, sir. What about your birthright?" I asked.

"They have no record of my birth or my baptism in the archives at the state capitol or diocese headquarters. I knew this. Once in about 1915 or 1916, before the First World War, my father and I went to Santa Fe to check on my records and see if they were recorded at the capitol or diocese, and they were not. So this was no great surprise."

Top spoke up. "That was a long time ago, Diego, and in those days maybe records weren't kept. But you're here. What other proof do they need? And for what reason do they need proof?"

"With that to explain, I guess I must start at the beginning. You are right. Absolutely right, Will." I thought to myself that it had been so long since I heard Top called by his given name, that I'd almost forgotten what it was.

"I am an old man, and I have lived on this ranch all my life. But you see, the problem stems back farther than that. If you care to hear, I will tell you the story." He got an immediate response. Everyone wanted to hear the story.

So, with a deep breath, he began. "My people have been in this country and New Spain or New Mexico for over two hundred and fifty years.

You see, I'm a fifth-generation Jaramillo to live in the New World. My ancestor, a young boy, was born in Spain and came to Mexico at the age of fourteen. He was a manservant for the Spanish territorial governor, Don de Vargas, in his second term in 1703. That is when he came to Santa Fe and there has been a Jaramillo in this country ever since.

"In 1788, Governor DeAnza made a land grant to the first Jaramillo grandson. And the land grant was out here on the prairie. You see, the Spanish and the Mexican people did not measure things by acres, and they didn't survey with transits and chains and measurements. They went by landmarks. And this land grant was probably thought to be useless.

"But what DeAnza didn't realize is, we Jaramillos are grazers, we graze cattle and sheep. Where most of the people wanted a land grant along the great river, the Rio Grande, this suited my people just fine. Isolated though it was, it was a large country. It could run many cattle and many sheep. The land grant was large in size. And as far as the physical boundaries went, the Canadian River was the western boundary. It bordered where the Vermejo runs into the Canadian up north below Raton, and ran in a line over to the Twin Mounds. From there it angled into what is now Texas to where the Rita Blanca Creek met the Punta de Agua. From that junction it ran back west to where the Mora Creek runs into the Canadian."

Somebody whistled, "Whew! That's a huge piece of land!"

Diego nodded. "Yes, it was a large piece of land. But, it was just in theory. Of course it was never fenced, because there was no one here but the Indians. This was Comanche country and was their prime buffalo ground. This land grant was made in 1788, but was not utilized until 1832."

"Why," Poke asked, "was this land given to your great-great-great-grandfather?"

Diego smiled. "As always, it was for services rendered to our holy faith and the royal crown of Spain. But deep in my heart, I think it was given to us hoping that we would settle on it and be a buffer between the Indians and the great Rio Grande Valley. We were an outpost, and it was dangerous living here. Also as an outpost to warn against the encroach-ment of the Texans, for at one time Texas claimed all of this country, clear to the Rio Grande."

Diego thought a minute. "We gathered up thirty-two families, many of them relatives, all young people who were strong, who had the same desire to graze sheep and cattle, and had a good pastoral background. They left Las Vegas, and trekked across the prairie, around the great gorge of the Canadian, until they came to this spot. We got along with the Indians. The Comanche learned to respect us. We traded with them. We were not Comancheros, we never traded whiskey or guns. But we did trade with them. On our trips back over to the capital we would stock up and bring back anything they wanted. We traded for buffalo robes and hides mostly. We were always wary, but always fair. And we lived in harmony for many years.

"You see, the Comanche really didn't get that hostile until they became infringed upon from the east by the white man, and by the plainsmen that began to eliminate their source of livelihood, the buffalo. Although they were savages, they were honorable men until they saw their life vanishing. That is when they became incorrigible and merciless in their killing."

"Well," Top said. "I still don't see the problem, Diego."

Diego nodded his head. "The problem is when the United States took over this land from Mexico in 1848. You see, the Spanish and the Mexican governments never had this thing of taxes. They just wanted people to spread the word of the church and settle the land. But in the treaty of Guadalupe Hidalgo, all Spanish and Mexican land grants were honored by the United States. So, when the United States took over, the grant was still, in effect, ours.

"I don't know which came first, the taxes or the surveying. About the same time, I imagine. They started surveying, and as they did so our land became smaller and smaller, at first without us realizing it. They were not honoring the land grants of Mexico and Spain as they should have. So, we objected. We hired lawyers and fought. But lawyers were expensive, and the government, as you know, is always strong. And we would lose. I have almost all the pertinent documents," and he pointed over his shoulder at an old safe. "They're in that safe. Even copies of the land grant. But, they're just copies. The main papers were at the capitol in Santa Fe.

"The United States territorial governors were not too concerned about all the documents of Spain and Mexico. And, I admit, they were foreign to them. Some plots were so small that it was hard for them to understand. The documents were not taken care of. They were left in basements to rot and mildew. And some said, even dumped down the holes in the outhouses. These were the governors before the territorial governor, Lew Wallace, became the governor of the territory of New Mexico in 1878.

"So practically all legal documents were lost, up until that time. But back to the taxes. They were sent out, again I say if, I have no record of them. The notices would have been in English, and we did not understand English and we did not understand taxes. So, we ignored them, if we got them. In 1880, my grandfather realized what taxes were, and that he should pay them. Of course, they have been paid since. Every year, up to the present time.

"So, you see, that is one problem. If they should come back on me to pay those taxes, plus the interest that has accumulated on those taxes over all these years, I do not know what the sum would be. But it may be way too high, and unaffordable. I don't know whether I can do it.

"But the problem doesn't end here. If you'll bear with me, I'll try to explain. We built a church here, as all Catholics must when they build a settlement. Then some of us wanted to break away and make another settlement. The Piedra that my friend, J.W., owns is where one of my relatives, Martinez, for which the Martinez pasture you have is named, settled up there at the village they called Peralta, and they built a church.

"But regardless of how we spread out and settled the lands, there were no fences. But they kept surveying until they whittled down the land grant to the size it is now and turned all the rest into public domain. And for this I have no bitterness. We have more than enough to be comfortable, and probably more than a man should have a right to own. But this is the problem. Since I am the oldest son of my father, at his death this land grant was passed on to me. And yet there is no record of my birth, at the capitol."

"Well," R.C. asked, "where were you born, sir?"

"Strangely enough I was born at the Martinez place, which you know as the Piedra. And I was baptized in that old church. But, around the year 1874, that whole village that we called Peralta was besieged by the Comanches. There had been great killing of the buffalo on the plains, and everyone thought that the Comanche had been taken to the reservation in Indian Territory in Oklahoma. I believe they broke out and made one last stand in 1873 or 1874."

Poke spoke up. "Eighteen seventy-four would have probably been the year, Diego, and was probably the same bunch of Comanches and Kiowas that formed the great war party and made the historic raid on Adobe Walls over in the northern Texas Panhandle."

We all looked at Poke, and he shrugged his shoulders. "Texas history. You know, like the Alamo." Then he realized what he'd said and glanced at Miguel and Joaquin, and said, "No offense."

They all smiled, shook their heads. "None taken."

I couldn't help but ask. "Baptismal records, would they be proof enough? Would they be the same as a birth certificate?"

Diego nodded his head yes.

"Where would the certificate of baptism be kept?"

"In the church," Diego said.

"You mean the church there on the Piedra, the old church?"

"Yes. Our whole life centered around the church. Our important documents or anything of value was kept at the church."

"Then," I said, "you think the Indian raid on the Peralta settlement destroyed them?"

Diego shrugged his shoulders. "What is paper to the Indian? They cared not for paper, gold, or silver. None of the sacramentals, or any of the official papers of the church, were ever found. I suppose they were just destroyed as an act of vengeance by the Comanche."

"Well," Top said, "how did you survive?"

"I am told we had left there and came back to this place two days before the Comanche raid. My father brought my mother and brothers and sisters back down here for no reason that I know of, a coincidence. But, we were not there."

"Were there any survivors of the Indian attack?" I asked.

Diego shook his head and said, "None. They were all killed. A surprise attack, I suppose. There was evidence that they tried to defend themselves, but were finally overcome. The Indians burned the village, but not the church. It still stands, as you well know. But the village was completely destroyed."

"How come this place was spared?" I asked.

"God knows. The war party split off. Some of them came here. I am told that they were probably just occupying us and acting as a decoy for the larger war party that went up and destroyed Peralta, and then left a path of destruction clear across the eastern plains of New Mexico into Texas."

Diego continued, "This is all really speculation. I don't know why there were no survivors at Peralta. We'll never know. But I remember my father talking of the total destruction and the many bodies that had to be buried."

Top had been thinking on this. He got up and poured himself another brandy. "This is hard to digest all in one sittin'. I'm gonna have to think about it awhile. Is there any chance that those papers or any of the religious artifacts could have been hidden? Your father would have known if they were going to hide something somewhere, wouldn't he have?"

"If there had been a plan of someplace to put the valuables and the things that needed to be saved, I would have thought that my father would have known. But he didn't."

Top shrugged. "Well, it appears they're long gone. But that still doesn't make any difference in my book. You sittin' in that chair is proof enough for me that you were born, and that you live."

"Yes," Diego said. "But it does not give any proof that I am my father's son, which would make me the legal heir to the land that we now run our cattle on."

"Oh, my God," Top said. "This is gettin' complicated."

"And that's not all of it yet, Top," the Boss said.

"No," Diego said. "Part of the land that was ours, that became property of the United States government and the territory of New Mexico that was not filed upon and not patented in the homesteading days, reverted back to the state and we leased it. Everybody that had a chance took state leases out on grazing land. Almost all the ranches in this country have some state land, and I admit, it is a cheap lease. Of course you know that every sixth and thirty-sixth sections are called 'school sections.' And the revenue from those sections goes to the revenue that supports our schools for our young people.

"And I will tell you that we have twenty-two thousand acres, including school sections, of state land that is leased from the state by us, and has been since New Mexico became a state. Now the problem is, if somebody wants that land, they can put it up for sale. It can be bid upon from the steps of the county courthouse, and bought by the highest bidder. And it appears that is what somebody wants to do. So you see, my friends, between having to pay back taxes and interest that has accumulated over all these years, somebody putting up our state land for sale and the high price that it will bring, and me not being able to prove my legitimacy toward the grant, it is causing me considerable problems."

"What," R.C. asked, "are you going to do?"

Diego shrugged. "We have consulted a lawyer. J.W. and I even went to Santa Fe. We had a personal meeting with the land commissioner to find out who is behind all this, and why now."

"And?" Top said.

"We found out that a law firm called Anderson and Associates, based there in Santa Fe, has filed the grievance and are the ones that started this whole thing. Now, who has employed them and who they are representing is yet a mystery to us."

"Well," Top said, "the mystery is beginning to clear up a little bit for me."

With that, he got all our attention!

"This Anderson and Associates that you mentioned," he said. "I've heard the Cannon brothers mention that very name as being the law firm representing the party that's interested in buying our outfit."

This was a surprise to everybody. The Boss said, "We need to find out who this is. If he could get hold of the Cannon place, and that state land of yours, Diego, joins the Cannon place, it would make him a pretty good spread. Not to mention, and I don't think it'll ever happen, this place thrown in."

And that stopped us all dead in our tracks.

CHAPTER

16

Although the accommodations were the best, I'd sure spent better nights. With all of Diego's situations to be sorted out in my head, and the damn mockingbird who sang all night, and R.C.'s moaning and groaning, I had a fitful night. When I figured it was about morning, and I couldn't lay in bed any longer, I hit the floor and did so quietly, as not to wake R.C. I slipped on down to the kitchen hoping that somebody might be making some coffee.

I was amazed to find out that the kitchen was abuzz. There must have been over a dozen ladies cooking up a storm, and Francesca right in the middle of all of it. She smiled at me and poured me a cup of coffee. "You're up awfully early."

I smiled. I told her I hadn't had all the sleep I wanted, but I'd had all the bed I could stand.

"Where's your partner?" she asked.

"He's had a tough night and I decided to let him sleep."

"I'll bet he is sore all over! You know, I'll make him another cup of tea."

When I shook R.C. to wake him up, he groaned terrible.

"Don't touch me, Frank."

"I've got some of your special medicine here."

"Oh, my God." He slowly rolled over and sat on the edge of the bed and held his head in both hands. Finally he raised the cup to his lips and drank a little.

I began to laugh at him and that made him mad. "Drink as much of that stuff as you can and go splash some water on your face and plaster your hair down. My God, you look like the afterbirth of a bastard rat!"

Painfully, "It isn't nice to call people names when they're standing on death's doorstep."

"Go look at yourself."

He eased up off the bed and walked over to the washbasin and looked in the mirror. "Oh! You're right."

But by the time he got the brew down, got his clothes on, he perked up. Which even made me more determined to get a recipe for the brew. A fellow needed to know a powerful potion like that if he could.

"Kika said we're gonna have a full day today. I have an idea you'll do a lot of watchin'. But, I think you'll enjoy it."

"What do you think is going to take place?"

"I don't rightly know. But I think you're gonna see some of the best horseflesh you've ever laid eyes on."

Then he asked me, "Have you been thinking about what Diego told us last night?"

"Very little else all night long. I'm havin' a hard time sortin' it out in my mind. It's all so damn complicated. How about you?"

"Last night, all I could do was lie down and conk out. But, it's beginning to occupy my mind now."

"I'd like to help, but there's nothin' that we can do."

"Well," R.C. said, "maybe there is."

That didn't make sense to me. "Hell, it happened so long ago, and we don't have any money or power to change anybody's mind. I don't know what we could do."

"Let me think about it. You do the same."

R.C. started drifting off again and since all night long I had dreamed I was awake, I did too.

When finally we got outside, things were picking up. They'd already gathered cattle, and were sorting the calves off the cows. As we drove by the arena just south of the stables, people were already backing pickups up to the fence and setting chairs in them. They were placing a low, flat-bed hay wagon alongside the fence and putting lawn chairs on it. I had a feeling that was where the king of this empire would sit, meaning Diego.

Up around the stables and pavilion, tables were being set up and chairs brought out. Just planks of wood on sawhorses. We milled around and it seemed like everybody on the place and all their kids had shown up for a big day of festivities.

We went on up to the kitchen. Found Poke and Top lounging around drinking coffee.

"What's the deal with you fellers?" I asked. "I figured you'd be out there helpin'."

Top shook his head. "We went down and tried, but, hell, we was just in the way. They know what they want done and how they want it done, so I reckon they're best left alone 'til they holler at us."

It wasn't long until we were all seated around the large arena to watch the parade. This was a chance to see how the five-year-old geldings had come along in their training. It was quite impressive to watch these Jaramillo cowboys put the horses through their paces, roping, cutting, reining, and showing off their general all-around cow work and cow sense. It lasted the entire afternoon and was highly entertaining.

Later, I asked R.C. how he was feeling. He had been asked to sit with Diego during the showing.

"I've forgotten all about it. This was a real education. I probably learned more than I could have learned from going to a hundred horse shows. I'll have to tell you about it sometime. He explained everything, the change of leads, conformation. Oh, Frank, what that man and the Boss don't know about horses, I don't believe anybody knows."

"They're about ready to eat now. Do you think you could eat something, R.C.?"

"Let me get another beer and I'll show you. I haven't had much to eat since my wreck yesterday. I swallowed so much blood that I didn't think that I'd ever be hungry again. But, between the old lady's potion and time, I'm feeling a lot better. I believe I can make a hand at the table tonight."

Directly there was a yell for silence, which had an immediate effect on the crowd. Diego gave the benediction and everybody crossed themselves, and then he announced it was time to eat. There was a rush for the line. The young people first, then older men and women. There didn't need to be any hurry and fight for us to get in line because there was going to be plenty of food and there was plenty of beer to drink while we waited.

As the line filed by, they piled your plate high with meat. It didn't even need to be cut. The servers could reach and grab hunks of meat with their hands and not even have to tear it off. It just melted off the bone. Next came the salsa that went on the meat. There were beans, potato salad, tortillas. Good things to eat clear down the line.

Most of the men sat around and drank their beer and talked about the happenings of the day and teased one another. And along with that some praise, comments about how horses had worked and what they could have done better. You could tell that the horse industry was a very vital part of this ranch.

You could hear the musicians tuning up down at the other end, and it wouldn't be long before the baile started. With all the people around, Diego was quite busy. He talked to everyone, some at great length. There were some questions in my mind that I'd have liked to ask. But tonight wasn't the night to bring up what we had discussed the night before. It would have to wait. Poke and R.C. and I walked on down to the stables, found a bench to sit on, and tried to relax and let our stomachs settle. It was twilight and in the distance you could hear the music. Sounded like guitars, maybe a couple of fiddles. And, if I wasn't mistaken, an accordion. Professionals they weren't, but good music they did make. And to think it was all homegrown.

As the three of us sat under the overhanging porch of the stables Poke said, "Are you going to town next weekend, Frank?"

"Yeah, I thought I would."

"How about catchin' a ride in with you and we'll throw a party and turn our toes out?"

"Well, I've got a commitment, Poke."

"How's that?"

"I've got a date with Roberta Chism Saturday night. We're gonna go to the show."

Poke scoffed it off. "Well, hell! That there will ruin a good weekend."

"For you, maybe. But I'm kinda lookin' forward to it."

"I suppose you'll take her to the picture show and buy her popcorn. And then go out to the fairgrounds and park for a while and play a little kissy-face, and you'll try to get in her pants and she'll fight you off. And you'll come back with a bad case of the blue balls."

"That's about enough, Poke. You're gettin' on a touchy subject now."

"Don't tell me Frank Dalton's fixin' to get caught in a trap!"

"Hardly. She's a good girl and I sure like her."

"Yeah. I can understand that. Are you gonna take her out to the Water Hole and show her the wilder side of life?"

I hadn't thought about that. "I don't know. I hadn't thought about it. We just might go dancin'."

"Well," Poke said, "reckon her mama and daddy would appreciate you takin' her to one of those dens of sin?"

I had to think about that. "I don't know. I've seen old Jingle Bob and his wife out there myself havin' a few and cuttin' a rug. Not often, but I don't think it's against their religion."

Poke studied awhile. "Well, if it was my daughter, I'm not too sure I'd want her to go out with a wild hombre like you. And 'sides that take her to a honky-tonk. You might send her down the road to damnation."

"Oh, bullshit, Poke. All you're tryin' to do is get in between me and Roberta, and I think it's a selfish move."

Poke got all indignant about the selfish bit. "What in the hell do you mean?"

"As long as you and I and R.C., we go out and drink and carouse and chase the ladies, that's all fine. But let somebody get serious about somethin' and you throw a fit."

Poke jumped on the word "serious" like a dog on a bone. "Ah, this is what it comes down to, huh? You're gettin' serious."

I'd had about all I wanted of this conversation. "I'll tell you what." I looked around R.C. where I could see Poke and looked him right square in the eye. "I've got one thing to say to you. Poke Ma-hone."

With that, Poke went to laughing and of course R.C. didn't understand. I sat back and leaned up against the wall. I think my point was well taken.

"Well, aren't you going to finish telling him what you're going to say?" R.C. asked.

"I just did."

R.C. got a puzzled look on his face, all the time Poke laughing and throwing a fit. "I don't understand," R.C. said.

"No, I suppose you don't. It's kinda an inside joke. We're not tryin' to leave you out. But, it's not my place to say anything. Perhaps Poke would like to shed a little light on it."

Poke shook his head. "No. I made a mistake and told Frank a secret one night, and he's never gonna let me forget it. Maybe someday, R.C." And he broke into another fit of laughter.

About that time Joaquin walked around the side of the stable. "There you are! What are you doin'? Hidin' out from all the señoritas?"

"No," I said, "we just came back here to try to let our supper settle."

"There's a lot of pretty girls up there that have kind of taken a fancy to you boys, so I hope you'll oblige them."

"We intend to," Poke said.

"Joaquin," R.C. said, "I can't really speak for these other two, but I think it would be fair to say that all three of us have been thinking a great deal about Diego's predicament and what we could do to help. And I'd like to get your input. What could we possibly do?"

Joaquin shook his head. "I don't know. If Dad and J.W. can't make headway through the lawyers, I don't know what you can do."

R.C. had done considerable figuring, evidently. "To try to make it as simple as we can, and it's not a simple matter by any means. Sifting through it in my mind, seems like there are three points that need to be clarified before action can be taken."

"Go on," Joaquin said.

"Number one, we need to find out who is behind this action, and what their plan is. Secondly, I can't believe that there wouldn't be some sort of record in Santa Fe that would clear up the title to this land. And third, if possible, we should try to figure out what happened at the old church at Peralta. It could be the documents that were at Peralta when it was destroyed would be the key to the whole problem. I don't know the laws here in New Mexico, but I think it's highly unlikely after all these years that your father could lose possession of the home ranch. There should be laws of prescription, or use of the land, or adverse possession. I'm thinking a lot of things. A quiet title, condemnation, a color title, I don't know. There's all these things running through my mind. I don't know what would apply."

"Jesus," Poke said. "R.C., you sound like a lawyer yourself!"

"No, I'm not a lawyer. And I don't ever want to be one. There was a time, though, when I thought I might take up the law profession. That has long since passed. I just can't see where at this late date they can do it."

"I hope you're right," Joaquin said. "But I do know that they can put our state lease up for sale, and bid on it and possibly buy it. Or run it up so high on us and make us buy it, that it could really put us in a pinch."

"Tell me," R.C. said, "twenty-two thousand acres is a large parcel of land. But what would be so attractive about buying that alone? Does it have a unique quality to it, other than just being a large size?"

Poke said, "I think this is what they're thinkin', that the state land joins the Cannon outfit on the north, and if you combine those two alone, you'd have a pretty good outfit."

"What if," I said, "they put it up for sale and bought it, made payments on it for a certain number of years, then turned it back to the state and leased it back? I wonder if there's anything in the state law on who gets the first option to lease state land."

"If we didn't buy it at the sale, then we would give up our rights to it. Those leases are as good as owning it, except you can't use it for collateral."

Poke spoke up and said, "Well, I'll tell you what. Because of the moisture this year, things are pickin' up for the Cannon boys. I think they still want to sell, but they're not gonna give it away. And I'm sure they can hold out until after we ship in the fall. I know for a fact that they've changed banks and got refinanced twice since they closed down the Tramperos bank, because of my paychecks. These Cannon boys have been around, up and down the pike a few times. They'll hang tough."

"Well," R.C. said, "it looks like, then, if the sale of the Cannon place doesn't fly, possibly your state lease might not be in jeopardy. It sounds to me like someone dug into some files and just blindly stumbled across the fact that there were no records on Diego and decided to make a grand-stand play for the whole thing."

"And that's where," I said, "the church up at the Piedra comes in. The old place, Peralta. That could help a bunch if we could find those lost documents. But one thing I didn't understand, Joaquin. And perhaps Poke, you could help too, bein' Catholic. Tell me about the sacramentals that were never found. What are we talkin' about?"

So Poke began to name over what he considered the sacramentals. Candlesticks, a tabernacle, a chalice, and a paten.

Joaquin said, "A monstrance."

"Yeah," Poke said, "that, too. I'd forgotten."

"Do these things have any value?"

Poke and Joaquin looked at one another, like that was the dumbest question ever asked. Joaquin said, "They're of great value. Not only the spiritual value, which is great. Everything that Poke named is made from gold, or in some cases silver."

I let out a deep breath. "Then they must be very, very valuable. Then who do these belong to? I didn't know that priests were so wealthy that they could afford these things."

"The priests themselves were not wealthy. They were men of God, but wealthy in the spiritual meaning. These were their set of tools to conduct services, and they were made from precious metals for the glory of God."

"How did he come by them, then?" I asked.

"Many ways," said Joaquin. "Perhaps he had a wealthy sponsor that would provide him with the sacramentals. Maybe the community would go in together and buy these fine objects of holiness."

"Is there a chance that the church would own them and give them to the priest?" I asked.

Both shook their heads. "Possible, but highly unlikely. The church didn't have that kind of money to outfit every priest that left the seminary to go out amongst the people."

R.C. had been studying about this. "Let me understand. Would the priest only have one set of these sacramentals and carry them from church to church, or did every church have their own?"

Joaquin shrugged his shoulders. "Who knows? If it was a wealthy parish, perhaps they had their own, and remained in the church 'til the priest came back for services."

Something struck me then. "You mean that the priest didn't live full time there at the church?"

"Oh, no. He would travel from church to church," Joaquin said. "It's well known that in the old days in the Spanish diocese, or Mexican if you prefer, that almost all churches were about twenty to twenty-five miles apart, meaning about a day's ride apart. So the priest would travel around to these different outlying churches on a regular basis to hold mass."

"Well, then," I said, "perhaps the priest had taken all his sacramentals with him and had left Peralta, when the raid and all the killing had taken place."

Joaquin shook his head. "I don't think so, because it was the priest himself that was buried on top of the Piedra."

"Then all official documents, like baptisms, births, would also be of great value?" R.C. asked.

Joaquin shook his head. "This is true."

"Then they were all probably kept in one place. But the problem is, we don't know where they went, and they have been missing for over eighty years?"

Again Joaquin nodded his head.

"I'll tell you what," I said. "Papers could be burned. They may be long gone. But the gold and silver, all these sacramentals, have got to be somewhere. They could be hidden. I have a feeling that they wouldn't be far from the church, because as we said the other night, the Indians had no use for silver or for gold, or papers for that matter, although they might have been burned just for destruction."

"This is true," Joaquin said. "But where would one look? The ground holds many secrets, and it has been so long."

"I don't know," I said. "We might never know. But at least we can give it some thought. We'll keep our eyes peeled."

About that time, Francesca walked up with a mock scowl on her face and her hands on her hips. "There you are! I've hunted all over for you. Aren't you going to come join us? I have no one to dance with. Are you just going to ignore me all night?"

I didn't have a feeling that she was talking to her brother, or Poke or me. Her eyes were on R.C. "Perhaps you are still too sore and too stiff for a slow waltz on the dance floor."

R.C. stood up. "I don't think so. I'm sorry we've been rude."

"Come on," she said. "I was just kidding. But you have been missed." She took R.C. by the arm and headed back to the pavilion. And so did the rest of us.

We entered the dance. I had to fortify myself with a couple of beers. Then I proceeded to dance with everything that wore a skirt. There were many brown Spanish eyes that were more than happy to oblige us with a dance. I even danced with the lady, Maria. To use the exaggerated phrase, she was two axe handles and a log chain across the butt, but while dancing with her she was light as a feather, and seemed to enjoy our dance immensely.

I was having the time of my life. The whole day had been a big family picnic, and we were a part. But, occasionally, the image of a tall, blond-headed, high-breasted, proud-looking young lady entered my mind, and it kept me on the straight and narrow. I'd fight it back out of my mind, but that vision reappeared several times during the night.

The music was, I thought, outstanding. What I enjoyed more than anything was the people singing. On some songs it seemed like everybody there sang in harmony, even the men. I'm sure there are a few cultures such as the Indian and the Irish that would sing. Possibly the Germans in their beer-drinking halls would sing. But I thought nobody could sing with harmony and with such feeling as these Mexican people.

It was late that night when I crawled into bed. I was happy, exhausted, and looking forward to next Saturday night.

CHAPTER
17

The next morning we packed all our warbags up. I told R.C. that I'd lead old Dunny back, and he could ride back with the Boss, Miz T., and Tres. But he'd have none of it.

"I rode him over here and I'll ride him back. I asked Pedro about him last night, and he said he's as sound as a dollar."

"I'm not sure you're up to it."

"I'm up to it. You can't leave without me."

I thought while we had the chance, R.C. and I would head on down south, bend around, and come back into the Piedra from there. It might be a little bit further, but I wanted to show him some new country.

At breakfast we thanked Diego for his hospitality, and Kika, too. We all had enjoyed it. The only thing to mar the whole gathering was R.C.'s wreck, and he didn't seem to be any the worse for it. The Boss asked one time for R.C. to ride back with him in the car. And when R.C. declined, he let it drop. Miz T. almost persisted and stayed after him until the Boss finally told her to let him go.

We said our goodbyes and told her we'd be in later that evening. Poke, myself, Top, and R.C. headed down to the horses. Kika came with us, and R.C. stopped with her out on the porch. We went on. I figured they wanted a private goodbye, and I didn't want to be standing around on one foot listening.

Directly R.C. came down. We were saddled, having a chew and a smoke among us. While R.C. got saddled up, Poke said, "Maybe I'll see you this weekend in town."

With that we told the boys we'd see them later. R.C. said, "Give my best to Ol' Tom."

With a wave of the hand we parted ways. The sun was just coming up and we headed out south through the sandhills. There was still a lot of this Jaramillo outfit that we'd pass through, and I wanted R.C. to get a true picture of just what this cattle domain really was. We hit a long trot down the road.

We came upon a church. A small church, almost identical to the old church up on the Piedra. We stopped and looked at it. Of course it was still in use. Beside it was their cemetery. It had been well taken care of. I'm sure it was made out of adobe, like so many other of the buildings, only you couldn't see the adobe blocks like you could on the old church at home. They had mixed up the adobe mud, and hand-plastered and smoothed all the sides. Kind of stuccoed it, you might say.

"I suppose this is where it all started," I said. "If Joaquin is anywhere near right in his theories, it should be about twenty, twenty-five miles from this church to the one at home. If you're a priest, how would you get there?"

R.C. looked around a little bit. "I'd just take off in that direction," pointing to the northeast.

"Well, let's head that way then, if we can find a gate to get through." We did, right to the side of the cemetery.

As we hit a trot and moved along the country, I had to repeat to R.C. some of the things I'd told him coming in from his wreck, about the cholla cactus and the plant we called soapweed, that everybody else called yucca. He said he'd missed out on some of that, and I told him not to feel bad, that I was just talking, trying to keep his mind off his miseries. It was a great feeling to be out in the open and ride along with somebody you enjoyed.

Riding along on good horses and having the feeling of being free as the breeze. This is what this life we live is all about.

R.C. and I were busy taking in the country at a trot, when all of a sudden old Gruyer snorted and jumped sideways, damned near plumb out from underneath me, then wheeled and started the runaway bit again. By steady pressure and a jerk or two, I got him back under control. R.C. and old Dunny hadn't moved. They just watched. I had to spank on the Gruyer a little bit to get him back to where we were by using rowels and the end of my rein. He snorted and blew those rollers, cocked his ears forward, and then got to running backwards.

R.C. said, "What happened?"

"Damned if I know! Silly bastard's got some kind of a wild dream and decided to leave the country." That was the second time he'd done it.

R.C. pointed down to the ground. "Maybe that's it."

And sure enough, there was a rattlesnake.

When the sun was high overhead we stopped, pulled some sandwiches out of our roll that Kika had made for us. And just biting into one of those sandwiches reminded me of the dance last night, the flavor of the meat. We sat down by the windmill to where we'd have water. Loosened the cinch on our horses. We were in no big hurry.

"You know," R.C. said, "one thing I can't get over is how big this country is, but you don't see any cattle in it. We haven't passed by or seen over a couple of handfuls of cattle since we left this morning."

"Yeah. To make sure that you have plenty of grass, in all kinds of weather, drought included, means it takes a lot of country per cow unit. Unless you have 'em all bunched up or they happen to be in on water, they have a tendency to scatter. They just don't stay in herds. I guarantee you, though, they're here."

We continued on and were getting close to our home fence, when I decided I'd bring up something that had been bothering me. "R.C., there's one thing that until the other night I'd never thought of. I didn't realize how old Diego was. He's an old man! He should be Joaquin, Miguel, and Francesca's grandfather instead of their father."

"I thought of that, too. I had a lot of time to talk to Diego yesterday while sitting with him. He married late in life and his first wife died. He had been married to her for a long while. She was, to put it in Diego's words, barren. They had no children. He said he loved his first wife very much and lived in grief after her death for many years, until he married the mother of his children. And she died of complications of birth with Francesca. So you see, Francesca never knew her mother."

"That's gotta be tough," I said, "losing two wives in a lifetime. But where they live and how they live kind of played a part in how things happened, I suppose. I'll tell you one thing on the bright side, though."

"What's that?"

"You've got to admire Diego. Even in his old age, he's a vigorous, prolific old booger."

"Yes. He is that. And it looks to me like he did a good job of raising his children."

"Yeah. With a family around you like he's got, though, he had a lot of help."

We had just come up on the fence and the gate going into the Martinez. We were home. We followed the road on down north into the breaks of the creek. "This is the wagon road that took people down to the ford to Peralta."

When we got on up ahead where we could look down into the breaks and see the church and the Piedra standing tall there in the valley, we both swung down off our horses, and squatted down on our haunches.

"Let's just suppose we were living down there in 1874. Which way would the war party come from, do you think?" R.C. asked.

"Probably right about where we are right now."

"I think so, too, only maybe a little farther east. And I don't think they'd be out in the open. I think they would try to sneak up on the village, don't you?"

"Yeah."

"All right. How far do you think it would be from the church or from the village to where the leading part of this war party could no longer hide?"

I had to think about that. "If anybody was payin' attention at all, it looks to me like they couldn't get any closer than a mile or two without being detected. Unless it was just a few."

"How far do you think it is over to the Piedra?"

"About a half a mile."

"Well, that would give the people a little bit of time in the village. The Indians would have to find out they were detected, cross the creek, and make a run at the village. If the village people headed to the Piedra, they had only half a mile to cover."

"What's your point?"

"That they could have had a hiding place over on the Piedra somewhere. Maybe that's where all those valuables were cached."

"If they were, surely someone would've found 'em by now. The people that found the bodies. Don't you imagine they looked?"

"I suppose so. I'm just trying to be logical about this."

"That's where you'll lose me. I've never been logical."

"Just think, Frank. What would you do if you had something that you wanted to hide, and here came a whole passel of Indians, ready to take your scalp?"

"My guess is that they had some secret hiding place in the church, some secret compartment somewhere in the floor or in the wall, and buried it or hid it there."

"That's a thought. Look around. Can you see any other rocks or trees or something that would give an indication of someplace where they might hide something?"

"Well, it wouldn't be in the bank of the creek, because the water gets up and the bank changes. Probably, it never even got out of the church. The people fled trying to save themselves and didn't give those sacramentals or official papers any mind at all. They were just trying to save their hides. Wouldn't you?"

R.C. looked crestfallen. "Yes, I suppose so. But, I can't help but think that they'd utilize that high-standing, huge rock, the Piedra, for some sort of defense or hiding place."

"Well, we've been on top, and there's no place to hide anything. There's nothing up there but the grave of one priest. And I know that the relatives and friends of the people that were killed here have had to look for what we're lookin' for, all these years, and they haven't found it. It looks hopeless to me."

We both crawled back on our horses and headed down the hill.

"Frank, let's come over sometime and see if we can find inside the church some secret hiding place or something."

"I'm with you. But I don't know where in the world it would be. It was just a thought."

"I feel like I've got to start somewhere."

We crossed at the ford and headed on down to headquarters. I could see a little black-and-white dot coming my way, and I knew it was Belle.

Jim and Tio met us. Both commented about the condition of R.C.'s face. Tio seemed quite concerned. "R.C., you should have put some beef-steaks on your eyes. That would draw out all the swelling and the colors from your eyes."

"Oh, hell, Tio," I said. "That's just an old wives' tale that you read about in Joe Palooka in the funny papers."

"No, no, eet's true. Anyways," he grinned, "I no read, even the fonny papers. I have seen beef used many times. The raw meat has great medicinal value."

"Oh, bullshit!" I said.

"I'll tell you what," Jim said, "if he needs to put anything on them eyes, it's a poultice of alum water. I know an old widow lady up in town that douches with alum water. Every time she gets through, she opens the back door and throws the water out. She's douched so much to tighten her old snatch up that it's drawed the back fence up so close to the back door, you can't get it open."

"What you been up to, Jim?" I said.

"Oh, just stayin' busy. But you might as well hang your spurs and chaps up for a spell. We got a fencin' job to do."

"Oh, hell! Where at?" I asked.

Jim pointed over east. "The Boss has decided that he wants to divide up our yearlin' pasture so we can put the shorts and the lightweights separate from the heavy cattle."

I nodded my head. "He's been thinkin' about doin' that for a couple of years now, hasn't he?"

"Yeah. I guess he figures this year will be a good time. We've had so much moisture, maybe the ground will be a little softer."

I squinted at him. "I doubt it. But for my sake, I hope so."

That night R.C. put up quite a fight, but lost. He objected, greatly, to Tio's raw-meat theory. But Tio was convinced that it would take all the swelling and discoloration out of his eyes. Even I agreed with Tio. Hell, I thought it was worth a try!

Tio slapped a hunk of what looked like raw round steak, crossed both eyes and the bridge of R.C.'s nose, and tied it down with an old Ace bandage that we used as leg wraps on horses. He went to sleep that night with us kidding him that he wouldn't even have to close his eyes to go to sleep. Even if he did open them, it was gonna be plumb dark!

The next morning we took the bandage off. It was amazing what it'd done! It'd drawn most of the discoloration out of his eyes, made the swelling go down. For the first time since the wreck he began to look like himself, except for the nose. The meat hadn't done a thing to straighten out his nose.

This was the day I'd been waiting for. Roberta Chism. I'd thought about her a lot and I'd even seen her in my dreams. It was going to be interesting to see if I had let my imagination run with me, or if what I'd remembered was really true.

R.C. asked if he could catch a ride into town with me. I told him he could. I didn't know exactly what I'd be doing, whether I'd spend the night in town, or come back home.

"It doesn't matter, Frank. And I'll get home by myself."

So I washed up Ol' Bullet. Even checked the backseat for pecker tracks. Mostly for my own self-esteem. It'd been so long since I'd gotten any nookie in the backseat of Ol' Bullet, I couldn't even remember when. It seemed like the only drought in this country was my sex life. I aimed to fix that first chance I got. But not tonight! No sir. Tonight I had a date with a fine young lady and I was sure looking forward to it.

I slicked up the best I could and put on my silver belly hat and my best pair of boots. Somehow I had a feeling it really didn't matter what I wore, that this Roberta Chism just might be more interested in the person than in the clothes. Leastwise, that's the impression I got from her.

When R.C. and I finally got to town, the first thing we did was go to the bank and cash our paychecks. I figured he'd want to go over and pick up his new boots right away, but the next thing he wanted to do was go to the post office.

I'd seen R.C. writing letters, but I never mailed anything for him, and he never got any mail there at the ranch that I knew of. But he got a passel of mail there at the post office. I had a feeling that he didn't want me to know where the letters he was writing were going and where the letters he was getting were coming from. It struck me as kind of silly, because I really didn't give a damn!

Then it was straight to Tony Bono's. Tony had sure enough done quite a job on R.C.'s boots. R.C. didn't even try them on at first. He just held them and looked at them, felt them. After a while he finally tried them on for fit. They fit him like a second skin. He pulled them off so he could stick his pant legs inside and walked around by the mirror and admired them. You could tell that Tony was quite proud of his work, too. R.C. paid for them, again in cash.

As we started to walk out the door, I said, "I don't believe I'd do that if I were you."

"Do what?" he said.

"Leave those pant legs tucked in," I said.

R.C. pulled his pant legs out. "I reckon you're right."

"That's a good word. Your vocabulary is increasin'!"

We walked out on the street. "Well," I said, "I don't know how in the hell I'm goin' to spend the rest of my day."

"Aren't you going down to Kitchins and have a little toddy?"

"Nope. I've got a date tonight. I'm gonna clean up my act. I'm not gonna show up with liquor on my breath."

R.C. shrugged his shoulders. "It's just as well. If you don't mind, you can go with me and help me to find a vehicle."

I looked at him in amazement. "A vehicle? A car?"

"No. What I really want is a pickup."

"What in the hell for? Where're you goin'?"

He just smiled.

"Are you thinkin' of leavin'?"

The smile left his face. "Well, there'll come that time before too long, Frank." But the smile returned when he said, "Really, I want to have a way to get over to Jaramillos' without going horseback or trying to get you to loan me Ol' Bullet."

"Oh, I see. Just what do you have in mind?" For all I knew, the way this guy operated he was going to buy himself a brand-new pickup. Not so.

"I don't really care what it looks like. Just so it runs good. Like a horse you know is sound."

"You're lookin' for a used pickup then?"

"Yep. That's what I'd like."

"Well, let's go see what we can find."

So we spent the whole afternoon going from one car lot to the other, all three, finding two that he was possibly interested in. Now these car dealers, like any in a one-stoplight town, didn't have salesmen. They were the dealer, the salesman, and their wife probably kept the books or they did it themselves. They did everything except the mechanic work, and some of them even did that. So R.C. knew the man he was dealing with was where the buck stopped. And he traded like it was the last penny he'd ever have in his life, and finally got a deal done. Shook hands on it and went in and filled out the papers.

Again, R.C. paid in cash. And it didn't take him long to pay for it. He laid down three bills and then a couple more. I knew he'd given over three hundred dollars for the pickup, so again we were back to those hundred-dollar bills I suspected.

He came out with a big grin. "What do you think?"

"Well, it looks like a pretty good deal to me. What was the final figure?"

"Three hundred and twenty-five."

"Well, you are now the proud owner of a 1950, three-quarter-ton, Ford pickup."

"Yeah. Let's drive it around awhile."

"Boy, you're a tough trader."

He looked at me with a knitted brow. "Isn't that the way you're supposed to do it?"

"I suppose so. Hell, I can't trade on nothin'. I won't try to jew 'em down any. Maybe a little on a horse or somethin' like that. But mostly I just pay what anybody asks."

"Everybody has a price and everything is overpriced. The idea is to get the closest to the man's price as you can get. Besides, what's wrong with jewin', or Jews for that matter?"

"Oh, hell. That takes too much finaglin' and too much time. I've got nothin' against Jews though."

"Good! But look at the money you can save."

"What's money to an Indian or cowboy?"

He took me back to my car. "Now," I said, "that you've got your own wheels, you're on your own. I guess you're goin' down to Kitchins."

"No, I'm going back out to the ranch."

"So early? How come?"

"Well, Francesca is coming over to visit her aunt tonight, and I thought I'd be there. We can spend tomorrow together."

"What you gonna call it, R.C.?"

"Call what?"

"Your new pickup. You gonna name it anything, or are you just gonna call it 'my pickup'?"

"Well, I suppose I ought to call it Old Red."

"That would be original."

He stood looking at the color of the pickup. "I don't know. You remember what the colors are as the sun goes down on the clouds? The sun's already down and it's still shining up on the clouds. That color?"

"Just at sundown."

"Yeah."

"Well, how about Sundown?"

The more I thought about it, it ought to work.

"Sundown, Sundown. Me and Old Sundown. I like the ring to it, Frank."

"Me, too. And let's leave Ol' Sundown and Ol' Bullet out here to get acquainted and you and me go get somethin' to eat."

When I finally got in Ol' Bullet and waved bye to R.C., I glanced over at the clock on the bank. It was five minutes to six. I didn't want to be early. I sure didn't want to be late. I wanted to be at the Chism house right at straight-up six o'clock. You might say I was a little nervous. I just hoped that the girl I'd last seen out at the Chism place was going to be the same girl that I was taking to the picture show.

I pulled up in front of their house and noticed a fairly new Chevrolet coupe sitting in the driveway. I had no idea what I was walking into, whether the whole family would be there, or maybe she came in by herself. But at least it appeared that somebody was going to be there.

I knocked and didn't have to wait long 'til the door opened. And I wasn't disappointed. She held the screen for me. "Hi, Frank. Come on in."

I took my hat off. "Hi." Walked in and stopped and waited for her while she closed the door. This girl was the prettiest thing I'd ever seen! When she turned back around, we were standing surprisingly close, and I looked down into those beautiful hazel eyes. And for the lack of nothing else to say, said, "How are you, short shot?"

A broad smile crept into her face and her eyes sparkled as she looked up at me. "You noticed I'm wearing flats, huh?"

I shook my head. "No. But I am lookin' down on you."

"Well, I could go in and put on some high heels if it would make you feel better."

"No, I think you're just right the way you are."

She casually reached over and grabbed me by the hand. "Come on in and sit down. If we have a little time, I have a few more calls I need to make for Daddy. I just came in."

"Are you here by yourself?"

"Yep. The girls and Mom and Dad stayed home."

"Oh?" Kind of with a question mark behind it.

"Now don't go getting any fancy ideas there, Big'un. This is our first date."

I stammered around. "Oh, Roberta, I didn't mean . . ."

"Frank, I'm teasing."

"Oh. Good." We both smiled.

As she made her calls, I got a chance to watch this lovely creature. Quite different from when I'd last seen her in work clothes. She had on a yellow summer dress that came I guess what you'd call fashionably, quite below her knee, with yellow flat shoes. She hadn't spent all her time in work clothes and with that hat on, because she had a suntan. Not dark brown, but just tan. And she was evenly tanned all over, at least the places that it mattered, I thought. Even her foot, as she had kicked off one of her shoes as she talked on the phone.

I hoped she didn't notice my intense appraisal, but I just couldn't keep from looking at her, admiring what I saw. In the horse world I would have said that she had smooth lines. She wasn't skinny. She was slender and very small at the waist. Her hips flared out just perfect, and had breasts to match. Her hair was hard to describe. Again, if it had been a horse, I could tell you in a second the color. Red roan, blue roan, blood bay, seal brown. I studied her hair, which was pulled back into a ponytail. Not the kind of a ponytail that you saw so many cheerleaders or young girls wear, that was high on the back of their head. This was pulled back and clasped at the nape of her neck. And I guess the color, the only color that came to mind, was honey-colored. I remembered out there at the ranch when the sun hit it, there would be even red highlights in it.

What was strange, but natural on her, she wore no makeup that I could see. Her nails weren't polished, her lips weren't ruby red, her cheeks didn't look like they had any powder on them, or eye shadow on her eyes. She didn't need any of this. Everything she had she came by natural. And nature, I always figured, was the best work of art that God ever made. I thought to myself, and I know it sounded like blasphemy, but I meant it reverently: Boy, when God made this young lady he did one hell of a job! It must have been like on Sunday when he rested and looked upon his work and called it good.

Finally she hung up the phone and came over to sit on the couch with me. "I'm sorry. I had to get those calls in for Dad."

"Oh, that's all right. We've got plenty of time." And I gazed into her eyes. Even her eyelashes and eyebrows were that same honey color.

"Well, you sure look nice."

She smiled. "Why, thank you, sir. You look nice, too."

I looked down at myself. "I look like any old boy standin' on any street corner in any western town in the United States."

She scowled at me. "Not hardly. I've always had a fondness in my heart for silver belly hats, shaped just right. Kind of like yours. And faded Levis."

With that we locked up and walked to the car. I opened the door for her as she got in. She smiled. "Thank you."

It surprised me when I got in on the other side and she scooted right over to the middle of the seat right beside me. She looked up at me as if to say "okay?" There was no need. I looked back at her. "Good move." And she smiled.

We went on down to the Luna Theater and parked. Saturday night would be a big night at our one little movie house in town. The movie was called "From Here to Eternity." As we had a little time before the movie started, we read the promo sheets out in front of the theater. A movie starring Burt Lancaster, Debra Kerr, Donna Reed, and Frank Sinatra.

"Frank Sinatra?" I said. "He's that skinny little singer that all the girls swooned over a few years ago. I didn't know he was an actor."

"I didn't either. But, I've heard of this movie. It's supposed to be a good one."

"I hope so."

She looked back. "Does it really matter?"

"No. Not really."

I asked her if she wanted some popcorn after we got inside.

"Sure. Sounds good."

So I bought two bags of popcorn even. We went in and found a place about two-thirds of the way back. I took my hat off and crossed my legs and set my hat on my knee.

She very casually linked her arm around mine and dug into her popcorn, just like we'd been going to the show together for years.

After the show we decided to tour downtown, which was all of two blocks long on one side of the street and two blocks long on the other. We walked up the street and I got on the outside, like a gentleman should. I had my hands stuck in my pockets and she linked her arm inside of mine, and we strolled slowly up the street looking in the windows. When she saw something that really caught her attention, she just stopped and pulled me with her. And I saw the fascination in the things that she did.

Things were going way too well in this relationship and this was just our first date. It was a relaxed thing and I enjoyed it!

We continued to stroll up the street. Few other people were on the street at this hour and it wasn't even late. The only cars that were parked on Main Street were down on the west end in front of the picture show, and across the street at Kitchins.

We stopped in front of the jewelry store and she pulled me over and made me look at all the goodies in the window. She exclaimed about a few things. "Oh, look, Frank. Isn't that pretty?"

I happened to notice that she didn't wear any jewelry at all. "I wouldn't think you'd be interested in jewelry. You're not wearing any."

"Oh, I have some jewelry and I wear it occasionally." Then she looked at me very coyly. "It would depend on who bought it for me though." And then the coyness was gone and the honesty was right back in her face and she smiled.

"I wish I could buy you anything you wanted in there. But I don't have enough money to buy feed oats for a nightmare."

And she laughed. "No, but you're rich, Frank."

"Hah! How do you figure?"

"Well, you're doing what you want to do, aren't you?"

"Yeah."

"I can tell by looking at you that you're in good health."

"That's true."

"And you're also a very handsome man."

"Well, thank you. I don't believe anybody has ever laid that on me before."

"Well, there's always a first time."

About that time a car drove in and parked at an angle, as did all the cars on Main Street. I didn't pay much attention, but I heard behind us, "My, what a lovely couple."

And I thought, oh, my God. It's Miz T.!

We turned around and sure enough the Boss and Miz T. were climbing out of their car and coming up to have a little visit with us. Miz. T. scurried over and gave Roberta a big hug and she said, "Land, child, I don't know how long it's been since I've seen you! My, you're a lovely lady."

Roberta smiled. "Why, thank you, Mrs. Stone. It's nice to see you, too."

How the ladies did carry on. I said, "Hi, Boss."

"Frank." And then he glanced at the jewelry shop window and glanced back at me and said, "Doin' some shoppin' are you?"

"Oh, we're just walkin' around after the movie. What brings you to town?"

"Oh, I had to come in and make some phone calls. But we're headin' back home right now."

About that time Miz T. turned around and said, "Frank, why don't you bring Roberta down to our place sometime? Remember, Roberta, you used to come down with your dad a lot."

"I know. But I've been away at school."

"Well, Frank, you bring her down now, hear?"

"Okay, Miz T. I'll bring her." And I might have known.

She said, "When?"

"I don't know. Whenever she can get away."

Miz T. turned around to Roberta. "Are you staying in town tonight, Roberta?"

"Yes, ma'am."

"Well, why don't you come down tomorrow?"

Roberta and I looked at one another and we hadn't made any plans past tonight. "I guess I could. What do you think, Frank?"

"That'd be great."

"Well, fine. We'll expect you then."

The Boss hadn't said much, just stood there and took it all in. Of course, he'd received a hug from Roberta at the beginning. The Chisms and the Stones had been friends for many years, and I suppose that Roberta had known them all her life. So, I was the one that was kind of an outsider on this deal.

After they left, Roberta held my hand and looked at me. "I hope I didn't get you in a trap."

"A trap? How?"

"Well, we just had a date for tonight and she invited me out tomorrow. You may have other plans for tomorrow."

I had to smile. "No. This pleases me plumb to death. I couldn't have planned it better myself!"

"Honest?"

"Honest."

"Okay then. I'm looking forward to tomorrow already."

"What do you want to do now?" I asked.

"I'm very happy, Frank, doing whatever you want to do." She thought about it a minute. "If it weren't for me, what would you do?"

"What do you mean if it weren't for you?"

"Like if you came in with some of your buddies, what would you do?"

I laughed. "Oh, I'd probably go out to the Water Hole, have a few drinks, visit a bit."

"So, having me around has changed your plans quite a bit?"

"Oh, no. Not really. I've enjoyed this evening very much."

"Frank, if you'd like to go out to the Water Hole and go dancing, then let's go."

"I just didn't want to get off on the wrong foot. I didn't know what you were used to and what you weren't used to."

"I know, and I respect you for it and I thank you for it. But I'm happy just being with you, wherever you want to go." Then she smiled. "Within reason."

"I've got to warn you. I've got a lot of rowdy friends."

"That doesn't bother me, as long as I'm with you."

We studied one another quite a little while. And then, like a couple of magnets, she leaned forward and I leaned forward 'til our lips met. A soft kiss.

I raised back just slightly. "Just one last thing."

She murmured, "Uh, huh?"

"What'll your dad think if he hears about this?"

"I'm old enough to make up my own mind, Frank. But, if it makes you feel better, I don't think Dad would care where I went, if it was with you." Our lips met again. Nothing wild, just a soft, tender kiss.

When we both backed off, I said, "Would you care to go dancing?"

"I'd love to!"

When we got to the Water Hole the parking lot was full and the joint was jumping.

I led Roberta out on the dance floor. That was the first time I'd gotten to hold her close. It was a slow ballad. I didn't even know the name of the tune. All I knew when I held her and she laid her cheek up against mine, she smelled and felt like heaven. And I didn't step on her foot one time.

I had just a couple of beers. When we got ready to leave, there was still half of Roberta's beer that hadn't been drunk. But we'd danced practically all the slow tunes, just to get close together. Kind of get used to one another. And some of the fast ones. She danced well, better than I did. But she was fun to dance with. As a matter of fact, she was just fun to be with.

We pulled up in front of Roberta's house. I turned off Ol' Bullet. "Do you want to listen to some music?"

She snuggled up to me. "Sure."

I turned on the radio and was just drifting down the dial looking for some good country music. I found a station that was playing some of the top twenties on the Hit Parade and I decided I'd leave it there.

This was the first chance we'd had to just relax and be with one another. And it felt good. I reached down and tilted up her chin very slowly so she had a chance to back away. Now was her chance. But she didn't. She responded by reaching her arm up and putting her hand behind my head and pulling me even closer.

I'd kissed many women and lots of girls, but I don't think anything had ever left an effect on me like this kiss did! Finally we came up for air. I had my arm around her and we leaned back on the seat. Just at that moment, we heard the announcer on the radio say, "And now, 'You Belong to Me,' by Jo Stafford." We sat there and listened to the song and didn't say a word until she was through. As soon as she was through, we both looked at one another.

I said, "I've heard that song before. But it never meant anything until now."

"Me, too."

And with that, we kissed again.

I'd gone as far as I needed to go, dared to go, or wanted to go. I felt like this was too important and just a shade delicate. So I walked her to the door, gave her a goodnight kiss, and told her I'd see her tomorrow.

She smiled and held both her hands up to my face. "I'll look forward to it."

CHAPTER

18

I got up and went down for some coffee and donuts and found Miz T., Francesca, and R.C. already at the table visiting over coffee. I listened to the conversation for a while, but I was looking forward to Roberta. I didn't know when she would be down this morning, but I'd be watching the road.

After a couple of cups of coffee and catching up on things that happened at the Jaramillos' and here at the Piedra, I asked R.C. if he wanted to help me go run in some horses.

I think he was glad to get out of there, for he said, "Sure!" When we got outside I asked him what his plan was for the day. "Oh, I don't know," he said. "Just spend it with Francesca and try and enjoy it. It's the first day we've had to spend together. How about you, Frank?"

"You know Roberta's coming down this mornin', don't you?"

"Yes. Miz T. told me."

"I thought maybe she'd like to go for a ride."

"Where are you going to go?" R.C. asked.

"Hell, anywhere. As far away from the house as I can get. I'm like you. Roberta and I need to get better acquainted."

We both saddled up and loped out into the horse trap and got around the band of saddle horses that we kept up. As we were bringing them down to the corrals, I could see off to the east the road coming into the ranch and there was a cloud of dust kicking up. I hoped this was Roberta.

And sure enough, no more than we had the horses penned and were pulling the saddles off our horses, than she drove into the ranch and stopped in front of the main house. I asked R.C. if he'd turn my horse out for me. I wandered on down toward the house. As she got out she saw me coming from up the hill and she stood by the car and watched me come, with a smile on her face.

When I got up close enough I said, "Hi."

She came around the car, which kind of shielded us from the main house. She reached over with her left hand and grabbed me by the little finger and stood on her tiptoes and gave me a quick kiss on the cheek. "Hi," she said.

I was kind of disappointed. She was wearing tennis shoes. I hoped she'd be wearing boots and planned on going riding. But it didn't make any difference. She looked great anyway. She had on Levis and a man's shirt that she'd rolled up the sleeves just below her elbows. She had left the shirttail hanging out and taken the front ends of the shirttails and pulled up around her waist and tied in a square knot around her middle.

Standing there looking at her, I thought it must be a miracle. The sun had risen twice in one day. Once at dawn and the other when I saw her bright and shining face!

"I had a wonderful time last night, Frank."

"Me, too. I have to admit, I've been watchin' the road for you."

"Good."

About that time, R.C. came down. She smiled and said, "Hi. Where's Miz T.?"

"She's inside waiting on you," I said.

"Well, let's not keep her waiting."

With that she linked her arm in mine and R.C.'s and we started for the house. When we walked into the kitchen we didn't see anybody. Kika and Miz T. had evidently moved to get more comfortable. When we hollered, Miz T. came in from the living room and gave Roberta a big hug and said, "We're so glad that you could come out this morning. It's been such a long time. Have you had breakfast?"

"Oh, yes, ma'am."

"Well, how about a cup of coffee and a sweet roll or donut?"

"Okay, that sounds good."

So Miz T. went scurrying around for a cup and saucer and Roberta pitched in and said, "Here, let me help."

R.C. peered around. "Where'd Francesca go?"

"Oh, we moved into the music room to get more comfortable. You fellows go on in. We'll be in in a minute."

Now I'd been in the living room and up in the Boss's office, but the doors had always been closed to the south of the living room. There was another room that faced the creek to the south. I guess it was used as a library and a sewing room and a so-called music room. It had glass windows all around the outside to where you had a view of Long's Creek, which was running clear and low this morning. You could see it through the cottonwoods.

We went in and sat down with Kika, and Miz T. brought Roberta in and introduced her to Kika. They smiled and knew one another, but not well. Of course, they were familiar with one another's families. But Francesca was a few years older than Roberta, and they didn't attend the same schools. Their families didn't mix in the same social circles.

So immediately the three of them, as women do, started talking about as fast as they could talk and seemed to be having a wonderful time. It always amazes me how women could find so many things to talk about and try to get it done in such a short time. They acted like they didn't have much time to get everything said that needed to be said. And perhaps there was some truth in this because R.C. and I both didn't intend to let our two ladies sit here and visit with Miz T. all day long.

R.C. noticed a piano over in the corner of the room. It wasn't one of those upright pianos that you see so many of. It was what I think they call a grand piano, the type that you can open the lid from the top and you saw people playing at concerts. Since we weren't engaged in the conversation, for that matter we could have been just decoration on the bookshelves, he sauntered over to the piano and raised the lid on the keys and lightly tapped a note. And then tapped another note an octave apart.

All of a sudden the women had stopped talking and were watching him. When he realized this he was rather embarrassed.

Miz T. said, "Why, R.C., I didn't know you had an interest in pianos."

"Oh, I don't much. I didn't realize you had a piano."

"Oh, yes. There was a time," and you could see kind of a faraway look in her eye, and she continued, "there was a time." She paused and I thought I'd help her out.

"There was a time what?"

"When I had hoped that our son or perhaps that we'd have more children, a daughter, that would play. But . . ." and then she seemed to come back to the present time. She smiled, "It never happened. The piano's really just for decoration."

"Can you play, R.C.?" Francesca asked.

R.C. kind of backed off and you could tell he was a little bit got by the question. "I used to, a little. But cowboys don't play the piano," and he looked at me, "do they, Frank?"

Of course I said, "Nah."

And all the women glared at me and said, "Why, I think it's a gift if somebody can play the piano. Sit down, R.C., and play."

"Ah, no. It's been too long."

Miz T. insisted. So R.C. pulled back the bench and sat down and fingered the piano a little bit, and low and behold he started to play.

Everybody sat, astonished, as he began to play some classical piece of music that I'd heard but didn't know the name of. He didn't stumble through it. He didn't hesitate. He played it like he owned it!

As he played I couldn't help but think about an old poem that had been a favorite of mine for years called "The Shooting of Dan McGrew." It took place in an Alaska gold-mining town. I once memorized the poem, I liked it so well. An old miner had come in all dog dirty and loaded for bear, spied a piano, and went over and sat down. If I remember right, the phrase went, "He clutched the keys with his talon hands, my God that man could play."

Finally R.C. finished and sat there kind of sheepishly, and the women and myself were astounded. Miz T. said, "I know the piece. That is 'Liebestraum.' Where on earth did you learn to play the piano like that?"

I could tell R.C. was embarrassed and wished that he'd never gone over to the piano. "Oh, my mother insisted that I take lessons."

"You read music, don't you?" Miz T. said.

R.C. nodded his head yes.

"You mean you can read those little dots on a paper?" I said.

R.C. again smiled and looked at me and nodded his head yes.

"That's amazing. I've always thought if you could read music and speak understandable English, you were bilingual."

"Do you play anything besides classical music?" Francesca asked.

And he just started out in a medley going back to "Alexander's Ragtime Band," "Bill Bailey Won't You Please Come Home," and kept coming without ever stopping, just going from one song to another until he got up into "Mona Lisa." He must have played all or part of a dozen songs. The ladies all clapped. And I had to clap, too. With an audience of four he had completely overwhelmed us.

"You wouldn't happen," I asked, "to know a song called 'You Belong to Me'? Jo Stafford sings it. It's been out maybe a year."

He sat with one hand and picked out the tune.

"That's it," I said.

He sat there and thought a minute and then started playing. I glanced over at Roberta. She was looking at me, smiling. Right in the middle of it, R.C. stopped and said, "Frank, do you know the words?"

"I think I do."

I had thought of the words and sang it all the way home from town last night. I have this knack for listening to the radio and if I hear a song two or three times that I really am interested in, I pick up the words very quickly.

So I walked over and leaned on the piano, facing the ladies, and just started singing. R.C. hit a note or two and told me to stop. "Try it right here. This is the key that will fit you best, I think."

He hit one note to set me on key. "I'll give you a little intro, a few bars," he said.

I'd sung with pianos in church and with dance bands before. So, it wasn't a new experience for me. But this guy was almost a pro and I'd had no idea he could do it! And when my cue came in, he looked at me and I began to sing.

I'll tell you what, we got the attention of those three ladies, and one in particular. As soon as it was over, I sat down. So did R.C. "I would appreciate it," he said, "if everybody didn't tell the Boss that I can play the piano."

And Miz T. was indignant. "I'd like to know why not?"

"Well, it's not something that I'd like to get around."

Miz T. smiled and shook her head. "We may be in the West, and a long way from what some people call real honest-to-goodness civilization. But, if there's one thing that everybody enjoys, it's music. And when we find someone as talented as you, both of you for that matter, it's like finding a lost treasure!"

We both mumbled, "Thank you."

"Speaking of things that are lost," Kika said, "if other plans aren't already made, I'll tell you what I'd like to do today."

And we both looked at her.

"I would like to go out to the old church and the mesa you call the Piedra. Do you think that could be arranged?"

And both R.C. and I shook our heads. "Sure."

"I'll tell you what," Miz T. said. "We'll pack the four of you a picnic lunch and you can go out there and look around and enjoy yourselves to your hearts' content. How would that be?"

I glanced at Roberta and she smiled and was agreeable.

So Miz T. shooed both of us fellows out of the house. "You fellows need to get out of our way now and we'll pack you a lunch. And that way I'll have time to visit with these two wonderful girls before you two ranch hands take them away from me."

Soon as R.C. and I were outside, "My God! You play great!"

"Sometimes I feel like it's a curse."

"I don't know why in the hell you'd feel that way. I wish I could play the piano like that."

"I wish I could sing like you. If you want to hear a terrible noise, just listen to me sing sometime."

"Well, between the two of us, you know what? We could make pretty good music."

R.C. smiled. "You're right."

"Where did you study?"

He looked at me with a shy smile and shook his head. "Oh, back home when I was growing up."

"Oh. That's right. Where was that?"

"Come on, Frank."

"Okay. So, it's none of my business."

"Right. Ask me no questions and I'll tell you no lies."

We sat up on the porch of the bunkhouse. I told him again that I'd like to take Roberta for a ride, but I didn't know where we'd find her a pair of boots. I couldn't imagine her riding in those tennis shoes. Asked R.C. if he and Kika wanted to ride with us. I'd noticed that Kika had on Levis, too. Funny thing was, she had on tennis shoes, just like Roberta did.

"No," R.C. said. "I thought I'd take my new pickup."

"Well, it's not far up there. Could you mess around a little while and take your time gettin' up there so Roberta and I would have time to kinda make a circle and get there about the same time you do?"

"I think Francesca and I can find a way to kill some time. Maybe we'll drive up the river and look for arrowheads and talk a little bit."

"Okay. This is the plan then. As soon as they're ready, I'll get Roberta and if she wants to, we'll go a-horseback. If she doesn't, we're gonna have to figure out another deal. I guess I could take Ol' Blue. I want to get Roberta off to myself."

R.C. looked at me. "I think in this situation, your words would be, 'same dog bit me'?"

"Yep."

I pulled out my pocketknife and whittled. R.C. fiddled around making small talk until finally the girls came out and hollered at us.

I don't know where Belle had been when Roberta drove up. Seldom did she ever miss a car that pulled into the ranch. She was our watchdog and unofficial guardian. But she was here with me now.

So when the girls walked up, Roberta bent down and Belle went running to her. "This must be Belle."

"Look out," I said. "She'll tear your arm off!"

"Oh, I can see how fierce she is."

Belle wagged her whole rear end. And it was an instant friendship. She talked to Belle just like she'd talk to another human being. She rubbed her ears and stroked her head. "I've heard about you, Belle. You're somethin' special."

Belle looked at her with the same eyes that she would look at me, with nothing but love and compassion.

"Roberta," I said, "I thought maybe you'd like to take a ride horseback, but I see you don't have any boots on."

She looked down at her tennis shoes. They were just the old canvas low-topped, slightly dirty, run-of-the-mill tennis shoes. "That's all right, Frank. I don't need boots."

"Well, I never like to see anybody crawl on a horse with tennis shoes on. Maybe you'd rather ride up in the pickup?"

"No. I'd rather go horseback with you," and then looked down and said, "and Belle."

"Okay. What are you gonna do, R.C.?" As if I didn't already know.

He turned to Kika. "Want to ride in my new pickup?"

Kika looked at the pickup. "It doesn't look so new to me."

"That's the point. It isn't new, but it's new to me."

Kika laughed. "Does it run?"

"Sure, let me show you."

"We'll see you in an hour or so up at the church," I said.

"Okay," R.C. said.

So Roberta and I and Belle started for the barn. Halfway up she reached over and took me by the hand. I was glad the Boss had left early. Me holding hands with a girl walking around on this place made me nervous.

I had her crawl up on the fence and look at the twenty or so horses that R.C. and I had run in. "Pick you out one. They're all broke to ride. Some better than others."

She pointed out to the middle of the corral and said, "How about the big, snipped-nose sorrel horse?"

She surprised me because that horse had a little more thoroughbred in him than the normal run of our horses. He was a long, tall, rangy type of horse, a good-looking thing. Easy riding.

"Okay."

I got his bridle, and got my own for my horse, and handed her the bridle. "Do you need any help?"

She looked at me out of the corner of her eye. "You've got to be kiddin'."

We walked in and slowly approached them. And after cutting them out a little bit, held our hands out and walked up and bridled our horses. As we both walked out of the corrals, she said, "What do you call this horse, Frank?"

"Oh, it's real original. We call him Snip."

She laughed. "That'll do."

"Come on in the saddle house here. We'll try and find you a saddle."

"I don't need a saddle, Frank."

"What do you mean, you don't need a saddle?"

"I grew up riding bareback. Dad was always afraid that one of us kids would get hung up in a stirrup, so we all learned to ride bareback before we ever learned to ride in a saddle."

"Well, that's where you've got me. I couldn't ride a hayrack with my shirttail tacked to the floor without a saddle. I use my feet too much and put too much weight in my stirrups."

"Well, it's all in what you get used to. 'Course it kinda makes my . . .' and she looked down between her legs and dusted off her butt with both hands. "Kinda makes my rear end dirty." With that she smiled, "And I'll smell like a horse the rest of the day, if you don't mind?"

"I don't mind, if you don't. As a matter of fact, you and the smell of a horse are probably two of my most favorite scents."

She laughed.

I saddled up. "Do you want me to give you a leg up?"

"Oh, no. I can get on him."

And I thought to myself, this I've got to see. A horse this tall, and she's going to get up on him Indian-style. I thought I'd just watch and see how she did it, and I'll tell you, it was the slickest thing I ever saw!

She reached up and grabbed a hank of mane, right on top of the withers. And with a swing of her leg, straight up, she was astraddle that horse in a split second!

I stood there. "That was amazin'!"

She shrugged. "Not if you've been doin' it all your life."

We rode north up on top of the breaks and headed west. There wasn't a cloud in the sky. The sun was so bright, shining off her hair. She looked like an Indian princess, sitting there horseback with her legs slightly in front of her and riding so relaxed.

When we got on top we hit a lope to where there was an outcropping of chalk-colored caliche rock that came out to a point. There we stopped, dismounted. I took the hobbles that I'd tied around Snip's neck and put them around his forefeet, and did the same to my horse and tied the reins up around their necks. We walked out on that point to sit and looked off into the breaks.

"What's this about the church and the Piedra rock that Francesca was talking about?" Roberta asked.

So I filled her in briefly on what had taken place over at the Jaramillos'. She thought it fascinating. I told her that we hoped to find these, but I doubted that it would ever come about. It had happened too long ago. I ran through the problems that might crop up if something didn't happen.

But this wonderful Sunday afternoon wasn't to debate history or to search for hidden treasure. As far as I was concerned, the main object was to get to know this wonderful creature that, I hated to admit, I was fast becoming very, very fond of.

As we sat and looked out over the valley, she linked her arm through mine, rested her hand on my forearm, and reached across with her other hand and put it on top of her own. Both hands were there on my arm. I liked that. And because touching and the familiarity of the way that she laid her head on my shoulder, kind of like snuggling and kissing, came so easy for her, made it easy for me, too. Was this something special? But something special hardly makes sense because we hadn't had enough time to really get anything established. I was by nature kind of standoffish and a loner and not one to show emotions. And I knew it.

She showed her emotions and didn't seem to care. And as I kissed her, I thought, thank your lucky stars she's here. Thank God for such a great day. Time will tell, anyway. So, I made up my mind to just enjoy the day for what it was and for whatever it brought.

CHAPTER

19

We stood and looked at the church. The adobe plaster had practically all fallen off to expose the adobe bricks that it was built with.

"Let's approach this church like it's the first time we ever saw it and we're very interested in every aspect of it. Be aware of anything that looks out of the ordinary. Be curious about anything that doesn't seem to fit, where there might be a door or an opening, or, I don't know, just anything. Okay?" I said.

"I had," Kika said, "an opportunity to talk to Abuela Elena. She remembers this church and village when it was a happy place."

"Who," I asked, "is this Elena lady?"

Kika laughed. "Remember the old lady that came up and gave the herb-tea potion to R.C. when you were over at our place?"

"Oh, yeah. I'll never forget her."

"That's Abuela Elena."

"That's her name, Abuela Elena?"

"Well, it means Grandmother Elena."

"Is she your grandmother?"

"No, it's just what we all call her. She only speaks Spanish. I think she can understand English, but she refuses to speak it. I had a talk with her and I couldn't believe that she could remember when this place was inhabited by our people and was a thriving community."

"My God," I said. "Do you realize how old that must make her?"

"Yes. Nobody knows. I don't even think she does. But she has given me some idea about what we might find and where we might find it. I'll explain as we go along.

"But, for just a moment," she said, "let's take a look at everything around and even outside the fence, soak it into your mind. This place may hold secrets we'll never know about and some that we may, if we're lucky.

If we take all of this in now, then we'll be able to at any time, at any place, talk about and bring up from our mind and compare thoughts with one another."

With that, we stood there and tried to imagine what this place must have looked liked seventy-five to eighty years ago, to transport our minds back in time to where we could almost hear children laughing and the breeze. The town of Peralta was populated with families and children and their animals; mass was said on a regular basis and candles were lit and prayers offered for loved ones. The hope of a better life and the great beyond, a certainty that beat within the heart of the people that used this church.

It was mostly like any other Spanish church that you would find around the state. Narrow to look at from the front, but long in length, with a tower above the entrance that still held an old cast-iron bell. It made you wonder where the bell came from and where it was cast and how long ago.

I had cast many a critical eye on everything from the ladies to horseflesh to cattle. But never had I looked with such intensity and thoughtfulness as I did at this old, dilapidated church. And the longer I looked, the more began to catch my eye.

You could still see the ends of the vigas, the pine poles that held the roof up, extending beyond the walls on each side of the church, weathered through the years as they were. The bell tower was a square structure above the door that had smaller vigas. On top stood a lone cross. Everything was flat-topped, nothing pitched in the way of a roof. The tower had four windows facing in the four directions to expose the bell. And, I suppose, to accommodate the sound that the bell would make when rung. There were no steps leading into the church. It looked as if it sat flat on the ground. As we entered the churchyard we could see that there was sandstone rockwork in front of the church, as if there was a floor to a porch, but no roof. The door had been carved at one time, but was terribly weathered and cracked.

All of us were taking our time looking over everything that our eyes could take in and etch it in our minds. The hinges on the door had been made many years ago at a blacksmith's forge and were rather crude, but quite functional. Also, the handle and the latch to the door were made out of forged iron. There were two windows on each side of the door, up too high for anybody on the outside or the inside of the church to see out of. And I suspected because it faced east, the windows were for the purpose of letting the morning light flood inside the church.

I reached for the door handle. But before I opened the door I said, "Be careful in here. There's no tellin' what you might find. I was in here over a month ago and it's a good place for snakes, large or small. So watch where you're walkin'."

Which made Roberta grab ahold and hug a little tighter. I opened the door with the creaky old hinges, which was expected as it had had no oil or lubricant for all those years. And we all walked into the front of the church.

The floor was littered with pigeon droppings. After taking my boot and scraping around on it a little bit, it appeared to be almost like cement.

"I wonder," R.C. said, "how they packed the ground so hard."

"You're not going to believe this," Kika said, "but I've always heard, and I think it can be verified, that in the old days they would take adobe or caliche mud and mix it with ox blood and smooth it out and let it dry. And it would set up a lot in the manner of concrete."

It crossed my mind that I'd heard the same thing, only it hadn't been used for floors. It had been used by the Comanches to seal up springs out on the staked plains and the High Plains, so that the white man couldn't find water. The Comanche could come back and find where they had done this and obtain the water. Then seal it up again and go on, hoping to drive the white man off of the buffalo grounds.

We all stood and just looked into the church. R.C. said, "I wonder why they made it so narrow?"

I looked up and the vigas of pine beams were plainly visible. "I don't know. But, I'll bet that they made it this width to accommodate the poles that hold up the roof."

"Oh, I think you're right. I wonder where they had to go to get the poles. Where are the nearest pine trees?"

I shook my head. "The mountains to the west, I guess. Or up north on Sierra Grande or on Johnson Mesa." Anyway you looked at it, they would have had to haul those vigas a long way. But, then, back there in that day and time, time wasn't all that important, I don't suppose.

The latias on top of the vigas that held up what I supposed was a sod roof were split wood poles of some sort, it was hard to tell, set at an angle kind of in a herringbone design. I supposed they could have been found locally.

What we were looking for, we weren't quite certain. A place, somewhere, that a box or a container of some sort could be hidden or sealed away in a short amount of time. There were any number of places that something could be hidden and the adobe dug out, something put in it and then sealed back over with adobe and made to look natural. But this would take too much time. We all realized that whatever took place would have had to be done in a great hurry.

Roberta and I walked back to the front door and looked to the south toward Long's Creek. I gazed out the door to the breaks and to the hills to the south and said, more or less to myself, "That's where they had to come from."

"Who?" she said.

"The Comanches. When they raided this place, the chances are that they would have come from the south."

"Why?"

"Mainly because it looks to me like that's the best cover. Wouldn't you think?"

She looked east down the valley and then back to where I had pointed out the breaks. "I suppose you're right."

Then we looked to the north and there stood the Piedra, high and mighty. I said, "To make it over there would have been the only salvation. Can you see that fault line running up the south side of the rock?"

She nodded her head yes.

"That's the only way I know of up there. Now, I don't know how long it would take somebody to get from here over to there. But from the time the attack was spotted, or the people here in this community suspected something was wrong, what would have been the first thing they'd have done?"

Roberta thought a minute, bit her lower lip. "I bet they would have rung the bell to give warning to everybody."

"That makes sense. Then what?"

"I don't know. Try to form some sort of defense, I would suppose."

"You're right. It's only the law of self-preservation. They would have to fight back in some way. And that would buy some time, wouldn't it?"

"From what you told me, that's all it bought, just time."

We walked back in the church. But we could find nothing. Nothing at all.

"I really didn't expect to find anything," Kika said. "I was just hoping. You can always hope."

R.C. said, "We've got to look at this logically. Maybe try to reenact what happened and what would have been done."

"Roberta and I have just been doing a little of that. We walked out the doorway, and it seems to me that the only way the Comanches could have come was from the south, across the river. The villagers would have rung the bell, Roberta thinks, to give the warning. Then they would have set up some sort of defense."

R.C. agreed. "Look up toward the bell tower. How would they ring the bell?"

"In most Catholic churches," Kika said, "there would have been a balcony back there where the choir would sing. There would have been a hole in the floor of the bell tower with a rope hanging down that you would pull to ring the bell." There was no balcony anymore.

"But how would you get to the bell tower in order to fix the clapper on the bell, attach a rope to the bell? Would you have to do it from the outside?"

R.C. was studying the ceiling. "I don't think so. Look."

Over in the corner you could faintly see, even though the latias were matched up, a trapdoor that either led to the roof or to some space that would take you over to the bell tower.

This gave Kika great hope. "Maybe that's what happened! That's the only place in this church that we've seen that's gone undetected."

As we examined the ceiling and the trapdoor longer, you could see where there were hinges attached to the wall and to the trapdoor. "Well, that's just great," I said, "but how do we get up there?"

"We've got to get up there," R.C. said. "Just to check it out. If no other reason, just to prove ourselves wrong."

"Maybe," I said, "I can get to it from the outside. Let's look. How far up there do you think it is?"

R.C. studied a minute. "It's probably twenty, twenty-five feet, I guess."

As we walked outside Roberta loosened up a little bit, and just held my hand. We walked around the south side of the church. As I examined the side of the church, I said, "I think I know a way to get up."

R.C. had just come around the corner. "What?"

"I think I can get up there on the roof, if that's where that trapdoor goes."

It was a little hard to tell because the walls extended higher than the roof itself. You could tell because there were drain holes between the vigas, spaced evenly alongside the wall.

"What's your plan on getting up there?" R.C. asked.

"Well, I've got a lariat rope. Maybe I can throw a loop around one of those vigas that sticks out there, and some way shinny up that rope and get on the roof."

"Get the rope. It's worth a try," he said.

I got the rope, shook out a loop. With a twenty-eight-foot rope, and me standing six foot tall and my arms reaching even higher than that, it looked like it wouldn't be too hard to do. But the angle of the viga sticking out was going to put a little test to my ability.

But after about a half a dozen throws, my loop settled over the end of the viga. I used the fishing method with the rope to get the loop closer to the building before I pulled it tight. At least the viga didn't look as rotten there. I pulled on it and it creaked. "Now, if I can just crawl up this rope. It's not big enough to get a real good hold on."

"I'm lighter than you, Frank, and I'll give it a try." R.C. walked back over to the pickup and got a pair of gloves. As he put his weight on the end of the rope he said, "The end of that viga might break."

"Well, it's not very far. I can't catch you, but I'll try to break your fall," I said.

He reached up high and said, "Are you ready?"

"I think so."

So with that he jumped and pulled himself up. With his feet on the wall and going hand over hand he started upward, at times his feet getting much higher on the wall than his head. It took great strength to pull on that small rope, hand over hand, to reach the viga. But he was successful. In no time at all he had ahold of a viga. Now if he could just get up on top of it and straddle it.

He was a wiry little booger. I'll give that to him. The girls all clapped when he finally slung his leg over and pulled himself up astradlle the viga, right side up. He turned his toes out and tipped his hat and smiled real big. "There's nothing to it!"

"Well, why don't you get on with what you're up there for?"

"Give me time." And he crawled over the wall of the church and was out of sight.

We backed off a ways from the church trying to see him. For a while he was completely out of sight. Directly he popped his head up over the wall. "This whole roof is just like the floor of the church. Must be that blood and caliche thing. It looks like it would hold water and shed it like a duck's back. The trapdoor just comes up on top of the roof. But let me check out the bell tower." And again he was gone.

Then to our surprise we heard the first ring. So clear and so mellow. Then the second ring. We all looked at one another and smiled.

"I'll bet," Kika said, "that's the first time that bell has rung in three-quarters of a century."

"Do you suppose that over a period of time a bell is like a violin, that the older it gets, the sweeter the sound?" I asked.

"I don't know," Roberta said. "But the sound is beautiful."

We all just stood and listened. And finally, it quit.

R.C. popped his head over the wall again. "What did you think of that?"

"That was beautiful," Kika said.

"It's amazing," R.C. said. "Everything still works. The rope is long since rotted off, but the chains still hang down from the rocker arm. But, I've also got bad news. There's nothing anywhere for something we're looking for to be hidden. But, I'll tell you what. This roof in itself would make a pretty good fortress. With enough guns and enough people, you could make quite a stand from here. And they knew it. Look what I found."

With that he began to throw things off to us. It was unbelievable! There was an arrow, warped and darkened with age. But definitely an arrow, with feathers on the end long since gone. There was a notch for the bowstring and tied on the end was a flint arrowhead. Even the rawhide that tied the flint to the shaft had survived the ravages of time. As I held the arrow in my hand I could feel my chest tighten and a lump come in my throat. My heart beat just a little faster.

Finally he said, "I'm coming down."

He scooted out onto the viga and took my loop off the end of it. He threw the whole rope over the viga and stuck his foot in the loop. He made sure it was tight and let himself down off the other side. Going hand over hand, keeping his weight on the other side of the loop, he lowered himself to the ground easily.

"That was pretty slick," I said. "You're always surprising me. How did you learn to do that?"

"I'll have you know I was a Boy Scout!"

I shook my head and smiled at him. "I'll bet you were."

"I know it's a disappointment, but there's nothing. No hiding places, no doors, nothing on the roof. And another thing, the bell was forged in Florence, Italy, in 1736. What a story it could tell, if it could talk."

"It can talk," Roberta said. "We just can't understand it."

We went back to the pickup and put away our relics, ropes, and gloves. "Well, what now?" I asked.

"We're not near through," Kika said. "Let's walk around the outside of the church. We need to go through the cemetery, the well. The well could be the place!"

"I hate to disappoint you," I said, "but not a chance."

"How do you know?" she asked.

"Because Jim and I have worked on that well a number of times. I wouldn't go down in it, but Jim would. Things have fallen into it and it needed to be mucked out. It's a real shallow well, just one joint of pipe. But if anything were down there, Jim would have seen it and so would've I. It looked pretty scary to me, like it might cave in at any minute. So, there's no sense in even looking in the well."

We split up in pairs and went around the church as thoroughly as we could, looking for a cellar, a cistern, evidence of anyplace where something might be stored. And found nothing.

When we entered the gate of the cemetery I said, "There's an identical wrought-iron fence around the grave up on top of the Piedra."

"Now, that's Dad's doing," Kika said. "He had our blacksmith make this fence in sections and brought it over and put it up around the cemetery. And up on top, too."

There were more graves than I had thought. We counted fifty-four in all. And out of those, thirty-three had identical dates: April 23, 1874. There were a few before that time, about a dozen, beginning with the oldest grave in 1833, up until the early 1870s. And there were a few graves that were relatively new, as compared to the others, the newest grave being 1926. On all the graves someone had remembered, because there were plastic flowers, some faded from the sun and from time, and others much newer. So, someone still came and paid their respects.

Most of the grave markers were made of sandstone but were engraved by someone that knew what they were doing and was quite artistic to record the names and dates into the stone. Sandstone is easy to cut into. But what instrument they'd used to make these engravings, I had no idea. I suppose a chisel of some sort. But it was done by expert hands.

Those crosses that were made of wood were by far the hardest to read any kind of inscription on. You had to run your finger almost along each letter, and it was all in Spanish. The wood had weathered and split and cracked with time.

I didn't know what we were looking for in there and what we could possibly find. We were just looking for clues, anything that might help.

"Is anybody hungry?" Kika asked.

"I don't know about anyone else," I said, "but I'm starved."

"Can you wait until we get up on top of the Piedra?"

"Sure. That'd be a great place for a picnic. What do you think, Roberta?"

She shielded her eyes against the sun and looked up toward the towering mass of stone. "I'd like that."

So Roberta and I let our horses graze and piled in the pickup, all in the front, and drove over to the base of the Piedra at the trail. R.C. and I carried the lunchbox and the Thermos jug, and we scrambled up the trail that led to the top.

Once on top it was like it had been before. A beautiful sight to look all around, see the country for miles in every direction. And to see the one solitary, lonely grave.

Kika went over to the grave and stood beside it. And like Miguel and Joaquin, knelt and crossed herself, and then stood holding onto the little wrought-iron fence that surrounded it.

"Have you ever been up here?" R.C. asked.

"No, never," shaking her head. I've heard my father speak of it. And I've always wanted to come."

"I'm hungry," I said. "How about eatin'?"

So we spread our blanket out on the sand beside the grave and all sat down, cross-legged, Indian style. They opened up the basket and brought out all the goodies.

As we all sat eating, each in our own thoughts, I hated to break the spell. But I said, "I suppose today has been rather a disappointment to you, Kika, not finding anything."

She shrugged her shoulders. "I knew when we started there was very little chance. But I had to look. Thank you for helping me."

We ate in silence for a while. I looked over at the grave and the fence. "Did you ever ask your dad how he got that headstone and fence up here?"

"Oh, yes. He told me that the trail was not always like it is now, that it was much wider and had even been cleared. In 1901, as a wedding present to his first wife, who was a Martinez, I think the Padre Martinez who is buried over there was her uncle, and as an act of faith to God, he erected the monument."

"That was over fifty years ago," I said. "I can see how the sandstone would flake and break off and clutter up the trail. I guess that explains how they got the body up here."

"There's another story about the body being up here," Kika said. "I'll get to that. Abuela Elena shed some light on that and I need to tell you what her story was."

"Well, before you do, how did your dad know where the grave was?" I asked.

"I'll tell you as best I can what Dad told me. The grave itself had been well known for years and it had a small, crude, sandstone marker. He just erected the monument. He assumed that the sandstone marker was at the head of the grave itself, although there was no depression or an outline of rocks to where the grave would be. He just left the old marker where it was and placed the new one there," and she pointed with her hand, "just west of the old one. Then he erected the fence around what would be considerable space for a grave. Of course, the fence was brought up in sections, and riveted after it was put in place."

R.C. had been listening intently. "Where did he come by the inscription he put on the stone?"

"He copied the exact words off the old sandstone marker."

"Has anybody noticed the date on that tombstone?"

We were sitting there so close that it could easily be read. We all looked. The date was April 20, 1874.

"Doesn't that strike anybody as odd?" Roberta asked. "He died three days before the massacre."

"It would seem that way," R.C. said.

"Kika, the inscription. Can you translate it?"

"Abajo verdad. Arriba cielo. Below the truth, above heaven."

"Well," I said, "I guess 'below' meant the village and how cruel this world can be, and 'above' in heaven speaks for itself."

"I suppose," Kika said. "But you know, in speaking with Abuela Elena I learned some things that puzzled me. I tried to cross-check some of her story with Dad, but especially on this first subject he was very reluctant to talk. Ashamed possibly."

"Ashamed of what?" I asked.

"Well, my people. When I say 'my people,' I'm talking about my ancestors who settled in the Ute valley in the beginning. We practiced the Catholic religion, but with Penitente influence."

"What is Penitente?" R.C. asked. "I'm not familiar with the term."

"History is not my long suit, but I'll tell you the best I can. During the settling of New Mexico the church played probably the largest part. If it weren't for the Franciscans and that order of the Catholic Church, I doubt if New Mexico, even with its prospects for gold and precious metals, would have ever been settled. Our culture has always been built around the Church.

"Around 1680," she continued, "the Pueblos up and down the river, which was the lifeblood of New Mexico, revolted and destroyed the churches. There was a general uprising, and they drove all the Spanish out of New Mexico and they didn't return until 1703. During that time there was no clergy. But the seed of Catholicism was here. Those who remained retained their Catholic beliefs. But without leadership it began to get confused with fiction rather than fact.

"So, without trained priests from the seminary to guide us in our religion, it began to be made up as we went along, remembering what we could from actual teachings and supplemented by what we thought would be the way God would want the Church to be. Although I'm sure this is true, as I've heard it from other people, Dad will not talk about it. But it all ended and the clergy came back, and the government, about when my first ancestors came to this land with De Vargas in 1703.

"Now the Penitente, some people think, is a radical branch of the Catholic Church. It still exists today in some parts of New Mexico, and I suppose in other places in the United States and Mexico. When the French bishop Lamy took over the church in 1850 he outlawed the Penitente faction, and was successful to a degree. But we lived so far away from the Mother Church and from the Rio Grande Valley that we continued the Penitente way.

"Grandmother Elena told me that Padre Martinez held Easter services up here on this mesa, where we sit, every year. And people would come from all over the surrounding country for these services. This trail was maintained for the pilgrimages, the holy treks that were done in the Penitente fashion. Like the suffering that Christ endured, people carried crosses on their shoulders and climbed this great rock. They beat upon themselves. Of course flagellation and a crown of thorns and the reenactment of the crucifixion were all part of the Penitente religion.

"So you see, this great rock, the Piedra, was used as a religious holy place back then. But I want it understood that the Penitente faction of our religion has not been practiced around here in years. Except, perhaps, in Abuela Elena's mind."

"How old was she," I asked, "when this tragedy occurred?"

"All she's said is that she was a young woman."

"Do you really think she could remember anything about all this?" I asked.

"Well, you know how old people are sometimes. They remember the past much better than they do the present. Now here is what she told me, that no one," and she looked all around as she spoke, "survived the massacre."

Kika went on. "She said that upon the discovery of the massacre by the people from our church down on the Ute, everyone who lived in the village was accounted for, except the Padre."

And we all looked at one another. We had all stopped eating and were listening intently to Kika. Roberta scooted around in front of me, sat between my legs, and leaned back against my chest. She leaned her head way back and looked at me upside down.

"Okay?"

I smiled and leaned down and touched my nose to hers. "You bet. Go on, Kika, you've got us in suspense now."

"They didn't know whether he might have been captured or whether the Comanches in their hatred for a man of the cloth had mutilated him and destroyed his body. Or, perhaps he had escaped some way. Then there was a thought that he had not even been here at the time the massacre took place. You see, he traveled from parish to parish. Grandmother Elena said it was not until much later, and she can't remember how long, that someone found the sandstone grave marker up here on top of the Piedra.

"But here is an interesting thing, possibly the most interesting thing I got from her. Now listen to this! There were no bodies found up here on top of the mesa. All the people of the village were accounted for and their bodies were all on the bottom. No one was found dead on the mesa. And yet, a Padre had been buried here."

"I'm really puzzled," R.C. said. "I can't keep from thinking about how the date on his grave is three days earlier than those who died in the massacre and were buried in the old churchyard." R.C. looked at me. "What do you think, Frank?"

"I don't know. I just don't know."

"Maybe he came up here under his own power and died or was killed up here."

"Well, you've found a way to keep from having to haul him up that steep trail, coffin, body, and all. But if you're right, then who in hell buried him? And then what? Did those that buried him go back down and walk into a massacre? They didn't stay up here and get killed. The old lady said there were no bodies up here."

R.C. shook his head. "I don't know. Wouldn't the Indians come up here and find the grave and maybe, oh, I don't know what they might do."

"I know about Comanches and I'll tell you what I think. I don't think Indians would desecrate a grave. They were capable of almost unheard-of types of torture and inhumane treatment when somebody was alive, and mutilation afterward. But after someone was buried on a piece of holy ground, I don't think the Indians would touch it. Comanches or whoever. The Comanches and Kiowas were by no means dumb or ignorant savages like so many back then would think. They had their god or gods, and they knew that these people who lived here had their god and a place of worship. They didn't destroy the church for fear that maybe the two gods were one and the same, or connected together in some way between the two cultures. If that makes sense."

"I think it does," R.C. said.

"On second thought," I said, "probably what makes better sense is that the church is made out of adobe, and mud doesn't burn real good. And they didn't have any way to tear it down. It wasn't worth the time and effort."

"How do you explain the village then?" R.C. asked.

"It probably wasn't built as substantial as the church. More like a *jacal.* They had more wood in the roof and that's probably what burned.

As far as the adobes, they sit out unprotected from cattle. For years cattle have been wandering in and out of them and rubbin' against 'em. Without a roof to protect the adobe, and with the rain, they just more or less disintegrated."

"That's one place we haven't looked yet," Kika said.

"Well, not today," I said. "I've walked through there and I've never seen anything that would indicate what we're lookin' for. But this has been quite an afternoon."

"I'll say," R.C. said. "I'm really puzzled. I feel like there's an answer in here somewhere. It just doesn't make sense."

I looked at R.C. "Well, maybe the reason it doesn't make sense, R.C., is that old Grandmother Elena was right. Maybe this Piedra is a holy place and a miracle took place here."

I felt Roberta's arms tighten around my knees and I looked at Kika and she raised both eyebrows. We all looked around to the outlying areas and to what was visible from there on top.

Just before we left, R.C. went over to the grave and I heard him say, "Abajo Verdad. Arriba Cielo. Below Truth. Above Heaven. April 20, 1874." He seemed to study awhile and kind of memorize it. Then he turned and walked back to us and we started on down the trail.

We wound down into the bottom and crossed the creek, went up through the breaks. When we got up on the prairie, we could look down and see the little dot of Sundown still parked where it was, now in the shade of the sun as it lowered itself behind the church. I had a feeling that they weren't still poking around in the old Peralta ruins, but they might be getting better acquainted, as R.C. said.

Roberta and I rode alongside and talked. "What do you think of my friends?" I asked.

"I like them."

"I hope we didn't bore you with this wild tale and adventure that's goin' on."

"Oh, no. I'm fascinated by it. I'd like to help if I could."

"Well, you helped by just bein' along."

She smiled. "Frank, will this snip horse I'm riding lead?"

"Sure. Why?"

"I was just wondering." And directly she said, "How about the horse you're riding? Does he ride double?"

"Oh, yeah. Why, what's the matter? Is Snip gettin' lame?"

"No. I am. Stop a minute."

So I pulled up and she slid down off Snip and handed me the reins. Looked up into my face and said, "How about a hand up?"

I leaned over and offered my arm, which she grabbed just above the elbow. She swung a leg up and I pulled, and the next second she was sitting behind me. She put her arms around my waist and pulled herself up as close as she could to my backside. I felt her lay her chin on my backbone. "Okay?"

I laughed and said, "You bet! I don't know when we'll see each other again. We have a fencin' job this week, so I expect I'll have to work Saturday, seein's how I'll want part of next week off." I turned my head and asked her, "Do you know what happens next week?"

"Sure. Cowboy Christmas."

I laughed. "You stole my line. Where did you hear that?"

"My daddy's a cowboy, too."

"Well, the Fourth of July is a welcome holiday for a man with a thirst and that likes excitement."

"Are you planning on entering this year?"

"I always do. I'm pretty sure that Dee Jensen will be in with his doggin' team. He and I go back a long ways, so if he's here I know I'll be mounted right and sure enough be a-horseback. Might get lucky enough to win a paycheck. I could use it."

We reached the point where we'd have to start back down through the breaks again where the headquarters lay below us, and it was Roberta's idea to get back on her horse, which I appreciated. I could just imagine what the Boss would think if he saw us riding double, leading one horse, coming into the house. I'd never live it down.

We stood out in front of the house and talked awhile. I think both girls liked one another very much, and that pleased me. They said that they'd see one another at the Fourth of July festivities in town. I walked Roberta over to the car. Nobody seemed to be paying any attention to us. So I leaned down and stuck my head in the window. She gave me a nice soft kiss. "I'll see you over the Fourth, in town." She held up her finger and said with the most serious face, "Just remember, darlin', all the while, you belong to me."

And I looked at her. "What?"

And then she smiled real big. "The song, silly." She started up her car and pulled out with a wave of her hand. I waved back, and only then did it hit me. The song, "You Belong to Me." What she had said was the last stanza.

I stood there watching her drive out of sight, when I heard somebody say, "Hey, cowboy, aren't you goin' to tell me goodbye?" and Kika in her car had pulled up and reached out and grabbed my hand. "Thanks. I enjoyed the day."

I squeezed her hand. "I did too, Kika."

She looked down the road and we could see the dust of Roberta's car kicking up. "Frank, there goes a dandy if I ever saw one. You better not let her get away!"

"I guess you're right. But before they can get away, they've got to be caught. And I don't know if I've gotten that done."

She shook her head and laughed. "Men! I've been around you two all day long, and believe me, she's caught! How about you?"

"I don't know. I'm awfully young, Kika, to get real serious." I was just joking, but deep down, it was serious. "How do you know when it's right?"

"You'll know." With that she, too, was gone.

CHAPTER

20

Building fence or fixing fence has never been one of my favorite forms of recreation. It was just plain hard work. But I imagine, since the XIT over in Texas started fencing in the range back in the late 1800s and with that everyone starting to fence off their own country, the biggest part of a ranch hand's time has been spent either building or fixing the damn things. As for me, I had to get into a fencing frame of mind.

If you looked at it as a job you had to do and went about it in a workmanlike way, not hurrying, just steady and stayed with it, really it wasn't so bad. But I always dreaded starting. I'd rather build new fence than fix old fence, but we were always doing either one or the other in the summertime. Jim had worked for the Boss for so long that he took great pride in it. I always figured Jim had kind of a fencing mentality anyway. He actually seemed to enjoy it.

But you talk about an eager beaver! Now R.C. just couldn't wait to get started with something he'd never done. And like everything else on the ranch, seemed to want to get started so he could learn how. But we'd see how long that would last. I'd seen many a feller start out on a fence and before it was over go draw his pay and head for the highway.

We had two miles of fence to build over in the MacGruder pasture. It was all going to be just as straight as a string, no corners. We were going to split that MacGruder pasture in half.

This was Jim's specialty. He'd never used any engineering tools in his life. If you'd showed him a transit, he wouldn't have known what you call it. But he could eyeball a fence in as straight and true as anybody there ever was. Jim went right to the spot where he and the Boss had figured the fence ought to start and pointed with his hand to the north.

"We'll take off from this fence line right here and run due north, plumb to the Barton pasture fence. I reckon that's about two miles."

R.C. stood looking off in the direction where he was pointing. He shook his head. "Good gosh, that's a long way. That'll take us forever!"

Jim just grumped. "It will if we don't get started."

It was hot and sweaty work, but there was always a little breeze to keep you cooled off. We took our lunches every day so we wouldn't have to go back to the house and waste time.

We had gotten down toward the MacGruder well and were having lunch by the windmill tower, when Jim said, "This used to be the only home I knew."

'Course, I knew the story. But I figured it'd get R.C.'s attention. "What do you mean, Jim?"

Jim pointed over to a depression in the ground that had a rock wall around four sides. "That used to be my home."

R.C. looked at him with astonishment. "Your home? You lived here?"

Jim nodded. "Yep. I was born right there. My daddy homesteaded this place, a hundred and sixty acres up here. In 1906 it was. Yessir. For a sixteen-dollar filin' fee, he and my ma come out here and tried to make a livin'. He died here tryin' to make a livin'! You know what, I guess I prob'ly will, too."

"MacGruder," R.C. said. "Jim MacGruder. I've never connected your name with this well or this pasture. Are they named for your dad?"

"I reckon. We're the only MacGruders hereabouts. You see that rock and that hole? That there was a half dugout. That's where I was born, and that's where I lived."

"When was that, Jim?" R.C. asked.

Jim looked back at him. "Huh, when I was born? Tell you what mister, that ain't none of your damn business!"

"Well, there isn't any harm in trying," R.C. smiled. "Was the Boss already here and ranching when your pa came?"

"Ah, yeah. They'd come sometime sooner and bought the place off of Martinez. Now that's the Boss's dad that did that. He was a mighty nice feller, a good man, like the Boss. You know you always hear a lot of stories about the animosity between the ranchers and the nesters. Well, with the Stones and the nesters, that just wasn't true. There'd been many a time we'd a'gone to bed with nothin' in our belly if it hadn't been for the Stones. Quite often they'd show up with a quarter of beef or bring us somethin' to eat, like good neighbors. They never acted like it was charity or anything. Just bein' neighborly. And Pa even worked for the Stones some, when he had the time."

"When did you start working for them?" R.C. asked.

"Oh, I was about ten years old, I guess. I think I got the job more out of pity than anything else. The Boss and his pa were always willin' to let us get water down on the creek, even though they owned it and controlled all the water. Yep, I'd walk down there ever' day and peel posts or do anything that needed to be done and walk back home at night. But finally it got where I just stayed over there."

"Whatever happened to your mother and dad, Jim?" I asked.

"Oh, Pa had almost lost his health by the time the thirties rolled around. It got so dry and blowin' so bad. That, hooked on to the hard life that he'd already lived, he just passed away. Then my ma moved to town. She didn't last much longer."

And with that he got up and walked over toward the old dugout and looked around. "You know, the Boss has cleaned up most all these old homesteads, except this one. Sometimes I wonder if he hasn't left this one alone just on my account. After he bought the place from Ma, he went in and reseeded back to gramma and buffalo grass all the country that my pa tried to farm and broke out. He didn't use the CCC, or any government program, like everybody else in the country did."

He looked down in the old dugout and there among the old weather-beaten, fallen-down roof you could see the corner of a mattress springs. "Looky there, them's the springs off my folks' bedstead. I reckon I was 'got' on them springs right there."

There were a few dwarfed trees that cattle had walked around and made deep depressions on. You could even see them standing up with a foot of root showing.

You could tell by looking at Jim that he was remembering back. "Ma tried to make things grow. Them trees. But there just wasn't enough moisture to make it." He reached down and picked up an old cast-iron wheel that was about six inches in diameter and smiled. "This came off a little red wagon that Pa bought all us kids. I think that was the only present he ever bought for any of us. We shore did love that wagon!" With that he pitched it back into the dugout. "It ain't very big, is it?"

We all agreed.

"It's funny how time changes things. One time it seemed a lot bigger. But I'll tell you what, boys. I felt safe and I felt loved and that there hole in the ground was home."

Jim just ambled off and started back to work.

We came in at night dirty and dog-tired. Cleaned up, lay down, and rested up a little before going to supper.

It was somewhere during the middle of the week when R.C. seemed to get a great interest in the upcoming rodeo that was going to be held over the Fourth of July in town. It started out as sounding like casual curiosity.

"Frank, you used to rodeo, didn't you?"

"Yep, used to. Still do occasionally."

"What did you do?"

"At one time I've worked all five major events, and then some."

"What are the major events?"

"Oh, there's bareback ridin', calf ropin', saddle bronc ridin', bulldoggin', and bull ridin'."

"Will they have those five standard events at the rodeo in town this Fourth of July?"

"Oh, yeah," I said. "A rodeo that size will always have the standard events plus they'll have a team ropin'."

"Are you gonna enter the rodeo?" R.C. said.

"Yeah. I thought I would. I always do. Just the bulldoggin', I imagine. I've quit almost everything else."

'Course he wanted to know why. "The main reason I quit ridin' rough stock, I was too big. Most everybody that rides bareback horses, saddle broncs, and bulls are built more like you."

He smiled. "You don't say?"

"Yeah, they're just little bitty fellers."

Jim had to put his two cents' worth in. "Yeah, R.C., Frank works the bulldoggin' event 'cause that's the only event he's qualified for!"

R.C. got a puzzled look on his face. "Qualified for?"

"Yeah," Jim said. "In order to be a bulldogger you gotta wear a size two hat and a size fifty-four jacket!" With that he let out a big guffaw.

"Shit, Jim," I said. "You're just sayin' that because you're jealous."

"How did you get started rodeoing, Frank?"

"What's your big interest in rodeo all of a sudden, R.C.?"

R.C. shrugged his shoulders. "No reason. Just curious."

"Oh, I thought maybe you were gettin' some wild idea. Well, I was always turned that way. Damn near ruined me, 'cause that's all I wanted to do. I liked the wild part of it. I started workin' what they call amateur rodeos. Then I decided I'd join the RCA, about four years later."

'Course, R.C. wanted to know what the RCA was. "It stands for the Rodeo Cowboy's Association. Now that there's professional rodeo, they have their own association and stock contractors. In order to compete in one of 'em you either have to belong or the rodeo has to be held in your hometown. The money's better in 'em. A lot of times they'll add money to each event. That's where you find the guys that strictly rodeo for a livin' and make it a business. Believe you me, it's a hard way to make a livin'!"

R.C. let it lay for a while. The next night he started again, very casually. "This rodeo in town over the Fourth. Is it gonna be an RCA rodeo?"

"No, it's just an open rodeo, an amateur rodeo. Of course, not really an amateur rodeo. They pay money."

So, over the next four or five days answering R.C.'s questions, we went through all the equipment needed and all the particulars of each event.

It was around two or three days later that he dropped the bombshell on me. And to tell you the truth, it was the last thing that I expected. Just clear out of the blue, R.C. said, "Frank, I'm thinking about entering the rodeo over the Fourth."

I looked at him like I was hearing things. "You what?"

"I'm thinking about entering. The bull riding, as a matter of fact."

"Jesus Christ, R.C.! That is the dumbest thing I ever heard of in my life! You have about as much business in the bull ridin' as a hog does wearin' a sidesaddle."

R.C. kind of got indignant over that. "I'd like to know why! A fellow's got to start somewhere!"

"Well, you picked a damn poor place to start!"

"Why? You said I was just about the right size. All bull riders are fairly small guys about my size. All I need is a bull rope, a glove, and some rosin."

"I know I told you all that shit. But I thought it was just your curiosity. I wasn't tellin' you all that to give you information so you could go get on a bull!"

"I don't care. That's what I want to do."

"Let me tell you some other things that I've neglected to tell you, now that you've gotten serious about this. Them bulls will be Bramer bulls. Not these gentle Hereford bulls that we've got runnin' around here. And them bulls will flat eat you alive, if you let 'em!"

"I don't intend to let them."

I can't remember ever being so exasperated. "I don't know how in the hell you're gonna keep from lettin' 'em! If you're capable of ridin' one of those bulls, which I seriously doubt, there isn't any way to get off of one of 'em without endangerin' your life!"

"What do you mean?"

"Even if you were a world's champion you could sit up there and ride him like you owned him, there's no pickup men that can come in and take you off of one of 'em. There's nothing that can get close to one of 'em. Gettin' off, that's the hard part! Ridin' 'em's easy compared to that! When you get on the ground you're on their turf. Never worry about one of 'em hookin' you or gorin' you. But he'll damn sure mash the hell out of you, knock you around. The worst thing of all, one of 'em could step on you. And them bulls will weigh anything from fifteen hundred pounds to eighteen hundred pounds. Just have one of 'em jump on you, there won't be enough left of you to soak up with a sponge!"

But I was talking to a man who wouldn't reason. No matter how hard I tried to talk him out of it, R.C. was insistent. He had his mind made up. He was going to enter the bull riding. I spent the better part of a couple of days, while we were working and while we were resting, and part of the night when we both ought to been sleeping, trying to talk him out of it. But there was just no way!

So, I figured if he was dead set on it, I'd better try to help him the best I could. I knew when I was beat.

So one evening I asked, "Have you ever even seen a rodeo?"

"I sure have."

"Where?"

Well, he mumbled around and shook his head. "Back East."

"Oh, that's just dandy! A rodeo back East."

And with that I went over to the closet and came out with an old warbag that I'd carried for years. I rummaged around inside of it a little bit and came out with a pair of bull spurs. "Well, if you're gonna do this, you might as well have the right equipment." And I handed him the spurs.

He fingered them a little, grabbed ahold of the rowel, and saw that it wouldn't move. "How come the rowels don't move?"

"Because in bull ridin' you can lock your rowels down. See that set screw on the shank?"

He turned it around and looked.

"It's legal, within the rules, to lock your rowels," I said. "This here's a bull rope." I pulled out an old bull rope that I hadn't used in years, but I'd kept it dry and put up right.

He uncoiled it and looked at the handhold in it, stuck his hand in it, fingered it all over until he came to the bell. A big cowbell was attached to it with a leather strap. "What's the bell for?"

"All bull ropes gotta have bells. Bells just infuriate bulls and it makes 'em buck harder. Didn't you know that?"

"No, I didn't."

Finally I said, "Nah, I'm just hoorahin' you. The bell's on there to give it weight. So after you turn loose you're either bucked off or you get off, the bull rope will come off by itself."

R.C. nodded his head like he understood.

I rummaged around in my warbag and found a glove that was all rolled up. "Which hand are you gonna ride with?"

"I don't know. I've got more strength in my right hand."

"Well, you may have more strength in the right hand, but you've also got more balance in your right hand. I'd recommend that you ride holdin' on with your left hand. Strength won't get it done. You're gonna have to use a lot of balance and keep your whole body in position. I don't know why I'm tellin' you all this. You don't stand a chance in hell of gettin' him rode!"

He looked at me. "I've surprised you before, Frank."

"Yeah. You've done that. Here's the glove and it's a left-handed glove." I unrolled it and he looked at the palm of it.

"My gosh! What'd you do to it?"

I had to laugh. "That's from takin' chunk rosin and puttin' it in my glove and pullin' on that handhold. It makes it real rough and sticky on the inside. That's why it was rolled up."

I tossed it to him and he tried it on. It was way too big for him. "That'll never do. You'll have to find one glove that you don't have any other use for. Then tie the end of that bull rope to a fence post."

I brought out a rosin bag. "Take these chunks of rosin and put 'em in your hand and start pullin' on that bull rope around the handhold. Get it real sticky so you can keep your hand in it. A bull is so stout, he'll jerk your hand away from you. If you're not careful, he's liable to stretch your arm a foot longer than your other one. Be a shame if it stayed that way."

R.C. was taking all this in. And like everything else, he was dead serious. So, every evening and what slack time we had in between, I tried to coach him on the art of bull riding. I tried to impress on him that even though I never had much luck riding them, I'd been on a bunch of them. I knew how it should be done, even though I couldn't do it.

"When you're ready for him, and if you can't talk, just nod your head and they'll open the gate. That first jump is gonna be mighty! Try to get your spurs in front of the rope. Keep your toes turned out, your knees flexed, bend and stay loose at the waist. That's the secret. Lean forward, throw your chest out," and then I happened to remember. "But leanin' forward. Don't lean too far forward, 'cause a lot of these bulls will throw their head. If one of 'em ever throws his head up while you're leanin' over with your head down, and he hits you with his poll, he's gonna coldcock you. You might even catch a horn upside the head! And try to keep your free hand in motion with him. Ah shit! I don't know what I'm even tellin' you all this for. You won't be there long enough to even get any of it tried out!"

"Don't bet on it!"

"I think we'd better concentrate on things that might go wrong. If he starts in a spin, do everything in your power from fallin' down inside that spin. If he's spinnin' to the left, for God's sake, don't fall off or get bucked off to the left, he'll be circlin' back over the top of you. Bull riders call it 'fallin' in the well.' There, mister, is where you can get severely damaged. You'll flat get the shit knocked plumb out of you!"

"You're talking awfully negative, Frank."

"I know it. I can't help it! That's my nature when it comes to bull ridin'. There's a lot of things that can happen to you and most of 'em are bad."

"What if I should happen to ride him?"

"Well, good for you!"

I told him everything that I could think of in the remaining days before we left for town. Every now and then I'd try to talk him out of it again. I told him if he got up there and saw a bull up close, maybe he'd change his mind. Nobody would think the less of him for backing out. But he just shook his head. "No chance!"

I had to smile inside. I thought, Wait'll you get up close to one of them boogers and see one! That'll test his grit.

I talked to him so much about bull riding that I felt like I was getting a knot on my tongue. I was coached plumb out!

CHAPTER

*2*1

We kept working on the fence right up until the first day of July. It was at supper that evening that the Boss asked me if I was going to enter over the Fourth. I told him I thought I would. As usual he grumped around. "Well, you be careful. We ain't got no use on this place for a busted-up rodeo cowboy. We've got work to do around here and we don't need to be nursemaidin' anybody!"

R.C. told him that he thought he'd enter, too, and this took the Boss back a little.

"What event?"

"Oh, I thought I'd enter the bull riding."

With that the Boss just looked down at his plate and shook his head. Then he looked up at R.C. and said, "Is there any way I can talk you out of it?"

"No, sir. Frank's already tried."

"Then, I don't guess there's any use of wasting my breath."

"How about you, Boss?" I asked. "Are you gonna enter?"

"I think I will. This will probably be my last go 'round. Top asked me to heel for him, so I'll put in an appearance."

Later up at the bunkhouse R.C. asked me what the Boss had against rodeoing.

"Oh, he always acts that way. Acts about half mad when I tell him I'm gonna enter a rodeo. But you can't hardly blame him. Rodeo cowboys are notoriously sorry ranch hands. What time they're not crippled up or sandbaggin' you, they're makin' plans to go off to some rodeo. Or they'll work just long enough to get enough money to go on down the road. As a matter of fact, there's a sayin' about rodeo cowboys that there's a lot of truth in."

"What's that?"

I laughed. "Well, they say if a man's too lazy to work, too nervous to steal, and too ignorant to be scared, he'll make a hell of a rodeo cowboy!"

"Do you believe that?" R.C. asked.

"What do you think? You've been workin' around me. I don't think I'm lazy. There is somethin' to be said for it, I guess. But for me it's more like a disease. You get the taste of it and hear the crowd, win some money and get in with the boys. Up at this rodeo there'll be some locals entered. But there's a group of cowboys that are kinda like wanderin' gypsies. They just go from town to town, rodeo to rodeo. And it doesn't matter where you're at, you always know somebody. Some places you almost know everybody, if you're in the bunch."

"Are you in the bunch?"

"I reckon."

"Well, that makes me feel good. What chance do I have?"

"Well, bein' with me will be a plus. I'll introduce you to some of these fellers, and they'll look on you with kinder eyes. So, I don't think it'll hurt you. But I don't know what in the hell we're talkin' about you winnin' anything for! Your first time out of the chute you'll be just lucky to save your hide."

I heard a car drive up but I didn't pay any attention to it. And directly who should walk in the door but Poke Mahone. "Howdy, boys. Thought I'd check up on you and find out how everything's goin' over here on the Cross S."

"I thought I smelled sheep-dip," I said. "What in the hell are you doin' here?"

"I was wonderin' if you could put me up for the night and give me a ride to town tomorrow so I can partake of the big festivities with you."

"It'd be an honor," I said.

"Poke," R.C. said, "are you gonna enter the rodeo?"

"Nah, I'm gonna let you boys make fools out of yourselves. Outside of the wild beer drinkin' contest, I think I'll just chase the dollies. Who knows, I just might get lucky and catch one of 'em!"

"Hell, you wouldn't know what to do with one if you caught her," I said.

Poke laughed. "That's just what you think. I've been dreaming about it at night."

"Poke," I said, "you just ought to keep dreamin' about it. It'll last a hell of a lot longer than the real thing!"

All of a sudden Poke got serious. "Say, did you fellers hear about old man Kessler that lived down south between here and Tramperos apassin' away last week?"

When he said that, I looked over at Jim and smiled, and Jim looked back at me and smiled. I knew then that we had a setup coming. "Lord, no. I didn't hear that he passed away. That's sure too bad." I said, "What happened to him?"

"Well," Poke said, "I heard it was just old age, that he just flat up and died."

"I'll tell you what," Jim said. "You had to admire ol' man Kessler. For a man with no arms, he was a workin' fool!"

I glanced over at R.C. and he was really taking it in. And, of course, that was our plan.

"Yeah," Poke said, "I didn't know the ol' man well. But for a man who didn't have no arms, he made a good livin'."

"Yeah," I said, "but, my God, I tell you what. He sure picked a tough way to make a livin'. Just imagine. Choppin' firewood for a livin' and not havin' no arms!"

Jim shook his head. "Yeah. You sure gotta admire a man with that kind of grit."

We sat in silence there for a while, kind of in reverence to ol' man Kessler, just waiting. And sure enough, it came.

"Just a minute now," R.C. said. "You say this man Kessler didn't have any arms?"

Jim nodded his head up and down. "Yessir, that's a fact."

"And he chopped wood?"

And I had to say, "Yessir, that's the way he made a livin'. Amazin', ain't it?"

We sat a little while longer and let it soak in on R.C. And finally it came. "I'd like to know how in the world a man with no arms could chop wood."

And with that Poke spoke up. "Why, it was plumb easy, R.C. His wife would just stick a double-bitted axe up his ass and ol' man Kessler would just turn flip-flops. God, could he cut wood!"

With that everybody just died laughing. And R.C. sat there with a blank look on his face. Then he got to laughing, too.

Finally when we began to quiet down, he said, "How long am I gonna have to be around you fellows before you quit playing these practical jokes on me?"

Poke laughed. "Until you quit bitin' on 'em."

"I don't know when I'm ever gonna wise up! But I'm gonna try hard."

Poke had a craving for guitar music and singing, so I hauled out the old Harmony and played until we went to bed.

The next morning we had another short clinic on bull riding, at my insistence. I felt like I was leading a lamb to slaughter. Really, R.C. had made up his mind and he was doing it himself. I don't know what made me feel responsible, but some way I did.

Poke sat around and listened to all the advice I was giving R.C., all the do's and don'ts. When I was finally through, Poke said, "R.C., you may get hooked on this bull ridin' and go on with it. It may become your profession."

"You think so, Poke? Think I really might be good enough, if I work at it, to win some money?"

"Only time will tell," Poke said. "Time and your eyes."

"My eyes?"

"You bet! The good bull riders you can tell, their eyes start gettin' closer together the more bulls they get on. And when they get really good you can take your finger," and he held out his pointing finger in the air and jabbed once, " 'til you can poke the eyes once and get both of 'em."

R.C. grinned. "Poke, you're putting me on again."

"No. Ain't it, Frank? Ain't that right?"

"Well, it sure gets your concentration narrowed down and it'll make you feel like your eyes are gettin' closer together, the more of 'em you get on. But promise me, R.C., if you get to town and you see those bulls and you change your mind, don't feel bad about it."

"I promise. But I don't think there's any way I'll change my mind."

When we got to town I drove by Roberta's place, but there was no sign of life. So we drove on down to Kitchins. I was keeping my eyes peeled for Dee Jensen, an old friend and traveling partner. He was of slight build and a bull rider by trade. He had, however, an uncanny way of training bulldogging and hazing horses. He could get away with using outlaw horses that others had given up on. As a hazer he was fearless, knocking steers to the dogger, never giving a thought to his horse stumbling over the steer and falling on him. As a steer wrestler, what he lacked in size he made up in technique. Rodeo was his life.

We walked into the bar and looked around. There were quite a few rodeo cowboys already in town. There'd be an afternoon rodeo tomorrow, and a night rodeo on the Fourth, and a big parade on the morning of the Fourth. The town was braced for a big holiday, and the rodeo cowboys had already begun to drift in.

There were quite a few I knew and hadn't seen for a long time. So it took a good while to get around and renew old acquaintances. Some of those fellows I hadn't seen for three or four years. That's what happens when a fellow takes a steady job and quits going down the road.

At four o'clock R.C. showed up and got himself a cold beer.

Poke said, "Aren't you gonna have R.C. take a gander at them Bramer bulls?"

"Yessir. That'd be a good idea. Come on. Let's go out to the rodeo grounds."

I drove in behind the bucking chutes and already there were horse trailers lined up from people coming in for the rodeo. I didn't know what Dee was driving. He'd wear a vehicle out in one season of rodeoing. The trouble of rodeoing was all those miles in between them.

I turned around down by the roping and bulldogging chutes and was going to make another pass by the trailers, when I heard somebody holler.

"Hey, you ol' gut-eatin' son of a bitch!"

And it was music to my ears. I stopped Ol' Bullet right there in the tracks and turned it off. I'd found Dee Jensen. I got out and stood there as he came from around the calf pens leading two horses, with a big grin on his face.

"What in the hell are you doin'?" I asked.

"I just been takin' these ol' horses over to the only water spigot in the whole damn outfit." He walked up and shook hands with me. "God, it's good to see you, you son of a bitch!"

"Thanks, Dee. It's good to see you, too. You remember Poke?"

"Hell, yes. How are ya, Poke?" and shook hands with him.

"This here's my friend, R.C. Roth."

Dee shook hands with R.C. and said, "Let's go on back to the trailer. God, we've got a lot to talk about! Pull down there, will you, Frank?"

"You bet."

And out from behind the trailer came another cowboy. His skin was brown, his hair as black as a no-moon night. His name was Amos Shooter and he was a full-blooded Lakota Indian, and one hell of a cowboy! He was a couple of years younger than Dee and me. I'll tell you what, he was a hell of a bronc rider, both bareback and saddle bronc. Could ride bulls, and he could rope and bulldog. He could do it all. He was a shade light for a bulldogger. He weighed about a hundred and sixty-five pounds and stood about six foot tall. Made him pretty thin and lanky. But, boy, could he jerk the air out of a bareback horse!

"Hey," I said, "the old buffalo shooter!"

"Frank. Goddamn, it's good to see another brother of the drum around!"

We shook hands, and I introduced him to R.C. and Poke. Dee finally got there with his horses and tied them to the trailer. "Goddamn, are you still workin' out there for the Boss?"

"Yep."

"Boy, I'll tell you what. A good rodeo cowboy is damn sure goin' to waste! Why don't you pack up and go with us?"

"Nah, I like the steady money."

"Shit! You can make more money than that in just a few seconds in that arena."

"If I'm lucky."

"You ol' son of a bitch, you don't need no luck. How about a drink?"

"Have you ever seen this Indian boy turn one down?" I asked.

"I don't know. Between you and Amos, goddamn, you keep me scared half to death. Everybody knows that whiskey and Injuns don't mix."

I turned and looked at Amos. He smiled back at me and winked. "It's just a myth, Dee."

Dee passed the bottle around and then pointed over to his horses. "What do you think of my new team?"

"Well," I said, "they ain't plumb new. Looks to me like you're still hazin' off of ol' SicEm. What happened to the Baron?"

When Dee talked he kind of nodded his head side to side. He never wore his hat straight on his head. It was always cocked to the side just a little bit. His nose was a little too big for his face, and had been broken a few times. I knew he had some false teeth, 'cause I'd been with him when a horn had caught him in the mouth abulldogging, along with a couple of "shaving nicks" from riding bulls. But he had a special way with bulldogging horses. Even though he didn't weigh a hundred and fifty pounds soaking wet, on small cattle he could sometimes beat you. But he made a living riding bulls and mounting fellows that could bulldog.

"What," I asked, "are you bulldoggin' off now?"

"That blood bay mare there." And he began to shake his head. "I call her B.B."

"What does that stand for?"

"Bay Bitch. And let me tell you, Frank, ol' B.B. is as good a son of a bitch that ever backed into a doggin' box! Scores real well, really goes to cattle in a hurry and drives by 'em. I started workin' her this spring. When I bought her I thought I'd paid way too much. It's more money than I ever spent on a horse in my life. But she's already paid for herself and now the money's goin' in my pocket!"

"I'm glad to hear it. 'Cause I aim for you to mount me if you got the notion."

He grinned at me and punched me in the shoulder. "You ol' son of a bitch! What do you think I'm doin' here in Dorsey? Does shit stink? Of course I'll mount you. And I guarantee you'll like her. B.B. will put you there where you can win somethin'."

"I hope so. I need to get back down there and enter. But first I wanted to show R.C. here the bulls."

Dee looked over at R.C. "Oh, we got a bull rider here, huh? That's all I need is some tough competition." Then he cocked his head and grinned at him. "I've never seen you before, but that don't mean nothin'. Are you pretty tough?"

"Tough?" R.C. said.

"He's talkin' about ridin' bulls, R.C." I said.

"Oh! No. This will be the first one I was ever on."

"Well let's walk over here and get acquainted with some of these. I know 'em all by name and know most of 'em's habits."

"I'll need all the help I can get, this being my first one."

Dee threw his arm around R.C.'s shoulder. "Hell, don't worry about that now. Everybody's gotta have a first one."

We walked over to the bullpen and it was entertaining to all of us to watch R.C. We all squatted down there by the fence. The bulls were just milling around. R.C. walked up and down the fence, along the backside, looking at them with a critical eye.

He came back and he said, "Ooh, some of those things look like they could eat a man alive!"

"Yeah," I said, "I want you to take notice of that. Look at them horns. Look at the size. 'Member gettin' hooked and stepped on like I was tellin' you?"

There were some in there with real high horns that curved right straight up, some with no horns, and a couple with what we call banana horns that curled down almost straight to the ground. These bulls were here because they could do one thing real well, and that was throw a cowboy down.

"What do you think, R.C.?" I asked. "Do you still have the hankerin'?"

"You bet. I'm gonna do it!"

"Well," I said, "then let's get back to the office and get entered!"

Amos, real friendly-like, said, "Frank, this white-eye friend of yours, when I first met him looked like a smart man. It's amazin' how a man can be fooled. Especially an Indian."

"Yeah, Amos. Don't feel bad. It happened to me, too."

With that we laughed. R.C. knew we were ragging on him a little bit. He was getting used to our hoorahing by now. But you could tell that those bulls had made an impression on him. We hardly got out of earshot when R.C. said, "I never thought I'd live to see the day when somebody would call you a son of a bitch, Frank, and you wouldn't take exception."

I laughed. "Once you get to know Dee, then you'll understand. You see, the way he figures it, everybody in the whole world is a son of a bitch. But they're divided into good sons of bitches and bad sons of bitches."

"Well, he called you a son of a bitch more times than I could count," R.C. said.

"That's just it," I said. "Did you hear him say he's a good son of a bitch, and he's smilin', he's sayin' it in admiration and friendship. He likes you. But if he's got a frown on his face and he calls you a counterfeit, no-good son of a bitch, or words to that effect, then he don't like you. And I'll tell you what. That's one feller you want to stay on the right side of. Even though he's little, he's mighty. And his runnin' mate, Amos Shooter, he's no slouch either."

We went and entered up. Got us a room. Hauled all our stuff up to it. We went back to the bar where we found Dee and Amos. We all moved to a table where we could sit down and visit a little bit, order some drinks.

"I notice you and everybody else are wearin' different britches nowadays," I said.

Dee looked down at his pants. "Yep. They're the latest thing. They're Wranglers. Bill Linderman and Jim Shoulders both are endorsin' 'em now. Bluebell Wranglers is makin' a real run at tryin' to get the cowboy trade. As a matter of fact, they've been givin' out red jackets with 'Bluebell Wrangler' written all across the back of 'em to travelin' cowboys so they can get some advertisement. They even personalize 'em and put your name in gold letterin' over the left-hand pocket. I've got one and so does Amos. Matter of fact," he shook his head and grinned at me, "I have one in a large size that says 'Frank' over the pocket."

"No shit!" I said. "What made you do that?"

"I knew I'd be runnin' onto you, and I thought while they was orderin' mine, that I'd just get one made up for you, too."

"I appreciate that. Where is it?"

"Up in the room. I'll give it to you first chance I git."

"I ain't too old to change my ways. I might give 'em a shot. I'm sure glad you came down here. I know you could have probably gone a lot of other places and made more money."

"Nah, Amos and I thought maybe it'd be easy pickin's here. Besides, haulin' a couple of horses don't make it easy to work two rodeos unless they're real close together. Around here there ain't nothin' close together! Have you been down on any cattle, Frank?"

"Not in a long time. You may be mountin' me for nothin'. I might have forgot."

"Well, if I mount you for nothin' it won't be for the first time, will it?" He smiled. "But I doubt if you've forgot. It's like gittin' a little nookie and ridin' a bicycle. Once you git the hang of it, you never forgit."

"I'm glad to hear it. It's been awhile since I got any nookie, either."

He laughed. "If that's what you're lookin' for, you just wait'll them camp followers start gittin' in! It ought to be anytime now. They've got some dandies runnin' with 'em."

"I missed that," R.C. said. "What's a camp follower?"

Dee threw back his head and laughed. "You're gonna learn soon enough, I guess. You've never been around rodeo before?"

"No, I saw one once. But I've never been around the chutes or associated with the cowboys."

Dee looked at me. "Where'd you find this feller, Frank?"

"Sittin' on a suitcase underneath a tree out in the middle of nowhere." I saw Dee look at me like I was kidding. I held up my hand. "That's the honest-to-God truth. I swear."

"Well, I'll tell you, R.C." he said. "Camp followers are girls that just love cowboys. You're gonna like this deal! We call 'em 'boogie mamas.' They like rodeo and they like to dance, and they like to party! They'll trip you and beat you to the floor. And, hell, they don't have any travelin' expenses except gas money. A lot of times they'll hook onto somebody and won't even have to pay that. They use a wife's pass to git into all the rodeos free. As far as a place to sleep, they ain't never lackin' somebody to sleep with. They're more than willin'."

He reached over and whapped me on the shoulder. "You ol' son of a bitch. We gotta show this feller how the world of rodeo works!"

I smiled at him. "All he'll have to do is hang around you for just a little while and he'll have a pretty good idea. How about you? You boys been winnin' anything?"

"Oh, we've been hittin' a pretty fair lick here and there," Dee said. "Ol' Amos here, he's too modest to say anything, but he's been pickin' up a paycheck almost everywhere we go. I've been hazin' for everybody I mount, and Amos, too. I've been pickin' up a few bull ridin' checks. But I ain't near as consistent as Amos here."

Amos would joke around with me, or somebody he knew, occasionally. But more often, he was the stoic Indian. He was a good-looking fellow with those brown eyes and jet black hair. Even though he had a nose like Sitting Bull, it somehow fit him. I knew for a fact he was real popular with the boogie mamas.

"There's one drawback to comin' here, though," Dee said. "I've known Jiggs Rankin for a long time and I've always gotten along with him good. Hell, you know me, Frank. I'm the easiest son of a bitch in the world to git along with. Ain't that right?"

"If you say so."

"You remember ol' Hooch Bray, don't ya?"

"Oh, yes. I remember Hooch Bray." He was a great big fellow. Bull-dogged. Never could get it down to a science, but kept on trying. But he was a bully. We were acquaintances, but we weren't friends.

"What about Hooch?" I asked.

"Well, he married Jiggs' and Dorothy's daughter, Alice. You remember her, don't ya?"

"Yeah. But I didn't know they'd gotten married."

"Well, they damn sure did! And as far as I'm concerned, that Hooch Bray is a counterfeit son of a bitch!"

"Why? What'd he ever do to you?"

"I'll tell you what the big son of a bitch done! We was at Espanola in May. That's the first time we'd cracked out with B.B. Jiggs was puttin' on that show and he promoted his son-in-law to chute boss."

"Well anyway, what happened?"

"I was gittin' down on my bull and you know how they generally Hotshot 'em just as they turn and leave the chute?" I nodded my head. "Well, he stuck that Hotshot right on my butt. Give me such a whammy of a shock, hell, I was bucked off before I ever knew I was out of the chute!"

"Maybe it was an accident," I said.

"Accident my ass! That's what he claimed it was. I told him that if he ever pulled another stunt on me like that again, I was goin' to beat the shit out of him!"

"When you start to do that, if you ever do, make sure you have ol' Amos handy or me. He ain't just all talk."

Dee downed his drink and called for another round. "So you're still workin' for ol' Boss Stone, are ya, Frank?"

"Yeah."

"How do you git along with him?"

"Oh, pretty good. As well as can be expected, I reckon."

"To tell ya the truth, I sure would like to git my hands on just one of those Cross S horses! A couple of 'em would be a dream come true. Do you reckon you might git a couple of his good horses worth the money?"

"Yeah, I imagine I could. He'd probably sell one to me as reasonable as he would anybody. But still, I know I don't have that kinda money, and I doubt if you have."

"Nah, I haven't. For me to git ahold of one of 'em, it'd just damn near have to be a gift."

I could tell that the lack of finances and the want of a Cross S horse was depressing Dee, so I changed the subject. "How long has it been since you've been home, Amos?"

"Oh, it's been a long time. Over a year, I guess."

"Well, it's been twice that long for me since I've been back to Oklahoma. Do you ever miss the drums?"

Amos shook his head. "Boy, do I! I'm gonna have to take a sabbatical one of these days and go back home and listen to the drums beat. Why don't you come with me, Frank? Maybe we can get 'em to throw a Ghost Dance. We can get rid of all these white-eyes and the buffalo will come back! You and me'll go huntin'."

"That sounds like a good idea."

Dee knew we were just hoorahing him. "Shit, you blanket asses wouldn't be where you are now if it wasn't for us white people. You Injuns is the shits! I don't even know why I put up with both of ya. You're just like pet 'coons. What you don't break, you shit all over. Especially when you're drunk."

CHAPTER

22

The bar was filling up with local people and a lot of rodeo cowboys coming in. I saw Jiggs Rankin, the contractor, come in. I got up and shook hands with him, just to make myself known. It's always a good idea, I figured, to promote yourself a little bit. If an opportunity came to give a break to someone, Jiggs just might let it fall your way, if you stayed in his good graces. Besides, I liked the man.

When I got back to the table, R.C. was talking to Amos and Dee. Dee laughed. "Oh, hell. If you've never been around rodeo people, you're in for a treat! A lot of wild things go on."

"Why?"

"I don't know," Dee said. "The old sayin', 'It takes a wild man to ride a wild horse'... To win anything you got to git pretty wild in the arena. Most of these boys is wild to begin with, and they just carry it on when they git out of the arena. You wait and watch. The next couple of nights this hotel is gonna look like the red-light district in Juarez. But don't worry. You'll git used to it if you stay around it long enough. Hell, for that matter, you might even join us!"

I could see that statement made R.C. kind of sit up with pride.

We hadn't been ignoring Poke. It's just that he had about as much interest in rodeo as he did in going to college. The only thing he enjoyed about rodeo was the parties and the dances and the women that came with them!

He'd just been sitting there having a few drinks, listening to us talk, when I saw his eyes light up as he looked at the door. "Oh, looky, looky what's comin'."

Dee glanced over at the door. "Oh, shit! Amos, I told ya they'd show up sooner or later."

I had my back to the door and couldn't see what he was talking about. I turned around. There were two honest-to-God boogie mamas that had just walked in and were surveying the surroundings.

"Dee," Amos said, "there ain't no sense in hidin'. They're gonna find us anyway."

"Let's palm 'em off on these boys here."

"Why?" I asked. "Is there somethin' wrong with 'em?"

"Hell, they've been after Amos and me ever since that fiasco up in Espanola. It was fun for a while, but it soon got tiresome. Take a look at that one with the dark hair, Frank."

Her tits hung loose like the balls on a goose, you can git her when the sun goes down, I thought. Everything she had on was double-tight.

Dee leaned over and whispered, "And I'll tell ya what, mister, she's got an ass that don't stop, too. Her problem is between her ears. She's as dumb as a goddamn post!"

"How about the other one?" I asked.

"I'm qualified to judge her," Amos said. "She ain't bad, kinda medio-cre. You can't win nothin' on her, but she will buck a little." And with that he grinned.

Sure enough, they'd seen Dee and Amos and here they came. The short, dark-haired one plopped down on Dee's lap. "Where have you been, sweetie? We went out to the Water Hole and to the arena and couldn't find ya."

"I've been right here," Dee said, "hidin' from you."

She playfully slapped him in the face, not hard. "Oh, don't talk that way. You know you don't mean it."

With a wink at me, Dee said, "Sugar, I want you to meet an old friend of mine. This here's Frank Dalton."

She looked over at me with real sultry eyes. "Hi, Frank."

And I never saw anybody change laps so fast! First thing I knew she was sitting in my lap. "My, you're a big fella. Are you this big all over?"

I kind of weakly smiled at her. "I've never had any complaints. What's your name?"

"Just call me Sugar." And then she pointed to the brunette that had her hand on Amos's shoulder. "This is my friend, Dolly. How come I haven't ever seen you around before?"

"Oh, I've been around before," I said. "It's just that our paths have never crossed, I guess."

She smiled sweetly at me. "Well, now that they have, will ya buy me a drink?"

"Sure. What the hell. But get off my lap and sit down. You're makin' me uncomfortable."

She smiled as she wiggled her butt. "I hope so."

Dee introduced Dolly and Sugar to R.C. and Poke. Poke showed a great lot of attention and interest, so Dolly kind of gravitated toward him. Much to R.C.'s relief, I think. They had on those real low-cut Levis that just hang on your hips and loud western shirts that they had unbuttoned, damn near to their belt buckle, and long dangly earrings. Both of them immediately plopped a cigarette in their mouth and lit up. I figured they both dressed alike, did things alike, and had the same set of morals. Which was all right with me. I'd seen a lot of them come and go.

But I knew one thing for sure. Even though it'd be tempting, I didn't want to get mixed up with either one of them. This was what you might call my hometown right now. And with the thing I had going with Roberta, I had way too much to lose for a couple of nights' fling in the sack. It just wasn't worth it.

After a couple more drinks, I had to excuse myself. I told them that I had to go see somebody about some business. I got up and R.C. said, "I've got to go with him."

The bar was so damned crowded you had to shoulder your way through. It took awhile to get to the door, stopping and seeing friends that I hadn't seen in a while along the way.

I ran into a fellow called Sonny Wade and he had a cast on his foot. Shook hands. "What in the hell happened to you?"

"Oh, I got hung up in a stirrup and broke my leg, Frank."

"What are you doin' here, then?"

"Oh, I'm judgin'. Me and Murph here."

"Murph! How in the hell are ya?"

"Oh, fair to middlin'."

"You two are judgin'," I said. "What's wrong with you, Murph? How come you're not competin'?"

"Oh, I'm gittin' a lung recapped. Got it punctured a month ago. Thought I'd let her heal up before I got on any more."

I introduced them both to R.C. I suppose they thought that R.C. and I were traveling together. I didn't tell them any different. I wanted them to think that R.C. was one of us. Maybe they wouldn't be so hard on him if he happened to get that bull rode.

When we got to the door, R.C. turned and started to go in the lobby, like we were going to our room. "No, sir." I said, "Let's walk out the front door."

He followed me out to the sidewalk. "Where we going?"

"We're goin' up to the room, but I didn't want to make them think that I was stayin' here."

"Who? Dee and Amos?"

"No. Them two damn barflies! We'll just walk out here and we'll circle back around through the lobby. That way they won't know where we're stayin'. But it won't last long. They'll find out!"

"I hope not. You know what, Frank? They're kind of scary."

"Oh, don't let 'em get to you, R.C. Just keep your cool."

After we got something to eat we finally made it out to the Water Hole about nine-thirty. And it looked like Independence Day had already gotten a running start! The place was packed. First feller I ran into was Hooch Bray. Damned if he didn't shake my hand and act like we were long-lost kinfolk! I had my suspicions, so I acted like I was glad to see him, too.

We went over and sat with Poke and Amos. A lot more girls had shown up. Girls I hadn't seen before and weren't from anywhere around here. Sugar came on awful strong. But I kept turning her away. She didn't have any trouble finding somebody to dance with, and Dolly didn't either. They were both real popular with all the boys that had blown into town for the pitching. They seemed to gravitate toward the rough-stock riders. And I'll have to admit they were more wild and wooly, by nature, than the ropers and bulldoggers. They created more excitement, and that's what these girls were looking for, I figured.

Poke was having himself a hell of a time. For once there were more girls than he could dance with and he still was chousing Sally pretty hard. But Sally was so busy toting drinks, she didn't have much time for chitchat.

R.C. and I quit them early. I'd come up there to win some money and I'd seen and been through all this scene before. I'd feel better about it if I had some money in my pocket, and a certain girl by my side, before I went to partying real hard.

I asked Poke if he wanted to go, and there wasn't a chance.

"Frank, you're gittin' old," Dee said.

"Nah," I said, "it isn't that, Dee. I'm just gettin' more careful." I don't think anybody even saw us leave.

What seemed to be practically all night you could hear all kinds of hell being raised out in the hallways, as drunks, girls, and a few fights carried on from room to room. A wild party was being had, but for once I was taking no part in it. I felt kind of proud of myself.

"Let's get around," I said, "so we can get down and see when we're up. And go get something to eat! It may be a long time in between beans today." I hollered at Poke and he just groaned. "What's the matter, Pard, is demon rum about to get you this mornin'?"

Poke covered his head with a pillow. "My head is hammerin'."

"A good cup of coffee and some breakfast'll fix you up."

Again he moaned. "You're makin' me sick just talkin' about it. You go on. Let me try to heal up. I'll be around later."

Down in the lobby everything was posted. It really didn't make any difference to me when I was up, but I'd like to get my deal out of the way first off, if I really had a choice. Make a good run and let everybody try to beat me. Sure enough, I was up in the doggin' this afternoon. I also saw where Amos was up in the bareback riding and bulldogging this afternoon. Dee had a bull today and the Boss and Top would be team roping today. I figured it would be an interesting day to say the least.

We looked over the list for the Fourth and R.C. found his name. I also saw where Dee was up in the bulldoggin' and Amos had a saddle bronc. So they'd scattered us out pretty good. The luck of the draw.

"I was hoping," R.C. said, "that it'd happen today. I don't know whether I can stand another day of suspense!"

"I think it'll work for the best," I said. "This way you can get to see some bulls in action, get to see some rides, maybe learn somethin'. What bull did you draw?"

"Well, it's number eighty-eight, a bull they call 'Snuffy,' " and looked at me.

I shrugged my shoulders. "I don't know any of the bulls or any of the buckin' stock. We'll have to talk to Dee and Amos."

We went and got something to eat, came back to the room. Poke was still suffering. We made as much noise as we could, just out of orneriness if nothing else. Poke was sleeping in spurts, and moaning and groaning in between.

I showered, shaved, put on a clean shirt, clean pants, and dug a pair of boots out of my old warbag that R.C. and I were sharing.

While I was pulling them on, R.C. said, "You're gettin' all dressed up like you're going to a dance."

"Yeah. I kinda got in the habit of that. You won't believe this, but I used to wear nothin' but white shirts and they even had French cuffs."

"Why on earth would you be wearing French cuffs?"

"Oh, I think it worked a little psychological advantage on my competition. It might get them to thinkin' that I didn't plan on gettin' very dirty or takin' very long gettin' my job done."

Roberta and her family still hadn't gotten to town, but it was early yet. It didn't even cross my mind that she wouldn't make it. I knew she'd be here.

I saw Dee out in the arena riding his hazin' horse, SicEm, and leading B.B. We parked by his trailer and walked out and hollered at him.

One thing about Dee, he could stay out all night, get knee-walkin', snot-flyin', rip-roarin' drunk, but the next morning he'd be out to take care of his horses. I admired him for it.

He rode over with a big grin. "I see you're up today, Frank."

"Yep."

"Well, set 'em a pattern."

"I aim to."

"R.C., I see where you've drawn Snuffy."

"Do you know anything about him?" asked R.C.

Dee shook his head from side to side, which was his custom. He wasn't shaking his head no. "I'd know his hide in a tannery. He's a pretty shiny bull. You can win it on him if you can ride him right."

"You better tell me about him."

"I'll do it. Frank, why don't you come over here and get on B.B. and check your stirrups out."

I got on the little bay mare. The stirrups were way too short. I got off, adjusted the stirrups. Since these new Blevin buckles, we called them quick-change buckles, adjusting stirrups was a cinch.

I normally bulldogged with my stirrups at one notch, which was three inches higher than I normally rode. Since there might be an occasion to jump a long ways, I like to keep my knees flexed.

I made a lap or two around the arena with Dee. I even jumped B.B. out a little bit just to see what kind of speed she had. She was warmed up plenty good when I did it. After I caught back up with Dee, he smiled and said, "What do ya think?"

"She's a good'un. We were really shittin' and gittin'."

"I'll tell you what, pard. She can do it!"

"I believe you. If I can just get this deal pulled off."

"Don't worry about it, Frank. It's just as natural as fallin' off a horse." And then laughed.

When we finally went back to put the horses up, a pretty good crowd had gathered around. Behind the chutes there was lots of visiting going on. It usually starts several hours before the rodeo starts. And the closer rodeo time gets, you find guys beginning to loosen up doing a few calisthenics. Some go at it harder than others. And some just limber up their elbows and get a little of that liquid courage down in them.

We were all squatting around and Dee said, "Let me tell ya about this Snuffy bull, R.C. I've had him twice. He bucked me off once and I got him rode another time. As a matter of fact, I won a second on him down at Carlsbad last year. When ya call for him, really jump out with him because he comes out real high."

"What does he look like?" R.C. said.

"Oh, hell. Come on. I'll point him out to ya."

I tagged along with them. We squatted down by the bullpen and you could see a good-sized tiger-stripe bull. Red with yellow markings like a tiger. A big bull. Wasn't the biggest in the herd, but had real high horns.

"That's him," Dee said.

R.C. studied him. He had a pretty good little hump. This crossbred bull, Dee said, could sure enough buck. He was quicker than you'd think he would be for the size of him. He always jumped out high. And that first jump he would sling his head up. So you had to watch out from leaning forward. Right out of the chute he'd always duck into a right-hand spin, and not a flat spin, but a high, jumping, snapping spin, generally.

"Let's check around," Dee said, "and see what else we can find out about him. But I know this. He'll git you, once you're on the ground. So, if you git him rode or git bucked off, go to huntin' you a hole. Better yet, a high spot. We've got two clowns here that are good bullfighters, and they'll keep him off of ya."

We got the same story three different times from three different bull riders. Everybody agreed that he was a headhunter. He'd go looking for you on the ground. And this just added to R.C.'s woes.

Before you knew it, rodeo time was drawing near. The grandstand was filling up and you could just feel it in the air. The feeling of a show. Rodeo people don't like to admit it, but it had a feeling of the big top. Circus time. And activity picked up quickly behind the chutes.

A lot of cowboys were wearing bronc chaps. R.C. got so involved in everything he completely forgot about his bull. That was a day away. He really seemed to enjoy just the moment. He commented about the chaps, the bright colors, the fanciness of the way they were made, and the designs they had on them, from shamrocks to initials, as a lucky charm to the particular fellow that wore them. In all colors, green, lavender, blue. Quite a showy bunch!

We got inside the arena to watch the grand entry and the introductions and so we'd have a good seat for the bareback riding. I turned around and looked at the bleachers. They were for contestants and contestants' wives. Nowhere did I see Francesca or Roberta. Sugar and Dolly stood out like a sore thumb. They'd helped some fellers make it through the night, and were in their rightful position. You had to love rodeo to do what they did.

We squatted down alongside the fence and watched the bareback bronc riding. You could tell R.C. was fascinated. A couple of boys got bucked off and a couple made pretty fair rides. When they got down to Amos I punched an elbow in R.C.'s rib and I said, "Watch this!"

My only concern was that I'd bragged on Amos so much it was probably bad luck. He'd probably get ironed out and stake a claim right out in the middle of the arena. Sure enough, Amos didn't disappoint us.

He reared back, had his spurs up over the points of the shoulders with his toes turned out the first jump out of the chute. And when that horse's front feet hit the ground, Amos jerked his legs, bent his knees to where his knees came practically clear back to his shoulders, threw them out wide in front of him, and came back to the horse's shoulders. The horse bucked good and bucked high behind, kicking high. And every time the horse would come down, Amos's feet would be in front. And every time he went to his back feet for another lunge, Amos would pop his legs. He put on quite a ride!

When the whistle blew, the pickup men moved in on him and Amos reached over, grabbed ahold of a pickup man's waist, and turned loose. The pickup man veered off and Amos hit the ground lightly.

"What'd you think of that?" I asked.

R.C. grinned big. "Boy, that was something!"

I told R.C. I was going to mosey on down to the roping chutes and get ready. I needed some time alone to think, warm up and get loose, and get it on my mind.

Dee had SicEm and B.B. out behind the roping chutes, walking in slow circles. Dee only had myself and Amos to mount this afternoon. He was pretty particular about who he mounted.

Amos was listed to go first, so when he showed up he set the stirrups for himself. I had to shake hands with him.

"Looks like you're winnin' the bareback ridin'."

"So far. We'll see if it holds up."

"I think it will. It'll have to be a double-tough son of a bitch in order to get ahead of you!"

"I hope so," Amos said. "I can use the money."

"Hell, couldn't we all!"

CHAPTER

23

When Amos's time came up, he and Dee rode into the arena, waited in front of the dogging box until the last steer turned out had gone into the catch pen down on the other end. This was going to be a tough run on B.B. She had Amos and then directly behind Amos, me. I just hoped that she was in good shape and ready to go.

As soon as the arena was clear Dee rode into the right-hand side of the box. Amos rode into the left-hand side, set her up in the far corner. They communicated well together. They talked back and forth until the steer was looking straight ahead and Amos nodded his head for him.

Amos got down in good shape, but they were big, stout steers. He was working at it, but had a time getting the steer shaped up and slowed down. Finally got him turned around and slapped a front hold on him and went to the ground. He'd gone nine-two on him.

Since I was up next, I jumped down to the ground and walked out while Dee went down and caught B.B., who had gone clear to the end of the arena. He led her back up the arena at a trot.

Amos came back walking toward the chutes and said, "Frank, hell. I haven't got enough lead in my ass for big cattle, or lumps in my arms, for that matter."

"You made a pretty good run."

When Dee got there, Amos took one side and I took the other. I said, "Second hole up from the bottom." And I knew that's where he'd set that Blevins buckle. I checked the cinch before I got on and everything was in good shape. There was a dogging bat hanging by a thong over the saddle horn.

I looked over at Dee. "You think I'll need the bat?"

"No. Just give her a whap when you go in the box, and then hang it up. She'll take you there."

I took the bat off the saddle horn, stuck it under my arm, and, as had been my custom for many years, spit in each hand, rubbed them together, and muttered to myself, "The luck of the Indian."

I took the bat and tapped B.B. on the butt. She lurched forward as we got in the box, and I stopped her and held her on a loose rein while they pulled the barrier and stuck the pin. Once they cleared out in front of the barrier, I turned B.B. around facing the dogging chute and backed her into the far corner. I looked at my steer and he had his head turned a little to the side. I told the boys working the chutes to straighten his head out. I kept talking to them 'til his head was straight and I said, "How are you, Dee?"

"Ready."

I nodded for him and let him move just about a foot when I let B.B. go and gave her a nudge. She blew out of that chute like a ball out of a cannon! It was a good thing I was hanging on. I was holding onto the horn with my left hand and carrying my reins in my right hand. Just opposite of the way I normally rode a horse. We were coming up on the steer in good shape. It looked like I had a good shot at a fast run. Dee was right in position to keep the steer from going wide on me. He was good at his job. But I was concentrating on what I was doing.

When we pulled up along the back end of the steer, I started down, turned the reins loose, laid my right arm over the steer's back, turned loose of the horn, and B.B. blew on by. I grabbed the left horn with my left hand and gathered up the right horn in the crotch of my right arm. Propelled by B.B.'s speed, when my feet hit the ground they were set at an angle and I'd already thrown my hip into the steer, pushed down on the left horn, and jerked up on the right one.

My steer shaped up nice. I couldn't ask for a.y better. I turned the steer and had his ass end swinging around and had his nose sticking right straight up in the air when I let go of the left horn to grab his nose in the crotch of my left arm. So far it'd been a perfect run. But, I missed the nose! And there I lay, flat on my back. All the steer had to do was straighten out his head, realize that he was headed in the wrong direction because I had turned him past the ninety-degree angle, and trot on down to the other end of the arena.

I got up and dusted myself off. Pulled my hat up off my head to where it wasn't so tight, and walked back to the dogging chutes in disbelief. Everything had gone so perfect, and I had missed his nose! I knew I'd blown it and so did everybody else.

As I walked out of the arena, I could hear several people telling me, "Tough luck, Frank." "You had a good run started, Frank." They were offering their condolences. Right now, I could never remember being so thoroughly pissed! The fact was, it was my own fault! That was the puredee truth!

I didn't even acknowledge those that had spoken to me. Just kept my head down and stared at the ground as I walked past. I was leaning up against the fence with my little fingers in both my front pockets, swearing at myself, and I heard Dee ride up behind me, riding SicEm and leading B.B.

"Easy come, easy go," he said.

"Shii-it! I can remember fuckin' up, but not like that."

"You just had one problem, pard." I didn't even answer him.

"You were in too big a hurry. My God, you handled him good. If you'da just waited a half a second longer to go to the nose, you'da ironed him out and won this punkin' rollin'!"

I knew it was the truth. I turned around and petted the little bay bitch. "I'm sorry, darlin', I let you down."

Dee laughed. "You don't have to apologize to her, Frank. She knows how it is, and so do I. Did I ever tell you about a ropin' horse I had once? When I made a good catch and started to get down, he'd squat and make a big eleven on the ground with those hind feet. And while I was tyin' my calf, he'd just nicker at me while he was workin' the rope and keepin' it tight. Talkin' to me he was. But if I ever missed one, the son of a bitch wouldn't stop, and wouldn't say a goddamn word to me!"

I could see the humor. But I just wasn't up to humor right now. "I tell you what. I'm as thirsty as a tied-up Indian pony."

"I can fix that," Dee said.

We walked on over to the trailer. He loosened up the cinch on both horses, changed their bridles into halters, and tied them to the trailer. He got a jug of bourbon whiskey out of the pickup. We squatted down in the shade of the trailer and had us a little snort. I swallered 'til the bottle belched. It tasted good and it set a fire in my belly. Maybe this would ease the dejection a shade.

As we passed the bottle back and forth I noticed Dee was just taking little short nips. He had a bull to ride this afternoon. I began to really make a hand at sucking on that bottle.

"You're actin' like a rookie, Frank. You know how it goes. Some days it's roses and some days it's cactus. If I was you I'd forget about it. There'll always be one more rodeo to get to."

"I know," I said. "This isn't the first one I've missed, and I'm sure it won't be the last. But rodeos are gettin' so far apart for me now that I don't have a chance to redeem myself as often as I used to."

"Well, we can fix that. Just pack up and go down the road with Amos and me."

It had been in the back of my mind, and I'd rolled it around. If I didn't do it before too long, it'd be too late. I'd have to think about it.

I finally answered Dee. "It sounds interestin'. I'm thinkin' about it."

"That's when you're gonna git in trouble. Frank, you know the more you think about things, the more confused you git and the more trouble you're apt to git into. Just make up your mind and do it!"

I had another pull on the bottle. "I'll let you know before you pull out."

Who was I kidding? Roberta was probably the biggest thing in my life right now! I don't know how she had become so important to me so quickly. But I was still fighting it. Somewhere in the back of my mind even I resented the relationship a little. And I didn't even know why.

But the whiskey made me feel better. R.C. and Poke came over. R.C. said, "You sure looked good, Frank."

"Thanks, you're makin' me feel a lot better."

"You know how it is, Frank," Poke said. "Some days it's bacon and some days it's beans."

"Shit! All I'm tryin' to do is have a little friendly drink here and I'm surrounded by a bunch of goddamned philosophers! Between bacon and beans and roses and cactus, you guys are gonna bury me! Have you got any cold beer in your cooler?"

"Always," Dee said.

"Well, that's just what I need right now to kinda cool the fire of that panther piss I've been swallerin'!"

With that Dee opened the cooler and handed me a beer. Poke and R.C. both went for the beer, too. Dee, for the time being, was going to walk the straight and narrow.

I looked at Poke. "How are ya feelin'? You healin' up?"

Poke grinned. "I believe I'm gonna live. Took a little hair of the dog this mornin'. But with this here beer and one little snort out of that bottle, I'll be fine as frog hair."

"I thought I heard a drunk stumblin' around in our room last night," I said. "It couldn't have been you, could it?"

Poke shook his head. "Nah. It's what you git for leavin' your door unlocked."

"Uh huh," I said. "Tell us about last night. Did you get your honky wet?"

Poke smiled. "Now you know I'm not the kind to kiss and tell."

I was feeling a lot better. As a matter of fact, I was feeling better by leaps and bounds. So I thought a little good-natured hoorahing was in order. "Ain't askin' you to tell me about kissin' her."

Poke grinned again. "I ain't sayin'."

I looked at Dee and he winked back at me. "That's a dead giveaway, ain't it?"

"You bet," Dee said. "I believe our man scored last night."

"I do, too," I said. "Come on now, give us some details."

Poke just shook his head and smiled.

"Come on," I said. "Hell, I'd rather hear a feller tell about it than do it myself. Besides it's been so long for me, I forgot what it feels like. Tell me what it felt like, Poke."

Poke rolled his eyes to the sky. "My, my. It was just like a whole covey of quail just flew out of my asshole. It's what you'd call a wonderful sensation."

We all laughed.

"This is getting too nasty for me," R.C. said. "I want to get back over to the arena and find out what's happening. I'm enjoying this."

"Yeah," I said. "The bullshit is gettin' a little deep around here."

I drained my beer. "Wait a sec, and I'll go with you."

When we got back to the arena I looked up and saw the Boss and Top coming a-horseback, back behind the chutes. If there'd been a place to hide, I'd have done it. The last person I wanted to see right now was the Boss!

So I stopped as they rode by. Top said, "Frank, you had a hell of a run goin'!"

I just shook my head. "My own fault. Just flat missed his nose, Top."

The Boss just looked at me with sad eyes and then looked away. I wished he'd say something. Anything! But he didn't. And that made it all the worse.

"Good luck to you boys in the ropin'," I said.

"Thanks. Appreciate it," Top said.

And the two of them rode on. I stood there awhile and watched them leave. "Goddamn! If I live to be a hundred I never will understand the Boss!"

"Peculiar he didn't say anything," R.C. said.

"No. It's happened before. Now if I'da won it, or made a real good run, he'da never complimented me on it. But he'd be real friendly. But if you ever screw up, whether it's your fault or not, he won't speak a word to you. And it goddamn sure irritates me! For two bits I'd quit and go on down the road with Dee and Amos!"

"Ah, you don't mean it, Frank," R.C. said. "You're just upset."

R.C. and I were squatted down alongside the fence, just left of the bucking chutes, when we heard a commotion up in front. We were sitting fairly close to the gate that led to the outside of the arena. Poke had gone back up to sit in the stands. Not being a contestant, I don't even know how he had gotten back behind the bucking chutes. Pretty soon we saw what the commotion was all about.

Hooch Bray had a cowboy by the nape of the neck and it was fair to say that the cowboy was a little drunk. Hooch was throwing him out of the arena, and about after every four steps, hauling off and kicking him right in the ass as he jerked him toward the gate. Someone opened the gate for him and Hooch gave him a shove outside the arena with one more kick in the ass. "And stay out, you drunken son of a bitch!"

R.C. looked at me. "That was a little harsh, wasn't it?"

I shrugged my shoulders. "Well, he is the chute boss, and a drunk doesn't have any business in the arena. He was doin' his job. But I have to agree with you, it looked like he carried it a little too far." Besides that, the way he'd done it in the arena looked like he was playing on the crowd a little bit and showing everybody how tough he was.

"I don't care if he is the chute boss," R.C. said. "He was twice as big as that fellow. And nobody should be kicked like that guy was!"

We could hear the bulls being loaded into the chutes and I knew the first section of the bull riding would be coming up as soon as they were finished roping. I was looking forward to that. This would be R.C.'s first glimpse up close at these bulls, and I wanted to see what his reaction would be.

For once R.C. didn't say anything. He was quiet as he watched the clowns position themselves, two of them in front of the bucking chutes. You could tell he was nervous and excited. The anticipation of watching was about to get the best of him.

When the gate came open for the first bull, he had to watch close because it didn't last long. Two jumps and the rider was flung off flat on his back, but didn't stay there long and was up and running back toward the chutes.

There were eight bulls in that section.

Eight times the bulls fired, eight times the cowboys went down. The bulls were winning eight to nothing.

I glanced at R.C. and his eyes followed everything. When the rider was down, he watched the clowns as they diverted the bull's attention. The two clowns worked in harmony. What time one wasn't circling the bull, almost laying a hand on his head, the other would circle in behind him and go the other way, confusing the bull and giving the cowboy plenty of time to make an escape. And as soon as that section was over, R.C. finally spoke.

"I've never seen anything like it," he said. "Do you suppose any of these bulls will be ridden?"

I grinned at him. "Jiggs has a good set of bulls. He takes pride in them. And there are some that look damn near impossible to ride. But the old saying applies here as well as to the buckin' horses. 'There never was a horse that couldn't be rode, and there never was a cowboy that couldn't be throwed.' As impossible as some of these bulls seem to ride, there will be some tough that comes along and either by luck or skill, and it won't make a damn to him how, he'll get him rode!"

R.C. was still going on about the size of the bulls and the wild and woolly first section, when the second section of the team roping started. The Boss and Top would be in this section, and I was anxious to see how they'd do. I finally had to tell R.C. to shut up and pay attention.

When the Boss and Top rode into the arena, you could tell the announcer had done his homework, because I heard him say for all to hear that entering the arena was J.W. Stone, a cowboy that had been roping in this same arena part of the last five decades. He gave the Boss quite a buildup. He asked for a round of applause which, much to my surprise, was very scattered and not very enthusiastic.

It was then that I realized that not everybody in the whole country was a fan of the Boss. And that's why we had to go so far for brandings and gatherings. He had his own little circle of friends. Outside of that, he wasn't real popular. I had never really taken that into consideration. Perhaps it had something to do with his status around the country, his good fortune, his wealth, and maybe just plain jealousy. I'd never thought of it or recognized the symptoms until now.

Top was doing the heading and the Boss was going to gather the heels. I told R.C. to watch. Even though the Boss had a lot of years on him, all he had to do was gather up those heels. Top was plenty sudden when it came to roping horns and his ground work. They could be fixing to win the whole thing right here.

Top nodded for the steer and it looked to me like they hit the barrier just right. Top gathered his steer up. Threw a real flat loop that fit right over both horns, pulled his slack, pitched it away, and turned the steer back. The Boss dove in on Spud for the heels. Two quick swings with the rope and it looked like he'd set a perfect heel trap. To my amazement, he came up empty! When he pulled his slack, the rope popped up into the air.

The Boss had heeled so many calves over the years, he could build a loop faster than any man I've known. He popped the honda (pronounced "hon-doo") back to him, grabbed it, shook out a loop so fast that you could hardly realize any time had gone by. Again he threw his loop. And again, came up empty! I was dumbfounded. That was the first time I'd ever seen the Boss throw two loops and not connect.

But if I was astounded, I wondered how the Boss felt. I wondered if he'd ever missed two in a row in his life! The crowd fell to a hush. Top followed the steer to the end of the arena so somebody could take the rope off. All ropers were supposed to leave at the far end of the arena, but the Boss just coiled up his rope and at a walk, headed Spud to the gate. He had his head down, and was slowly shaking it like he couldn't believe what happened.

I heard the announcer say, "Let's give 'em a big hand, folks. All they'll get today is your applause."

And again, there was a small smattering of applause. As the Boss left the arena, I couldn't help but feel bad. Not that he didn't win. He'd missed two loops in a row! I know that may seem trivial to anybody else, but to the Boss it would be a blow that would set him back more than a step or two.

R.C. didn't seem to grasp what had happened. He was as excited as I'd ever seen him, looking forward to the next section of the bull riding.

"You know," I said, "the Boss is apt to be a very difficult man to work for, for a while."

"Why?" R.C. asked.

"You just saw what happened."

"So," R.C. said. "You win some and you lose some. That's what everybody's been telling me."

"Yeah. That's true. The Boss, though, is a very prideful man. I've heard him tell me on occasion how he dislikes seein' anybody just clown. Even though his two misses were not by any means clowning, I know this is how he feels about himself."

When there seemed to be an altercation down around chute four, everybody began to push forward to see what was going on. There was kind of a V lined with cowboys coming out from chute four so they could all watch what was happening. And sure enough, there was Dee.

He knew he'd drawn a chute-fighting bull, but it looked like the bull was doing his dead-level best to keep from anybody even starting him. Every time Dee would get down on him, he'd throw a fit. He damn near tore the chutes up by the roots. They wiggled the slide gate in front of his head to try and keep his attention while Dee got down on him, but the old bull was smarter than that and had seen that before. He came close to throwing himself over backwards, which is unusual for a bull.

I noticed Hooch Bray mouthing off to Dee to get down on him, get his rope pulled, and get him rode. Dee, being preoccupied with what he was doing, answered him right back that he was doing the best he could and he'd do it better if Hooch would shut up.

Seeing as how there were eight chutes, and they wanted to keep the rodeo going, they moved Dee's bull up two more chutes so they could fill in behind him, and went on with the bull riding. If Dee could ever get down on his bull, get his rope pulled, and get a fair chance at him, they'd skip back to him and let him go when he was ready.

Now Hooch was directing all this that was going on. But he came back to Dee, every time getting meaner sounding, a little tougher talking, which didn't bother Dee any. He still didn't have any luck getting down on the bull. Every time he started to tighten the rope, the bull just blew up.

After what had started in chute number four, they finally moved Dee's bull down to chute number one, and there was nowhere else for him to go. They'd filled all the seven chutes up behind Dee when Hooch made his stand.

"Goddamn it, Jensen, if you ain't gonna ride the bull, I'm gonna turn him out!"

That got Dee's attention. He looked over the top of the chute right directly into Hooch's eyes. "Over my goddamn dead body!"

"I'll give you one more chance," Hooch said, "to git on him or I'm gonna turn him out. We can't wait all day!"

"I tell you what," Dee said, "you'd better give me a fair chance with this son of a bitch, or you'll be sorry."

But you could tell he was hurrying. He did get down on him, Amos started pulling the rope, and the bull threw a fit again, mashing Dee's legs against the chute.

About that time, Hooch Bray decided he'd had enough. "You chicken shit! You oughten to've even entered the bull ridin'!" And with that he unlatched the chute gate and flung it open.

Dee had his rope pulled, but had not taken his wraps, wasn't near slid up on his rope, had his feet back behind him, and, of course, didn't last one jump. The bull flung snot and scattered bullshit to the great beyond as he left.

But as Hooch left, Dee Jensen was coming right behind him. And I'm telling you what, he had a mad on you couldn't believe! He tied into Hooch with both fists swinging, never stopping to take into account that he was outweighed by possibly a hundred pounds.

As I watched all this take place, I wondered why that bull was so highly aggravated. There are a lot of bulls that are hard to get out on, but for some reason this wasn't quite natural. It seemed like the bull had been stirred up.

About the time that Hooch threw open the gate, it had crossed my mind that maybe, just maybe, somebody had used an electric prod on him as he was in the holding alley, as he was coming into the chutes, and got his blood hot.

The moment that Dee tied into Hooch, the whole arena seemed to explode. It seemed as though half of the cowboys in the arena were on Hooch's side and the other half were on Dee's side. It could've been some of them just liked to fight, if for no other reason, just for the hell of it!

Within a few seconds the whole arena had erupted into one giant fistfight. Everybody was swinging at everybody else. I made a run to help Dee, because I figured he was terribly overmatched and was going to get the worst end of it by far. He was a double-tough little bastard, but he was way in over his head. I took two or three licks just getting over to where I could find Dee. But anybody that's ever been in a sure-enough, Wild West, rip-roaring, free-swinging, haymaking, shit-kicking, free-for-all like what was going on knows what I'm talking about! Everything is just a blur. I got thumped pretty good before I reached where I thought Dee was. And when I got there, Dee wasn't anywhere to be found, nor Hooch.

I don't know how long the fight lasted. I just started swinging at anybody that was close, when all of a sudden it seemed like the whole arena was filled with horns, hooves, and bullshit. I saw a bull go by me, narrowly missing me, and had enough sense of mind to think, What the shit? and take a run for the chutes and crawl up on the gate. I turned around and looked back and there were cowboys scattering everywhere, clear across the arena, toward the grandstand and out on each end.

It damn sure stopped the fight!

Some were being carried by their buddies, others were limping, and a few crawled out of the arena, when I noticed that eight bulls had gathered up, as they will with their own kind, down on one end of the arena by the catch pens. Standing out in front of the chutes was the county sheriff, Dub McCanless, with his gun drawn, and standing right beside him, Jiggs Rankin.

Dub was hollering at the top of his lungs. "I swear to God, any more fightin' in this goddamned arena, and somebody's gonna git shot! And I'm declarin' this rodeo over for this afternoon. Everybody go back to where they come from and settle down!"

It was then that I began to check myself over, and I had what was becoming one hell of a headache. I reached up and felt the right side of my head and there were two lumps up there the size of goose eggs.

I looked out in front of the bucking chutes and I could see my hat lying out there, so I hollered out at the two men who had command of the situation at the moment. "Can I come get my hat?"

Jiggs walked over, picked up my hat, and brought it to me. "You better not, Frank. Dub's a little nervous. He might shoot ya. Worse yet, he might get that hat."

When I got back over behind the chutes where my bunch was, everybody was kind of taking stock of themselves like I was. There were a few bloody noses, split lips. The hide had been barked off a place or two on damn near everybody, except R.C. Dee had quieted down considerable, but he was still mad.

"What the hell happened?" was my first question when I walked up to the bunch.

"I'll tell you what happened," Dee said. "That son of a bitch turned a bull out on me when I wasn't ready. And I've got proof!"

"Ah, shit, Dee," I said. "Everybody saw that! You was well within your rights. You've got a reride comin'. But after that, what happened?"

"I think I can shed a little light on that," R.C. said. "Everybody just began fighting. I didn't know who was who, so I just backed off over by the chutes. The sheriff got in there as quick as he could, but it looked like he was one man against forty. He was screaming at the top of his lungs to stop, to break it up. But nobody paid him any mind. That older man, the producer, I can't think of his name right now . . ."

"Jiggs Rankin?" I asked.

"Yeah. It was him. I don't know whether he was talking to me or not, Frank, but he said, 'There's just one way to stop this.' And he just walked along opening every chute gate, and he turned every bull loose." And with a smile R.C. said, "And you know, he was right! That thing stopped in a hurry."

Everything had settled down pretty good. Sugar and Dolly were rushing around like they were kin to Florence Nightingale, taking care of everybody, passing out beer, passing the bottle around, talking over what happened.

Dee shook his head side to side. "I just don't understand it. I've drawn that bull at least a half a dozen times. He's always been bad to git out on, but never anything like that!"

When I told him my little theory his eyes lit up. "You've hit on it, Frank! That son of a bitch had them goose him with the Hotshot, so I couldn't git out on him. I'll tell you what, pard, this ain't over yet!"

I rubbed the knot on my head and shook my head. "I had a feelin' it wasn't."

I had been holding my head all this time, and believe me, it was thumping like a two-cylinder pump jack. I brought my hand down and saw blood on it. "Somebody take a look at my head and see what in the hell's wrong with it."

Here came Sugar eager to do her job. She parted my hair and looked at my scalp. "Oh my God, your head's been split open!"

"What do you mean?" I asked.

"There's got to be at least a four-inch gash here. I think you ought to go to the hospital and get it sewed up."

"Oh, I don't think so. Somebody else take a look that knows what they're talkin' about." I think I hurt Sugar's feelings. Several others looked. "Well, it sure split the skin, Frank."

They dug some ice out of the beer cooler and put it in a cellophane sack so I could hold it up to my head. I got to wondering about Dee. "Did Hooch do any harm to you, Dee?"

Dee grinned. "Ah, the big son of a bitch got in a lucky punch." He reached up and pulled out his upper front teeth. "This is what I hate. The son of a bitch broke my teeth."

With that I thought R.C. was going to go into shock. "Oh, my God, Dee! You've had all your front teeth knocked out!"

As bad as my head hurt, I had to laugh. So did Dee.

"Hell," Dee said, "these aren't my front teeth. Well, I guess they are. They're bought and paid for. But these is false teeth. Just the same, they're broke anyway. He broke them right in the middle."

Dee's lips weren't even split bad. All you could see was a slight abrasion on his upper lip. "Hell, I got these knocked out down at Socorro. I think you were with me, Frank."

"You caught a horn, bulldoggin', right in the mouth hole."

Dee threw back his head and laughed. "That's right. I didn't know you'd remember."

"Oh, yeah. I remember. I never forget funny things that happen like that."

We loaded up pretty good on the whiskey and beer and decided to head back to the hotel. I had a feeling that we had a war party that was fixing to go out tonight, and I was really getting cranked up for it.

After R.C. and I got in the car and started back to town, I said, "You know, the only really unfortunate thing about this whole mess this afternoon is, Dee didn't get to ride his bull, and they didn't have the bull scramble."

With a puzzled look, R.C. said, "What's a bull scramble?"

"That's where they tie a Bull Durham sack onto a bull's horns and tell everybody that it's got a fifty-dollar bill in it. They tie it on a bad head-fightin' bull, and turn him loose in the arena. And any cowboy that can grab that Bull Durham sack, they give him fifty dollars. With the way I bulldogged today, I was hopin' I could get that fifty bucks and maybe tomorrow, too, to kinda help take care of expenses."

"That looks like an awfully hard way to try to earn fifty dollars to me," R.C. said.

"What it takes, R.C., is agility, quick feet, nimbleness, being swift and brave and courageous."

R.C. looked at me out of the side of his eye. "Frank, you aren't any of those things but the last two."

"Well, those last two ain't bad. But the best way to put it is, every now and then a blind hog'll stumble onto an acorn."

R.C. just shook his head and grinned.

When we pulled up in front of Kitchins, there was Kika. Still no Roberta. Much to R.C.'s disappointment, she was more worried about me, or seemed to be, than she was glad to see R.C. She made a big to-do over my split head. I tossed it off as nothing, even though I had to wear my hat a little gingerly, cocked on the side of my head.

I asked her if she'd seen Roberta. She smiled and shook her head. "I was here all through the rodeo and looked for her, and Frank, she just never showed up. I don't know what happened."

"Did you enjoy the rodeo?" R.C. asked.

She smiled and clapped her hands together. "More than any rodeo I have ever seen. Especially there at the end when they turned all those bulls loose when the big fight was happening. I don't suppose any of you paid any attention, but the whole crowd stood up and cheered and gave you a standing ovation. That was the best closing of any rodeo I've ever seen!"

R.C. and I both had to laugh. "Well," I said, "let's go up to the room and have a drink."

R.C. kind of frowned at me. I knew what was on his mind. He didn't want to take a respectable girl up there among all those rodeo cowboys and boogie mamas. So he and Kika got into Sundown and left, and I went on up to the room for a war council.

CHAPTER

24

The whole upstairs of the Kitchins Hotel had turned into one big party. Everybody congregated in Dee and Amos's room. My head was hurting me so bad I lay down and thought about having somebody go down to the bar and get me a straw so I could drink beer without raising my head. Somebody came up with the theory that to make a split on my head like that, I'd have had to been hit with a baseball bat.

Then Amos came up with a solution. "Frank, there's only one thing in an arena that would lay open your head like that. A Hotshot."

A Hotshot was a trade name for those electric prods. They were about an inch and a half in diameter, about two and a half feet long, filled with batteries to give it the electric charge. And the only ones who had access to Hotshots had been Hooch Bray's chute crew.

I could feel myself getting madder and madder. The whiskey was helping a little of the pain, but it was also about to trip the trigger that held my temper in place.

Then I heard the room grow very quiet and I heard a woman's voice. "I hope I'm not interrupting anything."

I recognized the voice. It was Roberta.

About that time one of the boys in the room jumped to his feet, swept off his hat, and said, "No, ma'am, you're not interrupting anything." He reached over and grabbed her by the arm, pulled her into the room, and said in a very sweet voice, "Where have you been all my life, you little lotus blossom?"

I came off that bed like a shot! Roberta was standing there wide-eyed, beautiful as ever, dressed in a solid-colored western snapped shirt that emphasized her figure yet revealed nothing. She had on a pair of Levis like the rest of us wore, and good cowhide boots with heels on them that made her as tall as anybody else in the room, if not taller.

"Get your hands off her," I said. "This one belongs to me!"

Out in the hall I said, "My God, Roberta, I was worried about you! Where have you been?"

"That's a long story. The question right now is," with a little laugh, "where have you been? This place looks like a den of carnal sin."

"Yeah," I said. "I know. I apologize. Come on down to our room and we can get away from some of this."

When we got in our room she had regained her composure somewhat. "Do you realize what you said back there in that room?"

I reached up and felt my head and grimaced a little bit. "I don't know what you're talkin' about."

"You told that cowboy that I belong to you."

"Oh. Yeah. I'm sorry. I had no right to say that. It just popped out."

Roberta smiled and sat down in one of the chairs, and crossed her legs. "That's all right. I don't mind a bit. Frank, why were you calling that girl in there 'Sugar'? You seemed to be rather intimate with her." She had a faint smile on her face as she said this, and a twinkle in her eye. I didn't think I was in too much trouble, but I was on shaky ground.

"Oh, that. That's her name."

Roberta laughed. "I've never known anybody named Sugar, outside of a pet horse."

"She's Dee and Amos's friend. She's just one of the camp followers that goes from rodeo to rodeo."

"Yes. I've heard about those kinds of girls. In fact, I just saw another one. I've been around some, but that shocked me."

"What happened?"

"As I walked down the hall, a door was partially open and I knocked. And there was quite a commotion going on inside, so I just stuck my head in and I couldn't believe what I saw! There was a blond-headed girl and a cowboy with his hat on, ah, for the lack of a better word, making love. And there were two cowboys sitting in the chair watching!"

Then she giggled. "The funny part about it was, outside of his hat, the girl was chewing bubble gum, and while I asked my question she glanced over at me and blew a big bubble. And all this time they never stopped."

"Well, at least we know where Sugar's friend Dolly is. But what happened? I left tickets at your house."

She slumped back in her chair and rolled her eyes. "Wouldn't you know it? Dad went out to check some yearlings early this morning, and you know Murphy's Law. The one windmill we had in that whole pasture had broken down, so I had to go help Dad pull it. By the time we got all that done and came to town, we'd missed everything. I'm sorry."

"Well, you didn't miss much." And I recounted the entire day to her, my failure in the bulldogging and the big free-for-all that closed the rodeo down.

She walked over to me, held my head, and separated my hair. "Gosh, Frank, this looks terrible. I think you need stitches!"

"Nah. It'll heal up. It can't be very deep, bone's right underneath it."

She still had ahold of my head, but she put her hand under my chin and tilted my head up with a smile. "I'm serious about this cut on your head. Since I was a little girl, I've heard rodeo announcers say that the only way you can hurt a cowboy is cut his head off and go bury it somewhere where he can't find it." She smiled. "But you'd better have it sewn up."

So, reluctantly, I agreed.

We got back in the car and Roberta said, "I think we better go get something to eat. After all the disappointments you've had today and the trouble, I know you drank a great deal of alcohol."

Then the thought hit me. "I will go eat, but before we do, do you mind driving out to the rodeo grounds?"

She looked at me with a question in her eyes. "Not at all. But there's nobody out there."

"So? There's no chance of me gettin' into trouble, right?"

She smiled. "Right."

We drove on out to the rodeo grounds, and of course it was deserted. The Rankins had their own trucks to move their stock from rodeo to rodeo. We pulled up alongside of them. "I want to check something. It's a long shot, but I just want to look."

I was disappointed to find that they had locked the equipment truck up. It carried all the Hotshots, saddles, bucking halters, and all the equipment needed to put on a rodeo. But something caught my eye lying over by the corral fence. I walked over and picked it up. And sure enough, it was a Hotshot. Bent, practically in a forty-five-degree angle. It was no longer useful, so they hadn't put it in the truck.

Roberta was still sitting in the car. I walked back over with the Hotshot and held it up for her to see. "Now we know what put the dent in my head."

She took it from my hand and hefted it. "It's a wonder it didn't kill you, Frank."

I smiled. "Nah. They'd have to cut off my head and bury it, remember?"

But just for proof, I had her open the trunk of her Chevy and I threw the Hotshot in.

We went on down to Kitchins and ate. Although I was still mad, still half drunk, just being with Roberta had eased my mind a good deal. But I did have revenge on my mind. I tried to keep my temper under control every day of my life. I knew that whiskey aggravated it, depending upon the occasion. Sometimes it was a very needed ingredient that relaxed me, made me laugh, and no one ever thought a thing about it. There had been a few times in my life when whiskey turned on me, coupled with my temper, and made me an unholy terror.

Dee and Amos came down and joined us in the booth. I introduced Roberta. Dee, being the more gregarious of the two, was quite complimentary to Roberta.

Amos just smiled, and didn't say much.

"My God, Frank," Dee said, "you're sittin' here ruinin' a fifty-dollar drunk, with a damned old two-dollar chicken-fried steak! That don't make no sense. If you ain't careful, it might sober you up."

Roberta winked at him. "That's the idea."

"Well, drunk or sober, I want this man on my side. We've still got a score to settle, don't we, Frank?"

I glanced at Roberta and didn't see any reaction. All I could say was, "I reckon."

Roberta thought about it awhile. "Do you have to keep carryin' this fight on and keep holdin' a grudge?"

"Roberta," I said, "somebody bent that Hotshot over my head and I can't let them get away with that."

That raised Dee's ire, too. "This has been a runnin' battle now for a good long while, between me and Hooch Bray. I paid good hard money to enter this rodeo, and to ride that bull. Hell, I didn't even git a chance! And one way or another, it's got to be settled."

"But," Roberta said, "not tonight."

Dee shrugged. "If they go to the dance, it'll probably be settled tonight."

She looked at Amos. "What's your stake in this, Amos? Can't you talk them out of it?"

Amos just shook his head from side to side.

"Well," she said, "why are you getting involved in it?"

Amos looked at her, and as solemn as he could possibly say it in that Lakota way of his, said, "Two reasons. One, these are my friends. Two, I like to fight."

That kind of shook Roberta. She had no more questions.

The dance was going to be held at the airport hangar. I had made up my mind that I was going to try, try hard, to stay out of trouble. I'd take this up another day.

The music was good, plenty of room to dance, and everybody was having a good time. All the rodeo factions stayed apart. Hooch Bray and his bunch stayed in one end of the hangar and the traveling cowboys and Dee's bunch stayed on the other side. We made a run for the car quite frequently to have a snort of puddin', as Dee called it. We hadn't seen Poke. But one thing was very evident, Sheriff McCanless wasn't taking any chances. He'd been sorely outmanned at the rodeo, but it looked like he'd called everybody in; all deputies from surrounding counties, even in Texas, anybody with law experience he had deputized. He wasn't going to be caught with his pants down around his ankles again!

Poke turned up around ten-thirty. With a sneaky grin he said, "Frank, chances are real good tonight I'm gonna git lucky and I need a set of wheels. You think you could loan me Ol' Bullet? I won't git drunk and wreck it, I promise. You can catch a ride with R.C. Come on, be a friend, Frank."

How could I refuse? I fished out the keys to Ol' Bullet. "Treat her gently."

Everything went pretty smoothly, 'til toward the end of the dance a scuffle erupted out on the dance floor. They weren't all that uncommon, and anybody that has ever been to a rodeo dance knows there'll be a few fights.

Then I saw who was involved in it. Again it was Dee and Hooch. Hooch had Dee by the collar. Shaking him like a rag doll, Hooch flung him down on the floor and jumped on him and was proceeding to thump the hell out of him!

Out of the corner of my eye I saw somebody coming and it was Amos. He took a flying leap and grabbed Hooch on the back, arm around his throat latch, and hung onto him like he was riding a bareback horse.

Hooch's contingent all gathered up surrounding him. All I can remember was jumping to my feet and taking off running.

My entry into the fray was conceived from playing years of football. I had no intention of running over there and trying to hit somebody with my fists. My theory was to hit them at a dead run with a double-forearm shiver. My elbows stuck out on each side like I was trying to take off and fly. I waded into them at full speed.

Some of them I hit in the back and some in the front. But I scattered them like marbles! I also fell down. I scrambled to my feet again and made another run. This time I met a more formidable resistance. But I was still doing a great lot more than my share.

Between the whiskey and the temper, I just completely blew it! I was out of control. Punches that hit me did not hurt. All I could think of was inflicting the greatest amount of pain on anybody that got in my way. I wasn't very picky either. Even if somebody on my side happened to be standing in the way, I just coldcocked them.

Faintly, in the background I could hear sirens. But that didn't stop me. Nothing could stop me! I felt like I was being choked from behind and being drug to the ground, yet I kicked, struggled, fought. Then I heard a voice out of all the commotion holler at me.

"Frank! Stop it! Frank! Stop it now!"

I realized it was Roberta's voice. For some strange reason she had a power over me that nobody had ever had in my life.

I stopped struggling and relaxed and found that I was pinned down by policemen hanging on both legs, a couple trying to hold my arms down, and one lying on his back behind me with a billy club up underneath my chin. And I think all of them were relieved when I finally quit struggling!

All I could say was, "Okay, okay, okay. I'll quit."

I was stood up, handcuffed, and led to a police car. I glanced over at Roberta. She was biting on a knuckle with tears in her eyes. I felt about as high as the underside of a snake.

When they finally packed us off to jail, I wasn't the only one by any means! Amos, and even R.C., Dee, and several others, were in one holding cell. Believe me, Dub had a land-office business. His jail was full for the first time in years.

He had Hooch and his boys quarantined at one end of the jail and us at the other end. Everybody seemed to be taking it pretty well but R.C., and he was as nervous as a fart in a skillet. He could not believe that he was incarcerated! In jail!

He looked at me in disbelief. "What have I done? Will this go on my record? I've never been in jail before in my life! Have you, Frank?"

I glanced up at him. "I'm gonna take the fifth on that, R.C., on the grounds that it might incriminate me. Settle down. We haven't robbed a bank or killed anybody. There's just been a fight. You haven't committed any felony. R.C., they're not gonna keep us locked up in here. This isn't a prison. This is just a jail. They're just gonna cool us off for a while. I have a feelin' come mornin' they'll let us all out. The only thing is, it's gonna cost some money. And that's one thing I'm short of."

That seemed to settle him down a little bit. I glanced over at Amos and he just sat there. Stoic, in the Indian way. He never said a word, but with his hands he pointed a finger at me and took two fingers, pointing out from his hand, wiggled them in the air in a snakelike motion.

I smiled. I took my hand and made a cutting motion across my throat and pointed at him. And he smiled. If anybody had seen what the two of us had done, they would have thought we were deaf and dumb. Actually, he had given me the sign of my tribe, like "I know who you are," and I had given his back to him, saying, "I know you, also. And we will endure."

Amos winked at me and reached up in his shirt pocket and pulled out what looked to be about two-thirds of someone's ear. It still dripped of blood.

When everybody saw that ear, everybody reacted in his own way. Some were proud of him, some were disbelieving that he'd do that, and R.C. was mortified.

He rolled his eyes to the sky and said, "Whose ear is it?"

Amos shrugged his shoulders. "An enemy."

I had a feeling we'd find out in the morning.

Staying in jail all night is a sobering proposition. Which is just what old Sheriff McCanless had in mind. About seven o'clock the next morning Poke came around. The jailer let him in to see us. R.C. called him off to one side and talked to him. At the time I didn't think much about it.

At eight o'clock in walked the sheriff with a couple of state troopers and a couple of deputies. "Boys, we're gonna have a settlin' of the mind on this matter. This is my town and this shit has gone on long enough. I want everybody to file upstairs to the courtroom. I dare anyone to start a ruckus or a fracas of any kind, 'cause I double-damn guarantee you, I'll make 'em pay!"

He stated his case very well and none of us were tempted to go against him as we filed upstairs to the courtroom, our side on one side of the courtroom and Hooch's on the other. Jiggs Rankin was there.

Dub started out. "All right, I want this hashed out, now!"

It did me a great deal of good to notice that Hooch Bray had a patch of gauze damn near the size of another hat on the side of his face covering up his left ear.

After about two hours of wrangling, Jiggs made Hooch get up and apologize and said if he didn't, son-in-law or not, he'd fire him! But in the last of his apology, he said, "There's just one thing. I want whoever bit my ear off to be prosecuted. I want to press charges!"

There were a few snickers around the room as he glared at our side. Sheriff McCanless said, "Do you know who did?"

"Not exactly which one. Who could be sure in a mishmash like that? But, I know it was one of 'em, Sheriff."

Old Dub looked him in the eye. "Prove it."

Well, things weren't looking too good for our side about that time. However, Dee got up and said, "Well, if he's gonna do that, I'll tell you what. Frank Dalton here ought to press charges, too."

Dub looked over at him. "What in the hell for?"

"Because somebody split his head open in the fight in the arena yesterday."

"Can you prove it?" Dub said.

"Hell, yes. Come here, Frank."

I got up and walked over to the sheriff. "Bend down."

I lowered my head so our little, potbellied sheriff could get a look at the top of my head.

"Pretty good lick. Do you know who done it?"

I was standing right by Hooch. "No," I said. "Not exactly. But it was one of them."

"How do you know it was one of them?" the sheriff asked. "Can you prove it?"

Well, he had me there. It looked like a standoff to me at this point, when I heard Poke's voice in the back of the room. "Say, I think he can prove it was one of them."

Old Sheriff Dub made him state his name. When I saw Poke hold up the bent Hotshot, I thanked God Roberta was smart enough to get it out of her car and clue him into what might happen.

Dub turned the Hotshot over in his hand a time or two. "There's no doubt in my mind that this is what put that crack on your head, Frank. But we still don't know who was wieldin' it."

"I'll let it drop if Hooch lets his damn ear deal drop!"

Hooch backed off and the sheriff made his speech. "Boys, we've got another rodeo to put on this afternoon. There'll be no more settlin' of grudges. Understood?"

Everybody agreed, to the man.

"I've gone to considerable expense," he said, "bringin' in officers from other parts of the county. So, I'm finin' each side the sum of . . ." he put his hand to his chin, looked up at the ceiling, and wrinkled his nose. "Five hundred dollars, each side."

Well, it probably would have amounted to twenty dollars a man on our side, but that there was a blow in itself. I didn't know how we were going to scrape up any five hundred dollars.

Jiggs Rankin was the first one to step up. That old man always had money in his britches to bet on a horse race or to buy a good bucking horse. He stayed ready. He fished out five hundred dollars and handed it to Dub.

"This is for my boys. I'll take it out of their hide and out of their wages."

About that time Poke popped up. "And I'll take care of it for these boys over here." He had an unlit cigar in his fingers and was as proud of himself as he could be. He strolled up to Dub, reached in his pocket, pulled out a wad of bills, wet his thumb, and went to shuffling through them and pulled out five one-hundred-dollar bills!

"There, Sheriff, I believe that'll take care of it."

Dub seemed quite pleased. "Thank you kindly, boys. Now you're all free to go. Remember my warnin'. I want a good rodeo this afternoon and no more of this fightin'."

Sheriff Dub's speech had made an impression on us. All the fight was gone. The only thing that remained from the night before was a few pretty good hangovers and a slight bit of animosity.

When we got out to the street, we found Kika and Roberta there waiting for us. Amazingly, in the same company with Dolly and Sugar, and it looked like they were all getting along just fine. I reckon they had struck common ground.

Everybody that Poke bailed out wanted to make a little restitution, and if they couldn't make it all they'd give him a marker for it. And Poke refused them all. Now he had his cigar lit, was waving his arms with grand gestures. "No, no. I can't take your money, boys. I'm doin' this out of the goodness of my heart and because I think you boys was right."

I knew all this was bullshit. And even though I didn't feel the best myself, I couldn't help but grin at Poke. R.C. was another story. He couldn't even look Francesca in the eye. All he could mumble, looking down at the sidewalk, was that he was sorry and if she didn't ever want to see him again, he'd understand.

Kika just laughed it off and grabbed him by the arm. "Just don't make a habit out of it. You were doing what you thought was right trying to help a friend. How about a little breakfast?"

Roberta and I started out behind R.C. and Kika.

"I appreciate your sending that Hotshot up with Poke."

"I thought it might help."

I allowed how it did. "There's somethin' else I've got to thank you for, too."

"What?"

"I don't know how, but you seem to know me better than I know myself. You called the shots last night. I can still hear your voice callin' out to me to stop strugglin'. I don't know what it was, but yours was the only voice I could hear and it was the only voice that mattered."

She hugged my arm tighter to her.

"If you can put up with me," I said, "I'll try not to let that happen too much. I told you that's just the way I am. But I'll try to veer away from those circumstances if I can."

"I'm just afraid, Frank, that someday your temper is either going to get you killed or you'll kill someone."

I nodded my head. "Me, too. But, I am sorry."

As an answer, she just squeezed my arm.

Being out in the sunshine, smelling the great outdoors, was doing wonders for me and my mood lightened up. "God it's great to be free!"

I heard Poke hollering behind us, "Hey! Wait up. Don't run off and leave me."

"Where in the hell did you get five hundred dollars?"

"You know when this mornin' I went into jail to see you guys, R.C. called me over and told me to go git in his suitcase where I'd find some money."

He shook his head. "Frank, that five hundred dollars, he'll never miss it, even though he knows it's gone. There's no end to that boy's money!"

"Poke," I said, "how come you're takin' all the credit for bailin' us out and not, at least, tryin' to get back some of the money these boys have been pushin' in your face?"

"Hell, that's the way he wanted it, Frank. He said, 'Don't tell 'em where you got the money and I'll foot the bill. Don't let 'em pay you back.' "

What could you say to that?

CHAPTER

25

We were all sitting in a booth in Kitchins Saloon after the rodeo parade was over. The door to the street was propped open and there was one hell of a commotion out on the sidewalk. Who should ride in the front door of that saloon a-horseback but Egg Robbins! I'll tell you now, if I was going to get drunk, I'd have given fifty bucks for his start! I don't think he'd ever let up from the night before at the dance.

He rode that old horse like he was riding into his own barn. He rode it around the tables and squalled at the top of his lungs, "Wahoo! I'm a son of a bitch from Texas!"

I glanced over at Pete who was washing glasses. He never even looked up, but said in a loud voice, "I always wondered where you was from, Egg."

I believe Egg got the point. "Give me a bottle, Pete, and put it on my bill."

Pete walked over behind the bar, got a pint of bourbon, still never looked at Egg, just handed it to him. "I'd appreciate it if you'd be on your way."

Egg turned his toes out and with another squall went out the way he came. And the funny part about it was, nobody paid a great lot of attention to him, except R.C.

His words were, "If I live through today, I'll never forget this place as long as I live! I'm sure going to hate to leave."

I couldn't believe what I'd just heard. I looked at R.C. "I don't think I understood you. What'd you just say?"

"Frank, I'm going to have to leave."

I looked at Kika and she just shrugged her shoulders. I looked at Roberta and just got a faint smile.

"Evidently," I said, "everybody here knows somethin' I don't. Suppose somebody tells me. And why in the hell am I the last to know?"

"Frank, because it's going to be you that's the hardest to say goodbye to. 'Course, outside of Kika here. And I've already talked it over with her."

"But, I don't understand. Aren't you happy here?"

"Frank, I'm happier here than anyplace I've ever been. I can't tell you what I'm doing, or why I'm doing it. You've got to trust me. There's a purpose behind it. I've met Francesca here, who means more to me than any woman alive. All of you," and he looked at Roberta, "I've become very close to. But when I set out earlier this year, I was on a mission."

"A mission? What are you? A Mormon?" I asked.

"No, no. Not a mission like that. It was a commitment I made to myself and someone else. And I've already stayed longer than I'd planned, because I like it so well here. All I ask you is to be my friend and understand."

This really took me back because I had been toying with the idea of leaving myself and going with Dee and Amos on down the road. But if R.C. left and I left, that'd just leave Jim back there at the ranch. And that didn't hardly seem fair.

"Have you told the Boss yet, R.C.?"

He shook his head. "When I do it'll be the hardest thing I've ever done. But the sooner the better, I'll give notice."

"Well, I'll be damned! I thought you'd found a home here."

He smiled at me. "Maybe I have, Frank. But I've still got this commitment to myself that I've got to finish."

I had to order another round of drinks. "Well, you said it. To make this all work, you've got to live through today. So, let's just enjoy this day the best we can."

We all tipped our glasses in a salute to R.C.

Out at the rodeo grounds R.C. and I took our usual spot and watched the bareback riding. When it was over, I was pleased to realize that Amos had won it going away. Dee would be up in the bulldogging and as a settlement in the big discussion that morning, Jiggs Rankin had given Dee a choice of a reride on another bull or the same bull back again.

Strangely enough, Dee had chosen the same bull that he'd had a hard time on yesterday. Had it been me, I'd have looked for an easier route. But Dee seemed to think he could win something on this bull and he knew what he was doing.

Since the bull riding would be the last event outside of the bull scramble, R.C. had plenty of time to get nervous. And as the rodeo went on, he did just that.

Just before the saddle bronc riding, we walked out to the cars and Amos was sitting in his saddle, rosining the swells and his chaps, leaning over to one side swinging a foot back to the cantleboard and doing the same on the other side. When he was satisfied that he had his stirrups set just right, he threw the saddle over his shoulder and headed back behind the chutes.

R.C. said, "Frank, Amos's chaps have me puzzled. I didn't want to say anything. But curiosity has the best of me now."

I knew what he was going to ask about, and I was wondering how R.C. would take it.

"What I can't understand is the red handprint. See it? On each side of his batwing chaps." And they had indeed a handprint cut out of red leather and sewn on his chaps.

"That's the sign, the Indian sign, that he has killed a man in hand-to-hand combat."

R.C.'s eyes almost popped out of their sockets. "Really?"

"Yeah."

"Frank, are you hoorahing me again like you always do, or are you telling me the truth?"

"No sir. It's the honest-to-God truth."

"Frank, do you think it's true?"

"What is true?"

"That Amos has killed someone in hand-to-hand combat?"

I shrugged my shoulders. "He's a proud man, an honorable man. I don't think he'd wear it if he hadn't earned it."

"My God! I can't believe it. How'd it happen?"

"I don't know. I've never asked him about it."

Then I said, "I want you to watch this, R.C." This was Amos's best event. Even though Amos was one of the best bareback riders I'd ever seen, he was a natural saddle bronc rider. "If you thought that bareback ride was somethin', you watch this saddle bronc ride. This could really get wild."

We got back into the arena for the start of the saddle bronc riding and it looked to me like easy pickings for Amos.

It went perfect for about four or five seconds. Immediately, I saw what happened. Amos was getting too wild on his downstroke; instead of placing his feet just above the horse's shoulder break, he spurred high up on his neck and spurred over his bucking rein. And the next lunge of the bronc pulled his thighs out from the swells of the saddle and popped him out of the saddle like a champagne cork!

Amos took a high dive right straight up in the air, let go of the bucking reins, and lit on his feet, like he'd almost planned to do it on purpose.

We left the arena. It was time for R.C. to get ready for his bull ride, and we headed back to the car. I opened my old warbag up and pulled out the bull rope and the old glove and a sack of hard rosin, and handed them to R.C. "You know how to do it. Work it over one last time. Get her good and sticky."

The girls sat down in the shade of the trailer and drank a beer with me. Kika said, "I'm scared to death for R.C., Frank. Do you think he'll go through with it?"

"He's still got time to back out, but I don't think he will. He's got too much pride. And you know what? I think he'll be okay. You always got to get on your first one if you're gonna ride 'em. Now's as good a time as any."

Kika just shook her head. "Why does he want to do this? I don't understand you and your kind at all, Frank. You don't have to prove anything to us."

I looked over at Roberta and back at Kika. "As strange as it may seem, we're not doing it to impress girls."

This part had never entered Kika's mind. "I thought that was probably the whole idea, that he was trying to impress me with his bravery."

"No. I don't think so. Mainly, it's to test yourself. For R.C. it's something he's got to prove to himself. I don't think, even as much as he thinks of you, that you have any bearin' on what he's doin'."

Amos walked up with his saddle over his shoulder and his bronc rein in his hand. With a sheepish smile, cocked his head. "Did you see what happened, Frank?"

"Yeah."

"I should have known better!"

We got behind the chutes when they started running the bulls in. In the first section of bulls, R.C.'s bull hadn't come in. But Dee's had.

Again the bull fought the chute, but not nearly as bad as he had yesterday. And I couldn't help but notice Hooch standing out in front of the chute with that big patch on his ear.

Finally Dee was ready and had taken his wraps and I heard him holler, "Outside!"

Dee's bull was a good one. He went into a flat spin to the right and Dee never loosened up. He even used his left foot to hook him a little. The bull started back to the left and Dee changed feet and was hooking him with the outside leg when the whistle blew. It was by far the best bull ride of the rodeo.

Dee landed on both feet and took off to the chutes. He shinnied up the chutes, turned around, and sat on top of the fence.

"What do you think, Amos? Will it win a check?"

Amos just nodded his head.

By this time R.C. began pacing up and down in back of the chutes. At each end he'd stop and do knee bends. He began to pop his hands together at the thumbs, like he was trying to slide the thumb deeper into the glove.

After the first section of the bull riding was over, they moved down to the roping chutes for the team roping and began to fill the chutes up again with bulls. In chute two stood the bull called Snuffy, R.C.'s bull. We walked over and looked at him.

"Oh, my God, Frank! He's even bigger than I thought he was. And look at his horns!"

"You'll do all right, pard. Don't worry about it."

I threaded the end of the bull rope through the loop, slid it around to where the handhold was on top so I could pull the rope from the right side. Felt the bull's back and placed the rope right in back of his shoulder muscles. I was doing everything I could think of to help R.C. I wanted everything to be perfect. The rest was up to him.

When I got to the place that I thought was just right, I tightened the rope up with my right hand and held the handhold in position with my left. Then slipped the tail of the bull rope underneath, so it wouldn't slip off, and got out of the chute. The flankers were putting a soft cotton rope around the flank of the bull, in front of one hip and behind the other, and left it tied loosely until we were ready to go.

When they finally finished the roping, the announcer turned everybody's attention back to the chutes. They were going to start at chute number one.

R.C. got up on the platform that ran about two feet below the top of the fence in back of the chute. I said, "Climb aboard, pardner. You'll be second."

I don't suppose it helped a lot, but when they started in chute number one, they had a hell of a wreck right in front of the chutes.

The cowboy got bucked off and got mashed. The clowns got the bull off the cowboy, but the cowboy never moved. They had to call the ambulance in and haul him off. That, in front of R.C.'s eyes, didn't help at all!

After the arena cleared and the ambulance left, I heard the announcer say, "We move down to chute number two, R.C. Roth on the bull Snuffy."

R.C. sat down on the bull and I pulled his rope tight. He had his hand in the handhold and was taking his wraps. I was leaning over and showing him how to do it when R.C. looked up at me and said, "Frank, I'm not ready."

"R.C., bull riders are never ready. It just comes their turn. Keep your knees flexed, pardner, and turn your toes out, bow out at the chest . . ."

"No, no. You don't understand what I mean."

I looked at him and I could tell in his eyes. "Oh, no."

He nodded his head. "I'm very excited, and you know what happens when I get excited."

I laid my hand on his head so I wouldn't knock off his hat, and though I hated to do it, reared back and just slapped the snot out of him. This brought Hooch running up to the chute asking what the hell was going on. By that time the stars began to get out of R.C.'s head.

R.C. leaned over the chute gate. "No, no. It was something he had to do. We do it all the time. It's part of the ritual."

"Whenever you're ready," I said, and R.C. was looking down at his hand. "Get up on your rope."

He hunched up as close to his hand as he could get and nodded his head.

The gate came open and Snuffy came out as billed. He threw his head high, but when he came down, R.C. was still there, looking good. I was hollering instructions at R.C. I knew he couldn't hear me. The bull circled in great, high jumps to the right. The bull was bucking high, showy, double kicking. He switched back to the left, and I couldn't believe that R.C. was still there. He never moved from the middle. I don't know whether it was because of the pressure of landing, or on purpose, but both of R.C.'s feet would come out and he'd put them right back in the bull again.

It appeared like he was spurring the bull. I thought he was just trying to get his feet repositioned after getting them jerked out every jump. But nevertheless, it was showy. I don't know how in the world he managed it, but he put on a beautiful bull ride!

When the whistle blew, I was thrilled for him. I honest-to-God thought he'd won the bull riding. But it wasn't over yet. He swung the leg to get off, but that bull gave him a bounce and he lost all control of his body and lit in a heap back in front of the circle where the bull was coming! All of a sudden I realized this high-horned bull had my pardner and was mopping the arena floor with him.

Before I even knew what I was doing, and I had no business doing it, I vaulted over the back of the chute onto the arena floor, ran out and slapped the front hold on that bull, just like you would a dogging steer. I don't know what in the hell I thought I was going to do. But I jerked him just like I would a steer trying to shape him up. R.C. had time to scramble up, get to his feet, and make a run for the fence. And there I was out there trying to bulldog a fifteen-hundred-pound Bramer bull, when all of a sudden the bull realized somebody had ahold of him. With one giant swing of his head he turned me loose and sent me cartwheeling in a flat spin, belly button down, thirty feet across the arena before I hit the ground.

I could see that being flung thirty feet was a blessing! It gave me that much of a head start. That was all I needed 'cause the bull was headed my way to finish up the confrontation. I left. I reached the top of the chute gate just as the bull reached the bottom. Out of harm's way, I turned around and sat myself down on the top rung.

When I noticed a roar in my ears, and finally figured out it was coming from the grandstand, I didn't know whether they were cheering for R.C.'s ride, or my little derring-do rescue. Just to be on the safe side, I tipped my hat and crawled over the chute to the back where pandemonium was breaking loose.

All up and down the alley in back of the chutes cowboys were grinning, whopping R.C. on the back, shaking his hand, and giving him congratulations. He took it all with great modesty. Either that or he was dazed. If he heard the phrase "real shiny ride" once, he must have heard it a dozen times!

I waited until he worked through the crowd toward me and stuck out my hand. He grasped it with gratitude. I said, "Congratulations! How did it feel?"

R.C.'s eyes were wide with excitement. "Frank, it was exhilarating! But I don't remember a thing. How'd I do?"

"Hell, you got him rode! And believe me, it was a good'un."

About that time Dee walked up, slung his arm around R.C.'s shoulder. "Frank, your pardner here is a ringer. Why didn't you tell me the son of a bitch was sure enough a bull rider?"

I grinned and told Dee that I didn't even know it myself. Dee gave R.C. a big whop on the back. "You're a bull-riding son of a bitch!"

R.C. grinned at him. "Thanks. How do you think I did?"

Dee said, "Hell, didn't you hear? You're beating me by three points and I was winnin' this thing 'til you came around. You're takin' money out of my pocket!" Again he gave him a big shake.

"I may retire after this one. I think I proved my point."

Dee wouldn't stand for that. "Shit, with a lick like you've got, you'll never stop 'til one of 'em eats you or you git too old. It would be a waste of talent!"

We watched from behind the chutes as the last bull riders finished their ride. Nobody moved R.C. out of first. He couldn't believe it. To tell you the truth, neither could I!

"Well," I said, "it looks like you won it all, R.C."

"It didn't even cross my mind before, and the money's not important, but are they givin' buckles?"

"Sure! They always give buckles. You're gonna have a memento of this rodeo for years to come. Also, it'll sure be nice to press up against those girls and polish it on Saturday night."

A big grin spread across R.C.'s face.

We walked to where the girls were waiting for us. Both girls gave R.C. a big hug. You can't tell me that girls don't love cowboys! They also love winners, which set me back a little bit. I was going to walk away from here without a dime.

Just then I heard the announcer call out for everybody to get ready for the bull scramble, and I headed for the arena. I looked back over my shoulder. "I'll be back directly."

A good crowd was gathering up in front of the bucking chutes. They had run one bull in, in chute number four. I walked over to see where they were going to tie this Bull Durham sack. It was going to be on his right horn. I turned and walked back out toward the middle of the arena. I looked around at all the cowboys out there. There were only contestants.

I thought to myself, There are three kinds of people out here: stupid, broke, or brave, or possibly a mixture of all three. They were mostly rookies, the guys that were going down the road, weren't winning any money. I'd have to hustle to get ahead of these young fellows.

The announcer was still talking, giving out the rules. He stated there was only one minute allotted time that we had. If nobody had gotten the money at that time, the contest was over. Since they'd had to call off the bull scramble the day before, they were adding an extra fifty today. I noticed when he said that, a few more crawled over the fence and got into the arena.

A number of the boys were crowded up fairly close to the chute gate. The bull would come out and fling a few around. My plan was to stay back and hope like hell that nobody got that money until the bull put the fear of God in them and scattered a few around. And then I'd make my move.

The crowd in the grandstand hushed down and the announcer began the countdown, and on "three" Hooch slung the gate open and released the biggest, blackest, high-horned, man-eating son of a bitch you ever saw! As soon as the gate swung open, most of the cowboys charged him, putting their life on the line to get that hundred dollars. I never made a move. I saw one young fellow slung at least ten feet in the air and a few more scattered out in the air going sideways.

The bull was quick, but he'd concentrate on one fellow. He'd hook him and look for another. After a few seconds of this, everybody backed off of him. He slung his head and slung snot and pawed the ground. They made a run in at him and paid the price. Got hooked and flipped, but the bull refused to chase anybody. He just stood them off.

I thought it was time I moved in. Everybody was standing back wondering what to do when I started in a jog right straight toward him. I immediately got his attention. As I jogged toward him, he started toward me. If my plan worked, I could get in and out of there and be gone. If it didn't, I stood a good chance of either getting an axle broke or my frame bent.

All of a sudden I stopped and began to fake to the right, to the left, but the bull kept coming. Just as he got to me, I slipped off at an angle toward him to the left, close to his right horn. As he got by I reached over and grabbed him by the right horn and held on and circled him. But he was quick and turned to circle around behind after me. I wasn't running away from him, I was running toward his butt and was staying right up by his right shoulder.

I made one complete circle around him with him turning after me before I could reach down and lay my hand on the poll of his head between his horns. I felt desperately for the Bull Durham sack, finally felt it within my grasp, and jerked it. All this time, his right horn couldn't have been a half a foot from my butt. It had worked. Now all I had to do was get out of the well and make a run for the fence. Even if he caught me, if I held onto that sack, I was a hundred dollars richer! The first good chance, I broke out and ran to the fence.

There's no substitute for luck. Soon as I held the sack up to the announcer's booth they blew the buzzer. I stood down below on the ground, pitched the sack up to Dorothy, and said, "You owe me some money, Dorothy."

"We'll pay off tonight, Frank."

Roberta was so happy to have me out of that arena, all in one piece, she gave me a big hug around the neck. "You've got to quit doing things like that, Frank. Life's too short."

I gave her a squeeze. "Hell, that's why I do it!"

She had a funny look on her face. "Why?"

"Because life is too short. You gotta grab it while it's here."

With the rodeo over and the sun going down, we looked over the past couple of days and a lot of things had happened. But all in all, it had been pretty successful. The winners would hang around a couple of hours until the payoff down at Kitchins. The losers were already starting out on the road.

We got us a booth at Kitchins. R.C. and Kika and Roberta and I ordered drinks, and I noticed Roberta was clinging to me like she thought I might run away.

Dee walked over to the table. The first words out of his mouth were, "Frank, have you given any more thought to comin' with Amos and me? Hell, why don't both of you come? R.C., you come, too. We'll make a hell of a foursome!"

I felt Roberta's arm tighten on mine. "Yeah, I've thought about it. And, Dee, if I was gonna go down the road, there's nobody in the world I'd rather go with than you. But, there's been some complications arise. I'd like to make a run with you, give it a good, honest shot. But now's not the time."

Dee just shook his head. "Are you sure? Absolutely sure?"

"Yeah, Dee, I am. For now, at least."

"Frank," Roberta said, "I had no idea that you were thinkin' about leavin'."

"Oh, don't worry about it. I think about it every time I get to a rodeo and get around Dee. Someday I would like to go, but not right now. Don't feel bad about it. It's really not you."

When I saw the hurt look on her face I said, "I didn't mean it that way. I just don't want you to feel guilty of keepin' me from doin' somethin' I want to do. If I wanted to go, I'd go. But I do want to stay around here and see you some more this summer. Just see how this thing turns out. It's kinda like readin' a book. I want to see how it ends."

About that time Dorothy Rankin walked in with Jiggs carrying a big box. "We've got it all tallied up, boys. So step up and get your checks as I call your name."

When she called R.C.'s name, everybody whooped and hollered. They knew it was his first rodeo paycheck and everybody hoped it wouldn't be his last. As he walked back to the booth, he had a little blue box and a check in his hand. I don't think he even looked at the check to see how much he'd won.

He sat down and opened up the box and there was a buckle that said "Champion Bull Rider, Twin Mounds Rodeo, Dorsey, New Mexico."

R.C. passed his buckle around and let everybody admire it. Dee really went on about the buckle, saying it was the slickest he'd ever seen, how he'd be proud to have it. I knew he was just pumping R.C. because he must have a dresser drawer full of trophy buckles at home.

When they called my name I went up and collected my hundred dollars. "Well, it won't hold my pants up, but it'll put enough food in my belly to where I won't need a belt."

"That," Amos said, "is the worst thing about those buckles."

"What's that?" R.C. said.

"You can't eat 'em."

Dee shook his head. "Amos, let's git gone. We need to be somewhere else."

With that he shook hands with me. "I'll see you down the road, pard. Hopefully sooner than later."

CHAPTER

26

It was a real comedown. Everything was over. We parked in front of Roberta's house. She was going to leave and go back to the ranch to-night, too. But there was one little matter that we had to get straight-ened out first. "Frank, I had no idea that you were considerin' leaving."

"You and I are beginnin' to get somethin' goin'. If I left, I'd be runnin' from it. I've got to be honest with you, Roberta. I've run from it before. But somethin' tells me that this is too good a thing to pass up. I want to give it a chance. And there is some truth in that I just can't run off and leave the Boss. I'll tell you what, with R.C. leavin', that really set me back. I had no idea that it was even on his mind. What do you make of it?"

She put her finger to her lips and studied the question. "I can't make it out either. I know this, he thinks a great deal of Francesca and the feeling is mutual. She is genuinely fond of R.C. Maybe fond isn't even the word. I think she's falling in love with R.C. And I think the same thing is happening to him."

"I know. I suspected the same thing myself. But from the first day that I saw him, there was somethin' different about him." And I told her about the bank robbery down at Tramperos and about the roadblock and the desperadoes killed down on Highway 66 in Amarillo, and my suspi-cions, which all turned out to be wrong. I told her about his unending source of money. I even told her about the pistol that we knew he had in his suitcase. We talked about R.C. and found out that we knew very little if anything about him.

Roberta was a lot like myself. You gauge a person on what you see and how he acts and what he does, and not on where he's from or who he is. What you see is what you get.

With the end of that discussion, we turned back to ourselves. She tilted her chin up toward me. I kissed her, and she responded. Such warm, soft lips.

She seemed so easy to be around. She took everything in stride. And she took me as I was. I thought to myself, anybody that will give a man that kind of room has to have an awful lot going for her.

I pulled back from the kiss. "If we don't stop, I'll never get home. And if I don't get home, I'll be in trouble in the morning. More than I already am."

She smiled. "I know. When will I see you again?"

"Well, how about next weekend? It seems like forever, but I think I can wait."

"It's a date."

I walked her to the door, gave her another kiss, and while we looked into one another's eyes, she said, "Git!"

I went by Kitchins and picked up Poke and we headed south. I wanted to visit and talk. If I was going to have to take Poke all the way home, I needed the company. But I had a hard time keeping him awake.

We turned on the radio and caught everything that Clint, Texas, had to offer, in between five-minute commercials on how to stack BBs and peel raisins. They even gave you directions on how to buy a life-sized autographed picture of Jesus Christ himself.

When I finally pulled up to the Cannon ranch house, Poke muttered his thanks and stumbled off toward the house. I was having a hard time staying awake too, but I headed it back home.

I was just about half asleep, trying my best to stay on the highway, when I came up over a hill where I could look down into the Martinez pasture, and I'll be damned if I didn't see car lights coming up out of the breaks on the old feed road. This woke me up right sudden.

Before I could turn off my lights and stop so I could see whoever it was, he had seen me first and turned his lights off. There was nothing I could do but leave my lights on and drive right on past.

I wondered who had any business down there this time of night. I turned on the dome light and looked at my watch. It was a quarter to three in the morning. I figured anybody down there was surely up to no good.

So, when I got down to the crossroads, I pulled in where I'd picked up R.C. a few months before, and just waited. Sure enough, in about fifteen minutes I saw lights coming east down the highway toward me. I knew this had to be my man because I could see for ten miles behind me. I decided just to wait him out. At least I could see what the vehicle looked like and maybe who was driving it.

As he got closer to the main road, he slowed down and I kept low, down below the seat. I heard the car slow down and make a turn. I raised up and peeked over the doorsill, as it turned north. And I knew the pickup, without a doubt. It was Dolph Mueller's pickup.

I switched on my lights and took in after him. Whoever it was, and I supposed it was Dolph or one of his two boys, was surprised to find out that somebody was waiting for them. He stomped down on that old red Dodge pickup and took off for all he was worth!

I never could catch him, but I got up close enough to see the shape of the man's hat. And it wasn't Dolph and it wasn't the boys. Somebody else was driving that pickup.

I could see him take a cigarette out of his mouth, lean toward the ashtray, and bring the cigarette back to his mouth. I was trying to tail-gate him as close as possible, but we both had our vehicles wound up tight as fiddle strings. I thought I'd just follow him wherever he went. But I looked down at the gas gauge and I didn't have enough. So about a mile from our turnoff I slacked off and let him go ahead.

I tried to run it through my mind. Who in the hell was he and where was he going? And then it struck me! Maybe that's what he was doing, prowling down around the old church. But instead of heading north go-ing on a feed road, to throw us off he'd gone out the south way. I had no idea. It was Dolph's pickup. But there was no way I could find out who was in it. So, I just pulled into the ranch.

As we walked down for breakfast next morning I had a feeling that there'd be about as much conversation around the table as there would be at a prayer meeting. Besides that, I was dreading to have to take off my hat and sit down and eat. Where they'd cut my hair to stitch up my scalp was going to be very visible and I wasn't very proud of it. But there was no way around it. I couldn't sit at Miz T.'s table with my hat on.

The only bright spot in the room was Miz T., who for some reason had decided to get up and partake of breakfast with us. She and Tres seemed to be in good spirits. It crossed my mind several times to mention about seeing the lights coming out of the Martinez pasture, but I decided to keep my mouth shut. The Boss glanced up at my head and quickly looked away. I figured he already knew the whole story.

We all finished eating when finally the Boss spoke up. "Frank, you've put a good deal of mileage on the Gruyer since we had Johnny the Twist top him off, haven't you?"

I nodded my head. "Yes, sir."

"Tell me about him."

I didn't know what he had on his mind, but I gave him a fair description of the horse. "There seems to be no more buck in him at all. I've drug calves on him and I've headed a few on him."

And as I hesitated, the Boss said, "Are you sure all the buck's out of him?"

"Well, as sure as I can be, Boss. I've given him every opportunity to buck if he wanted to. I'll tell you, he's big and powerful!"

The Boss studied a minute. "How is he on his feet?"

"He seems to be surefooted. Can't ever remember him stumblin' with me. And like most Gruyers or buckskins, he's tough. He'll take you a long way."

I noticed Tres listening carefully as I spoke, taking it all in. And the Boss then revealed the reason for his questions.

"Well, Tres here has been on me to let him start ridin' the Gruyer, and I needed to know more about him first."

I looked over at Tres and saw a big smile come on his young face. Boy, in a few years this young man was goin' to knock the young ladies for a loop. He had rather dark skin for a blond-headed boy. He was sure handsome. I could see the reasoning behind him wanting to ride the Gruyer. Getting to ride a former outlaw with the reputation of having to be conquered by Johnny the Twist at his age would be quite an accomplishment. He'd have some bragging rights around his pals.

I wondered as I looked at him if he realized how lucky a boy he was. He was the apple of his granddad's eye. He got to ride the good horses on the place and learn about the business from the man who had written the book. And all of this would be his someday. A young man's future couldn't look any brighter.

Then I thought there were a few more things I could tell the Boss, that I'd better bring to his attention. "There is one bad habit that the Gruyer seems to have."

The Boss pushed back his chair. "Well, what's that?"

"I don't think he'll buck, but he's kinda, if you'll pardon me, ma'am," and I looked at Miz T., "he's kinda goosey. He's bad to shy at things."

The Boss wrinkled up his brow. "Give me a for instance."

I told him about the covey of quail that had gotten up in front of us over on Diego's place, and the snake that R.C. and I had run across on our way back. And of several other times that he seemed to have an inclination to have a runaway.

The Boss studied this for a while. He looked at Tres. "I don't know. Tres, he may be a little too much horse for you yet."

But Tres started in on his granddad. "Ah, Granddad, I can handle him. What horse wouldn't shy at a covey of quail that jumped right up right in front of him. And any horse is afraid of a snake. I'll be all right. Please let me have him, Granddad."

Miz T. chimed in with some doubt, too. "I don't know, J.W. The boy's awful young."

"Ah, Grandma, I'm not a kid anymore. I can handle him. Come on, please, Granddad."

The Boss looked at me again. "What do you think, Frank?"

Well, I didn't want to disappoint Tres in front of his grandparents, so I said, "I know Tres can ride him. But you just can't afford to make any mistakes on him. He's liable to blow up and take off on you."

Tres looked at his granddad. "See there. Frank thinks I can handle it."

"Whoa, Tres. Only if you're careful."

Again Tres pleaded. "Please, Granddad, I can handle him. I know I can."

The Boss smiled at him. "All right then. You can go to ridin' him. But you watch out for him now, you hear?"

"Yes, sir," Tres said with a big smile. With that he took his dishes to the sink and left.

"There's one more thing I should tell you about, Boss. I had to take Poke home last night over to the Cannon place and I saw lights comin' up out of the Martinez pasture on that old road."

The Boss considered this. "Have any idea who it was?"

"Yes sir. They turned off their lights hopin' that I didn't seen 'em, but it was Dolph Mueller's pickup. Funny thing about it, though. It wasn't Dolph or either one of the boys drivin'."

"How do you know?" the Boss asked.

"I chased him to our front gate. I could see the shape of the hat. It wasn't any of the three Muellers."

The Boss studied it a moment. "Hmm. Well, whoever it was, was up to no good. And I don't like it."

I was glad to get outside. Deep down inside I did have some reservations about Tres riding the Gruyer. But I'd told them as honest as I could what I thought he might do. The rest was up to them.

It was good to see Belle again. She gave me the best welcome of anybody on the place. She was so excited that she just kept making circles around me, wiggling her rear end.

Back up at the bunkhouse, I asked R.C., "When are you gonna tell him?"

"I don't know. I guess I ought to go down there right now and get it over with."

"What's this all about?" Jim asked.

By the time I'd told the story to Jim, R.C. was back. He couldn't have been gone over fifteen minutes. As he walked in, he looked kind of funny.

"Well," I said, "that didn't take long."

"No. He wasn't even surprised."

"Oh, I imagine he was surprised. He's pretty good at hidin' his emotions."

"I thanked him for everything he'd done for me and that I loved working here. But it was something I had to do. I was going to give him two weeks' notice. And you know what he told me?"

Both Jim and I shook our heads no.

"He told me that he appreciated the two weeks' notice, but that I wasn't in the army and I could leave anytime I felt like it. Either way, it didn't seem to me like he really cared. The only one it seemed to bother was Miz T. She felt rather bad about it and said she'd miss me. But the Boss just turned and went on about his business. To tell you the truth, I was surprised."

Jim chuckled. "I've seen it happen before. It's always been the Boss's notion that once a man decides to quit he won't get any work out of him during the period that he hangs on. I imagine he's pretty well bent out of sorts today anyway."

"This is not the way I wanted to leave."

"Ah, hell, R.C. Leavin' never is easy," I said. "If I were you I'd throw my stuff in Sundown and take off down the road."

"No sir, I'm going to prove that he's wrong. I'll stay and show him. And I'll make him a hand for a little while at least."

"Well," Jim said, "let's finish up that fence."

For the next few days we spent from sunup to sundown building a Cross S–style fence.

We were working on the north end of the fence and were about ready to quit for a little grub time, when I saw the Boss coming from over in the Barton pasture heading our way. He moved along at a slow, easy fox-trot, but it looked like he was coming to see us. But who in the hell knew! The mood he'd been in ever since the Fourth of July, to say the least, was cantankerous. He might ride on by us, not say a damn word. There was no telling.

But there's one thing for sure. Tres would probably be showing up from the south. The Boss and Tres always rode alone, and then met at a predesignated spot to talk over what they'd seen. The Boss pulled up and howdyed us. We stopped and wiped the sweat from our brow, and offered him a drink. "Thank you kindly, boys, but I just got me a windmill soda over at the Barton mill and that'll do me."

And just as I suspected, Tres rode in from the south coming downhill to join us.

"Been prowlin' around over in the Barton pasture," the Boss said. "One of our good, big heifers has got somethin' wrong with her right forefoot. It's swole up three times the size it oughta be. You two boys go on back to the house and get saddled up. We'll ride in with you. I'll get the vet kit and drive over there and help you boys doctor her. We don't want to chouse her much."

Tres spoke up. "Granddad, let me rope them heels."

The Boss looked at him and smiled. "I don't know, Tres."

And before he could finish, Tres started in on him again. "Granddad, I'm ready. I can as good as anybody. Please, let me rope the hind end."

It was then that I noticed the Boss. There was an emptiness to his saddle that I hadn't noticed before. He was not carrying a rope. I don't believe I'd ever seen that. A thought crossed my mind that after the Fourth of July he'd taken his rope off and hung it up for good, feeling that he had humiliated himself. But never, ever, had I seen the Boss a-horseback without a rope tied to his saddle or in his hand!

Finally you could see the Boss give in. He was proud of Tres. But like all grandfathers, a little bit afraid for him. Finally he said, "All right. Frank, just get a-horseback and come over into the Barton pasture, and rope that heifer for us. R.C., you bring the pickup. Make sure you get the vet case."

As R.C. and I got into the power wagon and headed back to the ranch, I commented to R.C. about the Boss's rope. He hadn't noticed it. But to me it was just like the Boss leaving the house without his hat on. It just didn't happen.

When we got to the house, I went to catch a horse after telling R.C. what to get. I hit a long trot and R.C. would be coming in Ol' Blue. The Boss and Tres had finished prowling the Barton pasture and were up toward the northwest corner sitting and talking when I saw them. R.C. pulled up a little later.

Since this was the north slope that drained down to the south toward the creek, there was a pretty good uphill grade going toward the north. In among the small rocks that covered the hillsides was lots of blue gramma, and especially in this rockier country, side oats gramma.

The Boss began to proceed on telling us how he wanted us to do this. I had thought, riding up there, that it was a hell of a note when it took four people to do what one used to do on the ranch. If I had the medicine in my saddlebag, I'd just rope her, lay a trip on her, tie her down, doctor her, and then go on.

"Frank, you head her," the Boss said. "And try to get her caught on the first loop. We don't want to chouse her any more than we have to. Tres, you heel her. And remember, two hocks is better than one. That way she'll lie down flat. As soon as she's roped, we'll drive over in the pickup. Tres, you keep that rope tight on those heels. Keep that Gruyer settin' back on it so we don't have to worry about them hind feet harelippin' us. Frank, you see about that foot, since my old knees won't take much squattin' down.

"She's right over the little knoll here, off by herself. She's on the prod, like anything that's hurtin' will be. So, get to her quick and get it done."

Tres and I turned and rode off. We took our ropes off our saddle strings, slipped the horn knot over our saddle horns. I said, "You better get off and tighten her up. She's a big'un."

So we stopped and tightened our cinches. "You've never roped outdoors at all, have you, Tres?"

"No, Frank, but I can do it."

"I know you can. But listen, if I miss the head you go ahead and head her. Turn her around and I'll build a loop and take the heels. I don't want to upset your granddad."

Tres nodded his head. "Okay. Ropin' outside's different from bein' in an arena, ain't it, Frank?"

"You better believe it. They won't run straight. They'll be duckin' and dodgin'. But the principle's the same. You're not worried about it, are you?"

Tres shook his head and smiled at me.

I had a big loop shook out and so did Tres as we came up over the knoll. And sure enough, she was lying down on her belly sitting up on her knees, watching us. She'd heard.

"Veer off to the right from her," I said, "like we have no interest in her and we'll try to get as close as we can before we jump her."

The closer we got to her, the more nervous she became. Finally she stood up, ass end first, then the front end. Her foot was swole up the size of a football.

"Keep up with me now, Tres. When I break for her, you go with me."

And I heard him whisper, "Okay."

The heifer switched her tail a few times, watching us, and turned around and started uphill, which is just the way I wanted her to go. It's funny how a crippled animal when chased can run like there's absolutely nothing wrong with them.

"Now," and I broke to her.

This pony I was riding could flat run and I was glad of it. We were up on her before she could really get strung out, and I just hoped to God that I didn't miss.

When I got up close enough I let her fly. And I was relieved to see the loop settle over her head as I jerked my slack. I could hear Tres pounding along beside me all the way. As soon as I had her stopped and turned back, Tres rode right into the heels, just like the pro that I knew he'd be someday, and set his heel loop. And he gathered up both of them.

We both went in opposite directions and stretched her out, and here came the pickup as fast as it could go over the bumpy terrain, with R.C. driving. He slid to a stop, jumped out, and ran over and jumped on her head. Grabbed the top foot and pulled it toward him and looked at me. I rode toward him and gave him slack. He took the loop off her head and threw it away. I rode on up to her and got down.

The Boss turned and looked at Tres. "Turn your horse around and face us, and keep that slack out of the rope now, hear?"

Tres was grinning from ear to ear. He liked it, and he nodded. "Yes sir, I know what you want."

I went to the pickup and got our medicine and vet box. Took the scalpel and spread her toes and began to probe between them. No doubt about it being infected. I could see where it was draining, kind of a yellow-whitish puss.

As I poked and prodded around, the Boss leaned over. "Whatever it is, Frank, it's down there deep. You're gonna have to cut. Don't worry about it. It'll make it drain better."

So I made a cut between her toes. She did struggle, but R.C. had his knee on her neck and Tres was keeping the rope tight. Finally I hit on something that felt like metal. I got a pair of needle-nose pliers out of the box and dug down in until I could get ahold of it. And with a mighty pull, pulled out just exactly what I thought I would, a fence staple.

"I didn't remind you to bring some sulfa. Did you?"

"You bet." I opened up a sack of sulfa powder and dumped some down in it, for all the good it would do. It would probably be gone in an hour, draining out with the blood. The bleeding didn't concern me. Just like dehorning cattle, I never saw any livestock bleed to death from anything no worse than this. But the Boss recommended that I give her a shot of Penstrep, penicillin and streptomycin combined. I gave her twice the recommended dosage, as the Boss told me to. It'd either cure her or kill her.

He turned and hollered to Tres, "When R.C. lets go of her head, come aridin' up and give her some slack so she can step out of it."

We all stepped back from her and Tres rode ahead quickly, about ten feet. The heifer got up. She stuck her tail up in the air and left the country!

"We'll take a close look at her," the Boss said, "for the next few days. If it don't get better, we'll have to do it again."

For the first time in days the Boss seemed rather proud. I guess he forgot his own vanities and was proud of his grandson.

CHAPTER

27

I walked back to my horse and took the horn loop off the horn and was untying the reins, as I watched Tres ride toward us coiling up his rope. He had his rope practically all coiled up, but was separating the loops as most ropers will to get every loop in the coil just exactly the right length, when he seemed to drop the rope. And with it went his right rein. It was easy enough to do. I must have done it a thousand times myself. With the rope lying on the ground, Tres leaned far forward to grab the rein on the right side that he'd dropped, and when he did, the Gruyer shied to the left, quick and hard, and spun Tres to the ground. Just flat jumped out from underneath him!

It was then that I looked up and saw that Tres had never taken his rope from the horn. Cold chills and fear ran through me as I just stood there and watched. When Tres hit the ground, his leg was tangled in the coils of his rope and the Gruyer quit running sideways and began to run backwards.

Tres reached down and was fumbling with the rope, but wasn't quick enough. The Gruyer took the slack out of it so quick, none of us could move. And the first thing we knew, he was dragging Tres by one leg.

The Boss started quickly toward the Gruyer, maybe too quick. Because the quicker he moved, the faster the Gruyer backed up. All I could think was, Oh, my God! When I saw the Gruyer turn and begin to pull Tres, the words "Oh, shit" came out of my mouth and I knew we just had one chance. I had to stop the Gruyer!

I mounted my horse as fast as I could, and by that time it was serious. The Gruyer broke into a run and was dragging Tres. In my hurry, I even forgot my rope. All I could think of was I had to catch the Gruyer. With the end of my reins going over the neck and under, I was whipping and spurring for all I was worth. I had to catch the Gruyer!

We were gaining on him, but not fast enough to suit me. It came to my mind, what can I do? I couldn't grab the pigtail and jerk the rope off the horn, not with pressure on it. As the Gruyer had turned, he'd stepped on a rein and broken it. I only had one option, and that was to do what I did best. That was to bulldog a horse, providing I could catch him! I had my horse flattened out running his dead-level best, when I pulled up alongside the Gruyer.

And I jumped. I got an arm around the Gruyer's neck, and somehow got ahold of the headstall of the bridle and held on. I felt myself slipping, turned loose of the headstall, and reached for my hand on the other side of his neck. I was up close to the throat latch. Thank God!

When I got my hands locked on the other side of his neck, I knew I had him, if it just wasn't too late. All I had to do was hang on and dig in. There weren't many horses that could run very far with two hundred pounds plus hanging on their heads. But it was a slow process slowing down. My feet hit the ground just about every ten yards. All the time I was hollering, "Whoa!" He shouldn't have had any trouble hearing me, because my mouth was right in his ear. Finally I got him stopped. I was almost afraid to turn loose of my hands, but I grabbed ahold of the headstall and a hunk of mane with my right hand, and started talking as slow and easy as I could, even though I was in a panic.

I never took my eyes off the Gruyer. I could hear R.C. come up behind me and grab the pigtail on the rope and slip it off the horn. "The rope's free, Frank. The rope's free."

And with that I turned the Gruyer loose and looked back to see what had happened. The Boss had already gotten to Tres, sat down beside him, and pulled him up in his lap. When R.C. and I got to him, there was blood trickling out of Tres's nose, out of his ear, and a slight bit out of his mouth. His head was skinned and bruised. His breath came in short gurgling rasps.

"Frank," the Boss said, "pick him up and put him in the pickup, in my lap. You drive. Get to town as fast as you can. R.C., go back to the house. Tell Mother to get to town quick."

I gathered up Tres's small body in my arms and thought, Oh, my God! He doesn't weigh a hundred and ten pounds. That blond hair and youthful face all bruised and bloody. All I could think was, Hang on, Tres, hang on.

The Boss was in the passenger side of the pickup holding out his arms when I lay Tres in his lap. I started up Ol' Blue and pushed the accelerator pedal to the floor. When we got up to the gate leading out of the Barton pasture, the Boss said, "Drive through it. Hurry, Frank, hurry."

When we got to the highway, for the first time in my life I didn't stop. I slowed down just enough to make it on two wheels and turned toward Dorsey. I never took my foot off the accelerator, which was plumb to the floor. I even reared back in the seat, gripping the steering wheel with both hands, trying to make it go faster.

I looked at the Boss and tears flowed down his face. I had never seen it before, nor had I thought it possible. He never took his eyes off Tres, and the tears dripped off his face and landed on Tres. He said not a word.

I went through town blowing my horn at the one stoplight and just kept on going. Pulled in behind at the emergency room, jumped out, and ran around. But the Boss shook his head. He'd carry him.

They tried to make us wait out in the hall, but the Boss would not leave his side. I just waited. Then it began to sink in on me. And the tears began to flow. What could I have done to prevent it? Tres had looked up to me. He should have known. When you're through with your rope, always take it off your horn. Never mess with it tied hard and fast! Hard and fast. That was the rule of the country, in more ways than one. I should have never consented for Tres to start riding the grulla. It was all my fault. All I could do was sit there and hang my head in shame and remorse.

And that's just the way I was when R.C. and Miz T. walked in. I pointed toward the emergency room door that had been closed for the past forty-five minutes, and Miz T. went in. R.C. put his hand on my shoulder. "Frank, are you all right?" All I could do was shake my head.

I don't know how people knew, but they began to show up and stand silently in the halls of the hospital. Perhaps my wild dash through town had sounded the alarm. One by one and two by two they came.

Directly Miz T. came from the emergency room door. I heard her speak to me. I dreaded to look in her eyes, but I did. I could see nothing but sorrow. "He's gone, Frank."

"Yes, ma'am, I know."

"I thought you did," she said. "He never made it to town. I can't get J.W. to leave his side. But we've got to be strong. I want you to listen to me, both of you. Frank, you go get the horse. I want him gone."

I thought about this a second. "Do you want me to shoot him?"

She shook her head. "No. J.W. knows that place like the back of his hand. Even if that horse's bones were to rot, he would always be reminded. And I'm not so sure it was completely the horse's fault."

"Ma'am," I said, "if it's anybody's fault, it's mine."

"Frank, I'll not have you sitting there telling me it's your fault. Inside that room with my grandson is a man who thinks it's his fault." She shook her head. "It's just one of those things that happens and we have to deal with."

Then she looked at me again. "But that horse must be gone! I don't care what you do with him, where you take him, because J.W. will kill him when we get home.

"We'll stay in here tonight, and I'll finally prevail. I will persuade J.W. to leave the boy. But that horse is to be gone and J.W. is to never see him again. Is that understood?"

"Yes, ma'am."

Then she turned to R.C. "R.C., go over to Diego's and tell him what happened, and tell Francesca I will need her help for a few days."

I don't know why, but out of the sorrow came some rational thinking. I looked outside through the glass doors at the sun shining and wondered how the sun could shine on a day like this, when through the doors in a great hurry came a tall, lanky shadow. That shadow turned into Roberta, dressed in work clothes. She ran to me, threw her arms around my neck, and hugged me close. "I know something bad has happened. Thank God you're all right."

Miz T. took Roberta into her arms. I couldn't say a word. I was glad to see Roberta, relieved. Tears streamed down Miz T.'s face. "We lost Tres today. A terrible accident." And tears came to Roberta's eyes as the two women consoled one another.

As I stood there and watched, I realized I'd always been under the assumption that men controlled the world, and just now realized that it wasn't so. When things got tough, men just stood around wondering what in the hell to do next, while the women gathered up, held everything together, and went on.

"Roberta," Miz T. said, "I'm sending the boys back to the ranch. This has been hard on us all, and I know it's especially hard on Frank. Francesca will stay with me a day or two and I wonder if you could come and stay with me, also? It would be a great favor."

Roberta smiled. "Of course."

"You boys know what to do. Now get at it. Roberta, make yourself at home in my home. I'm sure your folks will be in before long. They will have gotten word. I'll tell them where you are. Thank you, dear, for your help."

As we walked out of the hospital, the sunlight and the fresh air helped a little, but not much. What helped the most was having Roberta there. "Roberta, what brought you to the hospital? How come you're here?"

"I had to come to town for some vaccine for Dad. And it was all up and down Main Street. You and the Boss had come through town in a hurry. I knew something was wrong, so I came out to the hospital."

"I've got some phone calls to make," I said.

After about five phone calls, I finally located Dee Jensen in southern Colorado. "Frank, you old son of a bitch, you've changed your mind. When are you comin'?"

And then I told him the story. "I've got you an outlaw, Dee. He's yours, for one dollar, if you want him."

"Hell, yes, I want him, if he's carryin' the Cross S brand."

"He is. He's a grulla."

"Well, that explains it. Grullas and duns are mustang ponies. They're built out of different stuff than the run-of-the-mill quarter horse. They've always got a little wildness in 'em."

"I've got to git him off the place," and told him I'd take him over to the Cannon place tonight and they'd keep him until he could arrange to come get him.

"Hell, I'll leave tonight. I'll be there tomorrow and pick 'im up."

I gave him directions to the Cannon place and told him I'd leave a bill of sale for him. It was his horse.

On the way back to the ranch, R.C. drove. Roberta sat in the middle and held my hand. She gently pried the story from me. Again, I said it was my fault, I shouldn't have ever let the boy ride the Gruyer. R.C. chimed in, "Frank, there was nothing more that you could do. And thank God you were there. If not, the horse would still be dragging the boy."

Roberta didn't understand this, because I hadn't gone into detail on how we'd gotten the horse stopped. R.C. told her. She held my hand tight and said, "Frank, that was a brave thing to do. Not many people could have done it, or would have done it."

Through blurred eyes, "It was no big thing. That's the only way I could do it. It's the only way I knew how. It was the best that I could do. But it wasn't enough."

When we drove into the ranch, Tio, Lupe, and Jim were all waiting. All I said was, "Tres is dead."

And bless little Tio's heart, he cried like a baby. He came to me, threw his arms around my waist. His head didn't come close to my chin, just about the third button down from my shirt top. He just held on to me and cried. All I could do was pat him on the head, like a small child, and tell him that I was sorry.

Again the women proved the strongest. Lupe came, took Tio away, and said, "You must be hungry. I'll fix something to eat."

I told Lupe I wasn't hungry and that I had things to do. "Roberta, I've got to go catch the Gruyer and I'm gonna lead him over to the Cannon place. It'll be late when I get back."

"Frank, I'm going with you."

R.C. headed for the gas pump to make his run over to the Jaramillo outfit. Roberta and I headed for the barn, along with Jim. As we both saddled up, we filled him in on the details about what had happened.

"The Boss will shoot the son of a bitch, sure as hell."

"No he won't," I said. "Miz T. told me what to do with him. Jim, you're not to tell the Boss where I'm takin' the Gruyer. Act dumb, it shouldn't be hard."

Jim didn't even catch the pitiful joke I'd just made. He just sat on the bench of the saddle house in gloom.

Roberta and I started out to the Barton pasture in a high trot. As we neared the knoll where we'd doctored the heifer, a lump came up in my throat. The only thing that remained on the ground was Tres's rope, which I picked up and coiled.

We found the Gruyer grazing in the northwest corner of the pasture. When he saw our horses, he nickered and moved over to us. He was easy enough to catch.

I took his bridle off and haltered him, and hung the bridle over Tres's saddle horn, and we headed west. We'd have to skirt the ranch house. Roberta wanted to know what we'd do with the saddle. I said we'd dump it by the post pile and pick it up as we came back. I was afraid if we rode right to the ranch that Tio's emotions might get the best of him and he'd bring out that twelve-gauge blunderbuss and kill the horse on the spot.

As we headed through the Padre pasture, past the old mission, I looked at the sky and the sun had moved over to the west. We'd have a few hours of sunlight and that was all.

How lucky could a man be to have someone ride by your side like this and look like she did? She made life worth living, even in the midst of terrible trials and tribulations. I felt a deep love at that moment with the beautiful girl riding beside me. And I realized that I'd felt that way for some time now. It was time that I told her. I didn't know how, but I'd have to find a way.

It was late when we finally sighted the lights of the Cannon place. Just a faint glimmer of light remained on the horizon, and when we rode up to the house, Tom, Poke, and Top were sitting out on the porch. They all stood and peered out into the darkness, waiting for us to come into view. A broad grin passed Poke's face. "My, my. What are you two doin'? Elopin'?"

With that I had to smile and I looked at Roberta, and she smiled, too. And then that black cloud that had been hanging over my head most of the day came back again. "No. We've had a tragedy over at the Piedra."

Ol' Tom scowled at Poke. "Where's your manners, mister?" He turned to us. "Step off and git down."

Top had a terrible look on his face. "Is it the Boss?"

"No, it's Tres."

Tom again interrupted. "Come in and tell us what happened."

I introduced Roberta to Tom, and it was at that moment that I realized that I didn't know Tom's last name. He smiled and said, "Slaughter. I'm pleased to make your acquaintance, ma'am, and may I say that this gentleman has wonderful, wonderful taste in selectin' his travelin' companion."

Roberta smiled. "Why, thank you, Tom."

Top and Poke could no longer wait. So, I told them.

When I finished, Top rose from his chair. "I'll be headin' for town. Miz T.'s a strong woman, but maybe I can help with the Boss. That's where I need to be right now."

I took the bill of sale that Miz T. had written, and laid it on the kitchen table. "Sometime tomorrow Dee Jensen will be by. Poke knows him, but in case Poke's not here, I'll give you a description of him, Tom. Ask him what he thinks of me, and if he answers anywhere in the nature of 'he's a big, gut-eatin' son of a bitch,' you'll know it's him."

Tom smiled. "Sounds like my kinda feller."

"Roberta and I've got to be gittin' on back."

Tom shook his head. "You've had a tough day. Why don't you just relax a little bit? Grab some shut-eye here."

I glanced at Roberta. "Whatever you want to do is fine, Frank."

I thought about it and the more I thought about it, the more it made sense. "Are you sure you can spare the room?"

"How much room will you need?"

Without blinking an eye I said, "Well, two beds."

"We can handle it. Let's go out on the porch and look at the stars and let the world settle down for the night."

We moved out on the porch and for a while sat in silence. For the first time, Poke didn't have a lot to say. But I knew I could depend on Tom. As he pulled out his makings and rolled him one, he said, "You know, what happened today was a terrible thing. It's happened before, and believe me, it'll happen again. But it's the kinda life we've chosen. And personally, it's the way I like it. There's a sort of fatal charm to this life that keeps you stickin' with it. If it weren't for that fatal charm, I reckon I'd die."

The words "fatal charm" ran through my head, though I didn't understand exactly what he meant. I told him so.

"Well," he said, "you see, in our business, we're always overmatched. The cattle and horses we deal with are big and wild, and always unpredictable. It's a big country. And generally we work alone. When you're out there on the prairie, just you and your horse, and you see somethin' wrong, somethin' that needs tendin' to, you do it. Because that's your job. You can git tangled up in your rope, your horse can fall on ya, you can git rattlesnake-bit. When you do work like we do, you've got to expect that. Any day you saddle up and ride out, you might not ride back again. It's always been that way, and I reckon as long as there's cattle and cowboys, it'll keep on bein' that way.

"Why, I can tell you myself," Tom went on, "about a young man that met his death on the prairie." He turned and looked at me. "I hear you're a singer."

I nodded my head.

"Have you ever heard the tune 'Little Joe the Wrangler'?"

"Sure. I know it by heart."

He took another drag on his cigarette and leaned over toward me. "What would you say if I told you that I could show you the washout where Little Joe was crushed to death under his horse durin' a stampede?"

I laughed for the first time that day. "Tom, I figured that story to be a myth somebody just made up to be entertainin'."

Tom became indignant. "No, sir! Don't doubt my word."

"How," I asked, "do you know this, Tom?"

"'Cause I was there. I was with that bunch, pushin' them cattle, when Joe got killed. I can show you the washout. Hell, it was down in the south end of Chavez County, south of Roswell on the Pecos, just like the song says. A norther commenced blowin'."

"Tom," I said, "I believe you, and I want to hear the story. But I'm gonna have to hear it some other time. After what happened to me today, I couldn't handle it right now."

"I understand, Frank. Someday I'll tell you the story. Hell, maybe someday I'll even show you that place. Who knows?"

And with that he began to rise.

CHAPTER

28

It took awhile before Tom could stand upright, with his old bones creaking from years in the saddle. "There's two bedrooms at the top of the stairs. There's nothin' much fancy. I wish I could offer you more, Miss Roberta."

She smiled. "Thank you, Tom. I'm sure it will do nicely."

As he turned and went inside, he patted me on the shoulder.

It had been a day I'd never forget. And now it had to end. Life had to go on. But I wasn't sure what lay ahead.

As we were starting inside, Poke said, "You know, there's just one thing that bothers me."

Roberta and I stopped, wondering what was on his mind.

"Maybe it's just my Irish superstition. But Frank, have you heard that bad things always happen in threes?"

"Yes. I've heard it all my life."

"Do you reckon it's true?"

"God, I hope not!"

I thought about it. Bad things happen in threes. Oh, Lord. Everything had gone so well all summer. More rain than this country had seen in years. The cattle had done well. Everything had been going too well. Was now the time for everything to turn around and go the other way?

There were two bedrooms, one to the left and one to the right of the stairway. I could feel the moment getting awkward, and I didn't know what to do. But Roberta made it easier for me by putting her arms around my neck and hugging me close. Of course I responded. I needed it. I felt like hell. But holding her close and feeling her touch helped soothe me.

Finally she lifted her head and pulled away. She gazed into my eyes and slowly leaned forward and we kissed. Very gently at first, and then a little harder. Without even knowing the words were coming from my mouth, I heard myself saying very softly in her ear, "Roberta, I love you."

It didn't seem to come as much of a shock to her as I had thought it would, for I heard her say, "Oh, Frank. You don't know how I've wanted to hear that. I love you, too."

And we kissed again.

Pulling back, I smiled at her. "We both better get some rest. It'll be a long day tomorrow."

As she smiled and nodded her head, her eyes welled with tears. I reached over and gave her a quick kiss and crossed the hall to my room.

I thought sleep would come easily. I was so tired I could hardly keep my eyes open, until I crawled into bed. Then everything that happened that day crawled into bed with me.

My room was on the east side of the house with a window beside my bed. As the moon rose, it made it seem as light as day. I couldn't get settled down. I rolled and I tossed. I relived the fatal runaway in different scenarios on what I could have done differently to make things turn out better. I even dwelled upon the philosophy of Ol' Tom, fatal charm. The more I thought about it the more sense it made.

I heard the door open and watched as Roberta walked in with a quilt wrapped around her shoulders reaching clear to the floor. She walked to the side of the bed and looked down upon me. "Frank, are you all right?"

"Yeah. I'm just having a hard time putting today away."

As I looked at her with the moon shining upon her, it reminded me of something that I couldn't quite put my finger on. And then in a moment I knew. It was the silhouette of the Indian aunt that had cared for me so long ago when I was a child in Oklahoma.

That thought was quickly broken when Roberta said, "Frank, do you want me?"

I must have sounded like I had a shot glass stuck in my throat when I said, "Yep. Bad."

She released the quilt and stood for a moment, the moonlight shining on all the woman anyone could ever want or hope for. Then she quickly slid under the covers next to me.

I lay on my back and put my arm around her as she snuggled up close and molded her body next to mine. All thoughts of the past and of the future were gone. They were occupied only by what was happening now.

As I turned to kiss her, I began to stroke her breast. The softness of her skin, yet the firmness of that breast, had an overwhelming effect on me. I was starting to go too fast. I wanted to devour her for fear that she would evaporate and be gone, that this was just a dream. She whispered in my ear, "Frank, please be gentle. I've never done this before."

I realized I'd have to take my time. I thought back to a woman of my past who, despite her sordid reputation and being much older than I, took the time to show a fifteen-year-old boy where the pleasure spots were on a woman and that making love was a two-way door. You must give as well as receive. I thanked that woman at that moment from the bottom of my heart.

I slowed down and began to explore her body. I knew I had found those spots by the reactions I received. It took every bit of willpower I had to go slowly, to touch softly, to try to be gentle and tender.

Roberta was becoming more relaxed and willing. I could feel her passion mount as I worked away at those so-called secret spots, one in particular. With a sharp intake of breath and the stiffening of her body, and the rise of her chin and a low moan, I knew that I had succeeded in giving that which I wanted so much to do.

She began to explore with her hands my face, my chest, all the while with light, soft kisses, on my nose and on my lips and on my ear. She worked her hands downward. When she found what she was looking for, I heard her suck in her breath. "Oh, my."

She pulled back from my face and looking into my eyes, "Frank, I'm ready. I want you in me."

Believe me, her wish was my command. I positioned myself over her, resting my arms out straight on the bed, kneeling between her legs. "You'll have to help."

She reached and guided me to where I had to go. All the time in the back of my mind, I could hear a voice saying, Easy, go easy. Don't hurt her. Gently. And with that in mind, slowly and tentatively I entered her. There seemed to be one small moment of pain. I could see her teeth clamp on her lower lip, and I stopped and started to withdraw.

But she clamped onto me and said, "No. I want this." A slight smile came on her face. "And it's wonderful."

I withdrew and started slow motions. It was then she gave me a suggestion. "Come down here to me, Frank. You're bracing yourself on your arms. I want to kiss you, feel you next to me."

"Oh, but you should see the sight I'm looking at here. It's very stimulatin', to say the least. And if I come down there, I won't be able to move."

I felt her legs tighten around the back of mine. "I don't care," she said. "Come down here to me."

So with that, I relaxed my arms and rested on my elbows, to where I could kiss her full on the lips and hold her hair in my hands. To my amazement, I could move. And that movement continued and increased until we had finally got in time. She met me with every thrust. And when the time came, I felt like I melted and drained my whole being inside of her. I can't ever remember feeling as good in my life.

As I lay there in her arms, she whispered in my ear, "Now I feel complete. That was wonderful."

I had all good intentions of making a night filled with passion. All night. But as someone wrote in a book, sometimes the best plans of men go asunder. I don't know whether I passed out from ecstasy or went to sleep from exhaustion. The next thing I knew, there was a thin streak of light beginning to peak over the eastern horizon. I was pleased to find Roberta sleeping soundly behind me, cupped up next to me in spoon fashion as I lay on my side, with her arm thrown over my waist.

I could hear Ol' Tom's boots clumping around in the kitchen and knew we'd better get things straightened up and back in our own pens, in case somebody started a count.

I turned over and brushed Roberta's hair from her eyes. She did not awaken 'til I kissed her nose and her ear and kissed her lightly on the mouth. She opened her eyes, smiled, and said, "Good morning."

"Good morning."

"I love you very much."

"I know. Are you all right?"

She snuggled up again. "Never better."

"I love you, too. But I'll tell you what, you'd better get back to your bed. I'm gonna get up and get dressed and have a cup of coffee with Tom. Then you come down and tell them what a wonderful night's rest you had. We're gonna have to do some acting here."

"It won't be acting. I did have a wonderful night."

"Of rest?"

"Yes, that, too."

I watched her as she slipped out of bed, again picked the quilt up, threw it around her shoulders, smiled at me, and tiptoed out the door to her room. I immediately got up, got my clothes on, and headed down the stairs.

Tom was at the stove.

"Mornin', Tom."

"Mornin' back."

"How'd you sleep?"

"Fine as a fiddle, discountin' of course these creakin' old bones a-achin' and havin' to take care of my bladder ever' two hours. Hell, I might as well have been calvin' heifers. You gotta git up every two hours all night long, you might as well do somethin' else 'sides take a leak."

I laughed. "That bad, huh?"

With a lowered voice, "Frank, gittin' old is the shits."

"I think I'll step out and feed my horses."

"Poke's already out there. He'll take care of 'em."

"Well, he can't take care of my bladder."

As I started for the door, Tom said, "That's a right fine-lookin' lady you brought here last night, Frank. She's shore a dandy. Did I understand you to say her last name is Chism?"

"You did."

Tom scratched his whiskered chin. "That wouldn't be Jingle Bob's daughter, would it?"

"It would. Why?"

"Oh, I knowed old Jingle Bob a long time ago. A great big feller, ain't he?"

"Yeah, he is," and went on out the door, wondering what he meant by that.

At the barn I heard Poke holler at me. "Frank, it could have been my imagination, but I thought I felt the house aswayin' slightly last night. Kinda had a rhythm to it. Did you feel it?"

"I know one thing. It ain't too damn early in the mornin' for a man to git a bloody nose!"

Poke came out of the barn carrying two buckets of oats. "Goddamn, you're surly in the mornin'."

"I think you'd better shut up."

"Ooh. I reckon I better."

We were drinking coffee when Roberta came down the stairs with a bright smile. She said good morning to all of us.

Tom jumped up and got her a cup of coffee. The mood around the table had lightened up a great deal from the night before. What happened yesterday just seemed like a bad dream.

The sun was just coming up as we curried our horses and saddled up. The last thing Poke said was, "If there's anything I can do, let me know. Anything at all."

I could see Tom hated to see us leave. He hung around 'til we were mounted and headed back east. He took off his hat and tipped it to her. Roberta and I hit a fox-trot and started home.

We rode close, at the same pace. You can always tell when you're just at the right pace of a trot when you look down at your slack rein, and they're both swinging in time, side to side, underneath the horse's neck. For some reason, both our horses had hit the same stride, and those bridle reins, all four of them, were swinging in unison. It gave me a feeling of harmony.

299

"Frank, I know how big and strong you are. I know you can be very violent if need be. And there's not a doubt in my mind that if you thought a man needed killin', that you would do it. And yet, you can be as tender and as loving and gentle as I could imagine any man could be." She looked at me and smiled. "And, I love you for it."

"I'm glad that you understand me. And I love you for that. But, darlin', I sure would appreciate it if you wouldn't let it get around."

Roberta looked at me with wide eyes. "Frank Dalton, what do you mean? Do you honestly think I'd tell somebody what we did?"

Right away she had me on the defensive. "No, no. That's not what I mean at all." I smiled at her. "It's this tender, gentle side that you're talkin' about that I don't want to get around. It might ruin my reputation."

She broke into a wide smile. "Oh. I see." She shook her head. "Men!"

We talked and visited as we rode. I looked over at her wearing a soiled, silver belly-felt hat that had seen better days, pulled down low in front and low behind, with her hair tied back low with a yellow ribbon. And I realized it was just like talking to a friend, a partner.

It was a pleasant ride. I had practically forgotten all the tragic things that had happened just the day before, until we crossed over into the Martinez pasture and got back on home ground. Then I began to worry about what lay before us. And I hoped I could handle it.

As we came into the headquarters and passed the post pile, I looked down to see if Tres's saddle was still there. It was gone. We rode in and tied our horses to the hitch rail in front of the saddle house. R.C. and Kika came up. The girls greeted each other like long-lost sisters. R.C. said, "How'd it go?"

"Okay," I said. "He's gone. And he won't be comin' back."

As I jerked my saddle and went on into the saddle house, I looked at Tres's saddle on the rack where it'd always been, the rope coiled up neatly and tied to the saddle with the wang leather slipped over the horn.

"Has the Boss and Miz T. showed up?" I asked.

R.C. shook his head no.

"I'm not lookin' forward to that," I said.

"Nobody is," R.C. said.

Kika gave me a kiss on the cheek and a hug around the waist and asked how I was.

"Oh, fair to middlin', I guess. At least as good as can be expected. I sure feel bad about this, Kika."

"I know you do. R.C. told me what happened. Don't blame yourself. You did the best that you could do. Probably more than anybody else could have done in that situation."

With that we went down and sat on the low rock wall that enclosed the lawn around the big house, and waited.

We didn't talk about the accident anymore. We just made small talk and kept watching the road. Sure enough, directly we saw a cloud of dust.

"Here they come," I said. God, I was dreading this.

But I was surprised to find that it wasn't the Boss and Miz T. It was Jingle Bob and his missus. I thanked my lucky stars that we'd made it back in time before they came rolling in.

We all got up and Mrs. Chism gave me and R.C. a hug. They were introduced to Kika and even gave her a hug. Jingle Bob shook my hand. "It was a terrible, terrible thing that happened."

"It sure was, Bob," I said. "Have you seen the Boss?"

"Yes, we got word yesterday, late. And we went in to see him. He's taking it mighty hard, Frank. You're gonna have to help him. He'll be a long time gettin' over it, if ever."

Mrs. Chism looked at Roberta. "We realized that you had come down here in your work clothes, so I brought you a change of clothes. Tess told me what she requested of you. I think I brought enough where you can stay for a while."

"Thanks, Mom. I'd better excuse myself and go get cleaned up. They should be along in a short while."

"I'll see if I can't get things fixed up so they'll have a bite to eat when they get in," Mrs. Chism said. "And for the rest when they come."

It wasn't long before another cloud of dust came down the road. It was the Boss and Miz T. Miz T. was driving and when the Boss got out, his face was ashen. He came over to us, shook hands with Bob. "I appreciate your comin', Bob. If you'll excuse me, I need to go in, try to collect myself."

Miz T. came over and gave everybody a big hug. "Frank, you and R.C. and Jim, take what you need and go up to the old church. We've decided we'll bury Tres here at the ranch."

Her face showed the grief, but it also showed faith. She had to give the orders now, because it seemed like the Boss was incapable. "Clean up as much as you can of the old graveyard. Dig a grave on the northeast side, in the front row, only off by itself. That graveyard hasn't been used in years. But I know this is where Tres would want to be. He loved this place. We'll have a rosary tonight in town. And services tomorrow at eleven o'clock at the church. Will you do that for me?"

Both R.C. and I nodded. She took Bob's arm and they walked toward the house.

When we got to the bunkhouse, we found Jim just sitting in one of the straight-back chairs with a big chew in his mouth, just staring out into space. I told him what Miz T. had requested of us. He nodded his head.

We got picks, shovels, and rakes and got in Ol' Blue and drove up to the old mission. Jim lined out the grave, just like he would a fence. He drew lines with a shovel handle. "We've got to make the sides straight up and down. All the dirt we'll pile on the north side."

R.C. went to raking and cleaning up. Jim and I began to dig.

This wasn't the first grave I'd dug. It was common practice in the country to dig the graves for those that died. Nobody ever thought of having somebody come in with machinery and dig it. It was just one of those things that you did for your neighbors. But, I believed this was going to be the toughest grave that I ever dug. And I hoped it'd be the last one that I'd have to dig for a long time.

R.C. and I switched off. But Jim wouldn't quit. Couldn't get him to lay his shovel down. When we finished, it was just like the fencing job that he'd done. By using the sharpshooter spade it couldn't have been any more rectangular and perfect. I guessed that Jim had dug many a grave, because he'd lived here a long time and it was a hard country.

When we finally finished and had the old graveyard looking fairly presentable, we all stopped and looked around. I thought to myself, If you're gonna die, and sooner or later it was comin', a feller could pick a lot worse place to be laid to rest.

I looked up at the Piedra. It was Navajo sandstone, rising high out of the valley. I looked at the breaks with the piñon and cedar trees, and the creek with just a trickle of water flowing through it. I could see the beauty of the country and it did something to me.

Back at headquarters there must have been ten or twelve cars parked around the place. Some were leaving, and you could see down the road some that were coming. It was an age-old tradition that when somebody passed away you came over with food, paid your respects. They'd express their condolences, walk outside, maybe visit with one another for a while, and then be on their way.

Kika came out and called us in. "I bet you boys are hungry. Come in. We've got plenty to eat."

My first sight of Roberta almost took my breath away. That girl, who rode with me clear to the Cannon place and back and shared my bed, had changed from a cowgirl to a lovely beauty in a dress.

But me, I was just what I was. And it didn't make any difference what part of the country I was in. People would look at me once and they'd know how I made a living.

She came over to me and laid her hand on the back of my neck, as dirty as I was. "How are you?"

"I'm okay. Just a shade tired."

A cloud of sadness hung over the ranch that day as we sat and watched people come and go. In the early evening when it was time to go to town for the rosary, Miz T. approached me.

"Frank, we would like you to be one of the pallbearers. Would you do that for us?"

"Why, sure, Miz T. Anything that I can do."

"Well, Tres always looked up to you. We thought that we'd get you and Will," meaning Top, of course. "You and Will will be the older ones. The rest will be Tres's friends. We thought we'd get Wade Robbins, Clay Turner, and Ike Crocket. And then Miguel's son, Juan."

"But I don't have any nice clothes."

Miz T. smiled and reached up and patted me on the cheek. "It doesn't matter what you wear. It's who you are that counts. Tres wouldn't have wanted it any other way."

The next day Top and I sat with the four young boys, Tres's friends. We were all dressed, more or less, alike. I caught a glimpse of the Boss. He never shed a tear. His face was drawn and his color wasn't good. It looked like he had aged ten years in just the last few days.

After the services we carried the coffin to the hearse and all piled into the second car, the pallbearers' old Cadillac limousine, and we headed south.

I glanced back through the window and it was the longest funeral procession I'd ever seen. I wondered if the hearse and the limousine might high-center on the road to the old church. You could hear grass brushing the underside of both of our vehicles.

I opened the gate that led into the graveyard. Everyone else parked outside. A huge crowd gathered and the services began. All six pallbearers were lined up on the east side of the grave. It was midafternoon and a bright, sunshiny day. I couldn't help but think of an old Indian saying: "It's a good day to die." In this case, it was as good a day to be buried. I'd always wondered about the wisdom of that statement, and thought of it strictly as an Indian way of looking at things. But, I understood it better.

When the priest called for prayer, everyone bowed their heads. Everyone that is, except me. I had long ago taken on the Indian way. I lifted my eyes to the sky, which seemed more appropriate, and gazed at the beauty.

It was during that prayer that something happened that I couldn't quite figure out and wondered if my eyes were playing tricks on me. Off to my right, high on top of the butte, something had caught my eye. I thought I must be imagining things. But I saw a flash reflected off a rock. There seemed to be a reflection of light coming from the Piedra.

I found my eyes drifting back to the top of the Piedra, time and time again, as the service went on. And again, when everyone was called to prayer, I was watching the Piedra, the very top. And I saw it again. A flash. The sun had reflected off something, and this time there was no mistaking it.

I could see nothing on top of the big red butte. But what had made that flash? I had been up there, and to my knowledge there was nothing that would give off a reflection like that.

By the end of the service I was convinced that someone was up there on the top, watching. And since I couldn't see the outline of the form, they must be trying to stay out of sight.

As everybody began to leave, we hung around and waited. I saw quite a conversation going on with Miz T. and the Boss. The Boss wouldn't leave. And I could understand that. It's just that he wanted to stay until it was finally over.

When we went around to the side of the church to change into our work clothes, I told R.C. and Jim that I'd cover the grave. It would probably be easier on the Boss if I just stayed.

This didn't suit Jim too much. He thought if anybody stayed, it should be him. I wanted to stick around 'til whoever was up there on the Piedra came down. Out of curiosity, if nothing more.

Finally I convinced them to go back to the house. Evidently Miz T. decided to let the Boss have his way. She came over to me. "He wants to stay, Frank. I understand. Take care of him."

"Yes, ma'am. Don't worry about him. We'll be fine."

CHAPTER

29

I brought the wooden lid to the box and carefully put it down into the grave, and took a hammer and nails and attached the lid, just as it should be. When I crawled out of the grave and reached for the shovel, the Boss said, "Let me do it, Frank."

"Boss, you're in no condition to go to shovelin'. This is my job."

"He was my grandson, and the first dirt that falls will be of my do-ing."

So, slowly, but gently, he began to scatter dirt over the box that held the coffin. When he covered it up to where it could not be seen any longer, he handed the shovel to me. He squatted down, grabbed a long stem of gramma grass, stuck it in his mouth, and watched.

I watched the Piedra, and did not see a sign. I slowly filled in the grave. And occasionally I'd watch. Still nothing. No sign.

It was not until I had the grave practically filled that I saw a figure starting down off the Piedra. It appeared to be a man. It seemed as if he had a walking stick, or something, in his hand. And I didn't call the Boss's attention to it. I just watched.

As I began to mound up the displaced dirt on top and pack it with my shovel, the man made it to the bottom and disappeared. As I finished up I wondered. Had I made a mistake? Should I have told the Boss? Should I have gotten in Ol' Blue and driven over there and just found out who in the hell that was?

These thoughts were running through my mind when I saw a pickup coming around the Piedra and heading our way. It appeared to be a red pickup. I stuck my shovel in the ground and got the water jug and took a swig. As I watched, the pickup came forward, slowly, on the old feed road that eventually led up north to the Mueller place.

The Boss had not seen any of this, up to this point. As I laid down the jug and picked up the shovel again, I put the handle down on the ground and leaned on the metal part of it with my chin. "Boss, wasn't Paddy Mueller and his missus and his two boys at the funeral today?"

The Boss seemed to come out of a daze. "Ah, what?"

I repeated again what I'd said.

"I don't know. I think so. I'm not sure who was there."

"Well, I am. I'm sure I saw them. It's hard to miss a little short fellow with a big belly like him. And those two great big old boys. I know they were there."

"What difference does it make, Frank?"

"Well, it appears that they're comin' back again."

The Boss stood up and gazed to the north. He had a frown on his haggard face. "I wonder what they're doing?"

"Yeah, I wondered myself." I didn't say any more of what I'd seen on top of the Piedra. I'd just wait and maybe it would explain itself.

We both stood and watched as the pickup pulled off the old road and stopped outside the fence, about twenty-five yards from where we were standing.

"That's Paddy's pickup," I said, "but it sure ain't Paddy."

A fellow got out. Had a smile on his face. Wore an old slouch hat, a plaid shirt, faded Levis, and boots. He stood holding on to the door, looking at us and smiling. Then he reached back in and from the gun rack that hung over the back window, took down a rifle. I couldn't figure out what in the hell was happening.

The man took a few steps out in front of the pickup and just stood there, smiling. Then he spoke. "What's the matter, old man? Surprised to see me. I betcha thought I was dead. Well, I'm tellin' you, the past has come back to haunt you."

The Boss never said a word. I looked at him and his eyes narrowed as if squinting to see who it was. The shadows were beginning to lengthen out from the Piedra and from the old church. But the sun wasn't in his eyes. He was just looking to see who this was. I sure as hell didn't know!

The man stood there with the rifle held loosely in his right hand at his side. "With me gone, and now the boy, I suppose you think that you're gonna live forever. Well, it ain't so. I come back for what's rightfully mine. Hell, old man, I could have taken you from the top of the rock over there. I knew you'd hang around, just like when Grandpa died, and be the last to leave. I didn't count on this big fella here stayin' with you. But, I coulda taken you," and he reached with his left hand toward the top of the rifle and flipped up a peep sight.

I'd seen it before. It was a thirty-aught-six like they'd used in World War II. He said, "I'm pretty handy with this thing. I got me a Purple Heart. Even a Silver Star. I was a hero in the war. But you never knew that. Not that you ever cared. But I got to thinkin' while I was up there on that rock, it wouldn't be right to shoot you, and you never knew where it came from. I wanted to come down here so you'd know who it was."

The smile was gone. "I'm gonna send you to hell, old man! I've already been there twice, workin' for you and goin' through a war. But I just wanted you to know."

The Boss had not said a word. It occurred to me then that this son of a bitch, whoever he was, was going to kill the Boss, and me. And there wasn't a damned thing I could do about it! All I had was a shovel. I wasn't afraid. I didn't have time to be afraid. I was trying to think what could I do. With a fence between us, him with a thirty-aught-six and me with a shovel, there was damn little!

The Boss just stood there. It seemed like he was unafraid, or he was prepared. One or the other. It was then I realized that the man was about half drunk, or crazy.

But through clinched teeth I heard him say, "I've waited a long time for this. You think you're so goddamn perfect!"

And with that, he raised the rifle. If he was as good a shot as he claimed to be, the Boss would be dead in a second, with a shot through the heart. All I could think of was to move the shovel, the blade, over in front of the Boss, which I did just as I heard the damnedest blast that I'd ever heard. It sounded like a cannon's roar.

I must have had a death grip on the shovel because it knocked me down. I quickly looked at the Boss and he was lying on his back, and I knew I was next. I glanced back at the pickup and the man that had been holding the rifle was gone.

Still holding the shovel, I jumped up. And then I could see he was sprawled in front of the pickup. The rifle lay some five feet from his hands, and it looked like he'd been sawed in half with a buzz saw. There was blood everywhere!

I couldn't imagine what happened. I had no idea. My head spun. He was no longer a threat. But the Boss! I was sure the Boss was dead.

I quickly kneeled by his side and I could see no blood, no hole, no anything, except some dirt on his clean white shirt. I quickly got some water from the jug, wet a handkerchief, and wiped his brow. He was breathing, but he was unconscious.

Finally I began to see his eyelids flutter. I put my hand underneath his head and lifted it up. "Boss, are you all right?"

He looked me in the eye. "I think so. What happened?"

"I don't know. I thought the man shot you."

It was then that I looked at the shovel. It had done its work. You could see where a bullet had hit it, knocking it back into the Boss and knocking him flat. But, because of the concave nature of the shovel, it had caused it to ricochet, and the bullet had gone on off, spent.

"Are you sure you're all right?"

"I'm sure. Just let me lay here and catch my breath. My chest hurts."

"No wonder," as I brushed dirt off of his chest.

I was still trying to figure out what in the hell had happened. Even though I knew the man was dead, I approached him warily. I climbed over the fence, shovel still in my hand, and looked down on him. Whatever had hit him had knocked him to the other side of the pickup and had come from the east.

I looked over to see nothing but a windmill and a tank and thought I'd better investigate anyway. When I walked over to the east side of the tank, to my surprise I saw Tio with his old double-barreled shotgun lying flat on his back, out colder than a wedge.

I pickup up the shotgun and broke it open. There were two spent twelve-gauge, birdshot shotgun shells. Somehow, either on purpose or by a strange fluke, Tio had shot off both barrels at once. And the recoil had knocked him completely out. I ran back and got the water jug, and came back to Tio and began to pour a little water on the same handkerchief and wiped his face.

He was breathing. I thought he'd be all right. My God! How could something like this happen? Thank God for Tio! I had a feeling I should have been dead by now.

I went back to the Boss who was beginning to rise. He'd taken a terrific blow to the chest, but said he was all right. He walked out the gate and around to the pickup and stood there. I followed, about two steps behind. Finally he squatted down, took off his hat, and reached down and touched the man's temple. He shook his head.

"Who is this man? Do you know him?"

The Boss nodded his head yes.

I waited for an answer. It took awhile.

"This is Sonny."

"Sonny?"

"My son."

With that I had to lean against the pickup and hold my head. How could a tragedy like this happen? Why?

And I heard the Boss say, "Who did this?"

I had completely forgotten about Tio. "Over here," I said, and the Boss followed me.

Still stretched out on the ground was Tio. The Boss knelt down beside him and touched him gently and said, "He saved our lives, Frank. Can you help him?"

I again put water on the handkerchief and wiped his face, 'til he began to come around. It took a minute for him to get his bearings and to realize what had happened. But when his eyes finally focused on us looking down on him, he began to cry.

And when he spoke, he spoke in Spanish. All the words I caught were "muerte" and "Sonny."

The Boss sat down and put his arm around him like a small child, and consoled him and told him it was all right, that he'd done a brave thing and that he'd saved our lives.

He looked up at me. "Frank, get back to the house and get word to the sheriff. Then come back for Tio. I'll stay 'til the sheriff gets here."

I drove like I was carrying a bucket of fire.

Everyone had left except Diego and his family. It was one of the hardest things that I've ever done to walk into the kitchen and tell Miz T. what had happened.

She covered her face with both hands and sat down.

"We've got to get the sheriff," I said.

Diego spoke up. "The sheriff was here for the funeral. He's on his way back to town. Kika, run to the nearest phone at Cone. Maybe they can catch him by radio before he gets clear to town, and have him come back."

Miz T. arose. "Come, Diego, we've got to go to J.W. and Sonny. Frank, you drive us."

When we got there, both Tio and the Boss were sitting beside the body. Miz T. rushed to their sides. Diego and I hung back. Tio walked over to us. Diego put his arms around him and talked to him in Spanish.

I stuck out my hand, and Tio took it. "I want to thank you, Tio. That was a brave thing you did. I know that you were very close with Sonny. You saved the Boss's life, and mine. And I'm grateful. But what made you come back?"

Tio said in his halting English, "During the prayers I saw the light flash on top of the Piedra. Not once, but twice. And then I knew that it was Sonny up there. I did not know what he might do. So I thought I had better come back."

"How did you know it was Sonny? Nobody's heard of him or seen him since, when, 1940, '41?"

Tio shook his head. "Si! But I knew somebody had been down here, so I come look. And I find a bottle of this whiskey, Old Crow. He tried to bury it. I saw where the ground was disturbed, and I think I will look. The Old Crow, you see, that whiskey was the whiskey that Sonny drank before he left. I knew somebody had been coming here and something just told me it was Sonny. And with his terrible temper, something bad might happen. So I came back. But I am sorry this happened. Now I am in trouble."

"You're not in any trouble. The trouble has been taken care of. Isn't that right, Diego?"

Diego nodded his head. "The trouble is over. The sorrow begins. As if it hadn't already." And then he shook his head sadly.

As we waited for Dub McCanless to show up and inspect the sight of the terrible tragedy that had happened, the thought ran through my mind, again and again, Bad things happen in threes. Two of them had happened. We had one left to go. What in the hell could happen next? I wondered.

While I had been gone the Boss had been thoughtful enough to take off his suit coat and at least partially cover the body up. I fished around in the pickup and found a slicker and covered the rest of the body.

Miz T. took one look, turned her head and sobbed, then realized she had another problem on her hands. The Boss had broken out into a cold sweat and was sinking fast. He was having trouble getting his breath. When Miz T. opened his shirt she found a large bruise rising just above the nipple on the left side of his chest. It's where the shovel had hit him.

Miz T. and Diego thought it best to take the Boss back to the house. They also took Tio, who was badly shaken. I told them I'd wait for Dub and watch the body.

Although it seemed like a long time, it really wasn't, 'til I saw the sheriff's car being led up the trail by Ol' Blue. Kika, R.C., and Roberta were all in the pickup and Jim sat in the back.

Dub walked over to the body and removed the covers. "Jeeezus Christ!" He picked up the rifle, opened the bolt, and there was a spent thirty-aught-six cartridge. He looked over the gun at arm's length. "An old military rifle. Musta been used in the war."

Then I told him what Sonny had said to the Boss.

"He musta brought it back with him," Dub said. "Look at this."

I noticed on the stock were the initials "J.W.S." and carved into the wood were notches. Dub ran his fingers over them, and there were many. But neither of us counted them.

"Goddamn, Frank. You reckon these mean what I think?"

I shrugged my shoulders. "He claimed to be a sharpshooter, even a hero. And had won some medals."

As he put the rifle back on the ground, Dub said, "I thought that went out with John Wesley Hardin." He looked up at me. "Now, tell me what happened."

The girls had hung back, not approaching the body. But Jim and R.C. were there.

"You know," I said, "I've always heard that somebody that was gut shot died a slow, painful death."

Dub snorted. "Not when you've been gut shot with a twelve-gauge, double-barreled shotgun with both loads pumped into ya. Did anybody make an identification of the body?"

"Sure," I said. "The Boss and Miz T. both were here."

"Well," Dub said, "I need it confirmed in my presence."

"I can do that," Jim said. "We've known each other all our lives. And that's sure enough him, Sheriff."

With that, Dub got the keys to his car, opened up the trunk, and brought out a tarp. "No need in callin' an ambulance to come way out here. We'll wrap him up in this and put him in the backseat. I'll take him to town to Remington's mortuary. This case is fairly cut and dried. The little man had no choice. It looks like he was fixin' to kill both of ya." Then he stopped. "Why did you put that shovel in front of the Boss?"

I shrugged. "I don't know. It just seemed like all I could do. It was just an accident that the bullet hit the shovel."

Dub looked down. "There's no doubt about it, it saved his life. But then, what did you think you was gonna do?"

"It all happened so fast, I didn't know what to do. If old Tio hadn't been here, I'd be dead, too. Even though he seemed a shade drunk, he could still shoot. I figured he was gonna put one right through the Boss's heart."

Dub nodded. "I thought I could smell liquor. Let me look."

He felt the body, down around the boot top, and said, "Ah!" and slid up one pant leg, reached inside of the boot, and pulled out a pint that was half full of Old Crow bourbon whiskey.

Dub glanced up at the Piedra, which now was the only thing around that was catching light, for the sun had dipped below the horizon. "I reckon this is what caused the glint that you saw. He'd wait 'til everybody was prayin', then take a little snort."

He threw the bottle in the backseat, picked up the rifle, made sure it was empty with the bolt open, and laid it on the backseat floor. "Well, that's one gizzard that won't be oiled up anymore. I consider this case closed. If anything comes up, you boys let me know, hear?"

We all nodded. The car had already started to roll when Dub stopped. "You know, the thought just struck me. For a man that had such hatred for his father as this gentleman did," and he motioned toward the backseat with his thumb, "don't you find it kinda strange that he'd name his son after him? J.W. Stone III. Somehow that don't make sense." And then he left.

Only then did the two girls approach the spot. Jim got a shovel and began to cover up the great amount of blood that covered the sod. R.C. took the slicker to the tank at the windmill and washed it off. Kika folded the Boss's bloody coat over her arm and Roberta slipped her arm through mine and laid her head against my shoulder.

"Pretty grizzly, wasn't it?" I asked her.

"I didn't look. I just thank God you're all right."

"I'll tell you what I thank God for," I said, "Tio. It musta been hard for him. But if he had shot before Sonny did, who knows, he might have been in a world of trouble."

Roberta tugged at my arm. "Let's go back."

"No. You all go back to the house. I've got to return a pickup to its rightful owner. And believe me, there's a man that's got some explainin' to do!"

Roberta wouldn't stand for it. "No more today, Frank. Tomorrow you can do whatever you think needs to be done."

And Kika agreed. "I think our first responsibility is to see how the Boss is, don't you, Frank? And maybe get his opinion on what we should do next."

Then the happenings of the day began to creep onto me, and I felt a tiredness that I'd never felt before. Too much had happened in too short a time. I needed to sort things out in my head and let the shock of what just happened drain out of my body. And I knew a woman, a special woman, that could make that happen. Still in the back of my mind, the thought of bad things happening in threes, remained.

Back at the house, we found that the Boss had been put to bed, only after he had refused to go to town to the hospital. To lose a son and a grandson, all in the space of a few days, would tear any man. Both physically and mentally. That's what worried me most.

I told both Miz T. and Diego that I thought I should return the pickup and ask some questions. And I needed to talk to the Boss about it.

Miz T. shook her head. "I'd rather you not, Frank. If you can handle it for me, I would appreciate it. And Frank, if Sonny had been staying there at the Mueller place, please bring back any of his personal effects that you can find."

I assured her I would. Then she said, "I suppose I need to go to town tomorrow and make arrangements. And you boys will have to dig another grave."

Jim asked where she wanted it.

And without hesitation she said, "Right next to his son, where it should be. God forgive him."

The next morning R.C. followed me in Ol' Blue. I took the old Dodge pickup back to the Mueller place where it belonged. Gunther Mueller had homesteaded back in the early days. And like most people of German extraction, was a hard worker, would accept no charity, nor give it. According to most people, harsh and determined would have been a good way to describe him. His son Paddy had taken over the place at the time of the old man's death. Mrs. Mueller seemed like the one that held the place together.

The missus was a big woman with a rather pretty face, but showed nothing but hard work and no nonsense, while Paddy was much shorter than she, had a great, huge belly, and had a way about him of making everybody like him. Some people had wondered and perhaps accused him, myself included, of doing some things that were borderline illegal to plumb larceny.

He appeared not to have any enemy in the world. I know the times that I'd been around him he had been so friendly and glad-handed, that it made me think that there was a purpose behind it. I had asked the Boss once about them. All he said was, "Not everybody that lives across the fence is a neighbor. Neighbors are people that you can count on that will help you in a crisis." Evidently somewhere down the line the Muellers and the Stones had got crossways, but I didn't know why.

As I turned into their place, it was as different as daylight and dark from the Stone outfit. A lot of little buildings, a couple of houses; chickens, dogs, hogs, horses, and cattle roamed freely all over the place. Nothing was painted. They all served a purpose, but you could tell that there was no pride taken in the way things looked.

I knew I'd be lucky to catch Paddy at home. He had long since figured out that a good, strong wife and two big healthy boys could do the work on the place. And, he could make more money off trading. As I pulled up to their front door and turned off the pickup, the missus came out of the house, drying her hands on an apron. Behind her, dressed up like he was just fixing to go somewhere, was Paddy.

Big smile on his face, he shook hands with me. I introduced them both to R.C. And, of course, Paddy was full of compliments. "Say, I heard about this young man. Quite a bull rider!"

"I just thought I'd return your pickup," I said.

"Well, I appreciate it, Frank. Where'd you find it?"

"I guess you haven't heard."

They both got a concerned look on their face. "Heard what?"

And I told them what had happened down at the Piedra the day before.

The missus seemed astonished, and held both hands to her face. Tears began to roll down her face. Paddy tried to look astonished, but somehow it didn't come across as sincere as it should have.

I thought there was no other way to approach it but straightforward. So I asked the question that I had been wanting the answer to for some time. "How come Sonny Stone had your pickup?"

Paddy shrugged his shoulders. "Why, I've known Sonny all my life. He asked to borrow it, and I gave it to him."

"Where was he stayin'?" I asked.

"Here."

"How long had he been here?"

Paddy put his hand to his chin. "Ah, I don't know, Frank. Maybe a month, maybe longer. He'd come and go. There ain't no harm in that, is there?"

I had to admit that there wasn't.

Paddy went on. "Everybody knew that the Boss and Sonny didn't get along. Lord, I hadn't seen 'im in a coon's age. So when he came around, he was welcome to anything I had."

"Did you know," I asked, "that he'd been drivin' down through the place, goin' by the Piedra?" I told them about seeing him come out of there late at night on the Fourth of July.

Paddy shook his head. "I never asked him where he was goin' or what he did. It wasn't any of my business."

"Where was he stayin'?"

Paddy pointed his finger. "Over yonder, in the folks' old house."

I turned and looked at an old, unpainted shack. "Well, do you mind if I pick up his things, if he's got any? His ma would like to have all his belongin's."

"Shore, shore! Follow me, Frank. I don't know what all he's got. But you're welcome to go and take whatever there is."

There was a stove where he could do his own cooking, a chair where he could sit, and a single cot in the back room where he slept. Up against the wall was an old Servel propane refrigerator. You could see evidence in an old garbage can of a lot of now-gone headaches, because it was half filled with empty pint bottles of Old Crow whiskey. Over in the corner was what was remaining of a case of pints. The box was still half full. I told R.C. to gather it up and put it in back of the pickup.

I looked all around and there wasn't anything that seemed worth taking. In the closet there were a couple of suitcases, old and battered. I opened them up on the cot. Nothing was in them except a few odds and ends of clothes. I opened a drawer of a crude dresser and took out what clothes there were.

The only thing that held any interest to me was a shoe box in the bottom drawer filled with letters and different papers. I quickly thumbed through the papers and letters in the shoe box for no reason that I could think of except to satisfy my curiosity. But I did notice one letter addressed to Paddy. I pulled it out and said, "Here's a letter addressed to you."

Paddy smiled real big. "Oh, he got a letter mailed to him here and when I gave him his mail, mine must have got mixed up in with it. I didn't realize it."

He reached to take it, and I almost gave it to him, when I noticed it'd been opened. "Wait a minute," I said. It was just a plain white envelope with the name 'Sonny' in the bottom left corner. I pulled out a piece of stationery. I glanced at the handwriting and it said, "Dear Sonny."

"Wait a minute," I said, "somebody just wrote him in care of you. This letter's to him."

I could see a look of concern come on Paddy's face. "I think that letter's for me."

"I don't think so," I said, and put it back in the box.

Paddy stood and leaned against the door as I loaded the suitcases. I said, "Traveled light, didn't he?"

"Yep. He wasn't much on excess baggage," Paddy said.

R.C. and I took another look around, and outside of a half a sack of Duke's Mixture smoking tobacco and some paper "makin's," there just wasn't anything left. I walked out and threw the suitcases in the back. "Well, Paddy, I appreciate it."

Paddy came up and shook my hand again. "Frank, I want ya to tell Miz T. how sorry we all are. It's shore a shame that two deaths in one family should happen like this."

I nodded my head as I got in the pickup. "Well, I'll be seein' you."

"Boys, ya'll come anytime, hear! You're always welcome."

I gave him a wave with my hand, and R.C. and I turned around and went back the way we came. I glanced in the rearview mirror as we drove out and there was Paddy, still waving his hand.

As soon as R.C. and I were off the place, I relaxed a little. "Well, that was a disappointment."

"What did you expect to find?" R.C. said.

I shook my head. "I don't know. Somethin'. I just know that somethin' isn't right. There's more to this than meets the eye. And damned if I ain't gonna stay after it 'til I find out what it is! But I don't think anything we found up there is gonna help a lick, do you?"

R.C. shook his head no.

Back at the house, I took the two beat-up suitcases into the house to Miz T. As she looked at them and realized that this must have been all that her son had in this world, you could see the look of quiet remorse in her face. As tears streamed down her cheeks, she said, "Was this all?"

"Yes, ma'am," I said. "That's all I could find."

She thanked me, and as I turned to leave, she said, "Frank, sit down and drink a cup of coffee."

I poured myself a cup of coffee and sat down. "How's the Boss this mornin'?"

She shook her head. "Not good."

"Should we take him to the hospital?"

"No, I don't think it's that. It was just a deep bruise. It's his mind, Frank. And I can understand it, 'cause I have to battle for my own sanity. I don't know how I'd have gotten along without these two girls. They've been such a help and comfort."

She opened the suitcases and started to go through them, there on the kitchen table. Again I saw a look of sorrow on her face. "My God, my son didn't even have anything decent to wear."

"Ma'am, maybe that's the way he wanted it. No responsibilities. I could see where it'd have its good points."

She sighed deeply. "Maybe. But I can't help but think what might have been."

She reached for the shoe box and pulled it out. "I wonder what all this is?" There were some solid objects at the bottom of the shoe box. Cases of blue, with some kind of a gold seal on them. She opened one and I heard her breath suck in. "Oh, my, Frank. Look."

As I looked I realized that the man hadn't been lying. There was a Silver Star. There were other medals, also. Sharpshooter, Rifleman, and those campaign ribbons that they wore during the war that I never knew the meaning of.

"If," I said, "he had the Silver Star, there surely must be some kind of a letter of commendation or something that went with it. Do you mind?" as I reached for the papers.

She shook her head. She was still smiling at the medals.

I quickly searched through the papers, and sure enough found a letter. The envelope was from Washington, D.C., The White House, the office of the president up in the left-hand corner. I handed it to her. With a look of reverence she opened it. "Upon winning the Silver Star for heroism and gallantry above and beyond the call of duty," it went on, but at the bottom it was signed by Franklin D. Roosevelt.

By this time she had opened up another one of the flat boxes, similar to the one the Silver Star came in. She was gazing at a Purple Heart. I'd always heard about them, but this was the first I'd ever seen. "Wounded in battle." As I handed it back to her I said, "He was a hero, ma'am. You've got that!"

She smiled. "Yes, I do have that!" She shuffled through the papers. When she came to the envelope addressed to Paddy, she opened it and quickly read it, frowned, and handed it to me. "Frank, what do you make of this?"

I read it, then read it over again. "Dear Sonny, Received your letter. Don't worry about it. If you can't find it, they can't either. We don't need it, they do. We'll proceed as planned. Sincerely," and just the letter *B*.

"I have no idea what it means," I said. "There's nothing on the envelope." But I did notice a postmark, and it was of Santa Fe, New Mexico, origin.

Miz T. finally sat down. "I'll take some time and go through all these papers. But, Frank, I need to ask a favor of you."

"Anything. Anything at all."

"I'm worried about J.W. Until he's back on his feet, will you take over and see that things are running right?"

"I'll do the best I can."

"I knew I could count on you."

We stretched out in the bunkhouse. The letter written by this Mr. "B" was bothering me. So, I ran it by Jim and R.C.

"You know," R.C. said, "it didn't seem like Paddy wanted you to have that letter very much. If there was some way he could have taken it away from you, I believe he would have."

"Yeah, I got the same impression," I said. "But who in the hell is 'B'? What would they be referrin' to that we can't find, and they can't find, and that we need and they don't?"

"Frank," R.C. said, "you don't suppose it's those papers missing from the old mission, do you?"

And then it hit me. "Hell, yes! That's the only thing it could be. That's why somebody's been prowlin' around the old church. They've been lookin' for these papers, too. And it has somethin' to do with Diego's problem. Has to be!"

I didn't even think that Jim was listening. With a wrinkled brow you could see his mind go back in time. Then he started talking, more or less to himself. "'B', 'B' you say. My God, you don't reckon it's Bernie?"

"Jim, who in the hell is Bernie?" asked R.C.

"Bernie Mueller. Paddy's older brother."

"Shit, I didn't know Paddy had an older brother. I think you'd better tell me about it."

Jim started. "Old man Gunther Mueller had two sons, Bernard and Adolf. We all called them Bernie and Paddy. Both them boys had a ton of smarts, but Bernie, he was the smartest by far. Leastwise, he was smart enough to git out of this country. He knew that little place could never support both him and Paddy.

"He and Sonny were awful close. And when it looked like the war was comin', it just seemed natural that they'd join up together." Jim paused and put his hand to his chin. "I don't reckon I ever seen him since. Heard about him, though. He took advantage of the GI Bill, and went on to git him a high-powered education. I think it was Paddy that told me. As far as I know, he's never come back home, even to visit. But he and Sonny was sure good buddies."

"Jim," I said, "how come you've never told me this before?"

Jim tongued his chew into a new spot in his cheek and said, "You never asked."

About that time we heard a vehicle pull into the headquarters and stop in front of the main house. I could see Top headed for the big house and Poke coming up our way. Poke opened the screen door and came on in, wide-eyed. He looked at me and said, "Shit, hockey, hell, damn, poot, fart!"

Such an epithet coming out of his mouth rather surprised me. "Lord," I said, "that was a mouthful!"

"It's just my way of gittin' it out of my system real fast." Poke pulled up a chair. "Tell me what happened. From go to whoa."

I had a feeling I'd be telling this story over and over again for a long time.

CHAPTER

30

It was as I figured. Few showed up at the memorial service. And as we drove back to the ranch for the burial services, I couldn't help but notice the difference from the one I attended just a few days ago. There was no long caravan, just a hearse and a few cars. And mostly those filled with members of the American Legion. Miz T. had turned her boy over to the soldiers, where he had fit in.

At the old church, as I heard the bugler play taps and listened to the shots fired by the old warriors in his honor, I could see that she'd made the right choice. He was no longer a part of us, he more belonged to them. A man with a Purple Heart and a Silver Star should be attended to by his fellow warriors.

The Boss barely made it through the funeral, and as soon as it was over had to return to his bed. I didn't like his looks. His face was ashen, and I wondered how long the recovery would take. Or if he would ever recover.

Long after everyone left, only Top remained, as far as the outsiders went. Out of respect I think he just sat with the Boss and talked to him. I had a feeling that it was probably pretty one-sided. But it made me realize the relationship that the two of them had had for many years.

With Top staying, it gave me a chance to talk to Poke a little. The first thing I asked him was if the Gruyer was gone.

"Yep," Poke said. "Dee picked him up later the day that you left him there."

While waiting for Top we all killed time sitting out on the lawn. It was then that R.C. and I told Poke and the girls about our trip to the Mueller place and the letter that we'd found and Jim's story about a fellow by the name of Bernard Mueller.

When R.C. got to the part about a high-powered education, it made us all wonder. I reckon any kind of an education, including a high school diploma, would be considered high-powered by Jim.

R.C. wondered if maybe it wasn't Jim's words, but Paddy's words.

"Same difference," I said. "Neither one of 'em ever went to school for any amount of time, I don't think. Paddy probably went longer than Jim. But I bet he never graduated from high school."

But this didn't satisfy R.C. "No, what if somebody else told Paddy that it was high-powered. I consider a high-powered education for a man to be a doctor or lawyer. And according to that letter they were looking for something. They didn't find it, they didn't need it. But somebody does. Frank and I think they're referring to the lost documents at the church. And this man may be behind Diego's problems."

"Well, whatever this Bernie's occupation is, with his high-powered education, he must have made a hell of a bunch of money," Poke said, "'cause it would take a ton of it to pull off what he's tryin' to do."

"Not necessarily," R.C. said. "Maybe it's just a power play to get all that state land out of Diego's hands and turn it back to the state and lease it himself."

"What if it's the same people that's tryin' to buy the Cannon outfit?" Poke said. "That would take a bunch of money."

As I tried to put it together, all I could think of was, there was no way I could do something like that. I didn't have the smarts. Nor did I have the ruthlessness that it took to do something like that. Then I said so out loud. "Whoever it is, he'd have to be a shrewd cookie and kind of a heartless bastard."

It was Poke that finally said, "All right. Let's take stock of what we've got so far. If, and it's a big if, this 'B' is Bernie and he's got a high-powered education, he's shrewd, cunning, a heartless bastard, and has considerable wealth, who am I describing?"

A big smile came across R.C.'s face. "You just described a lawyer." And then he quickly qualified it. "I'm not talking about all attorneys, but it can be a powerful weapon."

I agreed. "For some it can be damned near a license to steal, if it's not used right."

"I agree," R.C. said.

As we sat there, all in our own thoughts, I wondered aloud, "I wish we could find out more about this Bernie."

"That shouldn't be any trouble," R.C. said. "If you can get me to a telephone and he's an attorney anywhere in the United States, I know somebody that can tell me where he is and what his specialty is."

About that time Top came out and I asked him about the Boss's health. All the cockiness had gone out of Top. "Frank, I'm worried about him. I don't know as to how anybody can help. It'll just take time, I reckon."

Top seemed to want to leave as quickly as he could. "Poke, are you goin' with me, or are you gonna walk home?"

"I'm comin'," Poke said as he rose from the lawn. "I'll see ya'll. Keep me posted, will ya?"

I nodded my head.

"Why," Roberta said, "don't you run this Bernie Mueller by Miz T.? Maybe she knows something that Jim doesn't."

At supper that night we did. She knew Bernie Mueller. But she hadn't seen him since he and Sonny had left to join the army. She asked why I inquired, but I didn't see any sense in alarming her until we had something sure enough concrete that we could prove.

It was that evening after supper and I was sitting on the rock wall out in front of the big house when I finally got to scratch Belle behind the ears. She seemed grateful. When Roberta came out and sat down beside me and put her arm up over my shoulders, I said, "Damn, I had more luck bein' alone with you when we'd meet in town on the weekends."

She brushed her cheek into my shoulder and I knew she was smiling, even though it was dark. "I know," she said. "But these have been tryin' times, Frank. Maybe now they'll settle down and we can get back to normal."

"When are you goin' home?"

Roberta shook her head. "Miz T. seems to need me and Kika. So as long as I'm needed, I guess I'll stay." Then she quickly raised her head and gave me a kiss on the cheek. "At least I'm near you." And then mockingly said as she leaned back, "I can keep track of you here, mister, and I know where you are."

I had to counter that some way. "Wherever I'm at, I'm not makin' much of a hand anymore. I'm spendin' most of my time just thinkin' about you."

The next morning I asked R.C. if he was really serious about being able to find out about Bernard Mueller.

"Sure. But I've got to make a phone call."

"Well, why don't you run to town and do that, then?"

"I was going to ask the Boss for a little time off."

It was then I told him what Miz T. had asked of me, to kind of take over while the Boss was recuperating. I was the head honcho now, and if he needed permission to do anything, he could come talk to me. Of course, the last part I said with a smile getting bigger and bigger and bigger as I emphasized my newfound importance. R.C. could tell I was just hoorahing him.

"Frank, I may have to wait for an answer. I don't know when I'll be back."

"Just go on. Find out what you can and we'll see you when you get here."

I really hadn't expected him back quite so early. I was halter-breaking colts up in the big round corral, under Roberta's watchful eye, when I saw R.C. return.

He slammed the door on Sundown and headed our way, with Kika meeting him about halfway to us. I let go of what I was doing and walked over to the fence by Roberta eager to find out if he had found any information at all.

I peered at him through the slats in the fence and gently held on to Roberta's legs. She was sitting on the top rail, and canted around to where she could see both R.C. and Kika.

"We were right," R.C. said. "There is a Bernard Mueller who is an attorney and resides at Santa Fe, New Mexico."

"Damn! Anything else?"

R.C. began. "Graduate of University of Oklahoma Law School, specializes in real estate. You know, titles, escrow, land law, things like that."

"How do you know all this?" I said.

R.C. smiled. "It's all in the big book. You can look up any lawyer in the country. He had been practicing in Oklahoma until last year when he joined the firm of Anderson and Associates in Santa Fe. The only cloud on his record, and it came in a roundabout way to me, was ethics."

I looked up at Roberta and she raised her eyebrows, looking at Kika. "Well," I said, "it appears like he's our man."

"Wait, Frank," R.C. said. "*If* it's the same Bernard Mueller. Maybe it's two different men."

"I think it's time we go to Santa Fe," I said.

"Me, too," said R.C. "I've already made an appointment."

This surprised me. "An appointment with who?"

"With a Mr. Bernard Mueller," R.C. said. "The appointment's tomorrow, at eleven o'clock in the morning."

"Good," I said. I took a deep breath. "There's no time like the present. I'm not much of a hand on waitin' around. Let's go do it. I'll ask Miz T. for permission."

"I thought you were in charge now," R.C. said, "and didn't need permission."

I smiled at him. "I lied!"

Kika insisted that we take her car. It was a much newer vehicle than either R.C. or I had. I gave Roberta a big kiss and asked her if she'd be there when I got back.

"I'll be here," she said.

R.C. was ready to go after a trip to the bunkhouse and back with one of his suitcases.

"Goddamn!" I said. "What are you doin'? I'm goin' just like I am and I'm not even takin' a change of clothes."

R.C. just smiled. "I've got a plan."

"Oh, good. I wish you'd tell me what it is," I said.

"I have to make it up as we go along."

So we headed south. The Cannon place would be right on our way. Since it was so close to midday, we found Poke at the house for dinner. We told him where we were going and he knew the reason why. He had a talk with Top and said he'd go.

R.C. asked how far Santa Fe was and how long it'd take to get there. I replied, "Four, five hours. Just depends."

"Depends on what?"

"Depends on how you let the hammer down on this fine, fancy new car, and how many Mexican wood haulers we get behind going up through Glorieta Pass."

R.C. had never been in this part of the country or been to Santa Fe. I thought he had a treat in store for himself, because he'd find it totally different from any town he'd ever been in in the United States.

Finally I talked R.C. into letting me drive, though he reminded me that, after all, the car was Francesca's and he was responsible for it. It had been a long time since I'd been in that fine an automobile. When we finally reached the pavement I thought I'd see what it would do.

It seemed to make R.C. nervous at first. It didn't bother Poke one bit. He sprawled out in the backseat, and as the fence posts went by faster and faster, he said, "I do believe, Frank, that this son of a bitch could run a hundred in plowed ground!"

Little by little the country changed as we continued west and then angled off to the south. You could see the mountains. "The Sangre de Cristos," I told R.C. "The blood of Christ."

By the time we crossed the mountains through Glorieta Pass and began to come down into Santa Fe from the east, you could see the wonderment on R.C.'s face. "It looks like another country."

"It is," I told him.

I cut off the main road. It was awfully easy to get lost in Santa Fe. But we still had plenty of sun and I thought I knew where I was going. I soon found out I didn't.

Streets ran in every direction. Nothing was square. It was completely unlike the conventional towns that R.C. was used to. I took the wrong road and we wandered around through low adobe structures of the Pueblo type. Although R.C. seemed to be enjoying it very much, Poke said, "Goddamn, Frank! Are we lost?"

"Hell, no, we're not lost. I just don't know where I am." Kind of irritated me. "What do you care? We ain't in jail."

Finally I found the street I was looking for. It was the old Santa Fe Trail, and I knew it led down to the square. I pulled up and parked on the corner of the plaza. I wanted R.C. to see this. We all three got out and walked to the corner where we stood on San Francisco Street on the southeast corner of the square.

I wanted R.C. to see the old cathedral and the La Fonda Hotel. Those were the only landmarks near the plaza, with the Palace of the Governors, that I knew about.

R.C. stood back and looked at the La Fonda with its vigas sticking out of the adobe walls. I said, "Let's go in and have a drink at the bar. I'm thirsty from trail dust!"

The bar was on the order of a sure-enough Spanish cantina. We had our drink and I began to wonder where we'd spend the night. I knew some cheap motels out on the highway to Albuquerque, on Cerrillos Road.

But R.C. shook his head. "No. We'll stay here."

I laughed. "We can't afford it!"

R.C. looked at me and with a smile said, "Yeah, we can."

"Maybe you can," I said. "But I damn sure can't. How about you, Poke?"

Poke shook his head. "I already spent half my wages on women and whiskey and wasted the other half. I'll just have to sleep in the car."

R.C. seemed to get exasperated with us. "I told you when we started, don't worry about money. I'll take care of it."

I looked at Poke. "All right," I said, "it's your deal. Play your cards."

With that R.C. seemed relieved. "Tell you what," he said. "You fellows stay here and have a couple of drinks on me. I'm going to go get the car and check in. Then maybe I can tell you a little bit of what I'm thinking about."

As soon as he left, Poke and I looked at one another and began to laugh. "I don't think he has any idea how expensive it is to stay in this place," I said.

"I don't know. Remember me tellin' ya about all the money he seemed to have?"

"Sure," I said.

"Has it ever crossed your mind that maybe he does know what he's doin', how much things cost. Hell, he might even be used to it, for all we know."

We let the matter drop. It seemed like it was out of our hands anyway. When R.C. finally made it back, he said, "We're checked in. Let's go and wash up."

When we walked to our room and entered it, I couldn't believe my eyes. The man had rented a suite for the night, a three-room suite, complete with its own bar, three telephones, and four beds. I walked across the room and looked out the window and realized that I was looking toward the southwest because I could see the capitol building. And closer still, the Loretta Chapel.

I noticed the suitcase sitting on a bench at the end of one bed and knew that R.C. had already been up and checked the place out. I didn't know what kind of a plan he had, but I did know one thing. It was an expensive plan.

Poke couldn't get over it. "Jesus Christ! I can't believe this place," as he wandered around from room to room.

"Me neither. I never thought I'd ever spend a night in an outfit like this!"

R.C. had already sat down at the desk with a phone book and was in the yellow pages. He acquired stationery from the desk drawer and was making notes.

I tried to talk to him a couple of times, but he was so deeply engrossed in what he was doing it was just like stomping sand down a rathole.

"You know, for what this place must cost," Poke said, "it looks to me like they could furnish it a little better, instead of these straight-backed, carved, funny-colored chairs. Blue chairs. Whoever heard of blue chairs?"

"Poke," I said, "you idiot! This is colonial Spanish architecture in design. What in the hell do they teach you at Texas Tech? Goat milkin'?"

Poke seemed to take offense at that. "Hell, I'm just jokin', Frank. Texas has more Spanish culture than New Mexico ever thought of!"

So a big friendly argument commenced.

Finally R.C. was through, smiled big, and said, "Nice place, huh? I especially like those fireplaces, one in each room."

"I'd sure as hell hate to haul wood up here for 'em," Poke said.

R.C. settled down in a chair and flipped a room key to both Poke and myself. "We've got to have a game plan," R.C. began. "And this is how it works. Any meals or any drinks that you have in this hotel, show them the key and sign the check with your name. I've made arrangements at the desk for it to be taken care of. And please don't answer the telephone. If I'm not here, just let it ring. I'll take all calls that come in."

Of course Poke and I didn't understand, but at this point we didn't care, either.

Finally I said, "What's your plan, R.C.?"

R.C. hesitated a minute. "I'm still working on it, but . . . I thought I'd meet the man, form an opinion about him, discounting the opinion I already have, and act as if I'm interested in the acquisition of a ranch with a lot of state land that goes with it. If he's as greedy as everybody thinks he is, maybe he'll tell me what he has on his mind voluntarily without having to pry anything out of him."

"Shit," I said, "in order to do that, R.C., you'd have to convince him that you're rich!"

R.C. shook his head. "I intend to."

"Dressed the way you are, he ain't gonna believe ya."

He winked at me and smiled. "Smart people never judge another person by the way they dress. However, I'll take care of that. My plan is to run a scam on him and get him to think he's on our side. I think we can pull it off."

"I doubt it," Poke said.

"I agree with him," was all I could say.

"Well, anyway, I'm starved. Frank, do you know of anyplace to eat around close?"

"Right down here in the hotel lobby would probably be the best place."

That night we ate good Mexican food, Santa Fe style, until we practically foundered. Of course, R.C. handled the bill. I admired the subtle way he signed the check. He must have added a hell of a tip, as the waiter seemed most grateful and obliging.

We slept in virtual splendor that night. And sleep came easy on a full stomach.

At breakfast as we lounged over coffee, R.C. explained, "I've got some telephone calls to make and some preparations to make this morning. I'd just as soon do it in private, if you don't mind. I'll meet you boys back here at ten-thirty, and we'll go have our little powwow with Mr. Mueller."

It seemed as if R.C. was getting rather secretive, but he said he had this plan, and I was willing to go along with it. Poke was willing to go along with anything, just for the ride.

Poke and I decided to stretch our legs and take a look-see outside, while R.C. went back to the room for his phone calls.

When we got to the plaza I could see on the north side, under the overhang porch of the Palace of the Governors, the Indians had begun to set up their marketplace. They had done this traditionally for as long as I could remember, and no telling how much longer. We began to walk underneath the porch of the palace, slowly inspecting all the merchandise the Indians were setting out for sale.

We made our way back up to the suite and waited for R.C.'s return. When he did come in he caught us both totally by surprise. He stood in front of us, spread out his arms, and said, "What do you think?"

And there he stood, decked out in the damnedest outfit money could buy. A brand-new silver belly hat shaped to perfection, a linen western suit, alligator boots with belt to match. He was a sight for sore eyes.

All I could think of to say was, "Goddamn. You look like you've got money in the bank and cattle out west."

"That's the idea. I'm trying to look the part."

I remembered our first excursion outfitting him in Steinbach's Mercantile, and had to admit he'd come a long way. I couldn't improve on what he'd bought a lick.

"I suppose," he said, "it's time we get over to the law office. I know where it is. It's just a short walk from here. No sense taking the car."

As we walked through the streets of Santa Fe, I'm sure it appeared to everybody that took notice that a wealthy man had brought his two hired hands to town for some special occasion.

We turned down Palace Avenue to the east. And right close to Sena Plaza we found the office of Anderson and Associates. It was built in the architecture of everything else in Santa Fe, and from the outside showed prosperity and class.

R.C. didn't hesitate at the door. He just walked right in. We followed him. He walked up to the receptionist at the desk, as we hung back, and in a low voice spoke to her with all the confidence in the world. I couldn't hear what he was saying, but it seemed that he laid enough charm on her that he certainly got her attention, for she was all smiles as she reached for the phone and dialed a number. With a point of her hand, she designated the way he should go.

R.C. swung back by us. "Boys, have a seat. Take your hats off, will you? I don't know how long I'll be."

The office was built in kind of a half circle, the lobby, that is, with hallways leading off of it like the spoke of a wagon wheel. He had just started down one of those hallways when the man we supposed was Bernie

Mueller met him and shook hands. As I looked him over, there was no mistaking, in my mind, that it was Paddy's brother. He lacked the big, overhanging gut, was slightly taller, but the facial features were there. And he was dressed not in western wear, but as most attorneys in a three-piece suit. He and R.C. disappeared down a hallway and Poke and I began our long wait.

Finally, after an hour and a half, we saw R.C. appear along with who I was sure was Bernie Mueller. We watched them shake hands, talk a few seconds longer. R.C. came out to where we were.

Right away I had to put in my two cents' worth. "That was him, wasn't it, R.C.? I know it was."

R.C. started back toward the plaza. "Be quiet until we get out of sight."

We followed him down to the corner and I figured that was enough. "We're out of earshot now," I said. "What'd he say?"

R.C. turned around, adjusted his lapel on his new duds, and said, "You're right. It was him. We had quite a conversation. Let's go back to the room and get comfortable. Then I'll tell you what I remember."

I thought to myself, Damn, I hope he remembers it all! I want to hear everything that I can about this man and what's goin' on.

R.C. opened the hotel suite and he seemed very pleased with himself. "I think the man bought it."

"Bought what?" Poke said.

"That I am what I appeared to be."

"Quit hedgin'," I said. "Tell us the whole thing. Sit down!" I was very impatient.

"Well, I told him I was interested in purchasing a ranch in New Mexico with a large balance of state land attached to it. Because of the cheap lease from the state, it seemed the way to go if it could be done. Of course, he agreed that it could be done. I let him tell me about large state land parcels all over the state, and acted like I considered them, before I asked about the northeast corner of the state. I told him I'd heard it was some of the better cattle country that the state held.

"He did have some ideas on the subject there. But he kept skirting the Cannon place or anything about the Jaramillo place. He had lots of questions for me. I just hope I passed the test."

"What kind of questions?" I asked.

"Well, he was interested in whether I was interested in running a cow-calf operation or a yearling operation and if so, what kind of cattle that I preferred. I think he was just trying to test me."

Then a look of doubt crossed R.C.'s face. "I hope I learned enough from you guys. I tried to talk as knowledgeably about the subject as I could. He wondered why I hadn't contacted any real estate agents. And I told him that I had, but with my inclination toward these cheap state leases, that I'd heard he was the man who might be able to furnish some insight, on state land in particular. He even asked who had referred me to him."

He had us spellbound, but Poke said, "What'd ya tell him?"

R.C. grinned. "I gave him a name. I also showed that I'd done some research on him, and told him what I knew about his background. Which didn't seem to surprise him. I finally mentioned that I understood that a place called the Cannon Ranch might be for sale. And that's when I got his attention. He allowed that he had heard that place was for sale, and was familiar with it.

"I asked him if it contained any state land and he told me, not to any degree. I asked the possibility of picking up some state land that joined it." R.C. leaned back in his chair and hesitated for a minute. "Boys, that's where I knew we had our man. I think he has plans to buy the Cannon place for himself, try to put up Diego's state land, and buy it himself. If he can cause enough worry for Diego with his land grant and birthright problems, he'll use them mainly as a decoy and confuse the old man to where the state land that Diego controls can be bought for nothing.

"I don't really think that he thinks he can pull off legally the deal against Diego. Diego's just been there too long. However, if the records are as screwed up and such a mess as Diego says they are, who knows? He might. But don't you see? If he had Diego's state land and he had the Cannon place, and he had Sonny Stone in with him being the only heir to the Piedra Ranch, if they were partners in some way, not to mention if his brother was thrown in with him, he'd have an empire! A veritable cattle empire!

"But," R.C. continued, "there's not a doubt in my mind that if he could turn this empire that he's trying to build and make good money on it, and I mean good money, that he would sell it. And maybe he thinks he's found a sucker in me. I have a feeling that he's going to play me to the hilt."

"What do you mean?" I asked.

"I think he's going to think about it for a while and probably check me out."

And that's when it hit me. "My God, what are you gonna do about that, R.C.? A man of any sense is gonna check you out. When he finds no record, your act is gonna be shot full of holes."

R.C. smiled and shook his head. "Not necessarily. I made phone calls to people and told them what I'm doing. I gave him some numbers to call and they will guarantee him that I'm a bona fide man of substance and wealth who is interested in buying a New Mexico ranch. I think it'll satisfy him. I hope it does," R.C. said, almost to himself.

"I expect him to get back to me. That's why we're staying in this suite. That's why I bought the new clothes. But I have to stick close to the phone, in case he calls."

R.C. seemed oblivious to us as he took off his suit and put his regular clothes back on. He seemed to be talking to himself when he said, "If he'll just make a phone call to us, we'll know we've got him! He's got to call."

"Well, I hate waitin'," Poke said. "I'm goin' down for a toddy and some female companionship. Frank, you wanna come?"

"No, I'll stay here with R.C."

After a good spell of anxious waiting, the call finally came. I just heard one end of the conversation, but R.C. handled it very well. The caller talked for about fifteen minutes, with R.C. adding words of encouragement occasionally. But most of the conversation came from the end I couldn't hear. R.C. closed by saying, "I'll be in touch. You know where to reach me by mail. There are a few other places I'd like to look at in west Texas and southern Colorado, so I'll be unable to be reached by phone. But, I'll call you and stay in touch." After a few more pleasantries, he hung up and smiled. "Boys, we've got him!"

He must have wondered about the puzzled look I had on my face. "He thinks he's got a ripe one with me," R.C. said. "I have a feeling the gentleman will tell us his every move from here on out. Now, it's up to us to stay one jump ahead."

That made sense to me.

Poke hadn't shown up at the room yet. Probably still sitting at the bar down in the cantina, three sheets to the wind, trying to turn everybody that would listen into admirers of Texans.

But as R.C. and I entered the cantina, he was nowhere in sight. We didn't think much about it, but if he didn't show up soon, he'd have to eat supper alone. Then I heard my name being paged by a Mexican boy walking through the lobby and the cantina, hollering at the top of his lungs, "Phone call for Mr. Frank Dalton."

I couldn't figure it out. Nobody knew where I was. I got to the pager as quick as I could and he told me I had a phone call. R.C. took care of the tip with a bill from his pocket.

I picked up the phone not knowing what to think, only to hear Poke's voice, and you could tell he was in trouble. "Frank, thank God I got ahold of you!"

"What's the matter?"

"It's a long story. I need some help. And I need it fast!"

"What kind of help?" I said.

"You know those Mexican knife fighters?"

"Pachucos?"

"Yeah. I'm gonna be butchered if you don't come and git me out of here!"

"Where are you?"

"I'm not sure. It's a bar called the 'El Gato.'"

"Stay in the bar. As long as you're in there, you ought to be all right. Just don't go outside. We'll get there just as quick as we can. I'll find somebody that knows where it is."

All Poke could say was, "Hurry, Frank. Hurry."

R.C. had a funny look on his face when I told him, "Poke's gone and got himself in a jam. We gotta get him out. Pachucos. Mexican knife fighters. I've gotta find somebody that knows where the El Gato bar is."

R.C. took off in a run.

"Where are you goin'?" I asked.

"I'll be right back," he said.

I went into the lobby and found a shine boy. He was working diligently on a pair of shoes that a tourist was wearing. I asked the young man if he knew where the El Gato bar was. He nodded his head yes.

"How would you like to make ten bucks real quick?" I asked. And he looked at me with a wary eye and said, "Doin' what?"

"All you've got to do is come and show me where this bar is."

The shine boy backed off a little more. "No fonny biznez?" in broken English.

I shook my head. "No funny business."

"Where's the money?" he said.

It was then I realized I may not be able to make the ten dollars without R.C., but about that time R.C. was coming down the steps. "Give the boy ten dollars," I said.

With the boy's instructions we got out of downtown Santa Fe in a hurry. And I knew we were heading in the direction of trouble. This was the wrong part of town for a gringo to be in.

We drove past the bar and parked the car. I told the boy, "You've got your money. You can wait here. We'll be back in a few minutes and take you back to the hotel, or you can go on your own." I had a feeling he'd go back on his own. The El Gato bar was not a place for people like us to be going into it. I knew it. He knew it. I just wished to hell Poke would have known it!

As R.C. and I approached the entrance to the bar, I began to look around on the ground. "I'm gonna need an equalizer."

"We don't have time," R.C. said. "Let's just go in and bluff our way through it."

I took a deep breath and said, "I'm with you."

It was a typical, low-class Mexican bar. If anybody ever wondered what these pachucos looked like, he had a perfect example out of any of a dozen that appeared in the bar.

Poke was sitting nervously at the bar with his back to the wall. With him was a cute little Mexican girl who seemed not to have a care in the world. We didn't enter the bar over ten feet, when I crooked my finger at Poke and made a motion like "come here." Believe me, Poke didn't need any prompting. The problem was the local toughs decided they'd come too.

I saw R.C. bend down as Poke and I went past him. I didn't know what he was doing. It appeared like he was pulling up his pant leg and adjusting his socks. I told him to come on, we didn't have time to waste.

But, just as we hit the door, I heard R.C.'s voice behind me, very calm and very cool, say to the patrons of the bar, "Now everybody just stay inside and everything will be all right. If you don't, I can guarantee the first one that sticks his head through that door will be deader than a wood-headed redpecker."

I didn't know what the hell he was talking about, but I hoped it worked! R.C. backed out of the bar and closed the door behind him. We all made a run for the car. The Mexican boy, of course, was gone. It didn't take me long to get in gear and get on down the streets.

I looked at R.C. "I don't know what kind of a speech you made back there, but it damn sure worked! You can be very convincin' when you try." Then as I remembered what he'd said in our hasty departure, I began to laugh. "Deader than a wood-headed redpecker?" The more I thought about it, the more I laughed. Poke, too. "Didn't you get that fucked up?" I said.

R.C. looked indignant. "I said what I meant to say. If it was confusing, it was for a purpose. And it worked, along with this." R.C. smiled and held up a Colt .45 semiautomatic. "I didn't do anything. This did."

"Where," I said, "did you get that?"

R.C. smiled. "There's more than a pint of whiskey that'll fit inside your boot."

I told him I'd remember that. Then we both turned our fury on Poke. I asked him what in the hell he thought he was doing. "I just made friends with a lovely señorita. She decided she'd show me some of the local night-spots. And before I knew it, I was in unfriendly territory."

"Jesus Christ, Poke," I said. "You're just like a goose. You wake up in a new world every mornin'!"

Poke was kind of sheepish. "But this little sweet thing didn't seem to mean me no harm."

"Ha," I said. "That's what you think. I swear to God, Poke, you're the shits!"

Then I turned to R.C. "And, do you realize what you did by pullin' that gun? I've always been told, if you pull a gun, you better be ready to shoot it. If your bluff don't work, you can be in a pack of trouble."

All R.C. said was, "I wasn't bluffing."

As usual, we were up before daylight, and on our way home. It was much easier to get out of Santa Fe than to get in. All we had to do was get on the Old Santa Fe Trail and follow it 'til we met the highway to Las Vegas.

Santa Fe at that time of the morning was quite peaceful. You could smell the piñon smoke coming from the fires of the adobe homes, not because of the chill in the air, because it was late July. It was because of the cooking fires. Even in this day and age, one would be surprised how much of the cooking was still done over woodstoves. Santa Fe seemed to be the one place in the world that I knew of that always stayed the same.

It didn't take us long to get over Glorieta Pass and down through the canyon that led to the prairie. The sun was just coming up and we could look over to the east at the vast expanse of prairie. "Look, fellas," I said. "The Great American Desert."

CHAPTER

31

It was early afternoon when Roberta and I saddled up and headed for the Barton pasture. It was just an excuse to get off by ourselves.

The Aguacita, the small creek that crossed the main road that we always had to ford, was a beautiful little creek. It wasn't a wet-weather creek at all. It was fed by springs, and meandered from the north carving out its own channel heading to the southeast, where it joined Long's Creek. The water was clear and there were even a few bass, and 'course, catfish that inhabited the small creek. It was lined in places by bluffs that it had cut through years ago. It also had large shade trees, cottonwood mostly, and a few brushy thickets, wild plums and chinaberry that grew along its banks.

As we rode, I told her of our experiences in Santa Fe. She listened intently, seldom interrupting me with a question.

When I told her about R.C.'s "wood-headed redpecker" statement, she laughed so hard she got a side-ache. I began to laugh, too, and things turned much lighter and brighter because of it.

When we rode up on the Aguacita, Roberta exclaimed how beautiful it was. The little valley and canyon that it sat in captivated her.

"This is beautiful, Frank!"

I had to agree. "Yeah, it's a dandy. It's more like a creek that you find in Oklahoma or Missouri. Don't you know that this must have been a welcome sight to some weary travelers a hundred years or so ago when the country was open, to find this fresh water and firewood out on the prairie."

I continued to lead her on up the creek until we entered a chinaberry thicket where we had to go single-file. It opened up into a grassy little park, shaded by cottonwoods that must have been hundreds of years old.

It was there I dismounted, loosened my cinch and hers, and hobbled our horses. Roberta eyed the creek, which at that particular place had widened out and deepened, and formed a pool before it meandered on its way.

"We have this magnificent pool of water in front of us. Why don't we take a dip?"

I eyed her a little suspiciously. "Ah, I forgot to bring my swimsuit."

She smiled and said, "Haven't you ever heard of skinny-dippin'?"

"Sure. But that's usually done at night, isn't it?"

"Only with people that are bashful. Are you too bashful, Frank?"

It seemed like a challenge to me. And I was never one to back off from a challenge. Finally I said, "I will if you will."

"You've got a deal."

So we both began to shuck. I slowly went about the task of removing my clothes. Roberta seemed in a hurry. It was a pleasure to watch her. As she stepped out of her panties, I was just stepping out of my Levis, and she stood before me just as God had made her. Without any false modesty, she made it seem as natural as the sun coming up in the morning.

I smiled and looked at her.

And with that, like a child, she ran to the creek. After taking two or three steps into the water, grabbed ahold of her nose, just like a young child, and jumped, making a huge splash. I was right behind her.

We played like a couple of kids, splashing water on each other and then playing a game of tag. She tried to stay as far away from me as she could.

Over on the far side of the creek it got quite deep and was in the shadows of a small bluff. She swam well. Grabbing air and puffing out her cheeks, she'd go underwater, only to come up in a different spot. And finally she let me catch her.

We were standing in water that was slightly over chest deep. "Ma'am, your assets are beyond belief."

As I held her outstretched hands, she walked toward me. She put both arms around my neck and let her legs drift up and encircle my waist. She was so willing and so ready, and so receptive, that it didn't take long.

"Darlin', I'm afraid you didn't receive the passion you were due," I said.

She relaxed and smiled and kissed me on the nose. "That's what you think, Big'un."

I was relieved. Then a funny feeling came over me. A feeling that there was someone watching. Most people will sometimes have that eerie feeling that they're being watched. I knew Belle, after a quick swim in the creek, had jumped out and was lying on the bank, panting and watching us. But this was not what I was referring to. It wasn't until I looked across the creek, up on top of the bluff, did I see what had given me that feeling. And it almost made me laugh.

"Darlin', it seems we have an audience."

Roberta looked at me with surprise. "Frank, what on earth are you talkin' about?"

I turned my head across the creek to the top of the bluff, as did she. And there stood a bunch of yearling heifers gazing down on us, out of curiosity. It made us both laugh.

Finally we disengaged and arm in arm walked up on the bank and dropped down into the grass to let the sun dry us off. I lay on my back with my eyes closed while Roberta lay on her side propped up on her elbow, with her hand wiping the water from my face, forehead, smoothing back my wet hair. For some reason, the penetrating eyes of the heifers had made me uncomfortable. I raised up and hollered at them, but they didn't move a step. They just stood there, chewing their cuds, and stared.

I took Roberta back to town early the next morning. When we got to her house, she didn't even go inside. She fished her car keys out and I could tell she was anxious to get back to the ranch. She felt like she was needed there.

I told her I loved her, and gave her a kiss and a hug. Evidently it was just the words she wanted to hear, because she smiled back and said, "Me too, you." And we parted.

On the way home I had a lot of thinking to do. I knew what was happening. I'd tried to fight it, but I was losing. And I didn't seem to mind a bit. We weren't engaged. I hadn't asked for her hand in marriage. Without ever discussing it, I realized that we just had an understanding. An understanding that she belonged to me and I belonged to her, and would remain that way until I got up the nerve to make a commitment. I knew she'd never force the issue. She just wasn't the kind. She had given herself to me completely. She was everything that a man could dream of. I considered myself a very lucky man!

Still, after running wild and free all your life, to have thoughts like I was having now was rather unsettling. Before you really got serious and made a commitment, in my mind at least, you had to have something besides just yourself to offer. The odd thing about it, it seemed to be just the way I felt. Roberta had never asked for anything, except just me. For the first time in my life, I was in love.

So far in our relationship we had never had a cross word. Which was highly unusual, thinking about my past track record with women. It was hard to explain. She just fit into my life and I to hers. She left no doubt in what she thought and she didn't try to hide her feelings. No doubt about it, I had found myself a dandy! Now, if I was just man enough to handle it.

As I pulled into headquarters, no one seemed to be around. Belle didn't even run out to meet me, which was highly unusual. I crawled up on the corral fence and stood on the top rung, held on to an overhead gatepost, and I finally saw somebody. Three people were out at the post pile peeling posts. That was unusual. There were Jim, R.C., and even Tio, peeling posts. I didn't understand why all three of them were out there together.

When I walked up to them, I asked, "What in the hell are you doin'? Are we startin' on another fence project right away? If so, we've already got enough posts peeled to build a five-wire fence from here to town."

All three stopped and looked at me. Finally Jim said, "Frank, we didn't know what else to do. The Boss hasn't said anything for days. So, we're just tryin' to stay busy."

I guess it was as good a time as any. So I told them to take a break and we'd talk it over. We all squatted down and I told them about Miz T.'s request and how she'd asked me if I'd kind of take over while the Boss was down. Try to keep the ranch on an even keel 'til the Boss was his old self again.

Surprisingly Jim said, "Somebody needs to, Frank."

So it seemed that I had a vote of confidence and full support of everybody on the place. And then it dawned on me. Except the Boss. I had not talked to him, nor had he been in shape to talk to. If I was going to take on any responsibility, in my heart I needed his permission.

I figured there was no time like the present. So I went down to the big house. In a way, I kind of dreaded it. It had to come from his mouth.

Miz T. must have heard me come through the back door into the kitchen. I asked how he was today, and she said, "A little better, Frank. But maybe this is just what he needs, someone like you to talk to. Try to draw him out. See if you can't get him up and going. I've tried everything, and I can't."

She poured me a cup of coffee and told me he was in the den. As I walked into the den, it kind of took me back. I don't know what I was expecting, but it wasn't this. He had aged considerably in just a short while. His color was bad and combined with his gray hair, gave him a rather ghostly appearance.

I stood as I good-morninged him and asked him how he was. His answer was, "Tolerable." I remained standing, sipping my coffee, until he pointed at a chair, a big leather, overstuffed comfort chair. He didn't look at me. He just gazed off in space, and never said a word.

"Ah, Boss, the boys and I've been talkin' and there's some things around here that need to be done. We were figurin' that maybe those steers need to be sorted and put into our new pasture. The smaller one, I mean."

The Boss nodded his head.

"Also," I said, "you generally sell your heifers in September, so it would seem that we'd better be cuttin' our replacements out and gittin' them branded before too very awful long. We were just wonderin' when you'd be gittin' out and doin' some sortin'?"

The Boss didn't answer. I guess he was thinking on it. So I continued, "We're checkin' on the cattle. Everything seems to be doin' fine. The grass is curin' out. Appears to be one of the better years we've had in a long time. The cattle are showin' it. They're sure layin' on the tallow. Of course, we've been checkin' windmills. The fences are up. Everything's runnin' fine. No need to worry about that," and I let my voice trail off.

Finally he looked at me. I could see in his eyes that he was a haunted man, undergoing a great depression. I felt bad for him. But for the first time he spoke to me in a manner that he'd never done before. He wasn't giving me instructions or an order to carry out, like he sometimes would. There had been times when he'd talk to me, I'd swear I'd been in the army. But this time he said, "Frank, I'm kinda off my feed, and really not feelin' up to par. I'd appreciate it if you'd do the sortin'. You're right. I plumb forgot."

"I'd be glad to do it," I said. "But I'm not sure that I have the experience to do it to where it would suit you."

"Just do it like I'd do it. It'll be good enough. And don't worry about it. They're paid for. You're a good man, Frank. I've watched you grow and I've watched you learn. Now it's time for you to step out and test your own instincts. All I ask is you let your conscience be your guide."

I was dumbstruck! That was the first time, ever, in my association with the Boss, that he paid me a compliment. I felt rather proud of myself. I felt everything that needed to be said had been so.

As I climbed my way out of that deep chair, trying not to spill what was left of my coffee, I said, "I'll do my best."

The Boss had shifted his eyes away and was again staring into space. Since I'd gone this far, I thought I'd offer another suggestion. "You know what they say, Boss, about gittin' outdoors and gittin' a-horseback, that the outside of a horse is the best medicine for the inside of a man. We'll git ol' Spud up ever' mornin' and have him penned. If you git the notion, maybe you oughta git out and take a ride. Kinda check on things and look 'em over. Might do you a little good."

He nodded his head. It was time for me to leave.

It took us all morning to gather the two pastures. After there was a count we knew we had them all. It was the first time I'd ever held the tally book in my own hand and knew for sure. Not bad for a short-handed crew with a green boss!

In the beginning the responsibility of sorting the cattle had been overwhelming, but I had been with the Boss and helped him so many times in the past, the further we went the easier it got. When finally we were done, I looked on our work and thought it was pretty damn good, if I said so myself.

That task was done, others awaited. It had always been my job to take care of the horses. Halter-break the colts and do all the handling and messing with them and give them their first saddling when they were four-year-olds.

R.C. was terribly interested in this and asked if he could take part in handling the horses. He'd made a statement some time back that had been on my mind. I hadn't brought it up because I didn't want to. It was the statement that he needed to leave. With everything that had happened, I'd forgotten about it. Like most things that you dread to happen, you put off asking.

But before I got into any more teaching and instructing as he was asking me to do, I needed to know the man's intentions. "I thought you were leavin'."

R.C. looked at the ground and nodded his head. "I was, Frank. And I meant it. You see, I had this big plan worked out for myself. Come hell or high water I was going to do it. But," and again R.C. looked down at the ground, "things change, Frank."

"How so?"

"Well, with the Boss being in the shape he is, I feel like I'd be leaving you short-handed. After all you've done for me and the Stones taking me in like they have, it doesn't seem fair."

I still didn't understand this commitment he was talking about, but I didn't feel like I'd press him any farther. He was right, we were short-handed. And I was damn glad to have him, for one. So I said, "You're sure?"

With a smile on his face, he looked up. "Yep."

"For how long?"

"'Til things let up a little, at least."

I didn't mean to say it, but before I could think, it already came out of my mouth. "You mean to tell me that you are gonna up and leave this country and never come back?"

That kind of took R.C. back. "Whoa, Frank. I said I was going to leave. I didn't say anything about never coming back."

"Well, it's your business. And to tell you the truth, I'm relieved. We can sure use you. At least 'til after shippin' time, and then if you've gotta go, I guess it'll be all right. You gotta do what you gotta do."

R.C. agreed. "'Til after shipping time then, for sure."

We had a lot of work to get done between now and Labor Day. Labor Day, for all purposes, signaled the end of summer. Even though there may be three more weeks of summer on the calendar, in this country Labor Day was it. The rains may do some good, they were welcome anytime. But it seemed after Labor Day no more grass grew.

The last days of August were hot and still. Hardly enough wind to turn a windmill. The grass was cured out and had already gone to seed. It was fairly easy to get up early in the morning and start, but if you ever stopped, it was hard to get going again. Even R.C. noticed this and wondered what it was.

Jim explained it as "dog days." It has something to do with the end of summer solstice. A phase the moon is in or some magical thing like that that happens yearly in August. Rattlesnakes strike blindly at anything that comes within reach, without warning. Dogs bark at their own shadows, and strange things happen during "dog days."

The Boss was still in reclusion. It seemed he'd ride early of a morning and take his rest through the heat of the day. It was up to me to get things done. The only thing we had to look forward to was the annual Labor Day fandango and wingding at the Jaramillos'.

Back in the early summer, about the time that we'd learned of R.C.'s piano-playing ability, he'd discovered that the Stones had a pretty fair library. Of course, a man reads what he likes. Therefore, the Stone library was filled with western fiction, western historical fiction, and books pertinent to their style of life and things that were of interest to them.

Surprisingly, R.C. didn't read any fiction that I knew of. He read the works of bona fide historical western writers, most of them pertaining to the cattle business in Texas. He read every book that J. Frank Dobie wrote, and also books by historian John J. Haynes, and *Log of a Cowboy* by Andy Adams.

When he first came to work on this outfit, since we got up so early and worked hard, after supper he fell into bed and into an exhausted sleep. But as time came around he began to get used to it and stayed up a little later. It gave us plenty of time after supper to read, play cards. Myself, I played my guitar.

R.C. chose to read. And believe me, he could work his way through a book faster than anyone I'd ever seen. He read steadily. On his trip over to the Jaramillo place to see Kika, I noticed that he was borrowing books from Diego's library. Just recently, the books that I had seen him reading tended more to New Mexico and the Mexican side of history, rather than Texas. Books such as Hall's *Mexican Law* that was written in 1881, and Matthew G. Reynolds's work known as *Spanish and Mexican Land Grant Laws.* I even saw a small book written by The Honorable Frank W. Springer about land titles in New Mexico. It was a document of public record. How he came by it, I don't know. I had suspicions that he might even be checking books out from the public library at Dorsey.

It made me wonder. Perhaps his interest was just because he wanted to know the history of the land that he was living in at the time. Then again, it might have something to do with Diego's plight on the Mexican land grant. But whatever it was, he took it seriously.

I saddled up a young horse and headed out west to the Padre pasture. There's an old saying that as long as you keep your older horses around, you'll never get your young ones broke. That was a luxury we couldn't afford. We needed these horses and we needed them well broke and savvy. And the more riding they got, the more savvy they got. 'Course, you always had to watch them and be on your toes. Lots of wet saddle blankets and making lots of tracks was a tried and proved method.

When I got to the old mission, instead of riding on by and going up into the Martinez break, I stopped and hobbled my horse and walked into the little fenced-in graveyard. I could see that a path had practically been beaten out in the buffalo grass that grew in the little cemetery. The path led to the graves of Sonny and Tres. I knew the Boss had been spending a lot of time there.

I realized that when the time came for the Boss and Miz T., they planned to be buried in that small, lonely cemetery, also. I knew they had contacted the monument works at Dorsey for the headstone. But I didn't realize that they had ordered one large headstone with the one name inscribed on both the front and the back. The name "Stone" stood to the left of both graves. This would be the family plot. Both Sonny and Tres had smaller headstones with their name, date of birth, and date of death. The family stone was large, out of gray marble, with the two smaller headstones matching in color.

The thought crossed my mind, It must be quite a feeling to stand and look at the place that you had chosen to lie for eternity. I knew people did it, bought burial plots before their death. But me, it had never entered my mind.

As I left I couldn't help but squat and look again at the church and over at the Piedra and wonder about the mystery that went with the old building. But we had looked everywhere possible. And I had resigned myself that what had happened would always remain a mystery, and nothing could be done about it.

We'd put enough time and effort into trying to find the missing papers. And if it were to have been so, we would have found them. So in my mind, it was a closed book.

CHAPTER

32

Outside of Jim's constant worry of something dreadful that was liable to happen during dog days, everything went along as smooth as silk. I kidded Jim unmercifully about this, which didn't seem to faze his strong superstition that it still could and probably would. He'd feel this way until the dog days were over, whenever that was. I didn't know, and he wouldn't tell me.

Our biggest surprise was on the day before Labor Day, to walk into supper to find the Boss seated at his normal place at the head of the table. He acted as if he had never left, when in fact he hadn't taken a meal with us in over a month and a half. We had scarcely seen hide nor hair of him during that time, much less shared a meal with him.

He looked as though he'd lost a considerable amount of weight. But his color was coming back and I attributed that to getting outside and getting a-horseback, which he seemed to be doing on a regular basis. The pain and the sadness that had been in his face for so long had seemed to vanish. His appetite wasn't much. But as the rest of us ate heartily, he made small talk and we knew that he had observed some of the things that we'd been up to, if not all.

He commented about how well the yearlings were doing. "Can't remember when they looked any better, Frank. Both sets. You done a good job sortin' those steers. Couldn't've done better myself. Yes sir," he said as we ate, "I believe the steers shipped off this year will be the heaviest that I can ever remember. Wouldn't be surprised if we could get fifteen for the big set, possibly seventeen and a half for the lighter end."

I thought this highly unusual, for this was the first time, ever, that the Boss talked cattle prices with me. It made me wonder if he expected me to show them and sell them.

But as we ate, the Boss continued. "I expect Mr. Kaufman to be showin' up before too long." Kaufman was a repeat buyer of our cattle that lived in Illinois. And each of them was as tight and headstrong as the other. I'd seen it with my own eyes. Kaufman would throw his hands up in the air saying, "That's all I can do," and walk to his car ready to drive off, only to turn around and come back and start the dickering again.

Maybe, and I had strong suspicions, it was a game with them and every year it was a ritual they observed. But, nevertheless, Mr. Kaufman ended up being the buyer, year after year.

While we ate, the Boss pushed food around on his plate, ate little, and made small talk. He paid us another compliment when he said, "You boys did a good job on our keepin' heifers. They look like the right kind."

I couldn't believe it! Two compliments at one sitting! It was sure unusual.

As we finished up we all made it a point to tell the Boss how glad we were to see him up and around and back at the table again. He thanked us all with a smile, then reminded us, saying, "Boys, tomorrow is Labor Day. Of course you'll have the day off. Spend it as you please." Then as an afterthought, "Frank, would you mind bringing your guitar down after your supper settles and playing Tess and me a tune or two?"

I told him I'd be glad to.

The Boss then said, "All you boys come down. We'll have sort of a celebration seein's how summer's over and the growin' season's gone." Then he seemed to say to himself, "Yessir, that's a good idea." Then he looked at all of us. "Will ya do that?"

We were all in agreement.

There wasn't a word said between the three of us 'til we got back to the bunkhouse and inside the door, when I turned to Jim and said, "Jim, you've known the Boss for a long time. Now tell me, wasn't that the damnedest thing you ever saw?"

Jim was filling his cheek with a big chew. "Frank, I don't know what to make of it."

R.C. looked at both of us, and finally said, "What in the hell are you guys talkin' about. I thought he looked great. I'm glad he's back. And I believe he's back to stay."

Jim was still shaking his head, adjusting his chew, when he said, "It just ain't natural."

R.C. still didn't understand. "What isn't natural?"

"That the Boss be payin' compliments. Most he's ever told me in all the years I've been here was, 'that'll do.' That there was 'bout his highest compliment."

"Not only that," I said, "but discuss business, cattle prices. He's never done that before."

R.C. sat down on the bed, leaned back against the headboard. "Have you ever stopped to think that maybe he's had all this time to dwell on the way his life has been? Maybe that was the problem between him and his son, and he's decided to change his ways. What's wrong with that?"

"Nothin'," I said. "It just ain't the Boss. He's never done it before and I don't expect him to do it now. In the first place, it's none of my business. It's his cattle, his money. I'm just a hired hand on this outfit."

"Yes," R.C. said, "but Miz T. put you in charge while he was ailing."

"That's true," I said. "But that's just to keep things on an even keel, workwise. I don't believe she intended me to have any say in the sale of their cattle. That involves too much money to be entrusted to an old boy with no more sense than I've got."

"You're underestimating yourself," R.C. said. "You know as well as I do you could sell these cattle with no problem at all."

"Well," I said, "I hope I don't have to. I've never had the experience of handling that much money."

Jim was lying on his bed, staring at the ceiling. "He was just way too talkative. It's like he's changed."

"Well, I'll tell you what," I said. "When we go down there for this little celebration and he breaks out the brandy and cigars, like he does with ol' Egg or Jingle Bob, we'll know somethin's haywire."

Jim laughed. "That there'll never happen. Believe me."

I got my guitar. "Let's go down to the celebration."

They were waiting on us when we walked in the kitchen. Miz T. was all smiles. To my surprise, the Boss and Miz T. sat on the couch, side by each, and let R.C. and Jim have the big, cushy leather chairs. Tio and Lupe were even there to enjoy this little celebration.

"Frank," the Boss said, "how about some old-time music? Do you know 'When the Work's All Done This Fall'?"

I nodded. "You bet!"

While I was singing I saw the Boss reach over and take ahold of Miz T.'s hand. This was highly unusual. I'd never seen any open display of affection between the two of them before. When I finished, everyone clapped. And lo and behold Boss turned to Miz T. and said, "Mother, I think this calls for a drink. I'll get the brandy if you get the glasses."

I was stunned! Miz T. seemed so pleased at the way things were going. The Boss ambled over to the big oak, old-time icebox that he used for a liquor cabinet, and brought out a bottle of his finest brandy.

When Miz T. set a brandy snifter down in front of Jim, he looked at the glass like it might explode if he touched it. "Ma'am, could I have a glass a little more stout than that? That's terrible delicate for a fella as rough as I am."

Miz T. seemed to find a great deal of humor in that, and said, "Of course," and brought him back a heavier water glass.

I held the snifter as the Boss poured. He went around the room and did the same to everybody's glass. I glanced over at Jim and he was staring at me, dumbstruck.

The Boss made a simple toast. With a slow, sweeping motion of his arm to everyone in the room, he said, "To you," then tipped his snifter up and took a swallow.

I glanced over at R.C. He held the snifter in the palm of his hand, the stem between his middle and ring fingers. He swirled the brandy around in his snifter, then damned if he didn't sniff it before he put it to his lips and took a sip! Hell, for all I knew, maybe that was the way you were supposed to do it. Jim threw his down like a shot of whiskey, realized what everybody else was doing, and wished he hadn't and sat there with the glass in his lap, both hands clasped around it so nobody could see that it was all gone.

Me, I'd sing as long as the Boss wanted. Certainly until he quit pouring. Without any prompting, I sang "Bury Me Not on the Lone Prairie." It seemed to have some moving effect on the Boss, and he again took Miz T.'s hand. She sat there beaming happily. It did my heart good.

R.C. seemed to take the notion that it might be a good idea if we could draw the Boss out a little. "You know, sir, most old-timers worry that the cowboy will die out. That they're a vanishing race. I just wondered what you thought. Is it true?"

The Boss shook his head slowly. "Things change, of course. But as long as there're cattle and people eat beef, there's got to be cowboys. There's got to be those that understand the cattle ways. I don't see that ever happenin'."

I played a few more songs, then got the feeling that we were just about to wear out our welcome. "Well, I guess it's about time we turn in."

The Boss said, "Just a couple more, Frank."

"Do ya have anything in mind?"

"How about 'Home on the Range'?"

I knew it, and I played it for him. I had no more finished that song than he asked with a question in his voice, " 'Peace in the Valley'?"

Of course I knew that old Red Foley tune and had sung it many times. I had the Boss and Miz T.'s complete attention as I sang that last song. And as I ended, I stood up and the Boss said, "I appreciate it, Frank. Them last two are my favorites."

"You're welcome," I said. "I'm glad you enjoyed 'em."

We carried our snifters to the sink as we left. The Boss followed us out, and the last words I heard him say were, "Thank you, boys. Enjoyed the evenin'. I appreciate it."

When we got back to the bunkhouse, as I was putting my guitar up, I said, "Jim, what do ya think?"

"If I hadn't a'been there, I wouldn't a'believed it. I've never took a drink on this ranch. Ah, maybe a few, but I was sneakin' around when I did it. But I was offered a drink in that house and never expected it."

"Me, neither," I said. "I don't know what to make of it. It don't seem right."

"Well," R.C. said, "he seemed in good spirits. I still think he's just gone through a change and things are gonna be different now. I don't see what you all are worried about."

"I don't know what I'm worried about, either," I said. "But, I am."

Next morning at breakfast there was just the three of us and Lupe. Miz T. and the Boss had not come down yet. It was early, just getting light outside.

We made small talk as we were finishing up our coffee, when R.C. said, "You know, the Boss never said a word about going over to the Jaramillo place today. Do you think he's goin'?"

"I reckon so," I said. "They're kinfolk, and it's a tradition at the Jaramillo place."

"Well, I'm sure lookin' forward to it. I'm headed over that way as soon as I get cleaned up."

"I'm lookin' forward to it, too," I said, "but I've got to wait 'til Roberta gets here."

"Believe I'll just hang around and take it easy," Jim said.

"Yeah," I said. "Probably sneak off to town and see that widow lady you've been keepin' company with."

Jim just opened his mouth to defend himself, when a blast broke the morning stillness. And the hair on the back of my neck stood straight up.

"What in the hell was that!?" I said.

Jim was staring at me with wide eyes. "I don't know."

I looked at R.C. and got the same look. We all three hit the back door running. The sound had come from up toward the barns and we ran that way. I could see a figure coming around the barn. The sun was just peeking up over the horizon. It was Tio. We all four met at the road. I asked Tio, "What in the hell was that?"

"Madre mío, I don't know," Tio said, breathless.

"Which way did it come from?"

Tio pointed toward the corrals. "That way, I theenk."

The four of us began to run in the direction of the corrals. We could see nothing wrong. Nothing was disturbed. We split up, each taking a different direction.

As I glanced through the fence at the round corral, I could see the Boss. He appeared to be leaning on the snubbing post. I quickly climbed the fence, and hollered at him. It was when I reached the top of the fence that I saw, and realized, what had happened.

I went over the fence in slow motion. I couldn't believe what had happened. But then, the reason would remain always a mystery. There was no reason to holler, for the Boss was plainly beyond help. He was slumped against the snubbing post, head bowed forward, sagging, but still on his feet. A look at the ground beneath his right hand told me what had done the damage. His papa's old six-shooter lay in the dirt. And an odd thought crossed my mind: Yep, he still had ammunition for the old pistol.

His hat, all sweat-streaked from years of wear, lay behind him some ten feet covered with blood. The only mystery was, what held him upright? And that was answered as I squatted down and looked up at him. He had taken a lariat rope, his steer rope, looped it around himself and the post, pulled it tight, made several more wraps, and taken a double hooey over the top of the old post.

I had said at one time the old snubbing post that his father had brought from God knows where had been practically sacred. And this made it seem even more so. There the Boss hung, almost liken to a crucifixion. He had swallowed the barrel and pulled the trigger. There were no visual marks on the front of his face, though blood flowed from his mouth and from his nose as he stared vacantly at the ground. But the snow-white hair was a mass of blood and partially gone from the back of his head.

As I squatted there and looked, I realized the others had found me, for I heard someone say, "Jesus Christ!" and it had to be Jim. Then Tio with his Spanish mumblings of prayer were evidence that he'd arrived.

"Oh, my God. Oh, my God," I could hear from R.C. Of the four of us there, three expressed their astonishment and their grief in the pronouncement of religion, or of a supreme being, while all that ran through my head, and had since I reached the ground from the fence, was, Oh, shit. Oh, shit, over and over. Whether aloud or subconscious, I didn't know. It was broken only by the calls of Miz T., who along with Lupe was headed for the round pen.

That brought action and motion from me in a hurry. I could see this dear little lady whose husband had just completed the final act of living. And all I could think of was she must not see this.

She was wrapped in her housecoat and scurrying as fast as her matronly body would take her. I left at a run, vaulted the fence, and intercepted her before she got a clear view of what had happened. I took hold of both of her shoulders with my hands as she looked wide-eyed and pleading into my face, perhaps for a statement that what was happening was a dream or an untruth. All I could say was, "You don't want to go up there." Still she looked and I shook my head. "You can't help. It's over."

Rather forcefully, I turned her around, told Lupe to take hold of her other arm, and led her back to the house. She did not weep. Perhaps she was in shock. But Lupe was crying enough to make up for it. Nor did she say a word as we led her up the steps to the bedroom. It was then that I noticed a folded note laid on the Boss's pillow. A pillow and a side of the bed looked like they'd been unslept on. In her haste and rude awakening she had not noticed the note. With Lupe's help, she lay back upon the bed. I picked up the note and handed it to her and said, "Maybe this will explain. God, I hope so. Don't worry. Everything's going to be all right. I'll get Diego." And as I left I said, "I'll take care of everything. Lupe, try to help her as much as you can. Stay with her. Don't leave." And I knew Lupe wouldn't.

As I went out the back door and headed back toward the corrals I could see Jim coming, holding the Boss in his arms like a child. With what must have been unusual strength, Jim proceeded to carry, by himself, the Boss down to the house. Tio was crying uncontrollably. R.C., with a look of great concern on his face, followed.

I put my arm around Tio. "Tio, you believe in heaven, cielo, don't you?"

And Tio nodded his head that he did. "Well," I said, "your friend has just now gone to that wonderful place. It's what he wanted." And then I asked him, "Can you get us some blankets?" With a nod of his head, Tio broke into a trot.

I looked at R.C. and he said, "I tried to tell him you shouldn't move the body until the law gets here."

Jim, with the veins in his neck sticking out with the effort it took to carry the body, lips grim, said, "Damned if I'd leave 'im hang there. Just hang there for what might be hours before the sheriff got here. I don't care what they say or what they do to me. I wasn't gonna do it. And I didn't."

I agreed. "Me, too, Jim. I'd a'done the same thing."

We took the Boss in the house, spread a blanket on the couch, put several dish towels behind the Boss's head, and laid him down. As a matter of afterthought, I crossed his hands and arms over his chest, took another blanket, and covered him up.

It was up to me now to get something done. But where to start? "R.C., get over to Diego's, tell him what happened, and tell him to get over here, he and Kika, as quick as they can."

R.C. wheeled and started for the door. As parting advice I told him, "Act like you are carrying a bucket of fire," and he was gone. It was plain that Jim had no intention of leaving the Boss's side. I told him that I'd run to Cone and make the telephone call to town. Whether Jim heard me or paid any attention, he showed no sign. I left anyway.

There was really no reason to hurry. The worst had happened. It was over. The sense of urgency had left me. My concern now was for Miz T. And as I drove to Cone I even stopped at the highway and looked both ways before pulling out on the main road. It occurred to me there'd be no baile, no celebration at the Jaramillo place today. Then the thought of why? And though it was a question I would probably ask myself the rest of my life, I'd never know the answer.

As I pulled in at Cone and stepped out of Ol' Blue, a car pulled up alongside me that seemed vaguely familiar. As I walked in front of the pickup toward the store, I heard a familiar voice call my name. I turned and there was Roberta with a puzzled look on her face. Again she said, "Frank! What's wrong? I met you about a mile down the road and waved, and you drove right by me like you didn't see me."

I stood and looked at her and realized I'd driven from the ranch to here without ever realizing what I was doing. It was a scary thought. And then I told her. "Roberta, I'm glad you're here. The Boss is dead."

Her eyes widened and she hurried to me. "Oh, no! No! What? What, Frank, a heart attack?"

"No. He took his life."

Roberta found this hard to believe. She shook her head as big tears began to roll down her cheeks. "How?" she demanded.

"With a pistol, early this morning." And with that, she broke down and cried.

I had to break into a conversation on the party line. With one call to the sheriff's office, I saw to it that he'd soon be on his way, followed by an ambulance. It was time to go back and do what I could. But I had Roberta with me. She'd follow me in and that would help.

When we got back to the ranch, Roberta went up to do whatever she could for Miz T. Jim remained at the Boss's side, sitting in a straight-backed chair that just last night I had sat in and played the guitar. There was nothing to do now but wait. And that was the hardest part.

Tio and I sat at the kitchen table and drank coffee in silence, 'til at last we heard a vehicle pull into the yard, and it was the sheriff. I met him before he got to the door. The only exchange of words was, "Dub."

He acknowledged my greeting, if you want to call it that, and said, "Frank. Where is he?"

I motioned toward the door. "Inside."

Upon reaching the couch, Dub pulled back the blanket, stared down at the Boss, then squatted down. Jim made a move to raise the Boss's head and Dub stopped him. "No need for that. I can see what happened." He covered the Boss back up, turned to me, and asked, "Where did it happen?"

I motioned for him to follow me and we started for the corrals. We were halfway there before I said anything to Sheriff McCanless, and that was only to say that we probably shouldn't have moved the body. "But damned if I was gonna let him hang there 'til the law got here!" If anybody was going to take any heat over moving the body, I decided it should be me. But it didn't seem to concern Dub. "Ah, that's all right, Frank. I'd have done the same thing." And then without, in my opinion, good cause, Dub said, "Has the Boss been despondent lately? Have you noticed anything unusual?"

I turned and looked at Dub with what must have been an icy stare, although I wasn't aware of it. But Dub's face showed it when I said, "What in the hell do you think, Dub? He's lost a son and a grandson this summer. Despondent? Hell, no! He was on top of the world!"

Dub got a pacifying sound to his voice. "Now, don't git on the prod, Frank. I'm just askin'. It's part of my job. And whether you like it or not, I gotta do it. I've gotta have somethin' to write down on the papers."

I turned away in disgust.

Upon entering the corrals, Dub just walked around looking at the old Colt pistol, commenting that he hadn't seen one like that in a while, but he didn't touch it, and the hat, filled with blood, bone, and brains. Then he turned his attention to the rope, which still lay encircling the snubbing post. I told him how I'd found him tied to the snubbing post. And you could tell that this puzzled Sheriff McCanless.

As he squatted and looked at the bloody rope and peered up at the bloodstains that ran down that ancient hunk of wood, he asked me, "Frank, why would he do this? I can think of a number of reasons why a man might kill himself, but why the rope? And why tied to the snubbing post? Any ideas?"

I thought about it for a while and shrugged my shoulders and said, "I don't have any idea. Except," and I stopped.

Dub waited for an answer for quite a while. And finally, "Go on, Frank, speculate. This ain't an exact science. Speak what's on your mind."

So, I did. "Well, you know how the Boss was with a rope. He was well-known for it. It was a tool of his trade. Maybe it was even more than a tool. Maybe it was like a fine instrument that he had mastered. I know this, he never went anywhere without a rope tied to his saddle. That is until lately, after Tres. But I have a feelin' that a good catch rope was a travelin' companion and a pard for the Boss. So maybe that's part of the reason. And as far as the snubbin' post goes, I've heard him tell many times the story about this old snubbin' post. It's supposedly been in the family for years, was his granddad's, then his dad's." And I told him about the wood and how hard it was. As a final statement, "I don't know, Dub. Maybe he'd given up on the future and wanted to be tied to the past."

Dub looked from the post to me quickly, and said sincerely, "Frank, that's damn near poetic."

I shrugged my shoulders. "That's how it seems to me."

As Dub rose from the squatting position he was in, he said, "Well, it's a damn shame. But I've got all I need to write a report." He picked up the pistol by the barrel. "I'll need to keep this, for a while at least. When I'm through, I'll send it back." He checked the cylinder, only one round was in it, and it was spent.

The ambulance and Diego seemed to get to the main house at the same time as Dub and I walked back from the corrals. I told Dub, "If only I'd've known what was on his mind, maybe I could've done somethin'." But I knew in my heart I hadn't had a clue. I thought he was getting better and I told Dub so.

But I'll say this for Sheriff Dub McCanless, he'd been around some and he'd seen a bunch. And he offered me a bit of wisdom that helped, that I would remember the rest of my life. "Frank, it wasn't your fault. It wasn't anybody's fault. And there's nothin' you could've done about it. Once a man makes up his mind he's gonna end it, there's nothin' you, I, or anybody else can do to stop it."

The ambulance crew, though arriving first, respectfully waited, realizing the car that had followed them into the ranch contained relatives of the deceased. With Diego was the old lady, Abuela Elena. As always, dressed in black with the ever-present black mantilla over her head. She carried with her a coarsely woven handbag.

No words were spoken between Diego and myself, just a knowing look and a handshake that was firm and compassionate, as Diego used both hands to clasp mine before he entered the house. The old woman was scurrying for the door to enter when Tio stepped out. They both stopped, looked at one another, and quickly embraced, speaking to one another in Spanish, in low soft tones. Finally the old woman pulled herself away from Tio, laid her hand on his cheek, and went on inside the house.

By that time R.C. and Kika arrived. I stood there as Kika approached me, and I thanked God that my britches had pockets in them, for I would not have known what to do with my hands. I felt terribly helpless. But without saying a word, Kika reached up and pulled me down to her and gave me a hug, patted my back, and said, "It's going to be all right, Frank."

I started to speak. "Francesca," and I couldn't go on. All words had left me. Then she, too, pulled away and went into the house. With R.C., I walked over to the rock wall that surrounded the lawn and sat down, neither of us speaking. What was there to say? Sheriff Dub finally came over and sat with us. But there were no more questions asked. We just sat.

After what seemed a considerable length of time, Diego came to the door and motioned to the ambulance personnel. They took the stretcher, went inside. And only then, after they were bringing the body out, did Jim leave the house to sit with us. Diego watched as the body was loaded into the ambulance, the doors closed, and it left.

It was then that Diego, very calmly and very sadly, wanted to know what had happened. Between R.C. and me, he got the story of the morning events. He also needed to know what I was struggling so with. And I opened up and told him about last night and the celebration and the singing, his good attitude and his display of affection toward Miz T. As I explained that I thought he was getting better, had finally turned the corner, a faint smile came across Diego's face.

"Don't you see, Frank?" he said. "He had already made his decision. He had already decided the course of his actions. And this brought him peace because he knew what he was going to do. You might say that he has finally found the trail herd, and the longhorn. You see, J.W. was born at the tail end of that time. He'd heard so much about it from his father that he felt that he had missed out on the greatest period of time in the cattle business, and always regretted it. Why else, do you think, that he would cling to the old ways so strongly? You, Frank, being Indian, would know what I meant if one of your people died and his friend said, 'At last, he has found the buffalo.' "

I understood then, exactly, what he was saying. But still one thing remained that I didn't understand, and I asked. "But he had so much. A wonderful wife, and this ranch. As good a ranch as lays outdoors. It wasn't enough?"

Diego shrugged. "Who knows what kind of demons he battled? After Tres and Sonny, it must have become unbearable. Perhaps he has found peace, a peace that could only be found in death."

I felt an uncontrollable urge to be by myself. I had to get away. So I walked up to the saddle house to find Belle lying on the porch. She was on her stomach with her head resting on her forepaws, staring out into the round corral. I sat down beside her, stroked her head, and talked to her. She seemed to know something dreadful had happened, for she never lifted her head, just continued to watch the round corral with baleful eyes.

I got a shovel, entered the round corral, leaned on the shovel as I looked at the hat, the rope, and the snubbing post, trying to figure out the thing to do. What would the Boss want me to do? Finally I picked up the hat and emptied it. The blood had started to congeal. But by shaking it, that which was going to come out came and fell upon the ground. Stained with sweat around the headband, it was now stained with blood, like the sweat, soaking from the inside out.

The thought went through my mind to dunk it in the horse tank a time or two, but I decided against it and hung it on a high peg in the saddle house. After picking up the rope and lifting it over the snubbing post, I noticed the blood that had soaked into the twist of the rope, knelt, and with handfuls of dirt slid the rope through my hand, blotting but not removing the stains. I coiled up the rope and each coil fell into place, evenly and neatly, just as if the Boss himself had directed it. I took it to the saddle house, removed the hat, put it on the same peg the hat had been on, and replaced the hat.

I took the shovel and began mixing the sand and dirt with the blood that remained on the ground. It only seemed fitting. The blood gave him life and so did the earth. The two could be mixed together in harmony.

The sun was now high in the sky and as I smoothed the sand around the post, the sun seemed to glint off the considerable amount of blood that stained the post. I knew wood had pores. But I also knew that this wood was so old and so hard that a nail could not even be driven into it. Yet, the blood was not as red as I would have thought. It turned brown and seemed to be absorbed by the wood itself. The post seemed to draw the blood into itself. I couldn't help but think, Perhaps for a reason.

I'd been so absorbed in my thoughts that I had not heard Roberta approach me, or know that she was there 'til I felt her hand around my waist and her head on my shoulder. Standing there leaning against the shovel, like the post, things were beginning to soak into me, too. And as they did, tears began to flow freely from my eyes, down my cheeks, and dropped to the ground. I was not ashamed. It was a relief. Roberta led me over to the saddle house porch where we sat in the shade on the bench, and let my grief run its course.

Early that afternoon the barbed-wire network kicked into gear, and the neighbors started arriving. Never empty-handed, some of them making their third trip to pay their respects in the last three months. Diego met them at the door and ushered them inside. And to my astonishment, Miz T. was up to receiving visitors.

I confided in Roberta my amazement that Miz T. could see anyone outside of close family, and that there was no doubt in my mind that women were the stronger of the two sexes. Roberta just smiled and said, "Maybe that's why God chose us to bear the children." Had it been me and such a tragedy had occurred, I would have crawled into a hole and pulled the opening in behind me.

Roberta commented about a special tea that the old woman, Abuela Elena, had fixed for Miz T. on her arrival. I told her of the similar incidents at the Jaramillo place when R.C. broke his nose, and what a calming, numbing effect it had on him. Perhaps it was the same with Miz T.

"Perhaps," Roberta said. "But tea or not, I believe that grand lady could hold up under any circumstances, if she had to. And believe me, this she has to do."

Tio stopped by. He was already lost. He looked like a forlorn puppy. To get his mind on a different subject, I asked him if he'd known Abuela Elena a long time. He looked at me with a surprised look, like it was something that I should have always known. "Si, she ees my seester."

I was the one that was surprised. And I thought, maybe he was talking in a sense that they had grown up together and been close, perhaps kinfolk, that he called her sister, more or less the Indian way. When I asked if Abuela Elena was his real sister, he got a puzzled look on his face and said, "Si, we had the same mother and the same father."

Later that evening when the flow of people finally stopped, Diego asked me to come inside. Miz T. was always so kind to me and treated me so well, it pained me to see her in her grief. And besides, I knew she had to be worn to a frazzle. But as I approached tentatively and with hat in hand, though she didn't rise from the chair, she reached out for me, took my hand, and pulled me close. She reached up with her other hand, and I bent down for a kiss on the cheek. She clasped both her hands over mine and with great sadness in her eyes asked me to sit, that they'd like to discuss their plans with me and see what I thought.

Diego was the only other that remained in the room as I sat. "Frank," Miz T. said, "Diego and I will go to town tomorrow and make the proper arrangements. Although J.W. was reluctant to talk about death, especially his own, over the past forty-two years I've gathered bits and pieces of what I think he would like to have done. First, we'll have no funeral in a church. If you and the boys could clean out the large barn, I think we'll have the services right here."

I nodded my head that I understood.

"Secondly," she said, "I know what good care you've taken of the harness and the wagon in the old barn. Of course, we'll have the burial there at the old cemetery. But I'd like to use the wagon to take J.W. to the cemetery."

I nodded. "Miz T., we need horses broke to pull a wagon."

Diego spoke up. "I'll bring a span of horses over, broke to harness. We use them all the time with our fence crew."

"All right," I said. "But you'd better send somebody to harness them. I've never harnessed a horse in my life."

Diego smiled. "Miguel and Joaquin will be bringing the horses. They'll take care of that."

I nodded. As an afterthought, I said, "Ma'am, the thought just came to me and I wonder if it would be all right with you if I saddled ol' Spud and tied him to the wagon?" I shrugged my shoulders as my voice choked. "Empty saddles, you know."

Miz T. smiled. "Frank, that's a wonderful idea. That would make J.W. very happy. Third, would you sing? I know this is a lot to ask, but it would mean so much to me if you would sing the two songs that you sang the other night. My God! It was just last night, wasn't it," she said with a frown.

" 'Home on the Range' and 'Peace in the Valley'?" I suggested.

"Yes. Those two he said were his favorites."

This put me on the spot. It's not that I wouldn't. The point was, if I could. And I told her so. "Ma'am, I'd be honored. But I don't know. I just don't know," and my voice broke.

She reached out and touched my hand again. "I know how hard it would be. But I think, knowing you, you'll find the strength if you just try."

Without any hesitation I said, "I will." Of course, I didn't know how I could possibly get through two songs, how a note would come from my throat. But I'd do it, by God! If it was the last thing I did.

"I don't think," she said, "that you need to worry about digging the grave. I have a feeling enough of his friends will show up tomorrow to take care of that chore."

I nodded. There seemed to be nothing else left to say. I rose, again took Miz T.'s hand as my vision blurred. "Ma'am, I'm so sorry."

With tears in her eyes, but a faint smile, "Thank you, Frank. Thank you for everything."

Since it appeared that Abuela Elena and Francesca would stay in the big house, there was no need for Roberta to stay. She would be back early for the funeral. As I held her close and breathed that wonderful fragrance that I now associated only with her, I said, "It's been a long day." Then added, "Today time just ran out."

CHAPTER

33

R.C. and I started in cleaning the barn early the next morning. We were practically done when we heard the sound of a truck pulling in over the cattle guard. Sure enough, as I expected, it was Miguel and Joaquin in a bobtail truck carrying two of the largest horses I'd ever seen.

R.C. and I marveled at the horses. They were both geldings of a light sorrel color with a flax mane and tail. Their feet were as big as skillets with flax fetlocks that feathered up to their knees and hocks. It would have been unkind, but truthful, to say that they had Roman noses. When I commented on it, Miguel told me it was a characteristic of the breed. But it was a noble head. I had long heard these Belgian draft horses referred to as "gentle giants." And I could understand why. They seemed as docile as lambs, despite their size.

We opened up the large swinging doors on the back end of the old barn where the wagon and the harness were kept. "Frank," Joaquin said, "it would have been much easier if we'd just brought their own harness with them. But Dad insisted that we use the Boss's. So, we'll have to make a few adjustments. But when we get through, everything, except the horses, will come from the Boss's past."

I nodded. "I think that's the idea."

Late in the morning the neighbors and close friends—Egg, Iry, Horace, Jingle Bob, and others—showed up with their womenfolk. I noticed they were in their work clothes. True to custom, they had come to dig the grave. When asked if R.C. and I could give them a hand, they declined. It was something that they wanted to do. And I let them. It seemed only fit.

R.C. and I sat on the saddle house bench, each in our own thoughts, when R.C. said, "Frank, have you ever noticed that people around here, when a death occurs, unless it's someone very, very close to you, they don't mourn for a long time? They express their grief to the ones close to the deceased. But as soon as they're out of earshot, they go on talking about things and visiting like it was a social gathering. They just don't grieve like people I'm used to."

What he said was true. I had seen it many times. And it would probably happen again tomorrow. Friends would come to console and offer their sympathy to Miz T. I believed it to be genuine when they offered it. It's just that they didn't dwell on it for a long time. And I told R.C. so. But it was a hard country, and people got used to death and accepted it more readily than perhaps people from other parts of the country. If you stayed in this country, sooner or later it would claim you, especially in the business we were in.

R.C. repeated the phrase, "Fatal charm."

I looked at him. "Yeah. That about sums it up, doesn't it?"

That night everything had been done that could be to ready ourselves for tomorrow. One concern was that Jim had disappeared. But I couldn't do anything about that. Maybe tomorrow he'd be here, just as he'd always been for so many years.

At the ceremony I sat in a straight-backed chair, one of the two that we'd brought up to the barn from the main house, one for the preacher and one for me. As I was introduced to the pastor, I was surprised. I had figured that he'd be a Catholic priest. But he wasn't. He gave me instructions that he'd nod to me when I was to sing. My guitar sat in its case with the lid open, at my side.

Miguel and Joaquin had gotten there early, brushed the big Belgians down, and combed their manes 'til they shown in the sunlight. I did the same with Spud. I hung the Boss's rope, bloodstains and all, on his saddle. The old hat that he was wearing the morning he died, and his spurs, I placed in the wagon while they were hitching up the team. We had parked the team and Spud on the west side of the barn out of sight. As an afterthought, I went back to the saddle house, got the Boss's chaps, and laid them across his saddle, a chap leg on either side.

The flowers on each side of the casket were the largest assembly of arrangements I'd ever seen. One even bore the brand, the Cross S made of red roses with a white background. The aroma of the flowers mixed in with the smell of the barn was quite pleasant. Chairs brought from the big house made up the front row on each side. The rest of the people would have to sit on makeshift benches.

I glanced down at the little memorial pamphlet and read, "John Wesley Stone." And I realized for the first time what the W. stood for. Hell, I thought, he's a Methodist, as I was. You can't be named John Wesley and not be a Methodist, in my mind anyway. I read on. "Born August 14, 1888." That, I had never known. His birthday was just last month, and I hadn't known it. It also had his date of death, but that was beside the point. That day would go with me to my grave.

I watched the barn fill. All seats were taken. Then it became standing room only. I figured a third of the people came out of respect, another third came out of curiosity, and the other and final third came to see who the other two-thirds were. This country was full of petty jealousy. The Boss himself had not been the type to go out of his way to make friends with just anybody. He picked and chose carefully. And I knew old feelings died hard. The animosity between the rancher, the cowman, and the nester, the farmer, was still there. Never to one's face, but deep down inside, resentment cooked slowly for years.

As soon as Miz T. was seated, the parson rose from his chair and stepped to the homemade podium. He started into a eulogy that was of great interest to me. I was finding out today more about the Boss than I'd ever learned from him in person.

I had been so engrossed in what he was saying, and thinking about it, that it almost startled me when he turned and nodded to me. I picked up my guitar, put the strap over my neck, and rose to my feet. As I looked out over the audience I almost froze. I averted my eyes to the open doors and could see the sunlight and the house. I struck a chord and began to sing. Only then did I realize the wonderful acoustics in that barn. It sounded as though both my guitar and my voice were amplified. Never once did I think of the Boss or picture him in my mind. If I had, I'd have been a goner.

It doesn't take long to have a funeral, thank God! And after my last song, people began to leave and I slipped out. As soon as I reached the outdoors, I took a deep breath.

Joaquin came around to handle the team. We waited until we figured most everybody but the family and pallbearers were outside before we started around the barn with the team, with me afoot leading Spud.

I led Spud up behind the wagon, tied him to a ring there by the tailgate, which appeared to be there just for that purpose. I stood back, searched out Roberta, found her, motioned at Poke to follow, and the three of us got in Ol' Blue and led the way.

We got to the church way ahead of the procession, and it was quite a sight. Led by those huge, gentle giants, the wagon would reach the church before the last of the cars would leave the headquarters. We stood in silence and watched as they came.

As the actual services began I found an uncommon peacefulness come over me. I paid little attention to what the minister was saying. My eyes lifted to the sky. As I looked higher I could see a red-tailed hawk circling high above us. To many this would have meant nothing. To me, it was a good omen.

I was still daydreaming when I realized the services were over and people began leaving. I told Roberta to go on back. R.C., Poke, Miguel, Joaquin, and myself would stay and cover the grave.

Only Mrs. Remington and the funeral attendants that she had brought with her remained. I had not expected any problem with what I was about to do, until I asked the simple question, "Would you mind waiting a minute, Mrs. Remington, and opening the casket?"

But to my surprise, she looked at me indignantly and said, "I will not open the coffin!"

Hell, I had to have a reason, so I asked, "Why not?"

"The services are completed. You are not part of the family." Then she gave the order to one of her employees to start the winch and lower the casket.

I told him not to take ahold of the damn handle. We both glared at one another, and I tried to reason with her. "Mrs. Remington, please open the casket."

She glared at me. "Why?"

So I told her. "There are a few things of the Boss's that I'd like to put in there."

Her eyes widened with contempt, and she said the wrong thing. "Frank Dalton, I'll not have you tampering with this coffin with any of your pagan ways."

That did it! I took a step closer until our noses were about six inches apart and said, "Lady, if you don't open the goddamned coffin, you're gonna see just how pagan I can get!"

I heard Poke's voice behind me say, "Mrs. Remington, if I were you, I'd open that coffin lid, right now."

Mrs. Remington backed off from me a step or two. The wide eyes remained. The indignation had gone, and fear had replaced the look, as she nodded to her employees to open the coffin.

With that I whirled on my boot heel and walked over to the wagon, so damned mad I could hardly see straight. I picked up the Boss's hat, rope, spurs, and, as a last-minute thought, took the chaps from Spud's back, marched back over to the coffin, and laid them each carefully in the coffin with the Boss: the rope coiled neatly over the top of his hands, the hat on his chest, chaps and spurs by his side. I closed the lid myself. They locked it shut. Not another word was spoken between Mrs. Remington and me. And it's a damn good thing! As soon as she had all of her paraphernalia gathered up, she left, in a hurry.

We nailed the box shut on the coffin, and began to shovel in the dirt. Not a word was spoken, and it was just as well because I was not fit to be talked to. I don't know as to how I could have been civil to anybody.

Back at the house, Diego's people had served everybody. They'd gone through the line, just as they would've at the big baile over at Diego's place. People stood around in groups visiting with one another. I didn't have much of an appetite, so I decided to mingle.

The mood of the crowd was astonishingly lighthearted, as they talked about everything from what a good year moisturewise we'd had to cattle prices. It was mostly the men off by themselves and the women to theirs. But, more than once, as I walked up to a group, I heard talk of how the ranch had remained the same size despite the Boss's obvious prosperity after he had inherited it from his father. Everybody agreed that it was probably the best-improved ranch in the country, but never gained an acre in size after it came into the Boss's hands. I found this interesting and was disappointed when the conversation shifted.

I tired quickly from that conversation and slowly moved on to another group, only to hear someone speaking as I stared at the ground. The unknown voice in the middle of his story continued, "Hell, it even got so bad back in the thirties that I decided to commit suicide. But I missed the first shot and from then on I just got runnin' shots."

There was laughter through the group until they noticed my presence. Then there seemed to be an unusual amount of throat clearing, and the feller that was doing the storytelling wisely shut it down. This was the wrong time to take exception or to make a scene, though I couldn't understand how people could take such a tragedy so lightly. I turned and left. Loyalty was a part of my nature and I'd heard all I could stand.

Since Roberta was helping in the kitchen, I sought a place where I could be alone, and found myself sitting on the bench on the porch of the saddle house, with Belle at my side.

R.C. walked up on the porch, sat down beside me. He sat there awhile without saying anything, then rather tentatively said, "How you doin', Frank?"

"Fair to middlin'. You?"

"About the same."

"Sure gonna miss him. I don't think this place can run without him."

"Sure it can," R.C. said. "You can do it. For that fact, you've been doing it, Frank."

"Ah, hell, I haven't been doin' anything. Just keepin' it rollin'. But we've got important business ahead of us, and I don't reckon I'm up to handlin' that. I imagine Miz T. will turn it over to Top."

R.C. shook his head. "I don't think so. I think she'll leave it with you."

"I don't know about that." When he didn't start talking, I finally looked at him and said, "Well?"

"Why did you put those things in the Boss's coffin with him? Why were they so important to you?"

I thought about it a minute. "Well, because he might need 'em where he's goin'."

R.C. thought about that. "How do you mean?"

"Well, it's custom. Indian custom anyway. A custom I believe in. You bury with the dead anything that might come in handy in heaven. And if heaven's anything like I think it is, the Boss is sure gonna need his hat and his rope, and his spurs and his chaps. Tell you the truth, if I'd a'had my way about it, I'd a'shot ol' Spud and left him lyin' there on top of the Boss's grave."

R.C. looked at me with rather a shocked look. "You mean you'd kill a perfectly good horse?"

"Sure, why not? It was his horse. He might need to be mounted where he's goin'. I'd hate for him to be afoot. It's an old Indian custom. Haven't you read anything about Indians?"

R.C. nodded his head. "Some. But I never had anybody explain it to me like you're explainin' it."

I could tell R.C. was pondering this mighty hard. You could almost see him thinking. "This is a custom of Indians you say?"

"Yep. Practically any Indian tribe that I know of have similar beliefs."

R.C. was deep in thought when he said, "Do you know any other people besides Indians that had this belief?"

I thought awhile. "I don't know. But I imagine other cultures did the same. Why do you ask?"

R.C. paid me little mind, when he said, "Oh, I was just wonderin'." Then he came up with the damnedest question. "What about the Mexican culture?"

"What about it?"

"Did they do things like that?"

I had to think about that one myself. "I don't know. To me all a Mexican is, is a Central American Indian crossed with Spanish blood. So it could be possible, I guess. Why?"

R.C. just shook his head. "Ah, I was just thinkin'.'"

"Well, we'd better get back down. People will think we pulled out like Jim if we don't make a showin'.'"

R.C. was still thinking when he said, "I guess so."

We had both begun to rise when we heard a footstep on the porch. Neither of us had been aware as Top approached, propped one foot up on the porch, and rolled a cigarette. "You boys holdin' a private conference or just hidin' out?"

As I settled back on the bench I shook my head. "Just gettin' away from the crowd, Top. They're a shade bothersome."

As Top swung a kitchen match against his Levis pants leg to light his smoke, he said, "Yeah. Same dog bit me."

The three of us remained in silence for a short while, when I said, "You know, I can't help but remember back when the Boss brought the Gruyer home. It seems like that's when things started goin' downhill. I know for a fact I've never been so humiliated in my life."

"How so?" Top said.

As I looked at him I knew that Top was aware of what had happened that day. But for some reason was drawing me out to make me go through it again. "You know as well as I do, Top. I got ironed out three times."

Top blew a smoke ring. "You coulda rode 'im, Frank."

I smiled and shook my head. "No way. Three times made a believer outa me."

"Nah," Top said. "You coulda rode 'im."

This was getting a little aggravating. It appeared that Top was either trying to pay me an offhanded compliment or knew something I didn't. And the possibility of the latter was what was irritating. "How would you know?" I asked. "You weren't even there. I'm tellin' ya there was no way."

Top stood by his convictions and let me in on a secret. "The Boss told me ya coulda."

I had to laugh at that one. "He told you I could? Hell, if he was gonna give any advice to anybody, it shoulda been me."

Top, still on top of the situation, flicked ashes from his cigarette. "You know the Boss. He taught by example. He wasn't no coach. He figured he started ya, just like he started me years ago. After a certain point he let you figure it out for yourself. If you couldn't, you had only yourself to blame."

I couldn't understand what Top was saying. "Well, I'd like to know what the hell I coulda done different!"

"Think about it," Top said.

"I did." I remembered that morning so well and I could remember thinking, I don't know how he's doing it. But he is.

"What was goin' through your mind when you first forked him, Frank?"

Without a moment's hesitation I said, "Tryin' to hold his head up to keep him from buckin'. You know how it's done, Top. That's standard procedure for this place. Always try to keep a horse from buckin' if you can. You never want him to learn how, because once he learns, he might like it and get good at it."

Top nodded his head. "True. When you left 'im, when you was throwed, what position were ya in?"

I wrinkled my brow, not at the question but in the manner at which it was put. "Well, the position I remember most was hittin' the ground. 'Course before that I was in midair."

"Nah. I'm talkin' about in the saddle. When you left 'im. How was you throwed?"

I ducked my head and looked at the ground and remembered back. "All three times over the back end. Damned if I can figure out why!"

I turned and looked at Top who was lookin' at me with a slight smile on his face. And all he said was, "Think about it."

I did. And when I put together what he'd asked me to, slowly a realization came to me. I'd been pulling hard on those cotton reins. I'd been bucked off over the back end. That meant . . . and then it came to me.

Top still had that slight smile on his face when I asked him, "Are you sayin' that I was pullin' so hard that I mighta got a little slack in those reins and gone out over the back end?"

Top nodded his head slowly.

"In order for that to happen, the Gruyer woulda had to throw me his head. I don't think he did."

"Are ya sure?"

As I thought about it, Top went on. "Maybe you were so busy tryin' to stay in his middle and tryin' to keep his head pulled up that you never saw the little trick that Gruyer pulled by throwin' his head up and givin' ya a ton of slack."

I had been concentrating so hard, trying so hard to get him rode, I had no idea where his head was. But the Boss had been standing there and had seen it all. And not said a word.

"Well, I'll be goddamned!" I said. It made me angry at first and as I turned again to Top, that slight smile had widened a shade. And I had to smile, too. "The Boss saw this happenin' and wouldn't tell me."

He shook his head back and forth. "You know the Boss. You had to figure it out for yourself."

I had to laugh. I don't know how many times those bronc rides had gone through my mind. And I'd never seen it. But now it was as clear as day!

"Top, I appreciate ya tellin' me. I never woulda figured it out. But now I can see the mistake I was makin'." People were beginning to pull out and leave. Hardly anyone was left except Diego's people.

Roberta found us and said, "Come on inside. Miz T. would like to see you."

I entered the house again with hat in hand, like I was walking on eggshells. She had gone through quite a strain the past few days, and how she held up was a mystery.

Then again, perhaps I wasn't giving Miz T. enough credit. There was sorrow in her face as she smiled at me and thanked me for the songs. "Frank, they were beautiful. I know J.W. would've been proud. The whole service was lovely. I want to thank you for handling everything for me."

I never could handle praise very well. I thanked her with downcast eyes and felt somewhat uncomfortable, until finally she invited me to sit down. She looked at me with a mischievous look and said, "I understand you and Mrs. Remington had a set-to at the cemetery after we all left."

There was nothing I could do but fess up. "Yes, ma'am, I'm sorry. I know I had no right . . ." but she interrupted me.

"That's all right, Frank. You had every right. I don't know exactly what you did, but whatever it was, I approve. And I know J.W. would, too."

I muttered another "thank you."

"Now that J.W.'s gone, it would be a great favor to me if you'd take over the management of the ranch. I know that you've more or less been doing this practically all summer. But now, I need you even worse. I need you to completely take over."

These were the words that I had been waiting to hear for years. But deep down I didn't know whether I was ready to accept the responsibility, and told her so.

Miz T. smiled. "You're ready, Frank. J.W. and I had talked many times about you."

I didn't know quite what to say, so I spoke what I was thinking. "Why, I'd be pleased, Miz T., to do the best job that I could."

Miz T. nodded her head. "When I said 'run the ranch,' I mean just that. I mean for you to take care of everything. Write the checks, sign the checks, sell the cattle, order the feed, buy supplies, everything."

I stood up and said, "Ma'am, you can count on me to do my best, right or wrong. Anything I do will be in the best interest of you and the ranch."

Miz T. smiled. "I knew I could count on you, Frank. Thank you." With a nod of her head, I turned and left.

Diego rose and followed me outside. There he stopped me, shook my hand with both of his, and said, "Frank, you will do fine. If you need help, call on us, and we will come. But I want you to know that you have my full confidence and respect."

"I appreciate it, Diego, but I hate to bother you. You've got your own troubles. By the way, how is this land thing coming? Any more word from Santa Fe?" As I said that a cloud came over Diego's face.

"I am afraid so. I heard from the state land commissioner and attorney general. It looks like we are going to court."

"Diego, do you have any idea who's behind this?"

"Who knows? Of course, it is the Anderson law firm in Santa Fe that is initiating the lawsuit. But we have never been able to determine who they are representing. That remains a mystery."

"Diego, I can't see how our government can do this. The treaty of Guadalupe Hidalgo, made when the United States won the war with Mexico, guaranteed that all Spanish and Mexican land grants would be honored."

A smile crept across his face. "Ah, but it would not be the first time that our government has gone back on its word, would it, Frank?"

"That's damn sure true, Diego."

"Those old land grants were too large and too vague," he continued. "I have enough now to make any man happy. The problem is how to retain it."

I walked toward the bunkhouse thinking of what had just happened. I realized that no mention of money as pertaining to a raise had ever been mentioned. I'd not thought of it, nor had Miz T. It needed no special arrangement. I knew that Miz T. would make it right for me, as she in turn knew I'd do my best for her. There was no need to discuss money.

CHAPTER

34

I awoke on Friday morning, the day after the funeral, a few minutes before my Westclock Scotty alarm clock went off, as usual. I reached over and slammed the alarm plunger down so I wouldn't have to hear the damned thing clang, when I had the strangest feeling that somebody was watching me in the dark. I rolled over to see R.C. sitting on the side of the bed, next to mine, fully dressed.

"What the hell's wrong with you? You sick?" I said.

R.C. shook his head no. I could tell he was in an excitable state. His eyes were big, but he tried to appear calm. "Frank, have you got anything special that has to be done today?"

I was still rubbing the sleep out of my eyes, propping myself up in bed, when I said, "As a matter of fact I do. But what's on your mind?"

"I've got a hunch. It's more than a hunch. It came to me in the middle of the night. And I know, I just know," and at that point I don't even think he was talking to me. He was talking more to himself. "I know," he repeated.

"What in the hell do ya know?"

"If I tell you, I'm afraid you won't believe me, and you won't help me."

"When did I never help you? But I'm damn sure not gonna help you unless you tell me what you're talkin' about!"

R.C. seemed in a big hurry. "Get up! And I'll tell you while you're getting dressed."

While I was washing up and pulling on my clothes, R.C. started in telling me of all the volumes he'd read. He wasn't telling me anything I didn't already know. Hell, I'd known what he'd been reading! I'd watched him. He was leading up to something, but he was having a hard time getting it out.

When I was finally dressed, I said, "What came to ya in the middle of the night?"

R.C. looked at me as serious as he could possibly look. "Frank, I think, I'm almost sure, I can solve," and he looked like he was searching for a word when he said, "the mystery."

"Mystery of what?!"

"The old church, Peralta, the papers."

I couldn't believe what I was hearing. "Where?"

"You're not gonna believe me."

"Goddamn! We're not goin' through this again, are we?"

"I need your help. But we need Poke, too."

"Why do we need Poke?"

"Well, he's Catholic. That might be some help. I don't want him to miss this."

Again I asked him, getting more irritated. "Miss what?"

"Let me go over and get Poke and I'll explain it to you both. That way I won't have to repeat it. Maybe I can get it straight in my mind while I'm goin' over to get him."

"Is it that important?"

"Didn't you hear what I said? I think I know where all those documents are located. And the sacred things from the church."

I still didn't understand. "Okay, go git him, then. Don't ya want to eat breakfast first?"

"I'm afraid I'll miss him if I take time to eat breakfast. I'd better get over there before he leaves the headquarters."

"I can hardly wait to hear what you've got to say."

R.C. looked back at me and smiled. "Neither can I," and out the door he went. He was heading out the road in Ol' Sundown before I ever got to the kitchen.

I was sitting up in the office, just getting myself acquainted with the Boss's records and where everything was, when I heard R.C.'s pickup. I was glad to have an excuse to get up and get out of the office. It would take some time before I became at ease around the Boss's personal domain.

As I walked out to the pickup, Poke got out, walked around in front. We both morninged each other. "What'd he tell you?"

Poke shook his head. "Nothin'. He said he needed my help. But he didn't say doin' what. But Top didn't have any objections, so here I am," and we both turned to R.C.

"We need some shovels," R.C. said. "Let's get Ol' Blue and I'll try to explain along the way."

When he mentioned "shovels," Poke and I looked at one another with raised eyebrows. It had crossed my mind that what we had been looking for had been buried. But where? There were just too damned many places to dig that all you'd come up with was just a hole. You'd have to have a reason to dig, and evidently R.C. had come up with a reason.

We had thrown three shovels in the back of Ol' Blue while R.C. was off on the other side of the barn rummaging around for something, and directly came back with a couple of trowels, cement trowels, and a big stiff-bristled stucco brush. When he dropped these in the back of the pickup, I said, "Looks like you're an anthropologist fixin' to excavate."

R.C. nodded his head. "That's the idea."

I drove. Poke had savvy enough to quickly get in the middle so he wouldn't have to open the gates, and left R.C. on the outside to tell the story and get the gates. Poke and I waited patiently as we started out the west gate toward the old mission and the Padre pasture, and waited 'til R.C. was back in the pickup after the first gate before we demanded an explanation.

R.C. started, "Well, you see, I've been doin' a little research. And I know that the day the massacre occurred," and then he stopped. "No, let me back up. The day they were buried was Easter Sunday."

Poke and I both looked at him. "How do you know that?"

"Well, in talking to Diego and what records he had, he thought it might. But I did some checking and I found out that April 5, 1874, was sure enough Easter Sunday."

Poke and I both said, "How?"

"I found out through research that Easter is always celebrated on the first Sunday after the spring equinox. So, that would make it fall between March 22 and April 25. Or you could say it would be the first Sunday after the full moon. So, I went to the encyclopedias and tried to figure out when the spring equinox fell in 1874."

"You mean to tell me you calculated and figured all that out by the moon?" Poke said.

R.C. was staring straight ahead, thinking, when he said, "No, I couldn't do it. I finally went to the library, asked for their help. We ended up calling the library in Denver, and there they had an old world almanac. It provided proof that Easter was April 5, back in 1874."

I had some questions and I was almost positive that Poke did too. But we both, I think, decided rather than interrupt to just let R.C. tell his story and let him run his course. He was intent!

"You see," R.C. went on, "the reason April 5 is important is because that being Easter, everybody came from other churches to celebrate Easter up on top of the Piedra. So, they came to Peralta, either on April 4 or April 5. That's when they found that the villagers had been massacred. And, of course, they buried them as soon as possible. They must have died on April 3, or possibly April 2. But, if you'll remember, Father Martinez, who is buried up on the Piedra, his headstone reads that he was buried April 2, 1874. Now, this coincides with the research that I've done on the last big raid that the Comanches and Kiowas made after breaking out of the reservation in Oklahoma, led by this famous Comanche chief, Quanah Parker. It's quite possible a splinter off that main branch swept through here on their way to the encounter that they call 'Adobe Walls.' It's well documented over in the Texas Panhandle.

"The way I've got it figured is, Father Martinez was coming to Peralta to perform Easter services when he ran into this band of marauding Comanches. Now, this is all speculation, but this is what I think happened. He was wounded or injured in some way but made it into Peralta to give the warning, either on the first or the second of April, the day they buried him. The wound was fatal. And people, knowing that a Comanche raid appeared likely, took Father Martinez to the top of the Piedra and buried him, along with their most prized possessions."

I had stopped at another gate, and while R.C. jumped out and opened it, Poke and I looked at one another with disbelief. As soon as R.C. hopped back into the pickup he started again.

"Remember the inscription on the tombstone: 'Abajo verdad, Arriba cielo'? They said that meant 'Below truth, above heaven.' I think in code they were telling someone where these prized possessions were. Now, heaven is above. But below is the truth? When I saw Frank put the rope, hat, spurs, and chaps in the Boss's coffin and buried them with him, it made me think. Then I talked with Frank about it and he told me these were the Boss's possessions, as did Diego say that all the possessions, the sacred vessels, the sacraments were actual possessions of the priest himself, not the church. I began to think. And then, all of a sudden, it came to me that I knew where these things are buried."

By this time I'd reached the church and started to slow down. R.C. pointed and said, "Drive over to the Piedra. We've got to go on top."

"Whoa, now," I said, "I'm not up to any grave robbin'."

"Me, neither," Poke said.

"There's a possibility that there's not a body in the grave, that they just did that so it wouldn't be desecrated by the Indians," R.C. said.

I had my doubts. It was the wildest damned story I'd ever heard. "If we're gonna do this shouldn't we get Diego, or perhaps Miguel or Joaquin? Or for that matter Kika. Some member of the family. Shouldn't we tell them what we're gonna do?"

R.C. shook his head no.

"Why not?" I asked.

You could see R.C.'s Adam's apple bob up and down as he swallowed. "I might be wrong. And I'd hate to look foolish."

Poke laughed. "Have you ever thought how foolish you're gonna look to us?"

R.C., still serious, said, "That's all right. You guys don't count."

I stopped at the bottom of the Piedra where the trail up began. I still was reluctant to go up there, disturb a grave for what might be a wild-goose chase. It wasn't my nature. Poke had reservations, too. I don't know about it being against his nature, but it was damn sure against his religion.

But R.C. insisted. "If I'm wrong, we'll just cover everything up. Never say a word. If we're right, it might save Diego a world of trouble. I talked to him at the funeral. He's got a lawsuit staring him straight in the eyes, and we know who's causing it. Now he might win the lawsuit and keep the home place. But you can almost bet that the state land is going to be put up for sale. But if we're right . . ."

And Poke said, "Where do ya git this 'we'?"

"All right then, if I'm right," R.C. said, "look at the time, trouble, and money we can spare Diego."

I considered it and so did Poke. With some reluctance we grabbed our shovels and started up the trail. Belle jumped out of the pickup and led the way. All the way to the top I kept hoping that we were going to do the right thing and that we'd get lucky. And if we didn't get lucky, that none of the three of us would ever open his mouth about this escapade again.

When we finally reached the top and entered the little wrought-iron gate, R.C. took complete charge. By the direction that the head-stone was facing, and by the information that Diego had given us when he replaced the old headstone with the new, R.C. drew two lines in the dirt where he thought the grave should be. The problem was, we had to be careful. We didn't know the depth. And we didn't want to disturb anything that had been put to rest over seventy-five years ago. Disturb it unnecessarily, that is.

All three of us started, with a caution from R.C. to go easy. It was slow going. We didn't know how much topsoil covered the rock itself, but it couldn't be much. We dug down carefully to a depth of two and a half to three feet when Poke's shovel touched something besides dirt, and he realized it. R.C. told him to wait, grabbed a trowel, and went to scraping dirt carefully away from the shovel mark. The first indication of anything that we saw seemed to be old, partially rotted canvas.

I got another trowel and did the same thing as R.C. started scraping dirt away carefully. And using the big, stiff-bristled brush, we uncovered what looked like the remains of a human being wrapped in what appeared to be a canvas wagon sheet. Nowhere did we see any sign of the lost treasure that we were searching for.

As we all sat on the edge of the hole and looked at our handiwork, I said, "Well, it appears we have just dug up the Padre Martinez. It's sure gonna look good on our report card when we reach the pearly gates."

Poke peered down on the shapeless form and muttered, "Oh, Jesus," then caught himself and said, "Excuse me, Father," and crossed himself quickly.

R.C. still didn't seem concerned. "I expected this. Frank, what was it you said about the scaffold and killing the horse and his belongings?"

"Oh. When they buried an Indian on the prairie they put 'em up on a scaffold and put all their possessions that they'd need in the afterlife," and then I began to realize what R.C. was thinking. And I said, "Underneath him?"

"Right. We've got to pick the body up and move it out of this grave."

I looked at Poke. "Come on," I said, "we've gone this far."

Carefully we dug around the body with the trowels. We excavated the body, in other words. It was surprising that the body had not deteriorated more than it had. But in this dry and arid country archaeologists had been finding things that lasted for hundreds of years in good shape, much less seventy-five.

As we got enough clearance to get our hands under the body, we were all surprised to find that there was no give to the body as we began to raise it up. Only then did we realize that the body had been placed on a board, then wrapped in the canvas. And, not only canvas. There seemed to be, through a few holes in the old wagon sheet, evidence of a rough-woven blanket or rug. As we eased the body out of the grave and placed it to one side, R.C. took a trowel, dropped to his hands and knees, and began scraping.

It wasn't long before we knew that he had either hit bedrock or something that was hard. Both Poke and I crawled out of the hole to let R.C. do whatever he was going to do. And, as he worked with the trowel and the brush, we could see the outline of a trunk or container of some sort.

Whatever it was had been made to last and built sturdy, for two straps of metal encircled it lengthwise and the same across its width, bradded down with rivets where the iron bindings crossed one another.

R.C. was frantically digging around the chest, muttering to himself, "I knew it, I knew it!" He was as excited as if he'd hit the mother lode. Which, after thinking about it, maybe we had!

"I need some help," he said. So I crawled down in the grave with him, and together we dug to find the bottom of the chest. I had underestimated its length. Two and a half feet wide would just about get it. Only it was in a rectangular shape maybe three feet long. We didn't know how deep, but it did have a slightly arched top, making it more of a chest than a box. I'd dig and then feel. And finally could get my fingers under the chest. It was no more than twelve inches deep. Even though it was sturdily built with copper mountings on the corners, and the iron straps, we had to be careful lifting it out. After practically eighty years in the ground, it would be a shame to break it, even though we had no idea of the contents, just hopes.

Finally we had it loosened up enough that I thought we could lift it out. Squatting carefully at each end, R.C. and I began to pull. Rather difficult at first, but by slightly wiggling we inched it out. And it was surprisingly heavy. We laid it on the other side of the grave from the body and stood and looked at one another with what you could only describe as shit-eatin' grins, the three of us as happy as pigs in the mud. R.C. took his stiff-bristled brush and gave it the once-over. It had a hasp and an old, tiny lock, and it was locked. On the back, two old, heavy-duty, hand-forged hinges kept the lid in place.

"We're gonna have to take it back to the house, clean it up, oil those hinges so they don't break, cut the lock off to see what's inside," I said.

"Oh, no, " Poke said. "You can't cut the lock. Everything needs to be preserved just as it is. And to my way of thinkin', we need to find out what's in the chest now!"

"Why?" R.C. asked.

Poke nervously looked over his shoulder at the shrouded body and said, "We've got to lay the good Padre back to rest. And if this chest doesn't contain what we think it does, we have no business taking it. And that'd mean we'd have to come back, put the chest back where it was, and do the whole thing over again. And I'm not up to that."

R.C. shook his head. "I know what's in it. It's got to be! It's what we're looking for, whatever that is." It was at that point that all three of us realized we didn't actually know what we were looking for. But at least two of us thought we had found it. Poke wasn't sure.

"What else could it be?" R.C. said.

"Personal belongin's," Poke said indignantly.

"I thought most priests didn't have personal belongings, or anything of value," I said, thinking about Diego's comments so long ago. "If they don't have some significance or importance, why would they go to all the trouble to hide it so well? Even if the Indians decided to rob this grave, when they uncovered it, all they would find was a dead priest. I doubt if they'd go to the trouble of looking any farther. Not only Indians, but anybody else for that matter. So, by the way it was hid, I would say it would have to be something of great value."

R.C. agreed. Reluctantly Poke began to come around.

I fingered the lock and said, "I don't know of any way to get into the chest without cutting the lock off. Do you?" speaking to both of them.

"I do," R.C. said. "It's simple enough. Use the key."

Both Poke and I looked at him, disbelieving what we'd just heard. "Now where in the hell do you expect we'd find the key? It's just a stroke of pure luck that we found the chest. Now we've got to find the key?"

"Think about it," R.C. said. "Where would the key be?"

So the three of us sat in silence as we thought. I think R.C. had hoped that someone besides himself could come up with the obvious. We didn't. So finally he said, "It has to be on the priest's person."

"Oh, no," Poke said. "Oh, no. I ain't gonna unwrap that body and go searchin' it. That's blasphemy."

"Don't you think," R.C. said, "that when they hid this chest that they meant for it to be opened? And wouldn't you think the good Padre would want us, or somebody, to open the chest?"

Poke's mind was closed. "Hell, I don't know what he'd think. I just know I ain't gonna do it."

R.C. and I looked at one another. "I tend to agree with him," R.C. said.

"Well, somebody's gotta do it," I said. "If nobody else will, I will."

We carefully moved the body a little further away from the grave. I squatted on the ground at the feet of the shrouded figure. "Everybody take a good look on how this gentleman's wrapped up, because I want to put him back the same way we found him," and I began to fold back the old canvas wagon sheet, careful not to damage it any more than I had to.

With the canvas laid back, it exposed the thick, rough-woven, woolen blanket. The colors still remained, though dull: a maroon blanket with what had once been white stripes, but had now turned a dingy gray. Carefully, I unfolded the blanket to expose the body of Padre Estabio Tomas Martinez.

Poke was about to have a conniption fit. R.C., squatting at the other end, had actually helped move the folds back. And there in a black robe lay the body of the Padre. The skin had drawn up on his face to where his teeth protruded into a perpetual smile. He had a full head of hair and a mustache, which at one time, I'm sure, had been black, but now had turned to a rusty reddish color. The skin on the hands, face, and feet was like leather, dark brown in color. But there was no skeleton. What we had was what I'd always imagined a mummy would look like.

There were pockets in the robe. R.C. carefully reached down into them from the top to find nothing. Then he opened the robe at the nape of the neck and there we found what we were looking for. On a gold chain hung a cross of gold. But with it a small, bronze skeleton key, if you'll excuse the expression. No one had said a word as we went about this task.

R.C. looked up at both of us when he discovered the key. Taking the chain on each side of the neck, with a little bit of back and forth pressure, the chain began to move. When the chain was free, R.C. slid it around the back of the neck until the clasp came to view. Just a hook, like a shepherd's crook, had fit through the ring on the other end of the chain. Undoing this, he reached down and slid the key off the chain, leaving the cross. Snapping the chain back in place, he recentered the clasp behind the neck and the cross over the chest, closed the robe, opened the flap on his shirt pocket, dropped it in, and buttoned the pocket. "That's it," he said. "Let's lay the Padre back to rest."

We folded everything back just as we had found it, as close as we could, and filled up the hole that the chest had sat in at the bottom of the grave to where it was flat. Then, working with our shovels from the top, gently began to fill in dirt, first around the body, then on top, working more rapidly after the body was out of view. Soon we had the grave filled in, smoothed over, and with a little wind, rain, and time, no one would ever suspect what had taken place.

CHAPTER

35

The chest had leather handles on each end, but they were much too weak, dried, and deteriorated to carry the chest by. It would take two of us, each carrying an end, to get it off the Piedra. Poke whistled low as we lifted it up. I was carrying the front end, Poke had it by the back. R.C. was packing the tools.

"I don't know how we're gonna hoss this thing off this hunk of rock," Poke said. "It's gonna be a hell of a chore."

To give him a little inspiration I said, "Hell! I can do anything a horse can do, except shit while I walk."

Poke's only reply was, "Uh huh," as we started down.

Poke and R.C. changed off halfway down. Trying to back up my statement, I was determined to hold my end up all the way. And did. But it felt like my arms were about to fall off when we slid it into the back of Ol' Blue. Belle jumped in the back and curiously sniffed the box. She had never whined, growled, or left the gravesite during all of this, just lay off to one side, her head resting on her paws, her eyes moving, never missing a beat.

On the way back to the headquarters there were three fellows who were pretty proud of themselves, but still a shade subdued. Getting the chest open, now that was another problem. We each had our theory on that, but finally agreed that a little cleaning up and some forced air from our air compressor would be a good start. But we'd have to go slow and easy to make sure we didn't break anything.

We all wondered what kind of wood the chest was made of. But what we all couldn't figure out was what made the thing so heavy. We did agree to go directly to the barn and keep out of sight until we knew what we had. There was a chance that we'd made fools of ourselves and done all this for nothing. But I don't think any of us believed it.

We removed the chest and put it on a workbench. The metal parts, actually, weren't rusted, for moisture hadn't penetrated down that far and there was no submoisture to come up from the bottom because of the rock base that it was sitting on. With an air-tip on the air hose, a surprising amount of dirt and sand came out of the keyhole. We brushed it down several times completely. Then blew it off with air, applied lightweight penetrating oil to the hinges and to the lock. While it soaked, we took a cloth of linseed oil and wiped the box down thoroughly.

"What do you think?" R.C. said.

"You've got the key. Give it a try," I said.

R.C. took the key from his shirt pocket, inserted it into the lock, and wiggled it around, minding Poke's advice not to force anything. And to add insult to injury he advised R.C. not to let me take ahold of the lock and key, for I'd break it for damn sure. Poke even went so far as to degrade my mechanical skills and make the statement that "old Frank could break an anvil, if you gave him enough time to mess with it."

Things had been so serious during the morning, I was glad to hear things lighten up a little bit, even if I was the butt end of Poke's hoorahing. But with just a little added pressure, surprisingly the locked clicked and the bale came out of its ancient seat and was removed from the hasp. With a slight wiggling of the hasp, its hinge began to move and gave the oil we had applied to it a chance to do its work. Finally it cleared the catch. R.C. used the same technique when he lifted the lid, no more than an eighth of an inch, and we heard the hinges groan. But as he worked them up and down and we applied more oil to the hinges, he got more and more movement of the lid, and less squeaking and grinding.

Finally, slowly, he opened the chest lid. When it was completely open we stared at the contents. The chest was lined with royal blue velvet. Everything in the chest was wrapped in the same type of velvet cloth, except a leather-bound book, perhaps an inch thick, filled with paper. I had an idea that this is what we had been looking for.

Ever since we had opened the top of the chest, a strange odor had drifted from within. I asked the others if they noticed it, and both did. "What is that smell? It's kinda familiar. It smells like that stuff you put on mosquito bites or chiggers."

"Camphor," R.C. said. "I think that's it. Camphor."

"Maybe it's to keep the moths from eatin' this velvet cloth."

I reached for the leather-bound volume. Then a strange thought crossed my mind. "You know, the last person to touch this book was dead within twenty-four hours, I would imagine. They must have buried the chest and the Padre, knowing what was coming, and went down off the rock to meet the challenge, only to die to the very last man, woman, and child. That's bravery. That's honor."

They nodded in agreement.

I opened the volume carefully, and it was written in a beautiful script in the Spanish language.

"This is it!" I said. "This has got to be it," as a smile spread across my face as big as all outdoors. "I'm not gonna try to go through and look up Diego's name or anybody else's. I'll leave that to somebody that can decipher this lingo. But I'll betcha that this is what Diego's been needin'."

I carefully laid it over on the workbench. I don't know why we were handling everything so carefully. Everything was in good shape and beautifully preserved. I reached in, took ahold of a blue velvet–covered object, and withdrew it from the chest, unfolded the velvet it was wrapped in to find what looked like a candlestick. I held it up and said, "Look at this."

"Let me feel it," Poke said. And as I handed it to him, he said, "Solid gold! There should be another one." He reached in, withdrew another object, uncovered it, and just as he had predicted it was the other solid gold candlestick.

"How'd you know there'd be two?" R.C. asked.

"One for each end of the altar. I'm the Catholic of the bunch, remember?"

"We remember," I said. "Why in the hell do you think you're here? You're gonna serve as our resident expert."

R.C. reached in and withdrew another. Uncovering it, I heard Poke's breath suck in as he said, "My God! A chalice." It was a cup with a stem, made of silver on the outside and what looked like pure gold on the inside, and extending an inch down from the top around the rim. "This must be worth a fortune!" Poke said. "I can't believe it."

I pulled out another object, and after uncovering it, I said, "Lookit, a plate."

Poke shook his head. "That's a paten."

"A what?"

"A paten, p-a-t-e-n. The chalice and the paten go together. The chalice holds the wine, the paten holds the host."

I didn't know what he was talking about, but I took his word for it. It appeared to have a silver bottom and an inlaid gold top. That was everything except for some object that lay on the bottom that appeared so large that the chest had been made to specially accommodate this object. I reached in to pull it out. It was quite heavy, and I took the velvet shroud from it, and stood in amazement. It was the damnedest thing I'd ever seen. The first thing that crossed my mind I said aloud. "It's a Zia, like that's on our state flag."

It did have a sunlike appearance. Moving from a round center of cut glass were silver and gold spires that grew from the center like the spokes of a wheel, only with more width, and alternated in silver and gold. It had a stem and a base. But the glass center was hinged and served as a door. "What in the hell is this?" I mumbled, and looked at Poke.

"My God! I can't believe it. It's a monstrance."

"You're damned right it's a monster," I said. "It's monstrous grande."

Poke shook his head. "No, not monstrous. Monstrance."

"What's the difference?" I asked. And he spelled it. I looked at R.C. and he shrugged his shoulders. "I never heard of it," I said. "What's it for?"

Poke wrinkled up his brow and thought a minute. "Well, this glass door in the middle, that holds the consecrated host."

"Explain," I said.

"The host. Ah," he seemed to be searching for the right word. "It's like Protestants in their communion when they drink their grape juice and have a wafer or chunk of bread. 'This is my blood, this is my body.' That's the host."

Poke still seemed to be thinking. "It's for the veneration of the faithful."

I looked at Poke and smiled. "I believe you just got an 'A' in a pop quiz in your catechism class."

Poke smiled. "It's been a long time. I had to think. It can be carried in a procession through the streets, or it can sit on the altar. It's very sacred. All these things, except for the book, were the Padre's sacraments. They belong to him. They were probably given to him by his sponsor. And he probably was from the Old World, Spain."

"Well, I'll tell you what, pard," I said, "he had a hell of a sponsor. If this is sure enough silver and gold, he either had a sponsor that was rich and religious, and as generous as Jesus Christ himself, or he was some old boy that had been the shits all his life and was gonna try to buy his way into heaven. There's gotta be a fortune that just came out of this chest."

It was sitting there on the table for all of us to view. We had done ourselves up right proud. That monstrance thing was something to behold. Even I held it in awe.

We wrapped it all back up, put it back in the box, and took it down to the house where Miz T., Kika, the old lady, Tio, and Lupe could view our discovery. I had an idea that it'd mean a lot more to them than it did to us, which was saying considerable.

"Kika," R.C. said, "call everyone. We've got something for them to see."

A frown came on Kika's face. She looked at the chest, but didn't comprehend its meaning. But she did as she was asked. I walked out back and rang the clanger. Tio and Lupe soon showed up. Miz T., still in her housecoat and looking very drawn, came with Abuela Elena in her ever-present black garb. R.C. looked at me. I motioned for him to go ahead.

"Well, it's kind of a long story. But we figured out where the lost, well, the lost," and at that he stopped and said, "You'll have to see for yourself," and he opened up the chest. It was Kika who moved to the chest and peered in, wide-eyed. She took the volume that lay on top. "My God." Laying it on the table she began to uncover all the sacraments. And as she did, disbelief went through everyone there, 'til finally the belief of a miracle came upon them. Seeing the object as Kika removed it, old grandmother Elena knelt on the kitchen floor, tears running down her cheeks, crossed herself, and began to pray. So did Lupe and Tio. Although they did not kneel, both Miz T. and Kika shed tears. Tears of joy, I suppose. It was hard for me to understand, and I backed out of the way.

After the first signs of reverence, all crowded eagerly around, handling the objects. And before I knew it, Abuela Elena had come to each of us, flung her arms around us, and gave us all a big hug. Tio and Lupe did the same. Kika came around, kissed R.C. lightly on the mouth and gave him a hug, then moved on to each of us with a hug. With tears in her eyes she said, "I don't know how you did it. It's truly a miracle. This, I think, will end the problems that my father is having with the government. We are all indebted to you." At that point, she had to sit down, and broke into great sobs, which concerned R.C. greatly and he went to comfort her.

Joy and excitement seemed to spread through the house as they inspected the newfound discovery. Miz T.'s eyes glistened with excitement and the color came back to her cheeks. And rightfully so. It seemed nothing short of a miracle that after so many years a chest filled with so many important and valuable artifacts was found.

"Don't you think the first order of business would be to get all these things over to Diego?" I said.

Miz T., coming down from the high state of excitement to reality again, said, "Yes, of course. That's the first thing that must be done. Why don't you all run that over right away."

"Good idea," I said. "Miz T., why don't you go, too." It seemed to fluster Miz T. "Why, I can't. I'm not up . . ." and I caught her in mid-sentence. "The trip, getting outside, and especially going to the Jaramillo place would do you a world of good. Besides, wouldn't you like to be there and see Diego's face and share in the joy?"

Miz T. seemed uncertain. But with the help of Kika you could see her beginning to come around and savor the idea of getting out. "All right. I think I will."

"Why don't you take a few clothes and stay a day or two and not be rushed?" I added.

Kika agreed. "I'll bet Daddy has quite a celebration. Why don't you, Aunt Teresa? It will be good for you."

After a few minutes' thought, "All right. I will go," she said with conviction.

Turning to Tio and Lupe, I made the same suggestion to them. Tio looked horrified at the thought. "Oh, no, Frank. I cannot go. Who would do the shores?" He pronounced "chores" with an *s*, almost making the word sound like the "shores" of an ocean.

"Tio, you and Lupe haven't been off this place that I can remember. I'll take care of everything." The thought had not entered Tio's head until I planted the seed.

At that he turned to Lupe and spoke rapidly in Spanish, then turned to me. "Are you chure it will be all right, Frank? Who will feed you?"

I laughed. "I'll get by. Go on now and gather up your things." With that, Tio spoke to Lupe, and in a comical way shooed her out of the kitchen to change her clothes and throw a few things together that they would need. Evidently he planned to go as he was.

Kika was carefully and slowly turning the pages of the manuscript. Finally she said, "Uncle Fracio, here's your name." She was referring to Tio, of course. He quickly went to her. "See?" Kika showed him with her finger resting upon his name.

"Si!" And he turned around with a broad grin, placed both hands on his chest, and smiled as he said, "My name is en thees book, Frank."

"My God, Tio! Were you born here, too?"

Wide-eyed, Tio nodded his head yes. "Si, Frank. I have been here forever."

I laughed. The little man didn't know how that sounded, or exactly what he had said. I edged closer to Kika so I could look at the written date and said, "Where?"

Kika pointed with her finger on the page. The only thing I could make out was the year, 1868. "My Lord!" I whispered. Now I knew how long forever was, at least in Tio's mind.

Kika finally said, "Frank," as she looked up from the book smiling, "here's Daddy's name, along with my grandfather and my grandmother. This is surely what he needs to stop all legal proceedings. I just knew it was here, and it is!"

I smiled back. "I had a feeling it was there, too, Kika." Then, again, speaking before I thought, "You know, I've never realized how old your father is. He looks younger than he is, and is in good health. He was no spring chicken when you came along."

Kika smiled, and with a gleam in her eye, "Jaramillo men have traditionally been known to be quite vigorous. Had my mother not died, there's no doubt in my mind I would not have remained the youngest in the family. Dad outlasted two wives, as did my grandfather. So you see, it runs in the family."

As soon as Kika was through, we replaced everything back in the chest, loaded it in the trunk of Miz T.'s car.

But something was eating on Poke terribly. "Frank, I'm glad we did what we did, but I'm sure uncomfortable about digging up that priest. I hate to be the one to give the details to the church authorities, but I guess it's my job."

I disagreed. "I don't think we did anything wrong, Poke. I'm like R.C. I think that this is the way it was supposed to work, that they left a message on the headstone. They hoped someone would finally interpret what they meant, then do what we did."

When Miz T. came down she looked nice. For the first time in months she had spring to her step and a smile on her face, but she was taken back when she saw that I wasn't going. "Why, Frank, you're not ready to go."

"No, ma'am, I'm not going. If I left, since Lupe and Tio are going, that would leave nobody on the place. The Boss told me long ago that he never left the ranch unattended, that somebody was always around. And I intend to carry out his wishes."

"Oh, Frank. That was J.W. He was so possessive. I don't know what he thought somebody might come and do. Steal something or burn the house down? But that was his way of thinking. He's gone now. So, it would be perfectly all right to come with us. After all, you had a hand in solving this puzzle. Please come!"

"Please, ma'am, I wouldn't feel right about it. And somebody needs to be here to do the chores. So you all go ahead."

Seeing that she couldn't change my mind, she gave up. Lupe and Tio came down with their meager possessions, and with Miz T.'s we loaded up the trunk. Tio tried to give me some last-minute instructions on what to do concerning his hogs and chickens, but finally realized I knew what to do, and climbed in.

It was not until they rolled across the cattle guard and I could see the dust whipping up from the caliche road that I realized I had a date with Roberta tonight, and no way of letting her know that I wouldn't be there. Oh, shit! With no telephone, either here or at the Chism ranch, there was no way to call. My options were severely limited. The only thing that I could hope for was when I didn't show up she would realize that something had happened and would drive down to find out what. I was desperately eager to see her, to share with her our experiences of the morning, but also to see her smiling face.

I prided myself on my punctuality. If I told you I'd be somewhere at a certain time, by God I was there. But this time it wouldn't be so, and it bothered me greatly. To occupy my time, and because it was needful, I went up to the Boss's office and began to go through his records to try to get an idea of how he did things. I still had the feeling that I was doing something illegal by going through his personal papers.

It got to the point where I was actually enjoying the peace and quiet and being by myself for the first time, ever, on this ranch. I seriously considered letting God and Belle take care of the ranch while I ran to town, but just couldn't bring myself to do it. It was as if I felt the Boss's presence and he was watching. I couldn't break with tradition.

As the time came and passed that I was supposed to meet Roberta in town, I grew increasingly irritated with myself for being so gallant and insisting that everybody traipse over to the Jaramillo place when I had an obligation to keep. I was about ready to give up and turn in, but I sat playing the guitar. I glanced down at Belle who was sleeping flat on her stomach with her head on her paws, and I saw her head rise and her ears prick up. Although I couldn't hear a thing, I knew somebody was coming up the road. I could only hope.

I walked outside and watched as the headlights, far off at first, came nearer and nearer. It wasn't until she pulled up in front of the main house that I realized it was Roberta's car. She quickly got out, glanced at the big house, which was as dark as the backside of the moon, then she turned and saw me coming from the bunkhouse. With apprehension in her voice I heard her call out, "Frank? Frank!"

Almost fearfully she said, "What happened?"

By that time I was by her side and took her in my arms. "Nothin', darlin'. Nothin' bad anyway. It's been quite a day," as I kissed her on the cheek. "I've got some story to tell you."

She let out a sigh of relief. "Oh, Frank, I didn't know what had happened. All kinds of things ran through my mind."

As we walked toward the big house, I said, "Like what?"

"Well, when you didn't show up, I thought maybe another horrible thing had happened. And then," and she hesitated as we entered the back porch and I turned on the lights.

"And then what?"

I heard her say, "I was afraid . . ." and again hesitated, as I led her into the living room and turned on the lamps.

"Afraid of what?"

As I turned and faced her, her eyes welled up with tears. As they dropped across her lovely cheeks, "That you'd be gone."

"That I'd be gone!" I laughed. "Where would I go?"

"Anywhere."

I sat her down on the couch and sat beside her. "Now, tell me. Why would I leave?"

She was crying by this time.

I took her face in both my hands, looked her square in the eye. "Don't you know that I love you very much? And would never do anything to hurt you if I could possibly help it?"

She nodded, still sniffling. "I know. But . . ."

"But, we haven't talked about it, have we? Everything has been taken for granted?"

Again she nodded. I took a deep breath. "Well, we need to talk about it. And I guess now's as good a time as any. Okay?"

"Okay."

I took a deep breath and began. I had her total attention. "Roberta, ever since I saw you this spring at your dad's brandin', you're the first thing I think of when I wake up in the morning and the last thing I think of before going to sleep at night. Around you everything seems so natural and easy. You demand nothing of me, you accept me the way I am. And I enjoy you. As a friend, but more than that. You're a very giving person, Roberta. And you've gotten very little from me in return. And you've given me the ultimate gift. Yourself, totally.

"I've fought it, for a while, the feeling that was coming over me. But I wonder if you know, really know, what you're getting yourself into."

Roberta watched and looked into my eyes as I spoke, not interrupting. "The first thing is that I'm a half-breed. But, I am what I am, and I can't change it. And wouldn't if I could. Then there's my temperament. You mix the Irish and the Indian together and you get what you see," as I pointed at my chest, "a high-tempered, unforgiving, bullheaded, act-before-you-listen, easy-come, easy-go type of character like me. Some folks will say that I'm not plumb civilized. And even I wonder if I'll ever amount to a hill of beans.

"I have nothing of my own but the clothes on my back, the tools of my trade, and a worn-out car. How can you expect someone like me to be taken seriously by a woman of quality, such as yourself? And I know quality. Believe me when I tell you, as far as you and I go, in quality I'm way overmatched. You could do so much better for yourself.

"I know you have strong ties to this country. I don't. Suppose I wanted to go to Wyoming, Montana, anyplace? How could I expect you to go, with as strong a tie as you have? This is your home." I noticed a smile beginning on Roberta's face and her eyes began to glisten as I talked. "Don't think I haven't thought about it," I continued. "I've considered, and played out in my mind going up to your dad and saying, 'Jingle Bob, I'd like to ask your permission to marry your daughter.' And he'd say to me, 'Why, Frank, I appreciate your straightforwardness. Now tell me son, what do you have to offer my daughter?' And I'd have to answer, 'Not one damn thing, except what you see standin' before you. And the fact that I love her.'

"And I was afraid it wouldn't be enough."

By this time Roberta had raised her hand to her mouth as if to stifle an outright laugh. I could feel my blood rising. Here I was trying to explain, and she thought it was funny. Again, without thinking, I said, "What's so damn funny?"

It was then she outright laughed. And though it made me mad, I was somewhat confused. She laid her hand on my arm and said, "Frank, I am not laughing at you. I'm laughing at the situation."

"What situation?"

"Here you are, telling me everything negative you can possibly think of about yourself, trying to make me believe that you're someone other than the man I fell in love with, not just last spring, but much earlier than that, and have truly come to love, deeply, this summer. Frank, I know who you are. And I know what you are. And don't you see that all these things that you've been talking about are the very things that make you so attractive to me? I'll admit, you're different from most people. But that only makes it better, as far as I'm concerned. I don't want a man who has everything already planned out, that already has his fortune made. As far as my roots in this country," she shrugged her shoulders and smiled, and said, "whither thou goest. Can't you see? I love you for who you are. Not what you're going to be or what you've got, or what I can make out of you." She smiled. "I just love you, and I want to be part of your life."

I took her in my arms as I said, "You are, darlin'. You are. Don't you know that?"

"Yes," she whispered.

I held her back at arm's length. "So the question is, what are we going to do about it?"

Roberta nodded.

"You know how most girls fare that are raised in this country? Their options are limited. It's either get married when they get out of high school, or leave and go to Amarillo or Albuquerque for a job. But you're different. You went off to college. You've got two years behind you. It'd be a shame for you not to go ahead and finish up. I think you'd like that. I know your folks would. And I would."

Roberta was listening intently. But when I mentioned college, I could see a look of disappointment on her face. "There's been some things happening around here. Miz T. wants me to manage the place. So, it's a step up. We haven't talked about money, but I'm sure she'll pay me what I'm worth, probably more. If I asked you to marry me today, we wouldn't even have a place to live. But perhaps if you go back to school, and I work hard, and get lucky, maybe we can start a life together and have something besides just dreams to found it on. What do you think?"

"About what?" she said.

I didn't understand. "About what I just said."

"I'm not sure I understood what you just said, Frank."

I started to repeat what I'd just said, but decided to cut it short and say, "Maybe we can get married on something besides just dreams."

Roberta's eyes opened wide. "Married?"

"Yeah. Married. Isn't this what this is all about? Don't you want to get married?"

"I've never been asked."

I was exasperated. "Well, damn it, I'm askin' ya now. Will you marry me?"

Roberta closed her eyes. "Of course I'll marry you. I just didn't want you to think I was trying to make you do something you didn't want to do. You have to ask before I accept. But now that you've asked, I accept!"

She came into my arms and kissed me with the warmth and tenderness that I had grown so used to, and that I wanted to enjoy for the rest of my life. I reluctantly pulled away from her lips and hugged her close, my mouth next to her ear. "That's settled then. The only question is when. Will you go back to school, please?"

She nodded. "It'll be hard, Frank, being away from you."

"Me, too," I whispered. "But, let's try it. If it doesn't work, we can always get married anytime. But this way, you'll never be able to look back and say 'I wish I had finished,' or have any doubts. I don't want to take that away from you."

"I'll never have any doubts, Frank. I've never been more sure of anything in my life."

"Do you want a ring, an engagement ring? Maybe I can . . ."

She interrupted me. "I don't need a ring, Frank. This is just an un-derstanding between you and me, that you belong to me and I to you. That's enough." She pulled back, put both hands to my face, and with tears welling up in her eyes said, "I love you."

"I love you, too. Why are you crying?"

"Because I'm happy."

"That doesn't make sense."

She smiled through her tears. "It's not supposed to."

A big wave of relief went over me as I realized that we had resolved a situation that had been bothering me for quite some time. Or at least I thought we had, until Roberta said, "Frank," and immediately I thought, Oh, my God! We left something out.

"What?" I whispered back.

"Where *is* everybody?"

I had to laugh. She had been so intent, as I, with getting our feelings toward one another out in the open and making some sort of commit-ment, that she hadn't realized that we were alone and I had not had time to explain.

"We found the lost papers and the church artifacts this morning," I said.

"Who did?" Roberta said with wondering eyes.

"R.C., Poke, and me. It was R.C.'s idea. He figured it out."

"How?"

I laughed and said, "It's a long story. You're gonna have a hard time believing it. But if you've got the time, I'll tell you about the damnedest thing that ever happened to me."

With a big smile, Roberta settled back down on the couch, kicked off her shoes, and settled in for this story, which I told her from beginning to end, trying not to leave out even the slightest detail. She was pleased and enthralled. I embellished on the story, as I was prone to do, and had her both shivering with fright and laughing with delight, as I described the details. And, I said on finishing, "I insisted that everybody go over to the Jaramillo place and take the chest. Only after they left did I realize that I was to meet you in town and couldn't leave. And, darlin', I had no way of letting you know what happened. So, I just waited, hoping you'd do what you did."

"I sat and waited too, Frank, not knowing what to do, and finally decided to come down and find out. And the farther I came, the more I let my imagination run away with me. I was afraid, and had convinced my-self when I crossed over the last cattle guard that you had packed up and gone, rather than face me with the truth."

"Well, I'm glad you came. We needed to talk. This understanding between you and me, it'll work, won't it?"

She smiled. "You bet."

I said, like the words in the song, "You belong to me?"

"And you to me," she whispered.

"Well, nobody's here. Do you want to set up housekeeping?"

Roberta quickly glanced at her wristwatch. "My land. Frank, I had no idea it was so late." It was after midnight.

"Who cares?" I said. "We're together, everyone's gone. Why don't we make the best of it?"

Roberta smiled. "If you're thinking what I'm thinking."

Quickly I said, "I am."

"I believe I could stand a whole mess of that, right now."

"Okay, then," I said, jumping up. "Let's go."

"Where?"

"Up to your room."

"Oh, Frank. I couldn't do that. We couldn't, not here in this house. At least not 'til we're, well, you know?"

"Miz T. has always told you you're welcome here. There's plenty of bedrooms. Matter of fact, you've been spending a great lot of time in one of them."

Roberta shook her head. "It wouldn't be right, Frank. Besides, what if they came home?"

"They're not gonna come home this time of night. If they were comin' home, they'd already be here. I really don't expect 'em back until Sunday evening. I would expect Diego will throw some kind of a celebration and they'd be home after that."

"Still," Roberta said, "I can't. Not in this house, Frank."

"Well, the bunkhouse is the only alternative. And wouldn't we look a sight in one little single bed. It wouldn't be very comfortable." And then a thought crossed my mind. "How long has it been since you slept out under the stars?"

"Not since I was a little girl."

"How would you like to camp out tonight?"

"Where?"

"I'll drag a couple of mattresses out and put 'em together, out in front of the bunkhouse. Nobody'll ever know, except you, me, and Belle."

"Okay, Big'un, you're on."

I found a tarp, and by dragging two thin cotton mattresses out to the side of the bunkhouse, covering them with spare blankets and a couple of pillows, we had our makeshift bed. I quickly ran to the saddle house and got two lariat ropes, and upon returning tied them together and encircled the bed with the rope.

"What's that for?"

"Snakes," I said.

"Ooh. Does it work?"

"I don't know. The old-timers claimed it did, said a snake wouldn't crawl over a rope. But don't worry about it. Nothin' will come near us, as long as Belle is here." I looked down at Belle, lying at the foot of the bed.

Even though it was still summer, it was September and at this altitude the nights were chilly. So, we had a race to get our clothes off and slide under the covers. It was about a tie, as we snuggled up together, and she threw one leg over mine to get just a little bit closer.

"When do you have to go back to school?" I said.

"Probably the middle of next week."

"I'm going to miss you, something awful."

She rubbed her hand on my chest and said, "Ssh. Don't think about it anymore. Let's just think about tonight."

CHAPTER

36

The next two days were filled with love and harmony, both with each other and the world. Since no one was around, we had only to think of each other and our own pleasure. We ate, slept, played, talked, and made love as the notion fell upon us, not held to any strict schedule. Knowing that we would not see each other for some time made it even more intense. We searched the radio dial up and down, waiting with anticipation for Jo Stafford to sing "You Belong to Me." It was now the song that we would identify with for the rest of our lives. And the long talks we had, we even speculated as to what the future might bring, knowing all the while no one could possibly know, or for that matter want to know, because then life would lose its luster.

All barriers and defenses that I had built up through the years as an excuse to remain footloose and fancy-free came down. It seemed like the thing to do. Everything with Roberta seemed so natural, and seemed to be right. I had learned long ago that if it felt right, in your gut, and it looked right, it probably was right. You better go for it before it was gone. I went for it.

Finally Sunday evening rolled around and it was time for Roberta to leave. She promised to write, and I promised to *try* to write. I wanted to drive up and see her off. But I would have to remain here to show Mr. Kaufman the cattle. It was probably for the best anyway. Anything after the past two days that we had spent together would have been anticlimactic. Hell, I thought, if we married and stayed that way for fifty years, we might never get another lick like we had these past two days.

As I mentioned this to Roberta, through tears of goodbye she smiled. "Don't forget the nights," I said. "If I die tomorrow, I die a happy man."

"Don't you dare" were her last words as she threw me a kiss and left.

As I watched her drive off in the blue evening haze, the dust rising and suspending over the road in the stillness, I wondered if I'd made the right decision in letting her go. I'd miss her something terrible.

I watched until she was plumb out of sight before I bowed my head and turned back to do my chores. A feeling of emptiness and loneliness, to the point of quiet desperation, began to creep over me.

Thank God for Belle! She stayed by my side as I went about my business. After I'd finished up and was sitting on the saddle house porch watching the sun sink below the horizon, a glint, like that of a mirror flashing, caught my eye. And though I sat there, same spot, same time of day, many times, never had I noticed this reflection of light. I tried to dismiss it, but again and again, it caught my eye. Finally out of curiosity, I got up and walked straight toward whatever was glistening. I came to realize, as I peered through the fence of the round corral, a ray of sun had caught the copper stain that now was a part of the old snubbing post. It was that which had caught my eye. I smiled as I thought of the significance.

I was absorbed in this phenomenon, this marvel of nature, when Belle let me know someone was coming. A little while after Roberta left everyone returned. Everyone, that is, except Poke and the old lady. Miz T. looked well, though plumb tuckered. She seemed happy. But between Lupe and Tio, and for that matter everybody, in an excited state telling me what had taken place over the past few days, everything was lost and jumbled.

Miz T. went to the house to rest. Tio and Lupe, still excited, returned to their home. And only then, with R.C. and Kika, could I ask what had taken place. Kika, surprisingly, reached up, grabbed me around the neck, and gave me a kiss on the cheek. "What's that for?" I said.

"That's for Dad. You made him a very happy man."

"*I* didn't have that much to do with it. This gentleman here," as I motioned toward R.C., "was the instigator of the whole thing."

Kika, with her hands still on my arm, said, "It took you both. And Dad told me to tell you that he sends many thanks and will forever be in your debt for this wonderful thing that you have done for him. He, like many, feel it was truly a miracle."

I dismissed all of this as modestly as I could. But I was curious as to what went on. We walked over and sat down on the rock ledge around the lawn, as first one, and then the other, told me about Diego's reaction to our discovery.

"Frank," R.C. said, "at first he could hardly believe it! Then I told him the story."

"What'd he say?" I asked.

"He said nothing. He just listened, shaking his head in disbelief."

"Did you tell him," and hesitated, "everything?"

"Everything," R.C. said.

"Well, I'm not too pleased with having to dig up a priest's body. He didn't object to that?"

Kika chimed in. "Frank, of course he didn't. He wondered why he hadn't thought of it. The message on the headstone, if you thought about it, was clear. But no, it doesn't bother him, Frank. The only one it bothered," and Kika and R.C. looked at one another and laughed, "is poor Poke."

"What about him?" I said.

"Well," R.C. said, "his Irish superstitions began to run away with him. He convinced himself that we had committed a mortal sin. He harped on it to the parish priest until I believe he's gonna get that priest over here to bless the grave. I'm almost sure he'll get it done. Either that or he'll drive the priest completely crazy. He seems obsessed with it, Frank."

I laughed. "That sounds like Poke all right. Then what happened?"

Kika said, "Dad sent Miguel to the phone and had him call the priest and tell him what we'd found. He in turn called the bishop, and from there it was just the grapevine. Sunday morning everyone showed up, including the archbishop, the vicar general, several monsignors from different parishes up and down the Rio Grande and through the Sangre de Cristo parishes. We had a fiesta, Frank, and rightfully so. A celebration was called for."

"And then," R.C. said, "the procession."

Kika smiled happily and clapped her hands. "Yes, a procession. From our house, down the road to the church, the archbishop carrying the monstrance that shone like a second sun in the sky. Oh, Frank, I wish you could have been there! It was truly something to see. The altar boys holding banners, the banner of St. James, Santiago, with the family crest on it, and the Virgin of Guadalupe banner. People came from near and far, Frank, and fell in behind the procession. The church couldn't hold them all."

"Every politician, too," R.C. said.

Kika smiled. "That's true. Especially those that are up for reelection next term. Then the archbishop held mass."

"What did he have to say?" I asked.

R.C. shrugged. "I didn't understand a word. It was all in Spanish. But Kika told me the general gist of the thing."

Kika frowned at R.C. "It wasn't a 'thing.' It was a sermon."

"Sermon, then," R.C. said.

"His sermon," Kika said, "was based on hope and faith, and the belief of miracles, and the power of the Lord. He was quite dynamic."

"Being archbishop," I said, "I can imagine. You don't get a position like that by luck."

"Then after mass," R.C. said, "the fiesta, the music. Everyone fixed their own specialty and brought it. Kind of a potluck, you might say. I ate until I almost foundered. Is that the word, Frank?"

I nodded.

"I wished you'd have been there. It was something," R.C. said.

"Yeah," I said. "I wished I could've been there, too."

Kika turned to R.C. "I'll bet Aunt Teresa would appreciate it if you got her things out of the trunk, R.C."

As R.C. got up to do her bidding, Kika looked at me and smiled. "It was a great tonic for Aunt Teresa. Both Abuela Elena and myself were going to stay with her this next week. She insisted that now she'd be all right. Sooner or later she would have to accept being alone, and insisted that we leave her."

"You're not staying then?"

Kika shook her head. "I just came back to get my car. The fiesta's still going on. Probably will all night. But tomorrow Dad takes the papers to Santa Fe. And there, we think, the land problem will cease to exist."

"Good. I'm glad to hear it."

Kika glanced over at R.C., who was carrying a bag into the house, and looked back at me and smiled. "Did you have company while we gone, Frank?" She caught me by surprise.

But I wasn't going to lie about it. "Ah, as a matter of fact, I did. How did you know?"

Kika, still smiling, said, "When I gave you a kiss on the cheek."

"What about it?"

She looked at me in a chiding, playful manner. "I smelled a mixed scent, not just yours."

"Are you saying I have a particular smell?"

"Yes. All men do."

"Well, I'll have to start being more careful around you. I'd hate to offend you."

She threw back her head and laughed. "You never have. Your scent is quite," and she searched for a word, "attractive, in its own way. But the other scent, the other smell, was that of a woman. I think of a particular woman."

I held up both hands like I was under arrest. "Okay, okay. Roberta was here."

Still smiling, Kika said, "I knew it! Did you have a good time?"

"Better than good."

"I'm glad to hear it. Very glad."

"Damn, Kika, you're better than a bloodhound. I'll have to keep this in mind. I'd sure hate to swallow something right before prayer meeting and have you come around. I could get in a great lot of trouble."

Kika just laughed. "I'm on your side, Frank. And trust me. I'll never tell."

I spent a great lot of time going over every scenario and every possible curve that Mr. Kaufman might throw me in the selling of the cattle. I was trying to prepare myself for something I'd never done before: deal with a traditionally tough negotiator when it came to cattle. I felt severely undergunned.

I found Mr. Kaufman much easier to get along with and to visit with than I had anticipated. He had a genuine interest in how the country looked, commenting on everything he saw. When we got to the ranch he immediately wanted to pay his respects to Miz T. Only then would we look at cattle.

As I drove him out to show him our yearlings, he made the comment, "Frank, I've never seen your country look better." It took me back. "My country!" It wasn't my country. I didn't own it. I just managed it. But as he continued, I realized it wasn't a quick flip-flop of loyalty from the Boss to curry my favor. It was simply a statement of fact. I lived in this country, and you might say, this whole part of the state was my country. I realized his meaning, appreciated it, and had to agree. It had never looked better.

We didn't talk money until after he'd seen all the cattle. And this was the part I'd been dreading.

"What am I gonna have to give to own these cattle, Frank?"

I shrugged my shoulders and tried the one thing that I'd decided, after his answer, that I'd never try again. "What would you give, Mr. Kaufman?"

With a smile and looking me straight in the eye, he said, "Frank, I can't buy 'em and sell 'em both. You've got to have a price. What is it?"

I could understand his reasoning. So I told him. He nodded his head and surprisingly said, "You're pretty well right on the mark, Frank. That's just about what they're worth." It was the "just about" that worried me.

He smiled. "I know it used to take J.W. and me all day to deal on his cattle, but we enjoyed it. But, Frank, I think you've got the cattle priced fairly and you've done a good job with 'em. So, except for a minor change I wanta make this year, we've got a deal, providing you are agreeable with the change."

This caught me by surprise. "What change is that, Mr. Kaufman?"

"Well, you know how you always used to weigh the cattle here with a three percent shrink, early of a mornin'?" I nodded my head to all this. This was standard. The three percent shrink took care of the water and feed in their bellies.

"This year," Mr. Kaufman continued, "I'll contract my own trucks. They will come here to the ranch, load up, and we'll not ship them by rail. I'll truck them back home to Illinois."

I had heard of double-deck trucks, but they were so top-heavy that they could not, in my opinion, negotiate the type of roads that we had in this country, and told him so.

"Frank," he said, "they've come out with a new cattle truck. They call 'em 'possum bellies,' where the bed of the truck dips down between the rear tires of the trailer and the front tires. It's double-decked in the middle, but with a low center of gravity. It's got compartments in it, and loaded correctly, will revolutionize the transporting of cattle."

This was news to me. I had never heard of a 'possum bellied' cattle truck, much less seen one. But he assured me it would work. "Can these trucks get down the hill and cross the ford?"

"No problem at all," he assured me.

"Then we won't have the expense of hiring trucks to take them to town?"

"Exactly. And I would like an adjustment in price because of it. It's less expense to you, the same expense to me. However, I think the cattle will arrive at my place in better condition in a shorter time than by rail."

I agreed. I understood his thinking.

He said he'd write up a contract. I told him there was no need. A handshake would seal the deal. But he wouldn't stand for it. "Just between you and me," he said, "and this being our first time to trade together, we don't want to get anything cross-threaded. I'll give you a ten-dollar deposit per head, and mark it part-payment, not forfeit," and smiled. "That way, we'll dot all the i's, cross all the t's, remain friends, and live to trade another day."

I had completed my first cattle trade, and I felt right proud of myself. And if the cattle weighed anywhere near what he thought they'd weigh, I'd really be happy. As far as I was concerned, I'd just killed a fat bear!

In the meantime, I had a bunch to do. It was almost overwhelming.

On Friday morning R.C. asked if he could run to town to pick up his mail. He still received no mail at the ranch. Everything came general delivery to Dorsey. Although we had work to do, I knew it was important to R.C.

It was late morning when he drove back into headquarters. I was up at the barns, and as I watched him come toward me, I knew something was wrong. He didn't waste any time or mince any words when he started talking.

"Frank, I hate to tell you this," and he seemed to be looking for an easier way to put it, couldn't find it, and continued. "I've got to go."

I still hadn't caught on. "Go where?"

"Go. Leave. Quit."

I couldn't believe my ears. "Quit work? Now?"

"I'm afraid so."

"Why?" I said. "And it'd better be a damned good reason. We've got cattle to ship, in just ten days! We've got a lot of work to do. Jim's gone. How can ya leave me now?"

"Believe me," R.C. said, "I feel as bad about it as you do. But, Frank, I can't help it. I've got to go."

"Well, couldn't you put it off 'til . . ." and he interrupted me.

"It can't be put off. I've got to leave. Today! As a matter of fact, right now."

This all took me by such surprise, for once in my life I was practically speechless. I just stood there and looked at him. I had not realized what an asset he had been until I thought about him leaving. Besides that fact, we had become good friends, even closer than friends if that's possible. But there seemed nothing that I could do to change his mind.

"So, you wanta draw your wages?"

He nodded his head yes.

"I'll go write the check."

"I'll pack," R.C. said.

While writing the check I decided not to prorate his month's salary, just give him the entire month as a bonus. He'd been worth it, even though he was leaving at the worst possible time. Miz T. wasn't even there. She'd gone to town that morning. This would come as a blow to her.

When I got back to the bunkhouse, I handed him the check. He looked at it. "Frank, it's too much."

"A bonus," I said. "You deserve it."

He hurriedly folded it, stuck it in his pocket, and said, "Thanks, but it wasn't necessary."

"Are you going over to see Francesca, tell her goodbye? You owe her that, R.C."

R.C. shook his head. "There's not time. You tell her, Frank. She'll understand."

"I don't wanta pry. I know it must be important, or you wouldn't do this. Is there anything I can do?"

"I can handle it, if I get there in time."

I didn't know what he meant by that, but I'd never seen him so deadly serious. "Will you stay in touch?" I asked.

R.C. gave me a quick glance as he threw stuff in the suitcases. "You can count on it!"

"Will you come back?"

R.C. stopped and said with conviction, "I'll be back, Frank. You can put that in the bank."

"Do you have any idea when?"

"As soon as I get this matter taken care of. But it might be awhile." And he said as an afterthought, "It might be a long while."

"Is there anyplace I can reach ya? Or Kika, if we wanta get a message to ya?"

Again R.C. stopped and thought. "No. I'm afraid there's not. I know this is sudden, and I know it sounds mysterious, Frank. But I think you know me well enough by now to understand that I just can't tell you everything. Perhaps someday I will."

"You're right. I don't understand. But I think I have an inkling. I don't understand the immediate problem, but I think I do understand why you came here and why you stayed."

This seemed to catch R.C. by surprise. "You do?" he said.

"Yep. I think Top hit the nail on the head. Remember back when he said he thought you were an author and writing a book? And the answers you gave him? It was the truth, wasn't it? You are writing a book. But you played Top off, and me, and everybody else for that matter, and fooled us with the truth."

R.C. smiled. "I told you, Frank, perhaps before too long I can tell you the truth. Beyond that, I won't confirm or deny anything."

That was good enough for me. Now I was almost positive I was right. "Well, let me tell ya somethin', pard. Most books written about the West and about the life of a cowboy have been written by men that came out here, observed what was going on from a Pullman car or the seat of a buckboard, went back, and wrote about it. Owen Wister, Zane Grey, just to name two. But few have come out and lived the life and tried to fit in. Hell, in your case, you didn't try to fit in, you did fit in. And whether you know it or not, now you're one of us. So, if that's what you're doin', when you write remember us as we are, R.C., and treat us kindly."

By this time R.C. had everything gathered up. With a smile, he said, "If that's what I'm doing, rest assured I'll treat you kindly."

"Not me. Us."

"Us, as in you and me?"

I nodded my head. "You, me, and all the other honest-to-God cowboys that live the life. What about your tack and all the belongin's up at the saddle house? You can't leave without all your belongin's. They're the tools of your trade."

"Where I'm going, I don't need 'em. Keep 'em, Frank. That's proof I'll be back."

True. No cowboy would ever go off and leave his saddle. If it had really taken on R.C., he would be back. And I told him, "You know, I've heard said that back in the old days on the cattle drives, most of the punchers were just kids. Once they got a few trips under their belts and got the wildness out of the blood, they took up another occupation. But again it's been said, if you stay in this business 'til you're thirty, or thereabouts, you'll remain in it or on the fringes of it for the rest of your life. You've got a few years to go before that thirty mark. But we hate to lose a good hand, just because he was a few years shy of an old wives' tale."

R.C. looked at me and extended his hand. "I don't plan to be on the fringes of it, Frank. I plan to be in the middle, 'til the day I die." He still had ahold of my hand, and we found that that wasn't enough. A quick embrace, a slap on the back, and he jumped in Sundown, cranked her up, and with a wink he said, "Look for me when you see me comin'."

My only reply was, "Swing a big loop."

R.C. nodded. "Always."

I watched as he drove off. His cowboying days, probably, were gone forever. But the phrase "swing a big loop" still applied. He knew what I meant.

CHAPTER

37

Ol' Blue groaned when I downshifted into low gear as I crossed the creek and started up the feed road in the Martinez pasture. I rolled down my window and squalled in a coarse falsetto, "Wooo," then quickly rolled up the window and began honking the horn. I was loaded down with cottonseed cake and trying to draw the cows out of the rough breaks of the Martinez and up onto the flat, tight country, before I started feeding. That way I wouldn't waste too much feed.

I'd heard the wind get up sometime during the night, and when dawn broke we had the makings of a honest-to-God blue norther. It was just a pup right now, but by the looks of it, it was going to be full growed before too very awful long.

"Shit!" I muttered under my breath. I looked down at Belle, who sat in the seat beside me panting. "Nothin' personal," I told her. It's just that the weather matched my mood. It was the last day of January, and quite possibly my last day on the job at the Cross S. I still couldn't believe it, but the Cross S, the Piedra, was in the process of being sold. Tomorrow being the first of February was the so-called closing date.

It was back in the latter part of November when Miz T. had called me in for a talk. It was then she dropped the bomb. She was lonesome and had a more-than-fair offer from an eastern syndicate out of Boston to buy the ranch. A turnkey deal, lock, stock, and barrel, including all the hired help to remain in their present jobs after the deal was finalized. I doubted that. I had a feeling soon as those Yankees saw the ink dry on the contract, I'd get hit in the ass with a paycheck.

I rolled down the window and squalled again, hoping that the wind didn't catch my voice and carry it on south before our cattle heard it. Could be that squall would end up in Mexico, and those people down there would be awondering why all their cattle were gathered up.

The visibility was getting bad. Snow wasn't falling down like most people think of a snowstorm. It was going by horizontally. Not much would accumulate on the ground. But anything of any size, from sagebrush to a barn, it would drift behind and build up to the same height as whatever caused it to start drifting in the first place.

Our first bad weather had started back in the early part of December. From then on, the storms were apt to come at any time. It was like somebody left the gate open at the North Pole. Once they started they wouldn't quit until late spring. It seemed that's when the worst ones happened, after the calves were on the ground. It could put a man out of business. But I don't know what in the hell I was worried about. I had a feeling I was going to be out of business anyway.

When we reached the top and the land flattened out, I stopped, left the motor running with the heater going full blast, and waited for the cattle. Even though the visibility was down to about two hundred yards, I reckoned, though I couldn't see any cattle, they'd come. That cottonseed cake was like chocolate bonbons to a chocolate addict.

I sat and brooded and scratched Belle's ears as she panted happily. Between the heater and her winter coat of hair, she was more than warm. Me, long handles and all, was just barely comfortable, so I left the heater on and let her pant.

It depressed me to think of the ranch selling. I'd gotten through the last couple of months by trying to keep it out of my mind. Not that I blamed Miz T. It was her ranch, her money, her life. I couldn't understand why she just didn't move to town and retain ownership. But then, who'd live in the big house?

So when she'd asked me for my thoughts, I had no option except to tell her, "Do as you wish and we'll all make the best of it." It was no time to be thinking of myself. Miz T. had been through a lot and I would respect her wishes, even though I was disappointed.

As I looked out the window I could see a few ghostly forms of cattle slowly making their way up out of the breaks and coming toward me. It'd be awhile before I had them all gathered. I had to wait 'til all that were coming got there before I started feeding.

No sense sitting here and brooding. I tried to listen to the radio but found that my tangled mind kept going back in time. It had been over four months since R.C. left, and I missed him. The only thing that held me together were the weekly letters that I got from Roberta. They were my chocolate bonbons. I read and reread those letters many times. Even smelled them. Not that she had dredged them with perfume or cologne. They just smelled like her, the scent. And that's what I savored.

But no word from R.C. Not yea, nay, go to hell, or nothing. Only two things had happened that I knew he was responsible for. One was about a week after he had left. Poke got a letter from the airport up in Dorsey. A fellow that owned the flying service notified Poke that there was a pickup being kept in a hangar for him. In that letter was the title to Ol' Sundown, signed over to Poke by R.C. Roth. I took Poke to town to pick it up and when we questioned the man he seemed as perplexed as we were.

He said a fellow drove up in that pickup, chartered a flight in one of his little puddle-jumpers to Amarillo, and asked him to send the title to Poke Mahone. The only thing the man remembered was R.C. saying, "I have a friend who's afoot. And since I won't be needing it, he might as well have it."

And second, around Christmastime, I got a notification from the post office in town that I had an insured package. I believe it was the day before Christmas that I picked it up. No card, no letter. Just a large cardboard box from Kalamazoo, Michigan. I got it home and opened it up to find a Gibson Super 400, the guitar of my dreams. I knew where that came from, too. It had to be R.C. But, shit! It seemed like he'd at least take credit for it or enclose a "Happy Holidays" or "Merry Christmas." But no. Nothing but the box. But what a guitar! I'd keep it forever.

Frequently when I'd see Kika I'd ask her if she'd heard from R.C. And always the answer was a shake of the head, no, with downcast eyes. Funny thing, she always remained happy and full of life. Just like always. Perhaps even more so. Now if that made sense, I didn't see it. Maybe she didn't care. But I could hardly believe that.

A fair amount of cattle had made their way up out of the breaks and began milling around the pickup. You could feel the pickup sway as they bumped into it trying to reach the sacks and get a little taste. It was time for Belle to do her job. I opened the door and let her out. She made one circle around the pickup clearing all the cattle back a ways, then made two bounds. A slick little trick she'd picked up: jump, front feet hitting the bumper that protruded from the back of Ol' Blue, then almost in the same motion bounding up on top of the tailgate to get on top of the sacks that were stacked upright in the back of the bed. There, wind, snow, and all, she patrolled. If any cow got too close, she slithered over on her belly, ears laid back, and nipped at the cow's nose. She was in full control.

My thoughts wandered off again, as it appeared only about half of the cattle were here yet.

No sooner had the dust cleared of R.C.'s leaving, than I realized that I was the foreman of a ranch with no crew, discounting Tio of course. He did just as he damn pleased. It was then I'd decided to go to town and try to find Jim. I had to order our winter supply of cake and hay anyway. I didn't figure it'd be too hard to find Jim, unless he'd completely left the country, which was highly unlikely. What shape I was going to find him in was the question.

I'd first checked in at Widow Hayes's home on the west side of the tracks. I knew that Jim had been spending time there on our little forays to town. And if I'm not mistaken, I think Jim and the widow had gone back a long ways to when they were kids. I'd heard it said that Mrs. Hayes's folks had homesteaded, like Jim's, down in our end of the county.

After knocking on the door, I was not surprised to see a woman who at one time must have been quite attractive, but a hard life and hard times had taken their toll. It was well known she took in laundry and ironing for some of the more prominent citizens of Dorsey. When I inquired about Jim, she looked at me with sad eyes, and said, "Yes, he was here. But I finally had to run him off." She must have seen a questioning look on my face and felt as though she needed to explain.

"I'm not big on temperance," she said, "but Jim kept drinking like they were gonna quit makin' it. And as much as I think of him, I couldn't sit by and watch him go to ruin. I had to ask him to leave. I don't know where he is."

I tipped my hat, thanked her, and said I'd try to find him.

"When you do," the widow said, "tell him I'd welcome him back if he'd just meet me halfway." I nodded in agreement.

I checked the jail, and sure enough, Jim had been a regular customer. He had not stolen anything or committed any crime other than being a public nuisance, a drunk, the jailer said. Not even disorderly. But they'd find him drunk, throw him in the tank, only to let him out in the morning. And this happened on more than several occasions.

So after tending to my business, I just drove around looking for him. It's hard to get lost in a little bitty town like Dorsey. And sure enough, I found him behind Kitchins in the alley going through the trash trying to find a little something to eat, or a little something to drink. And not necessarily in that order. He was filthy. For a moment it even crossed my mind that he might not even know who I was. But as I touched his arm, he raised his head out of the trash can and you could tell he was thoroughly pickled with alcohol, his eyes set in an alcohol gaze, unblinking.

I heard him mumble, "Frank."

I'd made up my mind that I was going to handle it as diplomatically as I could. But one way or the other, he was going home with me. Even if I had to deck him and load him in the back end of the pickup.

"Jim," I said, "don't you think this is enough? It's time to go home."

"Home?" like he didn't know what I was talking about.

"Yeah. Back to the ranch. You remember where that is, don't ya?"

"Uh huh," he said and pointed north.

Jesus Christ! He was so drunk he couldn't even point straight! The ranch was south!

He was in pretty good shape, though not real talkative, the day we delivered the heifers. It was quite a sight to look down the road and see these newfangled, shiny trucks coming one after the other, like a train down our road. It was even more of a wonder after we had gathered and penned the cattle and the first truck had backed up to the loading chute, to walk inside of what these Illinois truckers called possum-bellied trucks. They were the damnedest things I'd ever seen!

As you might have guessed, it was Egg Robbins who had seen one before, the only one of our crew who had.

"Shit," Egg said, "Possums are as scarce as hens' teeth in this country. That's what they call 'em back East. Out here people are just callin' 'em 'potbellies,' 'pots' for short."

Now that made sense.

By now it appeared that all the cattle that were going to come were here. The snow was flying by and the wind was blowing even harder, so I took off my wildrag, put it over the top of my hat, pulled the edge of my hat down over my ears, and tied my wildrag in a knot under my chin. I may not have looked too stylish, but it'd damn sure keep my ears from freezing and my hat blowing to hell and gone!

I put Ol' Blue in granny, compound, started it moving slowly, pulled out the throttle just a hair where the truck just crept along, and stepped outside. As the truck went by I climbed on the back end, cut the string, and started pouring out cottonseed cake, sack after sack, until they got their determined share of four pounds a head. We did this every other day.

When I was through, I stepped out on the ground and had to jog very little to catch up with the pickup, opened the door and stepped inside, made a circle, and came back along to count them. The cattle were strung out a good two hundred yards. I rolled down the window, stuck my hand out, and began to count. You have to use your hands to count cattle. As far as I was concerned it was impossible to count cattle any other way. For every head, you dipped your hand. When I was through I wasn't surprised to have my count. Every cow had shown up.

I let Belle back in the cab of Ol' Blue and we started back down into the breaks. We had to feed the south Tinsley pasture, but I'd have to go down where the cattle were and start calling them up. They'd never hear me in this wind.

As we crept back down the road, my mind wandered back in time to when Miz T. had asked me if there was a possibility that I could put in cattle guards, two of them, up to the old mission and graveyard. She'd said she'd like to go up and visit J.W., Sonny, and Tres's graves, but didn't want to have to ask anybody to go with her to open the gates. I told her I'd see to it.

Jim had been acting kind of surly up to that point. When I asked him about it he had said, "Ah, it's not you, Frank. It's just with the Boss gone I can't hardly stand it."

When I mentioned to him about the cattle guards, he said, "Frank, I'll tell ya what. I know delivery's startin' around the country and you're gonna hafta be gone helpin' our friends. So I'll build the cattle guards, dig the holes, pour the concrete, myself. I don't want no help. Because it's the last damn thing I'm ever gonna do on this ranch!"

This surprised me. I told him I'd help him and together we could get it done in half the time. But he declined, saying, "No, this is personal, Frank. I wanna do this myself. I still got some of that booze to sweat out of my system. It'll do me good."

When I asked about what he meant about the last thing he'd do, he'd said, "I'm quittin' as soon as I'm through."

I'd tried to talk him out of it, saying we couldn't get along without him and that this had been his home for too long. But his mind was set.

When I'd asked him what he would do, he replied, "It's just wishful thinkin' 'cause I don't have the money. But I'd sure like to open me up a windmillin' business. If there's anything I know about, it's fences and windmills. But I don't reckon it'll happen. It takes money that I ain't got."

After thinking on this awhile, I told Miz T. of Jim's intentions. She, too, was surprised but could understand. She called Jim in, talked to him, and wrote him out a check for five thousand dollars to get started on. Not a loan, and not a gift, but as a bonus for his faithful service for all these many years. Jim was speechless. And for the first time I saw tears well up in his eyes as he turned away, expressing his gratitude.

I let Jim go his own way then and took him to town to the Widow Hayes's house, after he'd finished the cattle guards. But during that time, through the last of September and practically all of October, I spent helping our friends deliver their cattle.

It was my favorite time of the year. Cold, brisk mornings, the leaves turning on the cottonwoods, and really nothing but cowboy work, a-horseback, 'til it was over. Our cattle, again, weighed heavier than any that had come off the place that I could find in the records. The Boss would have been proud. It was quite a feeling when I had the check in my pocket and took it to Dalhart to the bank.

It was easy to see how the song "When the Work's All Done This Fall" was put together out in cow country. It was a good time to be a cowboy. The sandhill cranes, with wingspans of over eight feet, flew in V formation toward the south, and you knew it wouldn't be long 'til the work would all be done this fall.

It was quite a shock to suddenly realize that I was driving up the feed road in the south Tinsley pasture. That meant I'd gone down to the bottom, through a gate, without even knowing it, like I was sleepwalking. I'd been so deep in thought, it was kind of scary. I began honking the horn and calling cattle, just as before, when my mind slipped back into the past again.

When I'd gone over to help ship at the Cannon outfit, it was a long, drawn-out affair. We didn't have those pot-bellied trucks, we had straight forties. And their cattle, being Corrientes, were not going to Illinois. They were going to the railhead at Tramperos to be put on the train for Bakersfield, California. So after we had all the cattle gathered, weighed, and the trucks loaded for the first time, because of the numbers of the cattle, we had time to sit around, take a chew, smoke a little, while the trucks made their way to Tramperos and doubled back. That continued all through the day and part of the night.

It was there that I found out that the Cannon place had sold. Top had got it straight from Jack Cannon himself. I was positive of who bought it: Bernie Mueller, hiding behind the Anderson law firm. Only to find out when the question was asked and answered honestly by Top, to hear Top say, "Eastern investors, I reckon. Anyhow, a law firm of Stein, Rothchild, and Kelly are representin' 'em. Two Jews and an Irishman," Top said. "That oughta be a piss-cuttin' outfit if I ever saw one," he laughed, and so did everybody else.

It was not uncommon for easterners to buy ranches. They were mostly absentee owners. For that matter, it was not uncommon in the early days for American ranches to be owned by foreign investors, especially from Scotland. For instance, there was the Matador, run by Murdo MacKenzie, a Scotsman and a hell of a cowboy in his own right. A legend, you might say.

Still, I wondered what position that left Diego's state land in. Perhaps Bernie Mueller was even in on that. There was no way of telling. We'd have to wait and see.

That's when the conversation turned to a lighter note.

Someone in the bunch said, "Say, did you see Fracus Daller and ol' Early Wright have a fight this mornin'?"

I knew both men. Both of them had to be in their seventies. They were what we called "commission men." Not order buyers. They got on the average a dollar a head as a kind of finder's fee for locating cattle for out-of-state buyers. I couldn't imagine the two old farts having a fight, so I just listened.

Someone said, "Surely you're puttin' us on. Neither one of 'em could whack the dust out of their own britches."

"Nah!" the one telling the story said. "I seen 'em."

"Who won?" I asked, trying to visualize the fight.

"Neither one, as near as I could tell."

"How'd it come about?" someone else asked.

"Hell, I don't know. I reckon they were fightin' over their cut of that dollar a head. Anyways, the funny part about it is, there was a fence between 'em!"

"Yessir," the storyteller said, "they both took off their jackets, spit on their hands, and went to tryin' to punch one another between the slats of the fence. They put their dukes up, danced around a little bit, and directly one of 'em would jab at the other through the fence. He'd back away and then ol' Fracus, he'd come up and swing a haymaker. Through the fence, o' course. I watched 'em there for a little while and said, 'Boys, you all are wastin' your time. There's the gate down yonder just a short ways.' Both of 'em looked at me and said, 'You fight your way and we'll fight ours. If we need any help we'll let ya know.' "

We all laughed. I hadn't heard of a fence fight before, but it sounded like a good way to keep from getting hurt.

Belle and I found ourselves out of the breaks and up on the flats in the Tinsley pasture, and again it was surprising how we got there, all the while me being so deep in thought. Cattle were beginning to come in, slower than ever because the norther was picking up steam.

Poke was in the power wagon over on the north side of the creek feeding. I hoped he wasn't having hell. Cattle would be reluctant to crawl out of a protected area and put their faces into a storm like this.

It was over at the Cannon shipping when I'd asked Poke what he was planning to do soon as the cattle were all gone.

Poke had just grinned real big and said, "Wait for you to come beg me to come over there and help ya out. I know Jim's leavin' and you need a top hand. And looks like I'm your man."

I'd studied on it a minute and allowed that he was right, the first time we'd ever agreed on anything. So I did offer him a job. And as expected, he'd accepted. And, he showed up two days later in Ol' Sundown with a suitcase, a warbag, his saddle and tack. All his worldly possessions.

When I peered in the back of the pickup, he grinned and said, "When I move I don't have to call the Mayflower van."

"Throw 'em in the bunkhouse," was my only reply.

What was surprising was the day after that, Top showing up. He knew as well as I did what needed to be done, some sorting and shifting around getting ready for winter. All of it horseback work. I think he'd have done it for nothing, out of respect for the Boss. But we paid him anyhow.

After the work was done, he'd shaken our hands, and with a wink, said, "I'll see you boys down the road," and pulled out, for God knew where.

CHAPTER

38

If I remember rightly, 'long about the first week in December when somebody let that gate down up north and the first storm hit, Miz T.'d called me in and asked me about my ideas on selling the ranch. From then on, it was kind of downhill until Roberta came back for Christmas. By that time I'd found out that money was in escrow and that same Boston law firm of Stein, Rothchild, and Kelly was representing the buyer. If what I'd heard was true, they'd damn sure bit off a chunk. They had the Piedra and the Cannon place. I waited to see what was going to happen to Diego's state land. I even went as far as to ask Kika about it. She shrugged and said that her dad hadn't heard a word. Things were going on just as they always had.

When Roberta came back on Christmas vacation I gave her all the details. As usual, she was more positive about the situation than I was.

"Frank," she said, "if they said nothing will change, I've gotta believe it."

Somehow, I didn't. It festered in my mind until it almost drove me crazy.

I'd been doing a lot of thinking this morning, but I was getting my work done. It appeared that I had everything gathered in the south Tinsley that needed feeding, so I went ahead, scattered the feed, and got my count. Came up a shade short of the count. But I wasn't too worried. I knew all the cattle were in good shape that were in that pasture, and evidently a few had decided they'd rather stay down and stay warm than to come up for their goodies.

So, I turned Ol' Blue toward the headquarters. It was way past dinnertime, but that didn't matter. When you fed, it was important and you did it right, however long it took. I just hoped Poke wasn't running too late.

When I pulled into the headquarters I noticed Kika's car parked over by the big house. Strange, I thought. A hell of a day for somebody to come visiting. I pulled on into the barn and saw that Poke wasn't back yet. I stacked all my empty cake sacks and made my way to the house. Tio, Lupe, and Kika were all having a cup of coffee with Miz T. I howdyed all of them and since it'd been awhile since I'd seen Kika, she came over and gave me a hug. We had become more than good friends and I expected and returned the affection.

As always, the first question I asked her whenever I saw her was, "Have you heard from R.C.?"

Although she shook her head no, she seemed rather flushed and excited about something. I'd heard them talking rapidly in Spanish as I came through the back door. Only when I entered did they switch back to English. Maybe something had happened that I didn't know about, but nobody seemed to volunteer any information. I got a cup of hot coffee, Lupe began to make me a sandwich, and I sat down trying to get warm, comfortable, and listened to what was going on. Most of the conversation revolved around the blizzard that was taking place.

It was not long before I heard Belle barking. I got up to look and I saw Belle heading out to the barn, and I knew Poke was back. I was kind of relieved. Soon he joined us in the kitchen. I asked him how it went.

He shivered his shoulders and said, "Whoo. It was a booger. But made out fairly well. Practically all of them came in to feed. If this keeps up, reckon we're gonna have to feed some hay, Frank?"

"Just depends. As hard as it's blowin' I don't think the grass will cover up. But we might have some trouble with our yearlings tomorrow."

Poke nodded his head. "Could be."

Poke and I both ate slowly, talking to one another, listening to the conversation between Miz T. and Kika, which involved nothing of importance as far as I was concerned.

Then that sinking feeling came back over me again as I asked Miz T., "Is the sale of the ranch, the closing, still takin' place tomorrow?"

Miz T. nodded her head yes. "As far as I know. Unless," she said hesitating, "the weather causes . . ." again she hesitated, "our eastern buyers problems." That's all I needed to know and I let the matter drop.

Again, I heard Belle barking. I got up, looked out the window to see a brand-new, red and white, four-wheel-drive Chevy pickup pull into the driveway by the side of the house. Odd, I thought. I don't know anybody that owns a red and white pickup, especially new. Most people coming to visit would have parked in front of the house. But whoever this was acted like he knew where he was going, assuming it was a man.

Belle was on the other side of the pickup. It was snowing so hard I couldn't see who was in it, but knew that they would probably be threatened by the dog if they didn't know her. However, whoever it was opened the door, climbed out, and bent over to where I couldn't see anything. Then I realized whoever it was must be petting my dog. Or, the dog had whoever it was down.

I started to call the dog off, or at least find out what was happening, when around the corner came a familiar face. Lo and behold, standing before me was R.C.!

"Hello, Frank," he said with a big smile.

I could hardly believe my eyes.

"Good godalmighty! Look who's here!" While shaking his hand and giving him a bear hug with the other, I expressed my delight in seeing him again. But I had to get out of the way fast because Kika was moving in swiftly.

She leapt into his arms, and we all had to stand back and give them a little time until they realized that perhaps they were making all of us a little uncomfortable. Then everyone greeted him with handshakes and with everybody talking at once. I realized that probably this was the reason Kika was here. She knew he was coming in today and maybe with a little apprehension over the weather.

Anyhow, we fired questions at him and didn't get an answer because he was firing questions at us just as rapidly. Finally we made our way off the back porch and into the kitchen.

"Stand back, pard," I said, "and let me survey you here."

The hat he was wearing was the best they made, shaped just right, a red wildrag around his neck, a fleece-lined leather jacket over his shoulders, Wrangler britches, custom-made boots.

I shook my head and said, "Bein' away hasn't damaged you any. It appears you might have prospered a little."

R.C. laughed and shook his head. "Now, Frank, you didn't expect me to revert back to my old ways, did ya?"

I grinned. "Not hardly. But what on God's earth brought ya back this time of year and in this weather?"

R.C. smiled and looked rather uncomfortable. "Ah, business," he said. He had everybody's attention.

"Well, if you're lookin' for a job," I said, "we've got some troubles, pard. I got news for ya."

"Oh, what's that?"

"The ranch is sold. We're closing tomorrow."

The smile never left R.C.'s lips as he said, "Is that right?"

"Yep. Far's I know. They say they're gonna keep everybody that's on the payroll, but maybe I can talk 'em into keepin' you. That is, if you're lookin' for a job."

R.C. laid his hat down on an empty chair and said, "Well, to tell you the truth, I'm not lookin' for a job."

I felt a sinking sensation in the pit of my stomach. But I thought to myself, Maybe this isn't all bad. If he's got something going somewhere, maybe I'll go with him. Maybe both Poke and I'll go with him.

R.C. appeared to turn serious all of a sudden, and said, "Frank, sit down. I've got some things I need to tell you."

I did, and he began.

"This is gonna be kinda hard for me to explain, so if you'll bear with me, I'll try."

Nobody said a word.

"I guess the best way to start is at the beginning and with the truth."

With the truth, I thought, as my eyebrows raised. It had never dawned on me that R.C. had ever told me anything but the truth.

R.C. began. "I didn't tell you the truth for a reason. And I hope you can accept my reason. My name isn't Roth. My name is Raymond Cornelius Rothchild."

When he said "Rothchild," it struck a nerve. But still I was confused.

"I'm from Boston, Massachusetts. I hope you won't hold that against me," he said with a slight smile. "My father is a partner in the firm Stein, Rothchild, and Kelly. All my life I was raised to be a lawyer. My father had big plans on me joining his firm. But all I ever wanted to be was a cowboy. A rancher. Frank, I guess I had the callin', like you. I read about the West, anything I could get my hands on. And it seemed like that was the only thing that would do.

"I was educated back East at Harvard University. I majored not in law but in business. I hate to tell you this, but money has never been a problem with my family or me. As a matter of fact, I have a trust fund that was set up for me when I was quite young, and it reverted to me when I was twenty-one.

"I told my father that I'd like to buy a ranch and he said, 'Raymond, what do you know about ranching?' And he had me. I knew very little except what I'd read.

"So he and I made a deal. I could go west, the plan being to get a job on a ranch. Several ranches for that matter, and see how I liked it. I was supposed to try west Texas, New Mexico, Colorado, Wyoming, Montana, work a month or two, and move on. See the different lifestyles and the different ways, and learn as much as I could. And at the end of that time if I still had the same dreams and aspirations, I could continue with this dream. If not, I would go back to law school.

"So I headed west. For some reason, and I have no explanation, I got off the train at Tramperos. You remember that day, Frank, when you found me down at the corner sitting under the tree?"

I nodded my head in acknowledgment.

"But that was as far as the plan went. You see, I fell in love with this country. I fell in love with the people, especially one," as his gaze turned to Kika. "I fell in love with Francesca and she with me. So, there was no sense in looking farther. I'd found what I wanted. To make a long story short, here I am. And unless Miz T. has changed her mind, we will close and I will own the Cross S."

Nobody said a word. And he still had not taken his eyes off Kika.

"I understand," I said in a choked voice. "But the Cannon place sold . . ." That's all I got out when R.C. nodded his head.

"I now own the Cannon place."

"What about Diego's state land?" I said.

R.C. looked at me and said, "What about it? Do you think I'd put my future father-in-law's state land up for sale and take it away from him?" as a smile crossed his face.

"Ah, no," I mumbled.

Then I began to understand. I turned to Miz T. and Kika and said, "You knew, didn't you?"

Miz T. smiled and nodded her head.

Kika said, "Yes, Frank. But not until the very last. Just before he left."

I looked at R.C. and said, "So now you own the Cannon place and the Piedra?"

"Yes."

"I'm afraid to hear what you're gonna tell me next," I said. "Are you in this with Bernie Mueller?"

R.C. shook his head. "Of course not, Frank. I used Bernie Mueller. But he's the only one I didn't lie to. I told him exactly who I was, and that I wanted to buy a ranch. I kept in close contact with him until I decided to make my move. And that kept me one jump ahead of him all the way."

"Thank God!" I said. "So, what's the rest of the story?"

"Well, what I want to do is make a proposal to you and Poke." Since he had our attention he went on. "I need you, Frank. You, too, Poke. And what I propose is a three-way partnership. The three of us equal partners. Now this might sound odd, but believe me, it'll work if we work hard and get along well. And I see no reason why we shouldn't. We always have. I want the three of us to buy the ranch, or ranches if you prefer, from me. A fair price, fair interest, amortized over a thirty-year period."

I was stunned! I think Poke was, too. "R.C.," I said, "you know as well as I do. I don't have enough money to make a down payment on a dead horse."

R.C. shook his head. "Frank, you still don't understand. You don't need to. We'll all work for a fair salary.

"Kika and I will be married as soon as we can make arrangements. I'd be honored if you'd be my best man," he said.

"Huh, of course. I'd be honored."

"Poke," he said, "I'd like you to stand up with me, too."

Poke, I believe, was in shock. He nodded his head.

"Kika and I will take this home, the headquarters. Poke can take the house at the Cannon place. We'll fix it up and make it nice. And how are things between you and Roberta, Frank?"

"Never better."

"Do you plan to marry her?"

"Sure. When we can afford to."

"Now," he said, "you can afford to. I thought maybe we could build another home down on Long's Creek where it passes through the north end of the Cannon place before coming into the Piedra here. How does that sound?"

"Terrific! But the money!"

R.C. smiled and shook his head. "The one thing I have never had a problem with, like I've told you, is money. This is not a gift. It's an opportunity. And I need you, both of you, to make this place work. We'll hook up both ranches with a main road cutting through, cattle guards so nobody'll have to open gates. Poke can run the cow outfit, 'cause that's where his heart belongs, in genetics. And we can even try to improve, if possible, what the Boss has started. And you, Frank, can run the yearlin' end of the business. That's where your interests lie. Am I right?"

I nodded my head yes.

"We can work out all the details later. What do you say?"

It didn't take long for both Poke and me to make up our minds. There would be a lot of wrinkles we had to iron out and a lot of things we'd have to understand, but we were both game.

R.C. said, "There is just one last thing that I need to tell you," and he hesitated. "I want everybody to understand that I am a Jew. This is the only thing that I can think of that might wreck the deal, is having a Jew for a partner."

I glanced at Poke, and he back at me. We shrugged our shoulders.

"Why would that change anything, R.C.? You're the same man that we grew so fond of last summer. It makes no difference."

"Me, neither," Poke said.

A big smile spread across R.C.'s face as he went over and put his arm around Kika. "Then it's settled. We'll be partners. Just don't anybody ever call me Raymond Cornelius. It'll always be R.C. Okay?"

About that time everybody got excited as it began to sink in what was happening. But just before the kitchen erupted in joy, I said, "Wait a minute. I need to tell you something."

The kitchen quieted down and I had the floor. "Everybody here has known that I'm a half-breed."

R.C. shrugged it off. "Frank, that makes no difference."

"Wait. I'm not through. You've got to hear the rest. The tribe I belong to, Plains Indians from Oklahoma, I've been rather vague about. For a reason. You see, the tribe I come from still sings songs about deeds of the past. And I acknowledge the past. But I need to let you know who I am and what I am. Within the tribe that I belong to there are many clans. I belong to the clan called the Quohada. My grandfather made many raids and was on many excursions into this part of the country. As a matter of fact, he was in that raid at Adobe Walls."

I could almost hear R.C.'s brain spinning.

"In other words, I'm telling you that I am a Comanche. Whether or not my grandfather was in the splinter band that passed through here killing the Padre and burning the town of Peralta and killing so many of your people, Kika, I have no way of knowing. But there's a good chance that he was with them." I looked at everybody slowly, and their mouths were open at this new revelation. Nobody said a word. I was a member of the tribe called Comanche, the dreaded terror of the southwest plains.

I heard somebody clear their throat and begin to speak.

It was Poke. "Well, I guess while we're all baring our souls here, I've got somethin' to tell all of you, too, that may have a bearing on how things go. My grandfather, Blue Mahone, was a Texas Ranger. And it was him and his company of Rangers along with the United States cavalry that hunted down the Comanches, found them in Palo Duro Canyon, killed their horses, and drove them back to the reservation and their agency at Fort Sill. So you see, as strange as it may seem, we're all tied together with the past."

Now it was my turn to look at Poke with astonishment. Only when I heard R.C. take a step toward me did I turn to look at him.

With his hand outstretched he said, "So be it."

Kika came, too, as R.C. and I shook hands, put her arm around my waist. "So be it."

Poke was still standing off as I turned to him and said, "What the hell!"

A big grin came across his face.

At last everybody's story was out. We made a pact. No more secrets.

The last voice to speak was Miz T. "However different we all are, this will make for a good bond, especially since you all belong to the same band."

A silence came over the room as we turned and looked at her. I didn't know what she was talking about. "What band is that?"

With glistening eyes, she said, "The three of you are cowboys. Clear to the bone and in the heart. The Boss would be proud."

The Boss. I'd never heard her use that term in relation to her husband. It made me proud. The three of us joined in a three-way handshake.

R.C. said, "We all have our callin'."

Had we been standing out on the prairie in this fashion, on a day like today, the snow would have drifted on our leeward side, a hundred feet high.